As a loving wife, mother, friend, and mentor to many, Karen inspired countless others through her love for life, her powerful story of hope amid adversity, and her abiding faith in Jesus Christ. I was moved to learn how she poured out her life in selfless service — developing and using her talents as a writer, speaker, and artist for the good of others and the glory of God.

MIKE PENCE, *48th Vice President of the United States*

PRAISE FOR KAREN O'NEILL VELASQUEZ

Well done, Karen, well done! I finished *The Rescue* in about 30 hours. I couldn't put it down.

DEBBIE HOPPER, *Ministry Coach & Consultant, Former Director Women's Ministry Seacoast Church*

Turn the first page and you won't be able to step away from the book. *The Rescue* reminds us that there is a much greater force at work and if we listen closely, we too, can hear God's voice.

JoDee WATKINS, *RFxCircle Achiever with Rodan + Fields Entrepreneur, Philanthropist, Special-needs Advocate and Adoptive Mom*

The first few pages grab you and never let you go. Shem Creek and the Low Country jump off the pages and into your soul as a place where patience and obedience are tested but friendships and faith prevail. Karen O'Neill Velasquez has shown her incredible talent by producing the great American novel. *The Rescue* is a remarkable read that I highly recommend.

JEB HENSARLING, *Former Chairman of the U.S. House Financial Services Committee and Congressmen from Texas*

The wisdom expressed through the characters of *The Rescue* is so profound that I began encouraging hurting friends with the quote: *"…who we are while we wait is more important than what we receive when the prayer is answered. Waiting matters. Waiting refines us. Waiting transforms us… the love I feel today… grew fresh and new from the ashes of suffering."* My grieving began about 2/3 of the way through as I wanted and willed there not be an end to this story. I felt a sense of bereavement when I turned the last page. *The Rescue* left me wanting more. This book is a wonder, and one that needs to be read. The prose is magnificent and it is beautiful. Karen O'Neill Velasquez is as gifted a storyteller as I've come across.

DARLA REESE, *Psychologist and Professional Counselor*

THE RESCUE

By

Karen O'Neill Velasquez

The Rescue

The Rescue is a work of fiction. Where real people, events, establishments, organizations, or locals appear, they are used fictitiously. All elements of the novel are drawn from the author's imagination.

ISBN: 9781737346708

For John Paul Velasquez

And these three remain: faith, hope and love.
But the greatest of these is love.
1 Cor 13:13

(NIV)

Special thanks to Michael Huh, Madeline Chuvalas, Kendra Gallegos, Christina Willson, and especially Jodi Mallon who quarterbacked the effort to have The Rescue released, all contributing out of love for Christ and selfless love for Karen

Table of Contents

~ CHAPTER 1 ~

December 2000

There is a precise moment when he knows he is going to die. It is as if someone flipped a switch, and he is dangling between two worlds. One minute, the pain is like a vice grip squeezing his shoulder, and the next, he feels as if an anesthesiologist has given him relief through his veins. Although his body is spent and he is sinking slowly to the murky bottom of the raging stream, he has the strange sensation that something—or is it someone? —is pulling him upward toward a light. He knows the fight is over; his physical body is willingly giving in to death. He stops trying to order his body to do what it is no longer capable of doing. He no longer feels the need to struggle to breathe. But, what about them? He feels like he should continue to fight.

His eyes are closed, and yet, he sees.

Colors and magnificent light.

His soul fills with an unfamiliar music. *He feels the music. He wants to be inside the music.*

He recognizes faces. He sees his grandpa.

Strong arms are pulling him up. He is being dragged from the water.

He is now on the ground, leaning up against a warm body.

Comforting arms are around him.

"Help us, *please!*" a male's voice screams. "Someone, help us! Lord, help us! *Please, God, don't take him!*"

He recognizes the voice. It's Jake. His lifelong best friend.

He knows he's dying, but he still tries to speak. He's not sure if words are coming out or not. He hopes they are because these are to be his last words to a living person.

"Tell him to take care of them," he chokes. *"Tell him … this … is why."*

"Who?"

"Tell him this is why he's always loved her." He coughs. There's no more air.

He feels the loving arms around him tighten. He is being held in a strong embrace as he dies. He's not alone. He feels the love of his best friend.

His last cognitive thought is a communication with God, without any words; it is like a soul-to-soul request to God, because his body can no longer speak. *Lord, please take care of them.*

With the last request of a dying man, a peace settles over him, and he has full confidence, God will take care of it.

A messenger from God is dispatched to usher him home to heaven. At the same time, the supernatural God of the Universe confirms that a significant transaction is about to take place. God releases an army of mighty angels to care for the wife and child of a man who has loved and served God with his life.

Almighty God sets out to answer the heartfelt prayer of a righteous man.

~ CHAPTER 2 ~

1970 Charleston, South Carolina

Katherine Grace awakens with a sudden jolt so powerful she feels as if a strong set of arms is shaking her awake. She opens her eyes, raises her head, and in one quick motion she reaches for the bedside lamp. She pulls down on the metal cord and the darkened room is instantly filled with welcoming light. She reaches for the notebook and pen on her nightstand. And just as she starts moving her pillow up against the headboard, her husband stirs. She feels his body move closer to her. She is sitting upright now with her head resting against the headboard and her husband of thirty years is snuggled up to one leg.

"Nothing scary, I hope," Neal whispers.

"Give me a minute," she says, not wanting to lose any of the dream. She begins to write quickly. Years of experience have taught her that if she doesn't write down the little details of her dreams right away, some of the dream's significance is lost. She's scribbling down a series of words. Christmas card. Dark-skinned child. And for some very strange reason, the color green. Once she has written down the small details in her head, she recreates the dream she's just had.

She turns to her husband and whispers, "it's Jeb." "The dream is about Jeb?" he asks, perking up. "Yes," she says, wiping a stray tear off her cheek. "Is he okay?"

"Yes, but in the dream I saw his Christmas card," she says. "I walk out to the mailbox and I remove a letter. It's a Christmas card from him but his return address is *South Carolina*."

"Okay, so our son is moving here? Is that the dream?" Neal asks.

"Not just that," Katherine Grace says, softly. "There's a picture in the Christmas card."

"Of he and Kathleen?"

"And their child," she says.

Neal sits upright and says, "are you serious, you've seen a Christmas card and the two of them *have a child*?"

"Yes," she says, crying. "After all this time it looks like he's finally going to be a father."

"And Kathleen," Neal says, softly. "She's suffered so much. And now, finally."

"I wonder if she will even believe me."

"Sweetheart, your dreams *always* come true," he says, smiling. "Did you see the date on the postmark? Like, is this happening soon?"

"The postmark is December 1970."

Neal rolls over on his back and whispers a prayer of thanksgiving.

"There's more," she says.

"Go, on."

"His skin is dark," she says. "I think he's is an adopted child." "*He*?" Neal asks. "They're getting a *son*?"

"An adorable little boy," Katherine Grace whispers. "Anything else?"

"Nothing that really makes sense other than the color green," she says. "And I have no idea what the significance of the color green is."

"I'm quite certain that in time we will know," he says. "Should I tell him?"

"You've always told the people involved about the dreams," he says. "So, I think this should be no different."

Katherine Grace smiles, knowing this dream is special. All her life she's had dreams. Her dreams are not like the kind other people have. When Katherine Grace dreams something, it happens in real life. And her dreams are vivid, involving all her senses. They play out like she's watching a movie.

Katherine Grace gets out of bed, puts on her slippers and goes downstairs to start the coffee. Today promises to be special. She can't wait to share this wonderful dream with her son.

******

"I had a strange conversation with my mom this morning," Jeb says to his wife, Kathleen. "Seems she's been having dreams again."

"What kind of dreams?" Kathleen asks. "Her dreams are usually spot on."

"I know," Jeb says. "Here's the thing ... She said she dreamed of receiving a Christmas card from us."

"Go on." Kathleen says. "That's no big deal."

"It's postmarked from Charleston, like we live there or something."

"Okay, that's not any big deal, we've been talking about moving for years."

"There's more," Jeb says. "And I hesitate to talk about it. Not easy stuff."

"Just spill it, Jeb" Kathleen says. "We've been through so much. I can handle it."

"The card is a photo Christmas card," he says. "It's a family picture."

"What's the big deal with that?"

"There are three of us in the picture, Katheen," he whispers. *"We have a child."*

"What?"

"We have a son in the picture," Jeb says, smiling. "And he appears to be an adopted child. He has dark skin."

Kathleen wipes a tear off her cheek. "After all this time?" she says, just barely above a whisper. "After three miscarriages and baby Chrissy? *Now*?"

"Yes," Jeb says. "Like soon, the postmark is *this year*." "But we haven't really talked about adoption," she says.
"Ironically, I had something I wanted to show you," he says. "I just wasn't sure how to broach the subject."

"Okay, go on"

"Well, I was paying bills the other night and a piece of junk mail caught my eye," Jeb says, walking over to his desk. "Here," he says, handing the envelope to Kathleen. "It's from an adoption agency in Guatemala."

Kathleen opens the envelope and a photo falls to the floor. She bends down and picks up a black and white photo of a baby boy in need of a home. He has dark skin and dark hair. Immediately, a swarm of butterflies take up shop in her stomach. Her heart is racing and tears prick at the corner of her eyes. *After all this time, God? Is this my son?*

"So, do you think this is a nudge from God?"

"I do," he says, "and I think my mom's dreams confirm it. We should probably move forward."

Kathleen looks at her husband, the man she'd been in love with since she was fifteen, and she finds herself falling in love with him in a new way. She knows she's blessed. And she *knows* there's no reason to doubt. Katherine Grace's dreams *always come true*. And she *knows* she's about to become a mother.

"Was there anything else?" Kathleen asks.

"Yes, one of those strange little details her dreams are famous for," Jeb says.

"What's the detail?"

"The color green."

"Just the color green? Nothing else?" Kathleen asks.

"Just green," Jeb says. "Maybe it's because green is a Christmas color. I don't know. I guess we wait for God to fill in the blanks on that detail."

******

Nine months later, Kathleen is preparing to meet her son for the first time.

The light from the large crystal chandelier makes the white marble floor sparkle like the sun reflecting on an icy winter road. Kathleen is people-watching in the busy lobby of a lavish hotel in Guatemala City. One by one, people walk by, seeming to flaunt their impeccable appearances. Kathleen struggles with the opulence in this lobby compared with the abject poverty outside the doors. Well-dressed, wealthy people march through the lobby with their expensive shoes tapping on the floor, sounding like the woodpecker outside her bedroom window back home. They all seem to have somewhere to go—the woman with the Louis Vuitton luggage, the man with the custom-fitted European suit, the little girl twirling in her pink boots and matching dress. A mixture of expensive fragrances tickles her nose.

Kathleen's stomach flutters as it did just before Jeb kissed her for the first time. The moment seems to have a romantic feel to it, as if love is in the air. She takes in her surroundings with the detail of a private investigator, knowing one day she'll sit at her kitchen table and attempt to recreate this moment for her son. She is about to meet one of the great loves of her life, and she can't quite wrap her heart around this.

Kathleen checks her watch and turns to face the revolving doors to the right of the reception area. As the woman walks in, Kathleen is struck with the notion that she doesn't look as if she belongs in this ritzy place. Initially, Kathleen is embarrassed for her. The woman's clothes match in neither color nor season. Her flowered cotton gauze dress is paired with a winter sweater. The heel of her shoe is broken, making the woman walk with a slight limp. It is unlikely she is the first owner of her clothes.

The woman is carrying the baby boy.

At once, Kathleen feels the need to rescue this woman, to somehow soften the blow of how she stands out. But upon closer inspection, Kathleen takes in the angle of her neck. Her head is held high, her chin up, and she smiles in greeting to those who pass her. Kathleen is struck with the notion that this woman is proud of who she is and what she's doing. She is a foster mother in one of the poorest places in the world. By her posture, it is obvious that she understands her work is important, and so is she.

Kathleen stands to greet this woman who is holding the baby who will become her son. The woman hoists the baby up onto one hip and stretches out her other hand in greeting. "I'm Marta," she says. *"Buenos dias."*

"Buenos dias," Kathleen says, trying out her Spanish.

"Este es tu bebe." Marta switches to broken English. "He is beautiful boy."

Marta places the baby in Kathleen's arms. The little boy grabs Kathleen's finger, just as she had imagined he would. Her eyesight goes blurry, and she struggles to see through her tears. She inhales the scent of him. The scent is very different, unfamiliar, yet not at all unwelcome.

As she holds the child, a warmth begins in her heart and slowly seems to travel to her extremities. She is bathed in a feeling of love. A desire to protect overwhelms her. She is struck with a well of emotion so deep and familiar, and it begins to pour out of her as she cries. One other time in her life a baby was placed in her arms. This baby had grown inside her; she was part of her physically; her tiny body felt like an extension of her. When she held her daughter for the first time, the attachment seemed to have existed already. There was no need to question what she would feel. Kathleen brushes a stray tear off her cheek. Four years later, the wound is still just as fresh. Just six short weeks after her birth, SIDS took baby Chrissy's life.

Kathleen had no idea what the moment of holding a newly adopted child would bring. She is shocked at the physical reaction she's having. She is overcome with the exact same motherly desires and instincts she experienced with her biological child. *How can this be? How can I love this stranger in my arms as if he were my own flesh and blood?*

"This doesn't feel different," Kathleen whispers, looking up at Marta. She wipes her eyes on the corner of his baby blanket. With dry eyes and clear vision, she looks at him closely for the first time. "Dear Lord, his eyes are magnificent. They're green?"

"I know," Marta smiles. "*El bebe de ojos verdes,* the green-eyed baby. His eyes are the most beautiful eyes I've ever seen. Green eyes are not common here in Guatemala, especially given how dark his skin is. All I know is that the doctor who delivered him said he is extraordinary."

Marta studies Kathleen for a moment. "His name is Joseph," Marta says.

"Joseph Lucas Nicholson," Kathleen says. "We gave him the middle name of Lucas because he's from San Lucas."

"You won't change his name?"

"No, we like Joseph," Kathleen says. "Jesus's adopted dad was Joseph. We will keep this piece of his life for him."

Marta kisses baby Joseph one last time. With tears in her eyes, she bids him farewell. Kathleen walks across the lobby and out the front doors into the waiting taxi. Joseph Lucas Nicholson is headed home to his forever family.

******

Kathleen and Jeb quickly forget what life was like before baby Joseph.

"You aren't even interested anymore, are you?" Jeb says, pointing to the TV. "You aren't paying any attention to David Cassidy and *The Partridge Family*. Your *back* is to the TV."

Joseph rolls over onto his back, squealing as he tries in vain to put his toes in his mouth. The two of them are staring as if it's a ticket-holder's event, patiently waiting for the next act.

"We are toast!" Jeb chuckles. "He is the best thing that's ever happened to us."

"What is?" They all hear a voice say as the back-door slams and Katherine Grace walks in.

"Well, hey Mom!" Jeb greets, getting up to hug his mother. "We were all talking about our little Joseph here. He's the greatest gift this family has been given."

"That's how I felt when I had you, Jeb," she says, kissing her son on the head. "I brought over a peach cobbler. Anyone need dessert?"

"You know how I feel about your peach cobbler," Jeb says, smiling. "Fresh peaches from the tree out back and my momma's good cooking, and we have the summer's greatest treat."

"I'm up for some," Kathleen chimes in, hugging her mother-in-law. "Thanks for bringing the cobbler."

Katherine Grace Sullivan Nicholson, in her mid-sixties, is still a stunning woman. With white-gray hair, blunt cut at her jaw, and California-girl boho-style, she's an eclectic grandmother. She and her husband, Cornelius, "Neal," bought the entire block of land twenty years ago when they arrived in South Carolina from California. The dream was to raise their family on a plot of land that sat on the water. Their goal was to parcel up the land for their children and grandchildren ... and great grandchildren, someday.

******

"Does it still feel like a vacation?" Jeb asks his wife during an early morning walk. "Does Mount Pleasant feel like home for you yet? I was raised here, so this is all familiar to me, but what about you?" he adds, taking a deep breath. "You've always been a Virginia girl."

"Home is wherever you are, Jeb," Kathleen says, smiling.

Jeb marvels at how easily they have adjusted to life on Shem Creek. He loves holding his wife's hand and making their way down the driveway, up Simmons Street, toward the mouth of the creek, where it spills into the ocean. He loves this time with his wife. Greeting the day with her is one of the greatest gifts of this move to South Carolina.

"I think the house is perfect for us," she shares. "I love the back porch on the water because when Joseph hits his teen years, we are going to be sitting out there watching him with all his friends. You know, we *are* going to be the home where all the teens gather, right?"

"We will be every teen's second home," he says, laughing. "I guess Mom really had a vision when she and Dad purchased all this land."

"Don't you hope Joseph comes to love this place?" she asks. "Like when he smells the air, don't you hope that down the road he will think about his childhood?"

"I keep thinking this is a place for happy memories to be made."

"Me too," she agrees, looking up toward the Atlantic Ocean. "Sometimes, when I'm doing dishes at the kitchen sink and I look out the window, I'm astonished at the colors of the sunset. I feel like the colors aren't even real."

"Winds of Fortune," Jeb reads out loud, looking at the name of the first shrimp boat parked on the creek. "Probably not a name I'd choose for a boat."

"Some of these names sound like somebody's ex-girl-friend."

"If we had a boat, we'd have to name it 'Joseph's Gift,'" Jeb jokes.

"Ha! Isn't that the truth?"

"I think Joseph is swimming really well these days. What do you think?" he asks.

"He's sure working on it," she answers. "But living on a tidal creek means that he needs to do a lot more than work on it."

"For sure. He can't seem to understand that sometimes he can touch the bottom and sometimes he can't," he says back. "That concerns me."

"He's smart enough to learn about the tides," she replies. "He's such a sponge. He remembers everything."

"You're right," he says. "Maybe I'll paint some colored lines on the posts holding up the dock. Kind of a visual."

"That's a great idea."

"We have a child who wants to live in that water," he says, laughing. "It's like he was born to play out back. Oh … and you know we've got no chance for a pretty backyard, right?"

"Oh, I can see that. There's already a dead grass baseball diamond forming," she says, pushing his arm gently.

"Hey, you wanted a little boy," he replies quickly, putting his arm around her at the same time.

Jeb knows he's the luckiest man alive. He has a beautiful wife whom he loves with all his heart. He has a son he adores. He lives in a pretty Cape Cod house overlooking Shem Creek, which is only steps from the Atlantic Ocean. Living in South Carolina provides a wonderful quality of life for his family. He gets to wake up every day with the smell of pluff mud and salty air blowing through the windows. He fires up the grill nightly, and the three of them have dinner on the dock overlooking the creek. Sometimes he feels like pinching himself to see if he's dreaming.

"I'll always love you." He smiles at his wife and places a quick kiss on the top of her head.

"And aren't you the lucky guy?" she says with a wink as she opens the front door.

"Oh, yes I am." he exclaims. "The absolute luckiest."

~ CHAPTER 3 ~

Joseph feels like such a big boy when Daddy asks him to walk out on the dock with him. He wishes that when he dangles his bare feet off the dock that his legs were long enough to dip his feet in the water. Daddy says that will happen soon enough. When he sits next to Daddy by the creek, he always has questions. Maybe it's because his dad is busy with work. And sometimes it feels like Daddy has less time for him. But today, it's just he and Dad, and this is good, because Joseph has some really big questions for Daddy.

"Why is my skin this color and yours isn't?" Joseph asks, poking his dad's pale leg with his index finger.

"Well, now, that's kind of a big question. I'll start by saying that this particular question will be answered little by little over the years," his dad answers, putting his arm around his son.

"Why not all now?"

"Some of it you'll need to be a bit older to understand."
"Ok, so what can ya tell me, Daddy?"

"You've heard us say you were adopted. Do you know what that means?" Daddy asks.

"Not really," Joseph answers.

"It's a little bit like the sticker on the underside of this toy truck of yours," his dad says, reaching for Joseph's toy fire engine. "You see this sticker?"

"Yeah, can I peel it off?" Joseph asks, distracted.

"Do you know what it says?"

"No."

"It says, 'Made in China.' So, you have this toy that you love so much, and it belongs to you, but it was made somewhere else. China is across the ocean and really far away."

"Okay, but what does that have to do with me?"

"If I had a sticker on the bottom of my foot, it would say 'Made in South Carolina'," his dad explains, "because I was born here. Momma's would say 'Made in Virginia'."

"Would my sticker say, 'Made in Virginia,' too, 'cause we just moved from there?" Joseph questions.

"No, yours would say something different, because you weren't born in Virginia. Do you know where you were born?"

"Oh, yeah, Guatemala. So that's not in Virginia?" Joseph asks.

"No, it's a couple thousand miles from here, and not even in the U.S. That's why your skin is darker than mine," Daddy gently explains.

"So, I was made far away from you and mommy?" Joseph asks, puzzled. "Then how did I grow in Momma's tummy if it's far away? Was Momma with me?"

"No, Momma wasn't there with you, but someone else was. We call her your birth mother, because you grew in *her* tummy and not your momma's."

"Neat!" Joseph says.

"Your momma says that you grew inside someone else's tummy, but you grew in *her* heart," Daddy says.

"So, she musta really wanted me?" Joseph ponders. "Because, like, she didn't go someplace else to get anybody else, right?"

"Exactly. And *that* makes you very special," Daddy says with a hug.

"Are you gonna get me a sticker?" Joseph asks.

"That's the funny thing about the sticker. I forget that you ever had one. It feels to me, right here," he says, tapping his heart, "like it should just say, 'Daddy's Boy.'"

"That's why you love me?"

"I love you, because of *all* the little boys in the whole wide world, God gave me you."

"And I'm the only boy," Joseph adds. "Do you think she misses me?"

"Who?"

"My other momma," Joseph says.

"Yes, I do. And remember when you first asked the question, I told you I would tell you more and more over the years?"

"Yep."

"That's the part I'll tell you more about in a few years. That okay with you?"

"Okay, but don't forget, 'cause she might wanna see me."

"Well, who wouldn't want to see a great little boy like you?" Daddy says, standing up. "Right now, I think I need an ice cream sandwich."

"Me too!" Joseph exclaims. He stands up and takes his father's hand, as he always does. "Sneak it, okay?"

"Okay, just us guys then," Daddy agrees, smiling down at his green-eyed son.

******

"Can I go out now, Momma?" Joseph pleads.

"Honey, give them a moment, moving is a tough chore," Momma replies.

"Can I at least put some stuff out near the fence?" "Sure, but don't bother them yet."

Joseph runs to his room and grabs his football, baseball, bat, and glove. He goes stomping through the house into the garage and grabs his life vest and his blow-up raft. He wants his best toys. He carries them all out to the edge of the fence, drops them in a large pile, and stands on top. He stares intently at the large moving truck in the driveway next door. He knows he needs to head back in the house so his momma will know he's obeying, but he's so excited that he stands there for just one more minute, hoping someone will notice him.

Reluctantly he returns to his house and stands in the kitchen, looking out over the front yard, watching the people begin to unload the truck, waiting to see. It's taking so long. All he wants to know is if there's a kid for him to play with. *Not a girl.* He wants a boy to play with. His momma thinks it might not be polite to go and ask. But if there *is* a boy kid, he'd want to play. Joseph is sure of that.

Joseph starts to bounce a rubber ball on the kitchen floor. He doesn't actually mean to bug his momma, but he just wants to be outside. Sometimes Momma will give in if he plays inside; she doesn't like that. And she really doesn't like balls in the house. She will usually tell him to take that ball outside.

"Okay, honey, why don't you go on out and ask," his mom finally says.

Joseph is out the door in an instant, barreling down the front steps, heading toward the fence that separates his yard from the yard next door. Once again, he stands on top of his pile of toys, hoping someone will notice him. He decides that maybe they can't see him, so he climbs up a bit higher, with his hands on the top rail of the chain-link fence. He sees a man unloading a box from the big truck.

"'Scuse me, Mister. Do you got a boy?" Joseph asks, leaning over the fence using his most polite voice.

The man stops, puts down a box, and laughs.

"Honey, what do you think?" he says, looking at a pretty, dark-haired woman carrying a small box.

"I don't know, have you seen a boy around here?" she says, peeking behind the big truck, smiling.

"Depends," the dad says. "Depends on if you're looking for a six-year-old boy or not."

"I am! I am!" Joseph calls out. "I'm a six-year-old boy. That's what I want, Mister."

"I think I can help you," the man says, hoisting a little blond boy up onto his shoulders and walking toward the fence. "I've got this boy right here."

Joseph jumps up and down, clapping. "I'm looking for a best friend."

"Me too," says the adorable blond boy.

"I'm Joseph, and I'm six."

"I'm Jake, and I'm six, too."

"Double Jays," Jake's daddy says with a smile. "The Double Jays."

"Daddy, can I play, *please*?" Jake asks.

"Sure, buddy, stay where I can see you," his dad cautions.

Jake climbs over the fence and steps into the yard.

"Why do I know that the best moments of his life are going to take place right there?" the new neighbor says to his wife, pointing at the yard in front of him.

"I was just thinking the same thing," she says back. "This is perfect."

"Is your mom or dad home?" the new neighbor asks Joseph.

"Yes, sir. My mom is. Want me to go get her?"

Joseph turns around to head toward his porch just as his mama is stepping out with a plate of warm cookies for the new neighbors. The boys take off playing, and Kathleen stays at the fence, talking to her new neighbors Pam and Paul. Both women are smiling, knowing they will be good friends.

******

"All right, Double Jays, go put on your trunks and meet me out back on the dock," Mr. Nicholson says a few days later. "We need to go over some house rules."

"Yes, sir!" the two young boys call back in unison as they take off running toward their rooms.

Mr. Nicholson, wearing his swimsuit, stands in the exact spot where the weathered boards of the dock meet the beaten down path to the house. His arms are crossed, legs parted, and his stance blocks the boy's entry to the dock.

A few moments later, two little boys come running out of the house, barefoot and ready for adventure. They both hit the brakes at the spot where Mr. Nicholson is standing as a human blockade.

"I want the two of you to observe something important," Mr. Nicholson says, turning around and pointing to the dock. "This dock does not have rails. Follow me," he says, walking down the dock towards the gazebo.

Mr. Nicholson stops about halfway down the wooden dock with old, misaligned boards and splinters sticking up. He turns and walks slowly to the edge. He stops just as his toes become flush with the edge. "This is the edge. Now both of you do the same. Line your big toe up with the edge here."

Both boys do as they are told. Up until this point, Mr. Nicholson had been very strict about being on the dock without an adult.

"Now, move your toes off the edge," Mr. Nicholson says, inching his feet forward so the edge of the dock is now where his toes meet the balls of his feet. Instinctively, his toes curl around the edge.

Both boys do as they are told, and they're having a tough time balancing on the dock. With their arms out for balance, both boys start laughing.

"Now, move your feet a few inches more," Mr. Nicholson instructs. The edge of the deck is now in the middle of his arches. At this point, even Mr. Nicholson is having trouble balancing.

The boys look at each other, and once again, do as they are told. With their arms out, attempting balance, bodies pitched forward and laughing, both boys go tumbling into the water headfirst.

Mr. Nicholson immediately jumps in. Both boys can swim, but he knows that pool swimming and tidal creek swimming are vastly different. Both boys are having trouble staying afloat as they search in vain for the bottom of the muddy creek. They are splashing and kicking and starting to be afraid. He grabs both sinking boys—one in each arm and swims toward the ladder at the end of the dock.

The three climb out and Mr. Nicholson turns to look at two scared little boys. "You both learned a powerful lesson just now. It's the lesson of the edge. Out here on the dock, we have no rails. Every time you come out here, you need to be aware of the edge or you will fall in. And this creek here isn't like the pools you're used to. Depending upon the tide, it might be shallow or deep. You must be ready for either."

Both boys, standing at full attention like soldiers, are hanging on his every word, their fear now slightly dissipated.

"The edge of this dock is just like life, boys. You can't go too far over the edge or you're going to fall in. You are going to be faced with the edge every day. You are going to want to take a closer look at bad stuff. It's human nature. You are going to be tempted to do stuff that you know you aren't supposed to do. That's the edge, boys. Don't even go near it. You hear me?"

26

"Yes, sir."

"What happens when you get too close to the edge?" Mr. Nicholson asks.

"You fall in," Jake answers.

"You fall in, and you could drown," Joseph says.

"Exactly," Mr. Nicholson says. "On a hot summer day, this water here is going to look really appetizing, and that's good, as long as you're careful. We are going to practice what safety here looks like, and both of you boys are going to need to completely obey the rules. For now, there's no swimming in the creek without an adult on the dock. And you must wear a life jacket every time. Understood?"

"Yes, sir," both boys answer.

"I guess we need to be careful, Jake," Joseph says. "My daddy won't always be here to rescue us."

"And if you don't go to the edge, you won't need a rescue," Mr. Nicholson adds with a smile.

That first summer in Mount Pleasant, South Carolina is life changing. After living in a household as an only child, Joseph finally has a boy to do boy things with. Every day from sunup to sunset, the boys swim, eat, fish, and play baseball. No girl games. Nobody yelling at him to take it easy. Just perfect summer fun for two little boys, running wild and free in the South Carolina sun.

~ CHAPTER 4 ~

1980

The ten-year-old Double Jays are lounging on the back dock dangling a couple of fishing rods into the water, when the screen door slams. In unison, two heads turn as a skinny child wearing a baseball cap heads down the path toward them.

"Who's *that?*" Joseph asks.

"My cousin from New York," Jake replies. "She'll be coming every summer."

"*She?*" Joseph asks, perturbed.

"Yeah, her name is Michelle," Jake says. "She's cool. She's a girl, but not like a girl. You'll like her."

Joseph sees his summer plans unraveling, and he isn't happy about it. The thought of adding a girl to the Double Jays doesn't seem to fit with his plans. His plan involves baseball, more baseball, and a whole lot of fishing and swimming. No pools. Just the creek. And no girls. Absolutely no girls. Because Joseph knows *all* about girls. His Aunt visits from Virginia and brings her three daughters. Joseph is always excited to have them come but quickly realizes it's no fun at all. Girls have dolls, hair ribbons, and pink stuff. Girls make a guy want to go outside and disappear. Girls don't like things that boys like, and they *always* complain and get their way. They get their feelings hurt, and you have to pretend you're sorry or they'll tell on you. They hate to get dirty, and they can't throw a football or baseball.

Plus, they definitely can't swim fast. *Girls slow you down.* Joseph secretly hopes that this Michelle girl will be hanging out with Jake's mom and not them. The last thing Joseph wants is to have to entertain some girl all summer long. He sees his big break from girls slipping away right before his eyes.

The girl walks up onto the dock and sits down next to Jake.

"Who's that?" she says, pointing to Joseph.

"That's Joseph. He lives right there," Jake says, pointing to Joseph's house.

Joseph turns to look at her. He doesn't want to encourage her. He wants to make her feel unwelcome, and then maybe she'll take the hint. *But* she is wearing a Yankees baseball cap, and he doesn't totally hate what he sees. She has a tomboy look, not all frilly like his cousins. Her long, dark hair is in a ponytail hanging out of the back of the baseball cap. No ribbon.

Michelle is wearing an old-looking, faded blue, oversized Bruce Springsteen concert tee that nearly reaches her knees. Her shoes are new and extremely cool, white Nikes with the red swoosh. Everyone his age wants a pair. Her body is long and skinny, and she's got knobby knees. Her skin is a summer-kissed deep brown tan color.

When she finally looks at Joseph, he thinks her face belongs on someone older. Her cheekbones are high, her eyes are a deep navy blue with a dark ring around them, and her eyelashes are so long and thick they could take the place of her baseball cap in providing shade for her eyes.

"He's rude," the girl says, poking her cousin in the rib with her elbow and turning to Joseph. "I'm Michelle, and don't look so ticked that I'm a girl. It's not like you're stuck with me or anything. I can handle myself." Michelle reaches up and turns her baseball cap backward and leans down to look closely at Joseph's face. "Cool eyes," she comments.

"Huh?"

"I said you have cool eyes."

"Thanks. *I think*," Joseph says, wondering what on earth cool eyes are. Joseph is getting tongue-tied, trying to find anything of substance to add to the conversation.

"Don't worry. I don't bite, and I'm probably better at most sports than you are, "she challenges with an infectious smile.

Her smile melts him. It pulls at something inside he doesn't yet understand. The butterflies in his stomach are making him wish he hadn't eaten that sugar doughnut an hour ago. She's way too cool for them, and Joseph feels divided. On one hand, he'd like her to turn around and head back to New York and not ruin his entire summer, but on the other hand, he's curious about her and thinks there might be a possibility that she won't be a complete pain. There's something about this girl that makes him want to be kind. He's trying to figure out what that means. She's been rude, and Joseph can tell she's the bossy type, and yet he wants to be nice to her.

"Do you play baseball?" Joseph asks, pointing to the well-worn glove she has in her hand. He's desperate to find something to talk about.

"No, stupid," she says. "Girls play softball."

Again, Joseph has no desire to say something smart or mean back. In fact, he's starting to reconsider his quick judgment.

"Want to play catch?" he asks. "I can go get my glove."

"Sure, I need to practice this summer. I want to make All-Stars back in *New York* next year."

"Okay, be back in a sec," Joseph says, and he takes off to get his glove.

Jake turns to Michelle and says, "Don't be so mean to him." "Why? He's just a stupid boy," Michelle retorts.

"No, he's not a stupid boy," Jake says. "He's a great guy, and I think we should always be nice to him. He's not like some of the other mean kids I know. Trust me on this," Jake adds.

"Okay, take it easy. I get it."

"He's my best friend," Jake says, meaning it with all his heart.

"Ok. If he's your friend, can he be mine too? It would be kinda hard for us to hang out if he isn't my friend too."

"Ask him yourself, but I know he will say yes," Jake confidently replies. "He's that kind of guy."

When Joseph returns, he has his glove and a softball. Not a baseball. He has frantically searched his house specifically for a softball. He has actually gone into the garage, rummaged through his mom's old boxes of stuff, and found an old softball.

"No point practicing with a baseball if you play softball," Joseph says, tossing the ball to Michelle.

"I accidentally left my softball in New York and thought I'd be practicing all summer with a baseball," she says, "Thanks." She catches his toss and smiles, and the two kids start walking up the dock toward the Nicholson's backyard to the homemade backyard baseball diamond.

"Go get your glove, Jake," Joseph yells over his shoulder as he heads to the backyard pitching mound. "We can play Hotbox."

Joseph is pretty sure nobody needs to take it easy when throwing with Michelle, but he doesn't want to look like he's showing off, so he decides to take it slow. He throws one, she catches it just fine. And then she throws it back. Hard. Stinging hard. Joseph smiles and realizes she is right. She probably does play sports better than most boys. And Joseph loves it. More girls should be like this. Life would be a whole lot easier if they were.

"Surprised?" she asks, after throwing another hardball.

"Yes, but good surprised," he says back to her. *Really* good surprised.

"My daddy says there's no point throwing like a girl," Michelle says laughing.

"Well, you sure don't," Joseph replies.

"I call Hotbox," Jake says.

"Guys on the outside, Michelle in the middle, running," Joseph says.

The competition requires two people to throw the ball between them and try to tag out a runner.

"Girl, you're fast!" Joseph yells.

"I know," she laughs. "Just try to catch me." And she runs off.

It proves to be a challenge to tag her out. Joseph loves it. No slowing down. No playing gentle because she's a girl. Not one item of pink clothing. Just fast-paced boy sports with a third person, who just happens to be a girl.

Within minutes, they are all dripping wet in the scorching South Carolina sun.

"Betcha can't!" Joseph calls out in a challenge.

"Bet I can!" Jake yells back.

To Michelle's surprise, both boys drop their gloves in the grass and take off running toward the dock in what appears to be a very practiced routine. While running, both boys strip down to their swimsuits and try hard not to trip and fall. They race toward the edge of the dock. By the time they hit the edge of the dock, they are laughing so hard they become clumsy. With a huge splash, they both tumble head over heels into Shem Creek.

Michelle doesn't merely stand and watch this spectacle, and when the boys resurface, they turn to see her reaction. But all they see is a ponytail flying high above her head as she comes running down the dock. She throws off her baseball cap and jumps into the water, fully clothed, hitting the water in a perfectly executed cannonball.

And this is the moment Joseph realizes this girl is cool.

******

Later that evening, Joseph is in the kitchen, grabbing a cookie. "Mom," he says, "what does it mean to have cool eyes?"

"You mean like one of the cartoons, like laser vision or something?" she asks with a chuckle.

"No," Joseph says. "Like if somebody says, 'cool eyes' to you."

"Oh," she says, shaking her head. "You mean like a *compliment*?"

"I guess," Joseph answers.

"Well, I wasn't there, but my best guess would be that someone thinks your green eyes are special."

"Why would someone think my green eyes are special?"

"Well, typically people with darker skin from places like Guatemala have dark brown eyes. Green eyes are rare."

"Then why are mine green?"

"I don't really have an answer to that. Daddy and I always just thought it was because God made you special." She smiles, ruffling his hair, and then she bends down to get eye to eye with him. "You better be ready to hear that lots more times, young man, because ever since I took you out in public, people have noticed your eyes."

"That's weird, Mom," he says, laughing.

"Who said it to you, sweetheart?" she asks, returning to a more serious tone.

"That girl next door, Jake's cousin, the bossy one, Michelle," he replies and stomps out of the room.

******

"What are your parents like?" Joseph asks Michelle the following morning.

"Never home," she says. "Dad is a big-time stockbroker, and Mom is a lawyer. I think they really don't want me."

"I'm sure that's not true. All parents want their kids," Joseph replies.

"That's easy to say when you have a great family. I just know they leave me with babysitters all the time, and when they come home, they're drunk. Not like fall-down drunk, but drunk like they tune me out. So, I've never figured out where they expect me to fit in. I'm getting used to it though. It's hard when no one is around but a babysitter. It's pretty lonely."

Joseph eyes her carefully, not wanting to push too hard with his questions before he says, "That doesn't sound like much fun. Who plays with you then? Do you have friends who come over?"

"I don't get to play with anyone. My life is totally different in New York. The big city is dangerous, and kids don't walk around alone or go over to see friends," she says. "The only thing my parents let me do is play softball on a team that meets in the park. The babysitter drops me off and picks me up. They don't watch games or anything."

"Do you like it in New York?" he asks.

"I've never really known anything else. Coming here is kind of my first experience outside a big city. And I've never spent any time around families who like each other." She pretends to laugh.

"What do you mean *like* each other? All parents like their kids," he replies.

"Mine don't. I think I was an accident," she says. "And my mom forgets me all the time."

"*Forgets you?*"

"On Wednesdays, we don't have a sitter, and that's her day to pick me up at school," she says. "But most of the time my mom forgets to come. And the school is ten blocks from our house near Central Park."

"Do they call her?"

"The first time they did, but she got mad. It embarrassed her that she forgot her own kid," Michelle says. "So, I usually slip out with my friend and her mom, and I walk home alone."

"*In New York*?" Joseph questions. "You walk home alone in New York?'

"Yep."

"Aren't you kind of scared?"

"At first I was, but now it's no big deal. I'm used to it, and we have a doorman who lets me in," Michelle says.

"But where's your mom then?"

"Usually asleep on the couch," Michelle says. "She says it's a nap, but she always has an empty glass of something on the coffee table."

"You mean like she's drinking during the day?"

"Yes," Michelle says. "She drinks a lot. But I'm totally used to it and can do everything for myself."

There is sadness under all her bravado. "Well, you're here," he says, "and it's going to be the best summer ever. We will make sure you have lots of fun. How does that sound?"

"I think it's going to be great," she says, sounding more confident than she felt. "As long as you remember, I can kick your butt in baseball!"

******

As Joseph is falling asleep later that night, he makes a decision. If this girl lives without love while she's home in New York City, then when she's in South Carolina, he's going to make up for that. He's going to be nice to her. Maybe his family can be her family too, because nobody should be alone when you're just a kid.

Michelle will be loved. Joseph will make sure of that.

~ CHAPTER 5 ~

Both sets of parents insist their children practice water safety at all times. For Joseph and Jake, this means that they are enrolled in the Junior Lifesaving program at the local YMCA, and both of them are required to be CPR certified. House rules.

Or no creek.

It isn't long after Joseph completes his Junior Lifesaving Program that things start to happen—things he didn't always understand.

"Why can't we just stay here and swim?" Joseph asks his mom. "I hate the pool, and so does Jake."

"Because we are all going, and it's important to spend time with the other neighbor kids once in a while," his mom says, gathering towels and sunscreen.

"Most of them won't even hang out with us, they're *girls* and all they want to do is look at boys."

"It's called friend time, Sweetheart. Besides, Michelle and Jake will be with us too," she adds, handing him a bag to carry.

"But I hate the chlorine. It stings my eyes, and the creek is so much better," Joseph complains.

"Well, the other kids hate the creek water, so you're even," she adds, smiling.

******

The pool is crowded. Moms and kids are everywhere. It's so crowded that Joseph can't find the space to do a cannonball.

Cannonballs are a must, or the day at the pool will be worthless. Another reason to hate the pool? Way too many girls. Joseph hates this. Water is for swimming and playing, not for watching from the sidelines because you're worried about your hair.

The Double Jays and Michelle are sitting on the concrete deck with their backs to the water, talking about the annual Fourth of July party.

The lifeguards stand in their chairs, blow their whistles, and yell, "Break!"

The entire pool empties as children and adults obey the pool rule of a break at ten minutes before the hour. Everyone is required to get out of the pool.

Joseph, Jake, and Michelle continue their conversation about the party.

Turn around.

Joseph is startled. Who is speaking to him? It's not the voice of a child or teen. It's a raspy baritone voice, a grown man's voice. No one else seems to hear it. Joseph turns around to

40

face the voice and the pool, expecting to see someone standing behind him. No one.

"Excuse me," Michelle says sarcastically, giving his arm a gentle shove. "I'm in the middle of something. That's kind of rude."

Joseph stays focused on the pool and ignores Michelle's remark. He scans the area. After a few seconds, he turns back to resume their prior conversation. "Sorry," he says. "I thought I heard something."

Turn around.

There it is again—the raspy voice.

This time Joseph knows he isn't exactly *hearing* the voice; it's more like a voice in his head or his heart. He *knows* he's supposed to turn around. Joseph stands and turns. Again, he sees nothing. He searches the crowd around the pool. Moms are feeding little ones, while kids are sitting on the side deck with feet dangling in the water, talking, and munching on snacks. Teen girls in colorful bikinis are face down on the lawn chairs, reading beach novels. Teen boys are laughing and roughhousing, pretending they aren't staring at the girls in bikinis. The pool is alive with conversation and the music from at least six different boomboxes. As far as Joseph can tell, not one person seems to be vying for his attention. But with this many people, he's concerned that he's missing something.

He studies the pool. It is empty; the lifeguards are on break in the pool house.

And then he sees it.

A small shadow in the deep end. A flash of blue at the bottom.

A child.

A drowning child.

Without another thought or a single word to his friends, Joseph throws down his towel and takes off running toward the other end of the pool. In the background, he is vaguely aware of a voice coming from a mom, screaming out to a child she cannot find.

A whistle blows. A lifeguard from the overlook deck, "No running!" The whistle again. "Stop! No running!"

Joseph ignores all of it and focuses on the mission before him.

He has trained for this moment, and at just twelve years old, he knows exactly what to do. Joseph dives in as everyone stands and takes notice. Within seconds, Joseph is back up to the surface with a small boy in his arms. He places him down on the deck of the pool. He gets out of the water to assess the child. The little boy in blue swim trunks is not breathing. His eyes are closed, his lips are blue, and his body is lifeless. Joseph begins to administer perfectly timed CPR, making all the adjustments for a small child.

"One, two, three," Joseph says aloud as he presses down gently on the child's chest. He holds the child's nose and breathes into his mouth. Again, and again, he repeats this process.

In the background, Joseph is aware that a woman is screaming and crying hysterically.

"*Somebody, help us!*" she yells. "Where's the lifeguard? I need a trained adult here, not some child." She screams in a voice that is more cry than voice. "Somebody, get the lifeguard!"

Within seconds, Joseph has the boy breathing again, and the small boy coughs and spits out a mouth full of pool water.

He sits up and reaches for Joseph's embrace, crying.

"*You saved his life,*" the mother whispers as she picks her three-year-old up off the cement.

Joseph is at a loss for words—completely stunned and filled with adrenalin. He isn't sure why, but he is fighting back tears. He feels a surge of power that is not his own, and it is strange and scary. He starts to shake. He feels the first tears sliding down his cheeks.

People are hugging him, calling him a hero, but he wants to be left alone. By this time, Jake and Michelle have joined Joseph near the small boy. Michelle sees the tears on his cheeks, grabs his hand, and pulls him toward the exit, where their bikes are parked. Jake walks behind Joseph with his hand on his shoulder, pushing him forward like a bodyguard moving a celebrity through a crowded scene. They take off on their bikes toward home and make it in record time. Joseph slams on his breaks, jumps off his bike, throws it down on the driveway, and then runs down the dock. By this time, he's embarrassed and crying uncontrollably.

"Go get his daddy," Michelle barks to Jake.

Jake runs toward Joseph's house, calling for Mr. Nicholson.

A few moments later, Joseph's dad arrives, and Joseph runs into his open arms, sobbing.

"What is it, Joseph? What happened?"

"Oh, Dad, I heard a voice, but it wasn't anyone's voice. I heard it here," Joseph says, tapping his heart.

"What did the voice say?"

"*Turn around.* Two times, it said *turn around*," Joseph cries. "I don't understand."

"*No one was there*, Dad. A voice told me to *turn around* because a little boy was drowning."

"Oh, my goodness! What did you do?"

"I saved him," Joseph cries, staring up at his father. "I saved him."

"You heard a strange voice and obeyed it?" "Yes," Joseph says. "I knew I was supposed to." "Are you sure no one was there?"

"Yes, I turned both times, but the voice was too close for me to have not seen the person."

"Did Michelle or Jake see anyone?" his dad asks looking at Michelle and Jake.

"No," Joseph says. *"There was no one to see."*

Mr. Nicholson holds his son and says, "What do you think happened, Joseph? Because I think it's possible an angel spoke to you. And I want you to remember who sends angels, Joseph. Be careful here with your pride, because lots of folks saw this and lots of people are going to want to pat you on the back. Just stay humble."

Joseph leans his head on his father's shoulder and continues to cry. "I was just talking with Michelle and Jake. If the voice hadn't spoken to me, I never would have turned around."

"I'm proud of you," Mr. Nicholson says, squeezing Joseph's shoulder.

His dad turns and sees young Michelle crying. Jake is standing beside her. His dad motions with one single arm, a gentle gesture of welcome, and Michelle and Jake run into his arms.

The four of them stand together in a circle crying, in an intimate embrace that touches Joseph in a place that as of yet, has not been reached. But it is the moment when a hand, similar in size to his own, locks its fingers with his, within that embrace, that he knows. This girl cares for him deeply … and that's more than okay with Joseph.

******

That night, Mr. Nicholson calls a family meeting. He often does this when he feels something significant needs to be shared. Mr. Nicholson does things like that. Sometimes he makes one of the kids do The Dock Walk with him. Mr. Nicholson knows that when you get to the end of the dock, sit down with your toes dangling in the water, and stare at God's creation, you are primed to hear a message or share a secret. He thinks that sometimes when someone isn't looking at you, like when you're riding in a car, the communication is better. The Family Meeting is the same, because with lots of people around, delivering a message is less intimidating. The Family Meeting and The Dock Walk are Mr. Nicholson's secret ways of imparting wisdom to the people he loves.

"Can you go get Jake and Michelle?" Mr. Nicholson asks Joseph.

"Sure, Dad, but what for?" Joseph replies.

"The Family Meeting."

Within a few short minutes, Joseph arrives back home with Michelle and Jake. The family is gathered in the Nicholson family room, sprawled out on couches, chairs, and the floor. Mr. Nicholson sits in his chair. Michelle stands just outside the opening to the family room.

"Come over here, Sweet Girl," Mr. Nicholson calls out to her, patting the empty ottoman in front of his chair. "You're family."

Michelle steps into the Nicholson family room as an official member. She quietly sits on the ottoman in front of Mr. Nicholson.

Mr. Nicholson begins, "Today, something extraordinary happened. It is likely that the voice Joseph heard was an angel and the angel gave him direction. As you all know, Joseph obeyed, and a little boy was rescued from certain death by drowning. While I'm extremely proud of my son's efforts, that's not all that this is about. I want all of you to remember that angels act because *God* wants them to. They are not God. They are not to be worshiped. So, I want us to think about what that means for this family circle here. I think it's pretty special, and I think it's incredible that God is using someone from this family. I'm honored. But I want you all to be careful how you talk about this. Because honestly, no one in this room really understands the how or the why. All we know for sure is that Joseph heard the voice of an angel, and he helped save a boy. This is how God works sometimes. Our job is to be grateful and humble." He finishes by making eye-contact with each child in the room, looking for their understanding. Mr. Nicholson has tears running down his cheeks as he watches each child nod their agreement.

"I don't understand," Michelle says.

"I'm not really sure any of us do, Sweet Girl," Mr. Nicholson says, placing a gentle hand on her shoulder. "I think that's what makes this so great. How about you and I do a Dock Walk and talk about this some more?"

"*Me*? You want to do a *Dock Walk* with me?"

"Yes, Sweet Girl," Mr. Nicholson says, pulling her into his arms.

"My daddy never hugs me," she whispers into his chest.

"Well, now that you're one of us, I guess you're going to need to get used to that."

******

Before sunrise the following morning, Michelle steps off the back porch of her house to see if Mr. Nicholson is up. To her great surprise, Mr. Nicholson is sitting on his back porch with a book open before him, having a cup of coffee.

"Hey there, Sweet Girl," he says.

"Good morning, Mr. Nicholson," Michelle replies with a smile.

"What are we going to do about that?" "Whatcha mean?"

"Well, the way I see it, if you're family now, you can't be calling me Mr. Nicholson anymore. It's too formal. How about you call me Mr. Jeb?"

"I can do that, Mr. Jeb," she replies, giggling. "Shall we?" he says, pointing toward the dock. "Yes, sir!"

Michelle woke up early, put on her best dress, neatly braided her ponytail, washed her face, and brushed her teeth. Today promised to be a very special day. When she remembers it, she wants to see herself as pretty—pretty for Mr. Nicholson, who she secretly wishes was her daddy.

Mr. Jeb holds out his hand to the young girl, and she places her small one inside his rough, calloused one. Michelle feels like a princess that summer morning holding his hand, but she has no idea what to expect. Her daddy has never done anything like this. In fact, most of the time, when her daddy speaks to her, it's to yell at her for doing something wrong. Michelle believes that he is most happy when she keeps her mouth shut. Her daddy doesn't seem to like her ... or her mommy for that matter.

When they reach the edge of the dock, Mr. Jeb sits on the side and takes off his shoes and socks. Michelle is barefoot, so she sits next to him.

"I want you to know that I pray for you," Mr. Jeb says. "Actually, I've been praying for you for a long time."

She turns to look at him and wonders if he can see the shock she feels. "How come you waited until today to tell me?"

"Good question, from a brilliant girl," Mr. Jeb replies. "Here's the thing, until yesterday, I didn't think you were ready. I watch you, and I can see the hurt in your eyes. Sometimes that kind of hurt can block your heart's ability to feel the love of people. And if you can't feel the love of people, it's even harder to imagine that God loves you."

"How do you know all this about me?"

"Oh, Sweet Girl, I know how hard your life is. I know how very much you love coming here for the summer, because it's a break from that life. Your uncle has told me about your daddy and momma. Honey, they aren't bad people; they're just sick people. When you can't stop drinking, everything else falls apart."

"I don't like to talk about my mom and dad. They don't act like your family, and I wish everybody didn't know about it. It's kind of embarrassing," she says.

Mr. Jeb places a protective arm around her and pulls her close. "I was very serious last night when I told you that you are family to us. I want you to know I am here for you, always. I also want you to know you have a home here and a place in our hearts here. You are always welcome, not just in the summer. My wife and I love you dearly."

Michelle looks up at him. There is tenderness and truth and kindness in his eyes. "You love me?"

"Oh, Sweet Girl, we've always loved you," he says. "But someone else loves you even more than we do."

"Who?"

"God," Mr. Jeb answers.

Michelle shakes her head as if to disagree. If there is one thing she is sure about, it's that God seems to love certain people lots and other people not so much. That's the only way Michelle can explain why people like Joseph get families like the one he has, and she gets two drug-addicted, alcoholic parents who hate her. Why would God make a mom who forgets her own kid? If there is a God, he must be mean. The way Michelle sees it, he should love everybody the same and give everybody a good family. Whenever she thinks about this, it makes her mad. That's why some people turn out good and some people don't.

"This is something you are going to have to trust me on for now," Mr. Jeb tells her. "Because you aren't going to be able to feel that love right away, but when you've believed for a while, it's amazing how you start to feel God's love for you in what He does."

A spectacular South Carolina sunrise, the kind where a few clouds provide a burst of color that no artist can ever capture sends light over the dock. The moment is magical, and everything seems to be perfectly reflected in the calm waters of Shem Creek.

"It's so beautiful," she says.

"It's beautiful for a reason," he says.

"What do you mean?"

"God makes this beautiful, so we don't have an excuse." "An excuse?"

"When you see a sky like this one, it's so spectacular that you know there must be a God," he adds.

"Maybe like his reminder?" she asks.

"Exactly. So, when we see His creation, we see Him." "You sure know lots of stuff, Mr. Jeb."

"I think you're a pretty smart cookie yourself, Sweet Girl," he adds, smiling. He looks over his shoulder. "I'm pretty sure I can smell bacon cooking. You got any interest in some breakfast?"

"Yes, sir!"

"Let's go help Miss Kathleen make breakfast."

"I know how to cook lots of stuff," she says, scrambling to stand. Mr. Jeb takes both of her hands and pulls her up then wraps her in a hug. "Thank you, Mr. Jeb."

"You're welcome, Sweet Girl."

~ CHAPTER 6 ~

Joseph looks up from buttering a piece of toast when Michelle and his dad walk in the back door to the warm, happy, family kitchen. Kathleen is busy frying bacon.

"Hey, Michelle," Joseph says with a big smile. "Hey, Dad." "Morning," his dad says with a pat on Joseph's shoulder.

"Joseph, can you set a place for Michelle, please?" his mom asks.

"Sure, Mom," Joseph says as he gets up to get the silverware and napkin.

"OJ or milk, sweetie?" Mrs. Nicholson asks Michelle. "OJ, please."

Soon, everyone is seated around the table for the big Saturday breakfast.

Joseph's dad says grace and plates get passed around. There is bacon, sausage, pancakes, scrambled eggs, and toast. There's so much food, Michelle says it's like eating in a restaurant.

"This sure beats cereal," she adds. "No one makes breakfast like this at my house."

"Anybody get the paper?" Mr. Jeb asks.

"I'll get it for you, Dad." Joseph rises from his chair. He makes his way to the front porch, retrieves the paper, and heads back to the table. He gives the front page a quick glance and is shocked. Staring back at him is a photograph of him doing chest compressions on the little boy at the pool. The headline reads, "The Twelve-Year-Old Lifesaver." Joseph is embarrassed and doesn't want to bring the paper to the table, so he places it face down on the kitchen counter.

His dad is just finishing his plate of food and says to Joseph, "Bring the paper over to me, would you, please, son?"

Reluctantly, Joseph brings the paper to his father. He looks at his dad and shakes his head, hoping his dad will understand his unspoken message.

But his dad doesn't catch his message and sees the headline and picture. "Well, look here," he says, handing the paper to Mom.

Joseph is so embarrassed that he can't even look up. If there is one thing he hates, it's when people call attention to themselves. He can't stand people who brag about themselves, like when someone plays a great game of baseball and they've got to tell everybody about it. His dad taught him that he's supposed to let other people do the bragging on him, not the other way around. It's making him uncomfortable to know that all his friends across Charleston are going to see this paper first thing in the morning. He's so glad it's summer, and he doesn't need to go to school and suffer all the teasing that would happen. He hopes this kind of thing won't stick around for long. Hopefully, everybody will forget it. He wishes the newspaper person had asked him before they printed the article. He would have told them that somebody told him to do it. *Find that person.* Even as he is thinking this, he knows he didn't see the person who called to him. He's not sure why he's wishing he didn't think it was an angel. Once someone thinks an angel is talking to you, they are going to expect you to always be good. None of it makes sense to him, and he wants to be left alone.

The article tells the story of the twelve-year-old lifesaver from Mount Pleasant, who single-handedly saves the life of three -year-old Justin Thomas. There are dozens of quotes from witnesses, all proclaiming him to be a hero. Joseph can't stand it.

"We should probably not make a big deal about this," Michelle says, turning to face Joseph. "I'm pretty sure it's gonna totally embarrass him."

Joseph turns to look at Michelle, and her eyes are squarely focused on him. It's comforting to have her on his side, and he knows she gets him. Knowing the room is filled with the parents he loves, and yet it's Michelle who understands him so well that she speaks up for him, fills his heart with something warm. He's glad she's a girl.

"Let's leave Joseph alone about this," Dad chimes in. "Michelle is right."

No sooner has Dad gotten the words out, the kitchen phone is ringing. Joseph, looking for a distraction, gets up to answer it.

"Hello … Yes, this is Joseph … Um, I don't know … Let me ask my dad." Joseph covers the phone with his hand and says, "It's a reporter from CBS, wanting to do a story on the 'twelve-year-old lifesaver'."

"Tell them yes, Joseph," his father says. "But only if you can tell the whole story."

Joseph smiles at his dad, gives him a thumbs up, and returns to the phone.

"Yes, my dad says I can do a story, but only if you let me tell the whole story," Joseph says into the phone. "Yes … 3:00 today is fine … You're welcome. See you then."

******

The reporter arrives promptly at 3:00 p.m. She's young and introduces herself to Joseph and his parents as Jenny Myers, CBS News.

"You sure you want to do this, son?" his father asks.

"I think so, if we can tell them exactly how it went," Joseph answers.

"Okay, did you pray about it?"

"Yes, sir."

The reporter watches this exchange and smiles. "Was there anyone with you when it happened?" she asks.

"Yes, ma'am, I was talking with my two best friends," Joseph replies.

"Are they around?" she asks.

"I can go find them," his mom volunteers.

"That would be great," says the reporter.

"Can you tell me a bit about your son?" she asks, now looking at Joseph's dad.

The cameraman points his lens at Mr. Nicholson.

"He is an amazing young man, special in many ways," his father answers. "We adopted him from Guatemala when he was just a year old. From the moment we knew about him, we knew he was to be ours."

"Can you elaborate on that at all?" the reporter asks.

"We received a junk mail ad from an adoption agency in Guatemala," Jeb says, smiling. "Both of us felt very drawn to the little baby in the photo."

"What did you do?" Jenny Myers asks.

"We both felt compelled to pursue the baby for adoption," Jeb says. "It was like somehow we both just *knew.*"

"You *knew?*" the reporter asks.

"Yes, almost as if God showed us this child."

"So, you believe God had a hand in his arrival into your family?"

"We believe He orchestrated the entire process."

"That's fascinating," the reporter says smiling.

The front door opens, and in walk Jake and Michelle.

The reporter asks them to bring three of the dining room chairs out to the family room. She asks Joseph to sit in the middle of his friends.

"I'm going to ask you some questions. Please just answer them honestly," she requests.

Each child nods yes, and the reporter begins.

She looks at Joseph and asks, "So, who are these people sitting with you?"

"These are my best friends in the world, Jake and Michelle," Joseph proudly states. "We have each other's backs, always."

Michelle and Jake nod in unison.

"What were you doing when this whole thing started?" she asks them.

"We were talking. I was in the middle of telling Joseph something. His back was to the pool," Michelle answers.

"So, you weren't even looking at the pool?" she asks Joseph.

"No, my back was to the pool, and the lifeguards had left their stands because they call a break at ten minutes before the hour," Joseph explains.

"What were you talking about?" she asks Michelle.

"We were talking about the annual Fourth of July party. We always have such a great time."

"Okay, so, Joseph, tell me what happened next," the reporter prompts.

"I hear a voice say, '*turn around*'." "Who was it?" the reporter asks.

"I don't know. I turned around to see, but no one was close to us, so I thought maybe I imagined it. I went back to talking with my friends," Joseph says. "But then I heard it again, and somehow, I knew it wasn't a person near me."

"What do you mean?" the reporter questions.

"I feel it here," Joseph shares, patting his heart.

"What are you saying?" she asks, leaning closer to Joseph.

"I'm saying that a little boy was drowning, and God, or somebody, spoke to me to turn around so I would see it," Joseph explained.

"Why would God or *somebody* specifically speak to you?" she probes.

"Because I'm CPR certified on both adults and babies. I was ready to respond. The lifeguards weren't. They were sitting in the pool house," Joseph answers without hesitation.

"Wow, well … that's quite a story," she says, and a touch of doubt rises in her voice.

"I didn't hear the voice," Michelle adds.

"Did you?" the reporter asks Jake.

"No, ma'am," Jake replies. "One minute we're talking about the Fourth of July and the next, Joseph jumps up out of nowhere and starts running toward the deep end."

"What happened next?" she asks.

"He dives into the deep end, even though the lifeguards are blowing their whistles to stop running." He shakes his head. "They didn't have a clue. Just a second later, he surfaces carrying the body of that little boy."

"You mean you didn't know him?" she asks Joseph. "No, we never met him or his mom before."

"You're saying you rescued a complete stranger?" the reporter questions.

"Yes, I did. I just saw this blue thing at the bottom of the deep end, and I knew it was a child," Joseph says.

"How did you know it was a child and not a toy?" she asks, scribbling something in her notes.

"Because an angel wouldn't ask me to rescue a toy."

"Did you know there was a birthday party going on, and a mom was running a video tape recorder, and she caught the entire thing on video?" the reporter asks.

"I didn't know that," Joseph says.

"Would you like to watch it? I think you might find it very interesting."

Joseph shrugs. "Okay, I guess."

Joseph's dad turns on the TV, and the reporter puts a tape in the VCR. The screen fills with a busy, noisy public pool. The image of Joseph running comes from the left corner of the screen. He dives in. And then ...

Everyone in the room gasps. A grainy image of an angelic being, dressed in a translucent white robe, and with human-like form, hovers over them. As the video continues, the being dives in behind Joseph. Immediately, Joseph resurfaces. At this moment, the angelic being holds Joseph up as a father might hold a child. Joseph is holding the lifeless child. He gently places the child down on the cement next to the pool. He begins breathing into the child's lungs while alternating with chest compressions, all done with perfect precision. The angel stands behind Joseph, seemingly ready to help if necessary. His arms are outstretched. His face is pointed toward heaven, and he is praying. Meanwhile, Joseph administers CPR. Moments later, the boy awakens. The angel vanishes.

Everyone watching the video understands that Joseph could not have gotten the child out of the water that quickly. Instead, it was as if the entire scene played on fast forward.

"Oh, dear God above, you sent an angel not only to speak to him but to assist my Joseph as well!" his dad exclaims. He is openly crying now.

"What do you think about this, Joseph?" the reporter asks. "I knew it ..." Joseph says, tears streaming down his cheeks. "How did you know?"

"I felt hands under my arms, propelling me up, faster than I was capable of swimming on my own, like I was a rocket blasting off, as if someone wanted to get him out of the water quicker."

"I've never seen anything like this before," the reporter says. "And I have to tell you, I begged the network to let me do this piece. I wanted to meet you, hear it from you. Off the record, I'm so taken by you and your friends."

"You must think I'm nuts," Joseph says.

"No, not at all," she replies. "I guess all my life I've been looking for proof. You know? I'm a reporter, and we usually want facts and information. Can I say something a bit off topic?"

"Sure," Joseph says.

"I think you have the most amazing eyes I've ever seen."

"Yeah, people say that a lot," Joseph says. "My mom says I'm just set apart."

"Interesting," she says, scribbling something in her notebook. "Very interesting."

She stands, tells the cameraman to turn his camera off, then walks over to the three kids and hugs them. "I've had my doubts about God. But today, I believe that this video was purposefully placed on my desk so I'd see it."

"Mission accomplished," Dad says.

"I would say so, Mr. Nicholson," the reporter agrees. "I think I have all I need here. It will air on the evening news tonight. Don't forget to set your VCR to record this. Someday, your kids will want to see this."

The reporter and cameraman pack up their equipment and leave.

Joseph's father turns to him. "How are you doing with all this?"

"I'm not really sure, Dad. On one hand, this is really cool. There was an angel with me," Joseph says. "But on the other hand, I'm scared, Dad."

"Why are you scared?"

"I don't know for sure. It's not like I'm scared like when you have a nightmare or something; it's more like I'm scared of what this might mean for me," Joseph says honestly. "I'm not sure I'm ready for all of this."

"None of us are ever really ready for what God asks of us. If we were, it wouldn't require faith. Why do you think God allowed you and the rest of the world to see this angel?"

"I don't know. What if He asks a lot more of me?"

"Maybe it's just about giving you a great story to share when people need a faith boost."

"Do you think people will believe me?"

"Some will, some won't, but I assure you, Joseph, this story will plant seeds. Those seeds will grow into something great someday."

"How do I not be afraid?" Joseph asks with fresh tears.

"Tell God you trust him, and call on someone to pray for you. Then here's the action part, you *choose* to trust God," Mr. Nicholson says. "You will find that every time you trust, the next time gets a bit easier, not in the sense of what's required of you, but more in your ability to just say yes."

"You mean like say yes and let God figure it out?"

"Exactly. And you'll find this to work with the rest of your life too," his father adds.

"Thanks for helping me figure stuff out," Joseph says. "I guess that's what dads are supposed to do, right?"

"This is an honor." Tears come to his eyes as he continues, "He chose me to be your dad. Today I am reminded that He let *me* find the picture of a baby boy. Yeah, the blessing is mine."

~ CHAPTER 7 ~

After the big news story, Jake starts to feel comfortable in the background, as if his role has somehow been clarified. He doesn't mind. Everyone needs someone to stand behind him and support him.

Being Joseph's best friend makes him wonder if things like the pool rescue could happen again. If Joseph is hearing from angels now as a young guy, what if this is just the beginning? Jake isn't sure why, but he doubts that the voice will stop. He's pretty sure this will happen again and again. Thinking about this gives him chills.

Time with Joseph and Michelle needs to be spent well. They can't get into trouble. What they do when they hang out with others matters. An overwhelming sense of responsibility hits him hard. God is using him too. It's a big role to be in the background, holding up your best friend who hears the voice of God. Jake decides to pray for Joseph. Something inside his heart confirms this as the right decision.

******

Joseph is glad when the summer craziness ends. He is not happy to see Michelle return to New York, but he is delighted to be out from under all the attention the news story provided.

The Double Jays start middle school the year that the boy with the stutter arrives. Mount Pleasant seems to be a place where the locals live and stay. It isn't often new families move in. The boys have spent most of elementary school with the same group of friends, and when Matthew arrives, The Double Jays are looking forward to the possibility of a new friend.

Matthew West lands in their homeroom class, and his first day is brutal.

"Okay, class, everyone, have a seat!" the homeroom teacher calls out. "Settle down, everyone. We need to introduce ourselves and lay down some rules to get started."

The Double Jays sit together, and they motion for the new kid to sit with them. The new kid puts his backpack down on the desk next to Joseph.

"I'm Joseph, and this is Jake," Joseph offers with an out-stretched hand.

"Matthew."

"Where'd you move from? Someplace better than this?" Jake asks.

"Greenville."

Joseph can't figure this guy out. He is a good-looking, athletic looking guy, but he seems to be more interested in cutting them off and not talking than meeting new people in his school. Maybe he's just shy.

"You play any sports?" Joseph asks.

"Baseball," he says.

"*Awesome,* so do we," Jake says.

"Okay, class. Now that you're all seated, let's go around the class and do introductions. I see a few new faces to Mount Pleasant, and we need to make them feel welcome here. Give us your name, and either where you've moved from or how long you've been here. Make it brief."

She points to the front desk in the right-hand corner near the door and indicates to the young girl that she is to start and then move down the row behind her and so on through the remaining rows.

"I'm Katie Wilson. I've been in Mount Pleasant all my life," the first girl says.

"I'm Sarah Briggs, and we've been here since I was five."
"I'm Sam Middleton, and I've been here all my life too."

"Dude! I'm the amazing Jeff Walker, and everyone knows me, so no additional info necessary."

"I'm with him," the next guy said. "We are both awesome, and my name is Kevin Brannan. The girls love me."

"I'm Jake Jackson, and I've been here since I was six."

"I'm Joseph Nicholson, and I've been here since I was six. I hope everybody had a great summer."

"Like everyone doesn't know *Joseph*!" a girl shouts out with a sarcastic tone.

"Oh, yeah! Our resident *angel watching* celebrity!" another student blurts out.

Joseph feels his face getting hot. Embarrassment settles in.

"Okay, everyone, let's stick to the agenda here," the teacher interrupts. "Next, please."

"I-I-I-I'm Ma-Ma-Matthew, and I-I-I-I'm from Greenville."

"Wa-wa-wa-wa- what did you say?" Jeff Walker blurts out in a high-pitched voice.

The class erupts into laughter.

Joseph begins to understand the one-word answers.

"Hey, stop it!" Joseph yells, slapping his hands on the desk. "Just stop it! Being mean doesn't make you all cool!"

"Have a seat, Joseph, and calm down," the teacher says. "Enough of the unkind words. We will not start the year this way."

******

After what seemed to be the longest homeroom Joseph ever endured, the bell finally rings. Kids pick up backpacks and look at printed out schedules, trying to figure out where their next class is.

Joseph catches up with Matthew. "Hey, man, we play baseball just about every afternoon in my backyard. You want to stop by?"

"Sure. Wa-wa-wa ... Where?"

Joseph hands him a piece of paper with his name, phone number, and address on it.

Matthew looks at the address and smiles. "Ju-ju-ju just dddddddd-down the street from me."

"It usually includes Joseph's mom's ridiculously great chocolate chip cookies and the remote possibility that someone will end up in the creek," Jake says, laughing. "Do yourself a big favor, put your bathing suit on under your clothes. You'll see why later!"

Matthew smiles, and it reaches his eyes. Joseph immediately sees the difference. Matthew is a really handsome kid, with sandy blond hair and dimples. His light blue eyes seem to perfectly enhance the ant-like freckles crawling across his nose and cheeks. The overall effect provides one of the friendliest faces Joseph has ever seen, and he instantly likes this new boy.

The boys ride their bikes home, and each part at the driveway to tell their moms about the first day. Both boys are anxious to get outside; starting school in the fall is always a big adjustment for the two outdoor guys.

"Mom! I'm home!" Joseph calls as he slams the front door.

"Hey there, Sweetheart. How was it?" his mom asks.

"It was great! There's a new kid, and he's coming over to play some baseball this afternoon. That okay?"

"What's the kid's name?" his mom questions. "There aren't very many new kids moving in these days; maybe it's his mom I met earlier today at the grocery store."

"Matthew."

"What's he like?"

"He's a blond kid from Greenville, and guess what?" "What, Sweetheart?"

"He plays baseball!" Joseph says, as if it was the highest single form of praise.

"Anything else about him? If this is the same kid, his mom seemed concerned that he'd have a tough time making friends."

"I just met him, Mom," Joseph answers.

"Okay, then, there must be a reason why I made extra cookies today. I guess Daddy isn't going to make the cut list for cookie distribution!"

"Thanks, Mom! I'm going upstairs to change."

A few minutes later, there's a knock on the door. A handsome boy with freckles is at the door, closely followed by the woman Mrs. Nicholson had met earlier at the grocery store.

"This is so wonderful," the woman says, tears filling her eyes.

"I'm Joseph Nicholson," Joseph says, reaching out his hand to Matthew's mom.

"I'm Mrs. West. It's so nice to meet you. Where's the other boy?"

"I'm right here, ma'am," Jake replies. "I'm Jake Jackson."

"And I'm the humble cookie maker!" Mrs. Nicholson says with a smile, extending her hand to Matthew. "Mrs. Nicholson."

The boys have their fill of chocolate chip cookies, and out the back door they go.

******

Joseph decides they will take it slow with Matthew. You never know if someone is good at a sport or if they just like it a bunch. Joseph doesn't want to make him feel bad if he stinks at it. They reach the spot in the backyard where the baseball diamond sits, but only because the grass has a personality of its own and refuses to grow after years of practice. Stepping off the back porch at the Nicholson house reveals nothing fancy. It's all about where kids can play and roam free. Once Mrs. Nicholson tried to plant flowers, only to have Joseph tell her that she'd planted them right in the first base line. You don't plant *pink flowers* in the infield, ever. The boys removed the flowers by having sliding practice over them. Joseph's mom only pretended to be mad because he saw her laughing. Joseph knows she still doesn't always get the boy stuff.

Joseph naturally goes to the pitcher's mound. Between the two of them, Joseph has always been the better pitcher. So, Jake has become the most incredible batter around. Frequently, they have to spend a couple of hours diving down to the bottom of Shem Creek so that they can fish out all the foul balls.

"Want to see what I've got?" Matthew asks. "Sure! You got anything good?" Jake asks. "I'll let you be the judge of that."

Matthew heads to the pitcher's mound, and Joseph takes his place behind home plate as the catcher. This leaves Jake up to bat. Joseph loves to watch Jake smack one over the backwards house two doors down. The backwards house judges if a hit is a home run or not. If someone hits the ball over it or even with it, you're home free. The boys carefully measured and determined that if you hit it over the rooftop, you would have hit a ball out of the average park.

The house is old, with shutters hanging off the hinges, and stairs that threaten to give in and drop you through the floorboards. The weathered wood siding is punctured with holes where unwelcome four-legged visitors have taken up shop. The house used to be white, but high humidity and rain have left a green fur-like algae growing up the sides. The roof sags near the top, and the gutters have become their own little garden with flowering plants growing wild in them. The windows do not need curtains, because the years of humidity and dust have built up a film coating that allows the boys to record their home run dates with a little spit on a finger. Each boy has his own window. The brick chimney is missing so much mortar that one side sinks into the moist ground like a tombstone leaning on its side.

The house dates back to a time before their town had roads. Dad says when people visited the backwards house back in the olden days, they arrived by boat, so the pretty front with the Southern plantation look faces the creek. But Joseph thinks there's nothing pretty about the house. Although an old man lives there, they have never seen him. Truth be told, the place looks a bit haunted. But the boys don't care, the backwards house serves one purpose only: It's the Home Run House.

Jake steps up to the plate with a single goal in mind. Every person who plays at the Nicholson diamond needs to know who the boss is when it comes to batting. Thus far, Jake has absolutely no competition.

"Give me a couple of warm-up tosses, will you?" Matthew asks.

"Okay, no problem," Jake replies, stepping away from home plate.

Joseph gets behind the plate, squats down low into the catcher's position, and smacks his fist into his glove. He holds his glove in the center of the strike zone.

"Show me what you've got!" Joseph says.

The ball comes so fast into his glove that Joseph is grateful he'd hit the target. It's a stinger. Joseph removes his glove and shakes the sting out of his hand.

"Give me an outside target," Matthew requests.

Joseph moves his glove about a foot to the left, holds it up, and anxiously waits for the next pitch. With a roaring rush of air, the ball hits the target with a velocity that causes Joseph to lose his balance in the crouched position. Joseph is on his butt, trying to figure out if it was just a lucky shot or not.

Joseph gets up, dusts off his backside, and goes along with it, moving his glove all around, up, down, wherever. Each and every time he moves his glove, Matthew hits the target square and stinging hard. He has heat unlike anything Joseph has ever seen on a kid their age.

Matthew holds the ball up and moves his fingers around on the laces, placing his knuckles in a weird place. He fires off another shot. He hits the target perfectly, but only after the ball has broken about six inches to the left at the very last minute.

"Let me at this!" Jake yells in amazement.

Matthew pitches to Jake, and Jake is missing everything he's firing at him.

"Who are you, *Matthew West*?!" Jake yells in disbelief.

"I'm just a stuttering kid who loves baseball. You can get pretty good at pitching when you don't have anyone to pitch to and when all you do is aim at targets for hours. When you don't have any friends to play with, all you can do is pitch," Matthew says.

"How come you're not stuttering?" Jake asks.

"When I'm nervous, I stutter. When I'm with people I know and like, I'm okay," Matthew explains. "Which usually means I stutter at school and don't with friends and family."

"I think you're going to make me a better batter, Matthew," Jake says. "Your heat is going to train my batting better than anything!"

"You think it's good?" Matthew asks.

"You're kidding, right?" Joseph says.

"Well, no, not exactly. I've been too scared to play on a team.

People are so mean about my stutter," Matthew replies sadly.

"Well, I'm pretty sure when you show them this heat, they will officially be silenced," Joseph says, laughing.

Joseph bats next and renames himself the strikeout king, unable to make contact with anything Matthew tosses.

"My dad gets home in a little while. Will you show him?" Joseph asks.

"Sure!" Matthew says. "My dad doesn't do sports. I love him and all, but he's an engineer. He really never played sports, so he can't tell if I'm good or not. In Greenville, I didn't have any friends, so I haven't been able to test my pitching on anyone."

"So, wait … Let me get this straight. You don't play on a team or anything?" Jake asks. "And, like, is this the first time you've pitched to other people?"

"Pretty much," Matthew answers.

"Oh, wow, Matthew! You got no idea, bro!" Joseph says, giving him a pat on the back.

When Mr. Nicholson arrives home from work an hour later, he steps out back to say hi to the boys. Joseph introduces his new friend.

"Dad!" Joseph says. "You gotta see this!" "See what?" his dad asks.

"This!" Joseph says, pointing to Matthew who is now, once again, standing on the pitcher's mound.

"Oh, I like the sound of this!" Mr. Nicholson says. "Show me what you've got, Matthew!"

"It's better if there's a batter up," Jake says moving toward home plate.

Mr. Nicholson stands on the back porch with his hands on the rails and gives the boys his full attention. Mr. Nicholson is aware that Jake is one of the best batters he has ever seen. He has power and control and can place a ball where the hole in the defense is. Mr. Nicholson is a real baseball lover. He played high school varsity and college ball. He played in the minors for a few seasons before he decided that his beautiful girlfriend, Kathleen, wasn't going to wait forever. So, he traded his baseball glove in for law school. There was always the lingering question in his mind, though: Did he stick it out long enough?

What Mr. Nicholson sees Matthew do blows his mind.

"Who has been coaching you, son? I heard you're from Greenville. Was it Mack?" Mr. Nicholson asks, because he knows all the key coaches in South Carolina.

"I've never had a coach, sir," the boy replies.

"You mean you haven't had a private pitching coach?" Mr. Nicholson asks.

"No, I've never actually played on a team, sir," Matthew says.

"Why not? Greenville has a great league." Mr. Nicholson questions.

"Well, sir, you see, I have this stutter when I'm nervous around strangers," Matthew says. "The kids have been really mean to me, and I got sick of it at school. I guess I was scared to try."

"Son, when the Good Lord gives you talent, it's sinful not to put it to use for Him," Mr. Nicholson says laughing.

"Honestly, sir, I didn't know if I was good or not 'til about thirty minutes ago, when I started playing with the boys here," Matthew says.

"Humility. That's an incredible trait, young man," Mr. Nicholson says, then adds, "But, son, you're joining our baseball team, and I won't hear another word about it!"

Matthew produces the full dimple smile and says, "Yes, sir; just tell my mom, please."

"Will do, son. Will do." Mr. Nicholson smiles as he heads inside to see his wife.

"Betcha can't!" Jake yells to Joseph.

"Bet I can ... and faster!" Joseph yells back.

Once again, the race begins. The boys abruptly leave the baseball diamond at breakneck speed, throwing off their clothing, running toward the dock. Each step closer to the dock, and ultimately closer to the water, means that another article of clothing is coming off, until both boys are executing perfect cannonballs into Shem Creek, stripped down to their bathing suits.

Like a certain girl before him, Matthew takes the bait. When Joseph and Jake turn around, Matthew is in the air above them, stripped down to his swimsuit.

"This is the best day I've ever had," Matthew says, laughing and splashing water in Jake's face.

"Life is good, bro! Life is good!" Joseph says.

Matthew West never stutters again.

~ CHAPTER 8 ~

The summer after they start middle school, everything changes.

"When does she get here?" Joseph asks, taking off his shoes and socks and putting his feet in the creek.

"Who?" Matthew replies.

"I keep forgetting, you never met her. We're talking about Michelle. She's Jake's cousin, and she comes every summer," Joseph replies.

"Oh, wow. So, you all have to play with a girl?" Matthew asks, throwing a rock off the dock into the creek.

"No, we don't *have* to play with a girl," Joseph explains. "We totally want to. Have you ever met a girl who doesn't throw like a girl, and who isn't into all that girly stuff? I mean she's cool. Seriously cool."

"No, can't say that I have. So, when does she come?" Matthew asks.

"Actually, later today," Jake answers.

Joseph smiles. He can't wait to see Michelle. Summer begins when she arrives. The three of them will run free all summer again—well, maybe the four of them if she likes Matthew. He has so much to tell her, so much has happened this year, and she is one of his best friends.

The backdoor slams shut, and all three boys turn.

It's Michelle.

A new and remarkably changed Michelle.

Gone are the skinny legs with knobby knees; gone is the straight up and down body of a little girl; gone is the face of a child. In its place is a woman—a woman with curves. She no longer has the gait of a little girl, her hips sway.

As she makes her way down to the dock, it is as if there is a shift in Joseph's world.

Joseph is stunned. He watches as this gorgeous woman-child walks toward him, and he can't even think. It is as if, in one single moment, he grew up, and all his hormones jumped into high gear. She is the most gorgeous human he has ever seen, but he can't actually think of another human he's seen like this before. The ponytail and baseball cap have been replaced by a wide-brimmed straw hat. She has tied her baggy bright yellow t-shirt in a knot at her belly button, revealing several inches of skin above her pink bikini bottom. Her heeled sandals accentuate her elongated, smooth, tanned legs adorned with a tiny ankle bracelet. Large gold hoops dangle from newly pierced ears. Her hair is all caught up on one shoulder, dangling in loose curls down the front of her. The image is topped off with gold aviator glasses. She looks so incredible that Joseph thinks this moment should be set to music.

Joseph can't even talk. On one hand, wow, he likes what he sees. On the other, what's going to happen now? How's she going to play with three guys now? Why did she have to go and become a *real girl?* Is she going to turn into one of those prissy girls who only cares about clothes and makeup? Is she going to be all worried about what she looks like and not want to swim and stuff? What about playing ball with them? How's that going to work out? But this new Michelle? He approves. He very much approves. Girls sure know how to confuse a guy.

From the back porch, Jeb calls to his wife. "Hey, Kathleen, I think you need to see this."

Kathleen rushes to the back porch with her mouth just hanging open. "Dear Lord, she's gorgeous! What are we going to do?"

Mr. and Mrs. Nicholson have always known the day would come when the gorgeous woman would erupt from Michelle's childhood body, but nothing prepared them for just how gorgeous. There's a moment for a young woman when everything is new and ripe, before she realizes her feminine power, when she is as beautiful as a woman can be. Michelle is in that moment right now.

"Well, I'm going to call a Dock Walk for tomorrow," Mr. Nicholson says.

"Any idea what you'll say?" Kathleen asks.

"Not a clue yet, but I know it will come!" He laughs. "I remember a certain girl I know having that kind of impact on a poor innocent boy." He pulls his still beautiful wife into a loving embrace. "Look where it got us."

"There has always been something special there with her and Joseph," Kathleen says. "I've always wondered if they will end up together."

"Whoa, let's slow this one down ..." Jeb says, smiling. "Give that poor boy a chance to digest the incredible sight he's just taken in. He won't know what hit him."

"You got that right," Kathleen says. "That one right there is a Mack truck." Kathleen gives Jeb a knowing smile, and the two of them sit down on the porch swing to watch this scene unfold.

Joseph stands up tall and walks toward Michelle. "How's my favorite New Yorker doing?" he says, pulling her into a stiff embrace that feels wrong and right at the same time.

"It's so great to see you." she exclaims. "I've missed you so much." She holds onto his embrace longer than necessary.

She takes a step back as if to examine him. "Wow!" she says. "You've *really* changed."

Nine months is a lifetime of growth for a fourteen-year-old boy. He hadn't even realized that the changes he was undergoing showed. But from the way she looks at him, he gets the impression she approves.

"You grew about a foot! You're so tall! And your shoulders are, like, super broad. And what's up with the peach fuzz?" she teases, touching his cheek with the back of her hand.

He hugs her neck and pulls her close. "It's great to see you. It's okay for summer to start now." The hug feels different. It's confusing because this is his friend who plays baseball with him. She's a girl, but not like a girl … and all of a sudden, she *is* a girl.

Joseph is trying to understand why he has butterflies in his stomach and why he is wondering if he smells okay. He rakes his hand through his hair and actually wonders if it's a mess. What is this girl turning him into?

She smiles, and it takes his breath away. "I'm finally here! This is where I'm the most me!" She lets out a big, happy sigh.

Joseph smiles. He knows exactly what she means. This is where she has the life she loves.

Matthew has no idea what she means by that.

"And you are …?" Michelle says as she makes eye contact with Matthew.

"I'm Matthew. We moved in down the street a few months ago," he shares. "Nice to meet you." He sticks out his hand. Matthew has a fleeting thought that this certainly did not appear to be this baseball-playing tomboy that was described to him earlier. For a brief moment, Matthew has a feeling of dread in his stomach. As he stares at this stunning girl, his heart skips, and there is such an intense attraction he's scared everyone will notice. His face feels hot, and he wants to reach up and touch her hair. He has a feeling of dread that only intensifies as he watches this beautiful girl look at Joseph. Matthew realizes in a moment of clarity that he is probably a couple of years too late. These two, whether they realize it or not, already have something for each other. Matthew doesn't really know how he knows this, but a realization hits him. She *belongs* to Joseph already. And Joseph is the most wonderful friend that a guy could ask for.

Matthew wishes he could *unsee* this moment that he fears will be etched in his brain. This is no tomboy; this is a beautiful young girl who just happens to have found his friend first. Matthew knows things just went from simple to challenging. It's going to be hard to pretend he doesn't think this is the prettiest girl he's ever seen. It's confusing, because he doesn't usually think of girls this way. He usually finds girls to be complicated and bossy. Then a thought occurs to him: *Maybe she doesn't always look like this.* Maybe she's just dressing weird to impress Joseph. After all, they *did* say she was a tomboy and plays baseball. How's a girl going to play baseball in that outfit?

But try as he might, Matthew could not imagine any situation where this girl would be anything but gorgeous. Truth be told, this is the first girl he's ever thought of like this. What is a guy supposed to do? He sure wishes they could go back to it just being three guys. Three guys are simple. *This … is not simple.*

"Has he been properly vetted?" she asks, utterly oblivious to the intense moment of confusion Matthew is having. She's laughing as she shakes his hand.

"Oh, yeah!" Joseph says. "This right here is a guy that we are lucky to know."

"Thanks, man," Matthew acknowledges. "That was a super nice thing to say." But this only serves to make the twinge of guilt over his reaction to Michelle feel even worse.

"He's great, and he plays baseball," Jake chimes in. "Enough said."

******

The four friends lounge on the dock for the rest of the afternoon until Mr. Nicholson comes out to light the grill.

As he lights the grill, he hears Joseph call out, "Who wants to go for a swim before dinner?"

"Betcha can't!" Jake laughs out loud.

"Aw, come on, guys! We're already on the dock!" Matthew calls out.

"What are you ... chicken? A girl might make it into the water before you?" Michelle challenges.

Joseph laughs out loud, because even gorgeous girls with perfect outfits on will look really stupid hopping around trying to get clothes off for the swim. He's looking forward to that.

"Bet I can!" she yells out as the yellow t-shirt slides over her head, and she kicks off her sandals.

Matthew can't move. As Michelle flings the last of her cover-up clothing to the side, she stands there in a pink string bikini that does absolutely nothing to hide the glorious changes that have occurred. He is so grateful when Jake comes up from behind him and encloses him in a bear hug tackle that lands them both in the calm waters of Shem Creek.

It would be years later when Jake finally confesses to seeing the look on Matthew's face and knowing the only thing to help him at that moment was the cold water of the creek.

As the afternoon moves on, Jake thinks about how complicated things will become between them if Matthew harbors some sort of a crush on Michelle. This is why girls make stuff difficult. Jake knows he is right in the middle of it, and if they are to all stay friends, Jake will have to play a significant role. He loves Joseph like a brother. They have been best friends for so long, Jake can't remember a time when he didn't feel the anchor of Joseph's friendship. He also has a respect for Joseph that isn't really common for kids that young. He doesn't want anyone to get hurt, especially Joseph.

Jake is happy when he sees Mr. Nicholson step off his porch and head for the dock. Jake has a feeling Mr. Nicholson didn't miss a thing, and knowing Mr. Nicholson, he will set them straight and help them out.

"Hey there, Sweet Girl!" Mr. Nicholson calls out to Michelle.

"Mr. Jeb!" she greets, folding herself into his bear hug. "Oh, how I've missed you! I think I need to call my own Dock Talk with you, please!"

"Well, that's a first. But how about tomorrow afternoon?" he suggests.

"Sounds great!"

******

Just after sunset, everyone retires for the night, and Matthew's mom picks him up.

Joseph is just about to doze off when his dad comes into his room. "Get your flashlight, Son. We need a Dock Walk."

Joseph has a fleeting thought that something might be wrong. Dock Walks were usually at sunrise and planned ahead of time. Joseph checks the clock on his nightstand, and it's 11:30.

"Sure, Dad," he says. "Give me a sec."

Joseph pulls on his gym shorts, grabs his flashlight, and follows his dad out the back-porch door, down the well-worn path to the dock.

When they reach the edge, both men sit and dangle their feet in the cool nighttime water.

"We need to talk about Michelle," his dad begins. "I'm quite sure I don't need to call your attention to the recent changes in her. I saw you and Matthew look at her. I want to tell you, that's the one and only moment I will tolerate you looking at a girl like that."

"I don't know what you mean, Dad."

"Do you know what the word 'vulnerable' means?"

86

"Yes, sir," Joseph replies. "It's like you're sensitive or something?"

"Not exactly. Let me explain," Mr. Nicholson says. "Vulnerable means that because of stuff that's happened, someone might have a tendency to do stuff that probably isn't good for them."

"Okay, but what does that have to do with me?" Joseph asks.

"Everything, absolutely everything," his dad answers. "You see, that sweet girl hasn't been loved well by her parents. And, in a girl like her, there's going to be a lifelong tendency to look for that love. "

"That's okay, Dad, because I'm already crazy about her," Joseph admits with a blush.

"I know that," his dad responds. "But when you're vulnerable, you're not ready, and so that changes what you are allowed to do."

"I don't understand."

"There are a couple of parts to this. The first one is that in the Bible there's a passage that says, 'Greater love has no one than this, that he lay down his life for his friends.' This means, quite simply, that we are supposed to love each other as Jesus did. And Jesus loved us so much that He gave his life. For us, it means that we love people sacrificially, that we put their needs above our own," his dad explains.

"So, let me make this simple: You may not date her, touch her, kiss her, or in any way act upon this physical attraction you have for her. Someday, she might be your wife, but if you show her lust instead of love, you'll never have her to love. Your job is simple: You are to protect her, love her as a friend, and do your best to guide her toward God. Do this God's way, and you'll have no regrets. You must treat her honorably and encourage her."

Joseph nods, and his dad continues, "For this big job, you're going to really need help, so I commit to you that you have my prayers."

Joseph can't believe what his father just said. It surprises him to realize that his dad already knew he had feelings for Michelle, especially since he just figured that out for himself. *Michelle might be my wife someday? That's a crazy idea, so far off. But what if my dad is right? What if these feelings are something big? What if she's here for a reason?*

In that moment, Joseph begins to understand that keeping his hands off her is important. He'd never thought that because Michelle's life was rough that she might have problems. He always thought she seemed just fine. But … if she needs someone to protect her? Joseph knows he can do his best to do that. He decides that although he doesn't fully understand what his dad is talking about, he's going to obey him. His dad is usually right about things. Maybe what you do today matters later on—maybe it matters a lot.

After a few moments of silent thoughtfulness, Joseph says, "Thanks, Dad."

"For what?"

"For always explaining stuff and helping me not to do something that I might regret later."

"You are to protect her. Do you understand what that means?"

"I think I do, Dad," Joseph answers.

His dad stands and stares out at the beautiful summer night and silently thanks God for the extreme privilege it is to be this young man's father.

"Hey, Dad, did God happen to tell you when?" Joseph says, with a grin spreading.

"When what?"

"When will the time be okay to … you know … date her and maybe kiss her?"

His dad smiles too. "When you're old enough and wise enough to not need to ask me."

"Ha! Okay, I get it," Joseph says, chuckling.

As Mr. Nicholson walks back to the house, he keeps wondering if Joseph will always be like this. *Will he reach a point where he questions God? Will life challenge his beliefs and cause him to change?* He ponders a feeling in his gut that sometimes this all seems too easy. *Will there be a day when he speaks harshly to me? Will he rebel, or is this budding faith I see here to stay?* Life and experience have taught him that, most of the time, childhood faith doesn't last, but only time will tell.

The Dock Walk with the rest of the boys goes well, although the content of the conversation differs significantly. Mr. Nicholson is aware that Joseph doesn't want any of his father's suspicions about his feelings for Michelle to be revealed. So, he makes the conversation about honor and waiting. He explains to the boys that lust and love are quite different. Lust is self-serving, and love is sacrificial. He tells them that as a group of brothers, they are charged with protecting this young girl and her purity. Hands off.

When Mr. Nicholson is finished with the Dock Walk with the boys, he is informed by his wife that Michelle needs a new bathing suit, and Mr. Nicholson wholeheartedly agrees.

"How will you keep from offending her?" Mr. Nicholson asks.

"I'm going to give her a dose of truth about what all teenaged boys want," she replies.

"She needs to know how to manage this woman thing, and she needs a woman to show her," Mrs. Nicholson says.

******

A few days later, Michelle and Mrs. Nicholson go on a girls-only shopping date in Downtown Charleston. Michelle has never done anything like this with her mom. Her mom is too busy with work and her wine. When Michelle wants clothes, her mom gives her money and drops her at the mall. She never asks Michelle to show her what she purchases, and she definitely does not have any wisdom to offer in clothing choices. Michelle is on her own, and most of the time she really doesn't know what to do.

The following day, when Michelle shows up to hang out on the dock with the boys, she looks a bit more appropriate. She is wearing a purple one-piece bathing suit with a matching pair of shorts and an absolutely adorable girly baseball cap. Michelle instantly feels more comfortable and she understands Mrs. Nicholson's advice when she dives off the dock, and all parts of her bathing suit stay in one place.

~ CHAPTER 9 ~

"What's for breakfast, Mom?" Jake asks, dropping his baseball cleats and bag on the floor next to the kitchen table.

"You okay with scrambled eggs and toast? I've got some homemade strawberry jam. Or are you in a sugar cereal mood?" his mom asks.

"Eggs sound good," he answers, and then asks, "Hey, what's this?" He points to the purple Jansport backpack with the mini Yankees baseball dangling from the handle. "Is *Michelle* here?"

"Yeah, your dad picked her up late last night from the airport. She's never seen the spring break baseball tournament, and since we are hosting it here, your dad and I thought we'd fly her here for spring break," his mom announces.

"Well, I know a couple of guys who will be pretty happy to see *her*."

Pouring orange juice in a glass, his mom gently explains, "She needs a break. Things are heating up at home for her, and your dad and Mr. Nicholson thought it might be nice to give her a break beyond just summer."

"Is she okay?"

"Yeah, but your aunt is really drinking a lot, and we're worried," his mom shares as she places a plate of scrambled eggs in front of him.

"Is there anything I can do? Or, like, is there anything I should know?" he questions, crunching on bacon.

"She seems good, but that's one of the reasons for the visit. We want to make sure she's okay."

"Can she come to the game this morning? It would be so cool to surprise the guys," Jake asks.

"That was our plan, to totally surprise the three of you, but since you know, do you think you can keep the secret until she gets there?"

"Absolutely! This is going to be so fun. Spring break is going to be great." Jake exclaims, just before filling his mouth with scrambled eggs.

"Remember the rules, please. Since you're the cousin, you need to keep your eyes on stuff, please."

"Mom, we aren't kids anymore. We're all fourteen. We get it. They get it. We're good," he says, rolling his eyes slightly.

"Okay, okay … just checking, Sweetheart."

"I know, Mom. Trust me, I know. With the two of them both crazy about the same girl, I'm a bit of a referee. I get it, but it is getting kind of old."

"Just keep doing a great job of being a referee. We all know she only has eyes for Joseph, though."

"Oh, I know. In fact, I won't be surprised someday when I'm asked to be the best man," Jake jokes, taking his last bite of toast slathered with strawberry jam. "They just seem like that kind of couple in books that meet as kids and never look back."

Jake places his empty plate in the sink, while his mother says, "Whoa ... Slow that train down, Sweetheart. We've got to get you all through your teens first. Anything could happen."

Jake shrugs with a smirk, and she smiles. "Well, okay ... we should probably get going, I know how much you guys love your warmup time."

Jake runs next door to get Joseph. Matthew is already waiting in the driveway. Jake smiles at his two best friends, knowing how much they are going to love this great surprise.

******

Michelle catches a ride to the game with Mr. Jeb.

"Go ahead of me?" she suggests. "If I come up with you, they'll notice too quickly ... and where's the fun in that?" She giggles. "I want to completely surprise them and catch them off-guard."

Plus, Michelle wants to observe and watch things for a minute. She leaves at the end of every summer wondering how Joseph acts with others and what he does during the school year when she's not there. At fourteen, she wonders if

94

he has any girlfriends. She's curious to see if anyone is chasing after him. After all, back in New York, she has lots of guys hitting on her—lots.

Michelle can't help but wonder, *Is Joseph a good guy all the time, even when I'm not there? Or is he the kind of guy who keeps lots of girls on a string?* She knows they aren't dating or anything, but it seems like it's understood that she shouldn't like anyone else and neither should he. She doesn't really know *why* it's understood, since they've never really talked like that, but she gets the feeling that Joseph probably likes her the best—at least she hopes so.

From her spot in the front seat of the car, she can see them in their uniforms, and they look older. So many changes in a few months. She notices that the bleachers are filled with people, but the front row seems to be occupied with girls— very pretty, typical, South Carolina blondes. Maybe they are watching other guys. She hopes so. She keeps her eyes focused on them. The coach hasn't called infield warm-up practice yet, so the guys are standing around outside the dugout. One girl, with honey-colored hair and long suntanned legs, gets up, and four other nearly identical blondes follow her. They head straight for *her* threesome. The girls are giggling and touching the guys on the arms, looking like they are marking their turf. The guys look happy to see them. Jake looks *especially* happy to see the blonde girls. Maybe he has a crush on one of them. They talk and laugh for a minute, and Joseph steps back and walks off, leaving Jake and Matthew to flirt with the girls. Michelle smiles. Even though he has no idea she's there, Joseph moves on. Michelle likes this. In fact, she might like this too much. After all, they can't date yet, so getting jealous doesn't make sense. Still, she's glad to know that he's not so taken with the blonde girls.

She glances back at Matthew. He's gotten taller. He's such a handsome guy. She sometimes wonders about him and what she would feel like if she had met him first. There's something about him. Maybe it's that she knows how he feels about her. Maybe it's just flattering knowing someone is crazy about you. He holds a special spot with her—not like Joseph, but still definitely not like the rest of the guys. She respects Matthew, because he's never let on about liking her, but a girl knows. She senses it when he's around.

Then there's Jake. Even though he is her cousin, Jake is the brother she was never given. She loves him. He's been so kind to her every summer, and he stays up late with her talking. He's heard all her family garbage.

She's so grateful for all of them. They are her family.

With a deep breath of anticipation, Michelle gets out of the car, opens the back seat, and pulls her glove out of her backpack. She puts on her Yankees hat with her dark ponytail hanging out the back. Wearing cut-off shorts, a worn Yankees t-shirt, and her really cool Nikes, she walks toward the guys.

"All right, everyone, take your positions in the field. It's time for infield warmup." the coach calls out.

Without seeing her, everyone but Matthew heads to the infield for practice. Matthew is looking around for the other catcher who hasn't yet arrived. The second-string catcher is responsible for pitcher warm-up. He is nowhere in sight.

"The catcher isn't here. What do you want me to do?" Matthew asks the coach as he rotates his shoulders to warm his muscles.

"I'll do it!" Michelle calls out.

He recognizes her voice without seeing her. A totally surprised Matthew turns around and sees Michelle walking towards him. Joseph, Jake, and Matthew abandon infield practice and run toward their friend. They encircle her in a gigantic three-man bear hug and lift her off the ground. This leaves them all laughing.

"What are you doing here?" Joseph asks incredulously.

"Oh, you know ... maybe your parents thought it might be a nice spring break surprise?" Michelle is smiling and drinking in the feeling of being caught up in their loving embrace. The scent memory hits her—freshly cut grass, leather baseball gloves, and teen guy smell. This is what home smells like.

Michelle is right where she wants to be. Joseph's arm is around her. Matthew is standing in front of her, arms crossed, and smiling from ear to ear. Jake is punching Joseph in the arm. She is with *her* guys. These guys don't belong to the blonde girls in the front row. They are hers, and she is happy in a way that defies words. She knows this is where she is loved, and this is where she is most herself.

"Okay, okay ... break it up! Break it up!" the coach yells out.

Jake and Joseph reluctantly head back to infield practice, but Matthew is still waiting for the catcher to arrive. "She can do it, Coach?" Matthew suggests.

"Your sting? *She* can do it? She can catch *your* sting?" the coach asks.

"Yes, sir, she sure can!" Matthew answers quickly.

Michelle heads to the dugout. She turns her Yankees hat backwards, grabs the catcher's mask, and puts it on over her face. She walks towards the bull pen, squats in the catcher's position, and smacks her fist in the glove. "Bring it," she says.

Infield practice comes to a halt, and Michelle knows all eyes are on her.

She moves through a practiced routine, where she knows the first pitches are slow and contain deliberate motions to warm up the arm and shoulders before the fast stuff. She calls the pitches out to Matthew.

"Give me the slider!" she tells him, with her voice filled with confidence.

Smack!

"Okay, time for the fast ball," she announces, punching her glove a couple of times.

The ball is fast and hard, but she doesn't blink. She catches each stinging ball and throws them back with the confidence of a baseball star. She moves the glove outside, inside, up, and down. She uses their two-finger signal between her legs to call out his famous pitch that breaks six inches to the left at the last minute. She is focusing on the ball, but she hears the comments coming from the girls in the bleachers—comments that she hears all the time. Girls don't like her. She smiles, knowing this is why her best friends are guys.

The coach is impressed, and with a laugh, says, "Please …
tell me she's on our softball team!"

"If she lived here, she would be!" Joseph calls from
shortstop.

After the warmup is finished, Michelle removes the
catcher's mask and smiles at her friends. Her confidence
is at an all-time high; she feels their admiration. She hopes
their teammates think she's cool too. She unties her ponytail,
shakes her head, and lets her mane of dark hair cascade down
her back, making sure that they all know she's still all girl. She
turns and looks toward shortstop, puts her hand on her hip,
and smiles at Joseph in a way that leaves no room for doubt
that *he* is special.

******

Back in the bleachers, a few minutes later, Mr. Jeb says to
Michelle, "That was quite a show, Sweet Girl."

"Too much?" Michelle asks.

"No, but tread lightly. Those boys out there are trying to
behave themselves."

"What do you mean?"

"I'm pretty sure you've figured out that two of those guys
out there are crazy about you. Be careful with their hearts.
Okay?" Mr. Jeb explains.

"Okay," she replies.

"You have an impact on young men, and with that comes some responsibility. You need to own your behavior, keep it friendly, brotherly, and not flirtatious. One of those guys might be your husband someday, and you really don't want to mess that up."

"I'm thinking that I'm kind of young to be talking about husbands. I probably should do some dating first," she says, with a laugh. "But I never thought of it that way ... Did I just do something wrong?"

"No, Sweet Girl, you did not. In fact, I think you made the three of them really proud. Just please understand that they know it's too early to date. So, help them stay away from that. It will make this foursome friendship a whole lot easier."

"Yes, sir. Got it. Thanks for the heads-up. And I think I'm going to pretend you didn't mention the word *husband*," she teases, laughing again.

Mr. Nicholson points to the field. "Watch this," he says, directing her to Matthew on the pitcher's mound. "Have you ever actually watched him in action?" Mr. Jeb says, noticing that after each pitch, Matthew looks up for Michelle's reaction.

"Not in a game. I'm always here in the summer after baseball season is over."

"See this guy up at bat?" Mr. Jeb asks. "He's the best batter in the state, and no pitcher can stop him, but Matthew does."

"So, he just struck out the best batter in the state of South Carolina?" she asks. "Like he's *that* good?" Matthew smiles at her from the mound again.

"Oh, yeah ... Our boy, Matthew, will be playing major league ball someday. Mark my words on that," Mr. Jeb notes.

"Seriously?"

"I've never seen anything like him. In fact, when you watch his games, they tend to be boring, because absolutely no one can get a hit off of him. His precision is remarkable," Mr. Jeb adds.

"I wonder where it will take him," Michelle ponders.

"Only God can answer that, but see that guy in a blue baseball cap about four rows behind you?" Mr. Jeb asks.

"Yeah, why?"

"He's a scout. He watches Matthew regularly, although Matthew doesn't know it."

"Why don't you tell him?"

"Because at fourteen, baseball should still be fun. He's going to have lots of years ahead of him for big competition. I want him to enjoy this last year before high school with his friends."

******

For the foursome, the afternoon plan is simple: the beach. The spring weather is a balmy seventy-five degrees, and the skies are Carolina blue. It's as if silent forces are pulling them toward Sullivan's Island beach. Life is good.

"Let's do it!" Joseph calls out. "Everybody line-up."

He reaches out his hand to Michelle; she turns and grabs Matthew's hand, and Matthew grabs Jake's. They stand perfectly still, toes aligned facing the salty Atlantic Ocean. A gentle breeze is lifting Michelle's hair, and the sun is kissing her cheeks.

"No chickening out," Joseph says.

"What? You're kidding, right? I mean who would *not* want to go headfirst into freezing cold water, seriously?" Michelle jokes.

"Just making sure everyone remembers the rules. Same pace. On the count of three. No cheating. Headfirst!" Joseph calls out. "One ... Two ... Three ... Go!"

The four friends run straight toward the crashing waves, and without breaking their hold on each other, they dive headfirst into the ocean.

The guys are splashing each other as another wave hits them. Matthew swims up to Michelle and grabs her by the waist and dunks her. Michelle comes up for air to find Joseph paying Matthew back. They are laughing, splashing, and loving the day.

"This water is too cold, even for this New Yorker!" Michelle calls out as she heads toward the towels.

Joseph turns as Michelle exits the water. She is stunning in a wet bathing suit with her hair slicked back behind her. As she walks toward the towels, Joseph is struck with a jealousy he's never felt before. He watches as several older guys on the beach check her out. He is uncomfortable as he contemplates their motives. In a moment of clarity, it occurs to him that he's feeling something he's only beginning to understand. Instinctively, he wants to protect her, but at the same time, he wants the world to know she's *his*. But he's not supposed to feel this way. His dad cautioned him to keep it friendly, but what is he supposed to do?

Joseph's stomach is nervous and feels like it's full of a flutter of butterflies. *This girl is so beautiful. But I know her. I know she's kind and gentle. I know she throws like a guy, but laughs like a girl. I know she loves my family. I know she has a tender heart. These other guys on the beach just think she's a good-looking girl.* And something dawns on him at this moment. He can hear his father's words, loud and clear. For the first time in his life, he begins to understand the difference between love and lust. Because as he watches this gorgeous girl walk on the beach, an overwhelming desire to protect her overtakes him.

While the guys on the beach are busy lusting after Michelle, Joseph wants to hand her a t-shirt to cover up and wrap her in a towel, because she's cold. He wants to be a different kind of guy for her. She's going to attract all sorts of bad news guys, who will never see past the gorgeous outside package. His job is clear: He is to love her and protect her.

As Joseph is lost in his thoughts, he notices Matthew. He, too, is staring at Michelle. Joseph knows his friend has a thing for Michelle, and he's grateful for the friendship that keeps Matthew from acting on his feelings. But today, Joseph begins to realize that Matthew has a tough job, trying to hide his feelings every day.

What if Michelle knows Matthew has feelings for her? he wonders. Joseph knows firsthand how tough it is to care for someone you aren't allowed to react to. He wonders what it's like to not even be able to acknowledge those feelings.

Matthew is such a great guy, but he seems to have eyes for only one girl.

Joseph hopes this doesn't cause the foursome to split apart.

Maybe Jake can help Matthew find another girl.

******

As the sun is dipping on the horizon, they gather their things to head home. Their bikes are parked on the other side of the sand dune. There's a chill in the air as they make their way inland towards Mount Pleasant.

Michelle is on the back of Joseph's Schwinn banana seat Beach Cruiser bike. The two of them are last in line as Joseph peddles toward home. His scent is an intoxicating mix of salt water, Coppertone, laundry soap, and Joseph's man scent. Michelle is perched on the seat behind Joseph, and she leans into him. She allows her arms to encircle his slim waist, and she moves in close behind in search of his body warmth. In response, she feels him take in a quick breath. She rests her body behind him, with her cheek resting on the back of his t-shirt. He takes his one hand off the bike handles and covers her hand with his as he sits up straight and rides.

She is completely attached to him. The wind is blowing through her hair, and the smell of the salty ocean mixes with the scent of Joseph. All her senses come to life. She feels a warmth travel through her as she snuggles close to his back. She has never before felt this content and safe. She wishes this bike ride would last forever.

As they pull to a stop in the driveway, she feels the loss of his warmth as she separates from him and gets off the bike. "Thank you for the best ride ever," she says.

"Yep, this day is a keeper," Joseph says. "Don't ever forget it, okay?"

"Something changed," she says, searching his eyes for confirmation.

"Yeah, and I like it."

"Me, too."

"Hellooooo ... we're here too," Jake says, laughing. "You can say goodbye to us too."

Michelle turns around to respond to Jake and sees Matthew. The look in his eyes tells his truth. It's as if the look confirms something Michelle has long suspected. Matthew cares for her in the very same way Joseph does. Somehow her moment of elation over holding Joseph close diminishes. Two wonderful guys, who are her best friends, both love her, and she cannot imagine how this can turn out well.

******

As the sun sets over Shem Creek, Michelle finds herself on the dock, thinking and wondering what today's changes would bring. Would Joseph become her boyfriend, or would they remain the same, but with a secret between them? She isn't sure she understands the change. Was her father a great guy at one point too, but life changed him? Or was he always a mean drunk? Do all men become bad, or are guys like Joseph for real?

The porch door slams, startling her out of her thoughts, and she turns to see Mr. Jeb heading toward her.

"Hey there, Sweet Girl ... Whatcha doing out here by yourself?" he asks.

"Thinking about things, but the more I think, the more questions I have," she answers.

"Can I help you sort through your questions?" He sits next to her and dangles his feet in the creek.

"Maybe, but they're about Joseph."

"Okay, I know him pretty well," he says, smiling. "Ask away."

"Well, when do men change?"

"You mean when do boys become men?"

"No, like, when does the being nice stop and the meanness start?" she asks. "Because you're not normal."

"Oh, gotcha. Well, it might surprise you to know there are lots of men like me. I'm not perfect; I've just learned a bit about how to treat my wife and kids. Is that what you mean?"

"Yeah, but how come you learned it, but my dad never did? And will I grow up to be just like my mom?" she asks.

"My faith in God changed me," he explains. "I feel like I have to answer to God for how I run my family and treat the people around me. Does that make sense?"

"Yeah, I think it does. But how come my dad and mom don't answer to God then? Aren't you supposed to do that when you have kids?"

"I can't really answer that, but I do know that God loves your mom and dad very much."

"Seriously? God loves them?" she asks. "Yes, He does. And He loves you too."

``Then why didn't He give me parents like you and Miss Kathleen?"

"Let me turn that around for a minute. Don't you think God brought you to us?

"Yes."

"Then He's busy helping you, giving you what you need. Can you feel Him taking care of you?" Mr. Jeb questions.

"I guess I can," she replies. "But what about Joseph? Will he be a good man, or will he change like my dad did and become mean?"

"I can't say for sure, but I'm doing my best, with God's help, to raise him right so he will be a great man."

"That's good, because you know that I kinda like him," she shares.

"Yes, we all kind of figured that out, and we are okay with it, as long as you wait for the right time—God's timing. Do you understand that?"

"I think I do, because I don't want to mess it up." "So, did something happen today?" Mr. Jeb asks.

"Yes, a little. I think it was how I felt when I was riding back behind him on his bike. I felt safe and protected, and it felt good," Michelle says.

"That's heading in the right direction. Young people need to know the person before they love the person, and not the other way around. If you felt protected, then Joseph is doing something right."

"But I really wanted him to kiss me," she admits, then quickly adds, "but don't worry, I know the rules."

"Well, you're supposed to want to kiss the man or woman you love. That's a gift from God. But you have to wait for the right timing. In the meantime, just know that Joseph loves you, and our family loves you, Michelle. You are always welcome with us. You are family."

"Thanks, Mr. Jeb."

Mr. Jeb puts his arm around Michelle and pulls her close. He places a kiss on the top of her head. She breathes in the scent of Mr. Jeb. He smells like a dad should smell. He doesn't have disgusting booze breath mixed with onions from his lunch, and his clothes don't reek of stale cigarettes. Mr. Jeb smells fresh, like Irish Spring soap and peppermint. For the second time in one day, Michelle feels protected and loved.

~ CHAPTER 10 ~

At sixteen, the foursome begins to realize nothing lasts forever.

"A moment of silence, please, 'The Boss' is on," Joseph says, looking to the right at his three friends, smushed together in the front seat of his old red truck. "It's the Matthew song!" he calls out, and they all laugh.

The day is typical of an early June day in Charleston. The scorching heat of the late summer has yet to arrive, so the typically tourist-filled beaches are occupied with just the locals.

The foursome is beachbound, cruising down Coleman Boulevard toward Sullivan's Island in Joseph's red truck. The sky is a brilliant blue, not a cloud in sight. A warm breeze is keeping the temperatures at a balmy eighty degrees. The windows are open, the muscular guys are shirtless, and Michelle's tanned legs are sticking out of her cut-off Levi's.

She has a habit of using his dashboard as a footrest. He smiles because she's the only one permitted to use his dashboard like this. It's all about her legs, and Joseph is more than happy to watch her tanned legs propped up like this. Jake is using the dashboard as a makeshift drum set. The music is loud, the day is beautiful, and life is carefree.

"Sing it out, people!" Joseph yells out above the music. *This* is our anthem to Matthew." He smacks Matthew's leg across the front seat, as Bruce Springsteen's "Glory Days" blares out.

They are singing out about high school baseball. They all think of Matthew when they hear this particular song. Unofficially, it's "The Matthew Song." Matthew turns to Joseph and rolls his eyes.

They all know the words to this song by heart. The windows are open, and the sea wind is blowing through their hair. They all sing along loudly.

"You know, when I'm old and gray, one day I'm gonna be out somewhere, and this Bruce Springsteen song will come on. I'm going to stop wherever I am, probably fight off tears, and remember these summer days with you all. I sure hope God will keep us friends always," Joseph says, turning the volume down a bit.

"You all know this song isn't going to be how it goes, right?" Matthew says as the song ends, and he turns his Yankees hat around backward.

"What do you mean?" Michelle asks as they reach the bridge to Sullivan's Island.

"Matthew is trying to remind all of us that he's going to leave us and go play Major League ball. He knows this is not going to be all there is for his life," Joseph explains protectively. "He's going to leave us and make it *big*."

"Yeah … sort of," Matthew responds.

"Right, because we are all planning to build houses on Mr. Nicholson's land on Shem Creek, get married, and raise our kids on the same block," Jake adds.

"Nice dream, guys, but how is a guy supposed to commute from a traveling baseball team like the Yankees back to Podunk Shem Creek every night?" Matthew teases.

They continue for a few more minutes enjoying the music and the moment.

It had never occurred to Matthew that he'd do anything other than play professional baseball and that he would leave this place for greener pastures. From the first day Mr. Nicholson watched him throw in the backyard, everything seemed to point toward that belief. Of the four of them, he seemed to be the only one with a dream of leaving South Carolina. But they don't understand. How can they? They don't have to look forward to a future where the girl you love marries your best friend. He pushes those thoughts out of his head. *Enjoy the moment,* he tells himself. *Enjoy it because you just never know how things will turn out.*

"I think you should have a house here, kinda like a home base," Michelle says, giggling at her baseball reference.

"What if it's lonely?" Joseph asks.

"I hope it isn't, but if I'm playing baseball, and if it's for the Yankees … *I'm good.*" Matthew says with false joy. It will always be lonely, he knows this. How can he leave this place, these people, and ever come close to replacing it?

"Okay, but maybe let's take a moment and just be thankful. Do we all realize what an amazing gift all of this is?" Joseph asks, sweeping his hand across the front seat. "That we all have each other, that we know we'd do anything for each other? How often in life do you get this?"

"Amen, JoBro," Jake says. "The older we get, the more I think about the sad truth that this might come to an end. Like, what if we do go off in different directions, more than just Matthew?"

"I'm staying here," Joseph says.

"Me too," adds Michelle.

"I always thought I would too," says Jake.

"Well, I guess it is just me then," Matthew says.

"You'll be back," Michelle says. "This is a once in a lifetime foursome. It will keep 'til your baseball career is over. Then, you can return home the hometown hero."

"But what if I marry a girl from someplace else?" Matthew asks, chuckling.

"Not gonna happen, MatMan. Not gonna happen," Joseph says, leaning across the seat and smacking Matthew's stomach. "You've got an eye for the Southern girls."

He had that right, Matthew thinks, *one in particular.*

"Okay, new song, and another moment of silence, please!" This time Michelle is the announcer. "A moment of silence for 'The Dogs'."

They all laugh as the old song "Joy to the World" by Three Dog Night starts up.

With music filling her soul and summer filling her senses, Michelle looks across the front seat at the three. She understands things these three cannot. She knows that when friendships become your family, because you don't have one, their value is immeasurable. She wants this memory forever. She wants to pack this moment up for the future.

She takes a deep breath, inhaling the scent of salt mixed with the musky scent of teenage males. She reaches across the front seat and grabs Joseph's hand, for just a second, and gives it a squeeze.

When the song is over, Michelle says, "I promise you all that I will never forget this moment. We are all happy; life is so good; and we have the best friendships here in this truck that anyone could ask for. When I'm an old woman, pushing my grandkids through Walmart, and this song comes on, I will forever be sixteen, in an old red truck with the three guys I love the most."

"Everybody in?" Joseph asks.

"What do you mean?" Matthew questions.

"Can we all do that? Promise to remember this, and know how great this moment is?" Joseph asks. "When we get older, life might not always be so great, and there might be days when we need this memory."

"I'm in," Jake says. "Totally."

"Me too," Matthew replies. "Whenever we hear 'The Dogs'!"

Joseph rewinds the cassette, and they play the song again, singing it out, knowing every word. Matthew is playing air guitar; Jake is pounding drums on the dashboard; Michelle is singing into her hairbrush fake mic; and Joseph is tapping the steering wheel as he drives. They are young, free, and happy on an endless summer day. With the ocean out the window and love in their hearts, nothing can spoil the magic of this moment.

******

The following morning, the four of them are out on the dock, talking about the upcoming annual Fourth of July party. They are deep in their discussion when they see the two dads walking down the dock towards the edge where they are sitting.

Michelle turns around just in time to see the look of worry cross Mr. Jeb's face. Michelle's uncle looks absolutely devastated about something. Fear creeps up her spine.

"Hey, Michelle, your uncle and I would like to talk with you. Can you come with us for a minute, please?" Mr. Nicholson asks.

Michelle looks at Mr. Nicholson with a strange expression. "What's wrong, Mr. Jeb? You never call me Michelle?"

"Sweet Girl, would you mind coming with us?" he rephrases.

Michelle gets up, and the two men each grab a hand, landing the young woman between them as they make their way towards the Nicholson home. They go straight to the family room, and Michelle takes her seat on Mr. Jeb's ottoman, while her uncle sits on the adjacent couch.

Mr. Nicholson gently takes Michelle's hand and begins to speak: "We need to talk to you about something important. Before we do, both of us want you to know how very much we love you," Mr. Nicholson says.

"We love you like our own," Uncle Paul adds.

"You're scaring me," Michelle responds, with fear registering in her eyes. "What's going on? Did I do something wrong?"

"No, Sweet Girl, you didn't do anything wrong. But we have some sad news to share with you." Just then, Mrs. Nicholson joins them in the family room.

"Michelle," her uncle begins, "your dad called this morning and said that he found your mom early this morning in her bed. They were not able to wake her up. They aren't completely sure what happened, but your dad thinks she probably had too much to drink, fell asleep, and never woke up."

"You mean, like, my mom is *dead*?" Michelle asks in a voice just above a whisper. A burst of panic adrenaline causes her heart rate to speed up. She feels lightheaded.

"Yes, Sweet Girl, she died," Mr. Nicholson explains, with tears in his eyes, reaching out to pull her into a hug. "Your dad thinks that it was peaceful, and she didn't have any pain."

Michelle leans into Mr. Nicholson. She's crying. She's scared. What will happen to her? She has no sadness for the loss of her mother, and she does not want to live alone with her dad. Who will care for her? The last bit of brave resolve about her broken family is shattering. She now *knows* she's completely on her own. She sobs. All her life she's lived with a dream that her mom would eventually get her act together and start being a mom. Now it's too late. She will *never* have a mother. She's choking down sobs of fear and anger.

As she cries, she sees Joseph standing in the family-room. He has heard the conversation. Joseph walks over to the ottoman, sits down next to her, and puts his arms around her. Father and son, like book-ends, hold up the broken girl and don't move as the magnitude of the loss begins to sink in for her.

Michelle sobs in grief—but not for the *actual loss*—she cries for the loss of the dream that one day her parents would get better and that they could be a real family. She weeps for the sad truth that her mom never wanted her. She sobs for the uncertain future before her. Now that her mom is gone, will her dad ever let her come back to South Carolina?

As she cries, she prays hard to the God who seems to have forgotten her, the God who seems to pile on good things for some and not for others. She cries out to God to please let her be able to stay in South Carolina; she cannot not imagine how terrible life will get with just her father. If she thought her mom didn't want her, her father takes that to a whole other level. She doesn't like the feeling of fear and loneliness that is setting up shop in her soul. Even Joseph's protective arms around her can't touch the fear in her heart. She is utterly alone. What will become of her?

Mr. Nicholson gets up and leaves the two teenagers alone. Michelle leans into Joseph. As Mr. Nicholson stands at the doorway to the kitchen, he feels in his gut that change is in the air. He knows for sure that Michelle will never again call New York home. He will make sure of that.

******

The following morning, Mr. and Mrs. Nicholson, Uncle Paul and Aunt Pam, Joseph and Michelle board a plane bound for New York City. When they reach the apartment where Michelle lives, her father answers the door. He is a mess and so is the gorgeous, opulent apartment overlooking Central Park. He reaches out for Michelle, but she stands firmly in Mr. Nicholson's grasp and makes no move forward.

As Joseph watches this exchange, things start to become clear. He knows two things for certain. First, this is not a good man. He is drunk. It's not just that he's a drunk; he doesn't react to his daughter the way a man who loves his child should. Joseph notices the sofa table has the remains of white powder on it. A razor sits on the table. There are several other people in the house, wearing wrinkled business clothes like her dad, but looking strung out, like they haven't slept for days. Her father has dark circles under his eyes that remind him of smeared mascara. His hair is greasy, and he has several days of dark stubble decorating his ashen face. He doesn't look sad, like a man who has just lost his wife. He looks like somebody might look the morning after a huge party. Joseph has heard that Michelle's dad is a prominent stockbroker in New York and that he never has time for Michelle, but this is a different scene than he had imagined. He'd thought that maybe her dad was just hardworking and maybe he came home late most nights. He didn't realize her father was a complete drug addict, and most likely, her mom had died of an overdose.

The second thing Joseph realizes is that this can no longer be her home. She absolutely cannot stay here. Joseph needs to talk to his dad about this. They need to bring her back with them. He can't protect her from this if she's far away. Something has to change.

The funeral is a showcase of all the prominent people in the New York financial world. Well-dressed people with blank faces stare at Michelle, offering her condolences, as she stands next to her shaking father. When the spectacle is over, the family heads back to the apartment.

"Joseph?" Mr. Nicholson says. "Do you mind staying with Michelle while we all go out for a few hours to talk about things." He motions to Mrs. Nicholson, Uncle Paul, and Michelle's dad.

"Sure, Dad," Joseph answers, looking around at the now clean apartment. His mom and Aunt Pam have cleaned the place from top to bottom.

The front door closes as the adults leave, and Joseph turns to look at Michelle. She is standing in the apartment that is supposed to be her home, wearing a black sheath dress and black pumps, looking more like a twenty-five-year-old than a sixteen-year-old. But it is her eyes that scare Joseph; they are vacant and empty. He can see that she is trying to be brave, but she is afraid.

She begins an anger-filled tirade, as if she needs to take it out on someone: "Now you've seen it all. This is the real me, not the girl who comes to South Carolina and pretends that it's her life. *This is my life.* Look, Joseph. Come over here and look in the refrigerator; inside there's only wine and long-expired Chinese take-out boxes. That's how it is. *Nobody loves me,* and nobody ever wanted me or took care of me. My mom never came to my school or watched anything I ever did. She was too drunk. And probably if she had come, that would have been worse, because who wants a drunk mom showing up at your school play?"

Michelle walks across the room and faces the window overlooking Central Park. "Do you know what a crappy mom she was? She never told me about girl stuff. Can you imagine that?" she says, turning back to face Joseph. "A preteen girl not knowing about *woman* things? I got my period in seventh grade and thought I was bleeding to death. I was crying in the girl's bathroom, and an older girl came in and saw my destroyed jeans and tied her hoodie around my waist."

Michelle wipes her eyes on the back of her hand, smearing mascara over her pale cheeks. She faces Joseph and looks into his eyes. "Do you know how horrible it was to admit to someone—that my mom didn't even tell me about my period? She *hated* me. And she just checked out. I really can't say that I'll miss her."

"I'm so sorry," he says in a whisper, gently wiping a tear off her cheek.

"*Don't you do that, Joseph Nicholson.* Don't you feel sorry for me? I'm not your charity case. I'll be just fine," she says, taking a step back putting her hands on her hips.

"Now you know the truth. Do you know that my dad has a drug dealer that delivers *like a pizza guy*? My parents function in their jobs—my dad, the big important drug addict stockbroker, and my mom, the power lawyer alcoholic, who was tanked most days by noon."

She takes the tissue he hands her and continues, "Do you know how horrible it felt every summer to come back to *this* after my time in South Carolina? Do you know that Uncle Paul set up my coming to South Carolina every summer just to get me away from his addict sister? Do you know that when I come back here after a summer in South Carolina, your mom calls me two or three times a week, and I absolutely *live f*or her calls? It's a voice on the other end of the line who cares about me. Do you realize that when your father told me I was part of your family I just wanted him to ask me to stay forever?"

She holds back a sob and says, "Look at me! I'm damaged goods, Joseph. There's no way I'm going to be a normal, loving woman, because nobody ever loved me. What's so wrong with me that they didn't want me?!" she cries.

Joseph can't stand to see her in so much pain. He closes the distance between them and takes her in his arms in what he hopes is a reassuring hug, but he's never done this before. She rests her head on his chest, and he holds her head in his hands as she cries. He kisses the top of her head. They stand that way in the apartment, holding on to each, and Joseph begins to rock her back and forth, in the way you'd comfort a small child. The unfortunate truth that this kind of comfort has never been offered to her stabs Joseph in the heart.

"It's okay, Michelle," he says. "I'm here for you. You have me."

She holds him tighter, and he senses a mood change. He feels stirrings that will only lead to trouble. He is alone with her in the apartment, and temptation is all around him. He feels desire stirring. He can feel his body reacting to her closeness.

Her body fits perfectly up against his, and no one is around. His heart is racing, and he is experiencing what feels like a magnetic pull toward something more. His breathing speeds up. She is moving her body against his, and he knows he must stop.

He can hear his dad's voice reminding him that she is vulnerable, and today, she is *completely* vulnerable. She moves her head away from his chest and looks up at him. Joseph gazes into her sad eyes, and he feels the pull. There is no doubt that she wants him to kiss her, and he knows where that will lead. She is leaning into him, searching for his kiss. She closes her eyes in anticipation. She's waiting.

In a moment of sweet clarity, Joseph takes her face into his hands with one protective hand on each cheek. But rather than moving down to touch her lips, he pulls the top of her head toward him and places a gentle, tender kiss on the top of her forehead. Michelle steps back, looking hurt, as if she feels his rejection.

"Michelle," he whispers, with tears streaming down his own cheeks. "There's nothing I want more than to kiss you in a way that makes up for all the love you've never been given. I want to show you what love looks like, but this isn't the time for that. I promise, I will never take advantage of you, and right now, you are lonely and scared. What we can have in the future is too important to start right now. Please, just trust me, there will be a day for us," he whispers. *"I promise you."*

Michelle feels his breath against her forehead as he speaks, and something deep inside her feels protected, even amidst the utter chaos around her. In this tender moment, she doesn't know how things will turn out, but she does know something for sure, something she has long wished for, and it gives her hope.

Joseph Nicholson loves her.

She takes a step backward, feeling the cool vacancy, where his body once leaned. She looks up at him and whispers, "What would I do without you?"

"You don't ever need to worry about that," he says, grabbing her hand. "I'm not going anywhere."

Michelle turns when she hears the lock click on the door. The adults have arrived home. Mr. Jeb walks across the room and takes her in his arms. She rests her head on the lapel of his suit, and it smells like rain and Old Spice. She feels so safe in his arms. She steps back as she sees the look on her father's face.

"You're coming home with us," Uncle Paul says. "Your father says it's okay for you to live in South Carolina … if that's what you want."

Michelle runs into her uncle's arms. "Thank you, Uncle Paul," she sobs.

"You're coming home, Sweet Girl," Mr. Jeb says. "Home," she whispers. "I'm finally going home!"

"You'll be better off there," her father says, without emotion. "I work too much to take care of you."

"I know, Dad," she says, giving him an awkward hug. "I know."

The feelings of doubt and fear disappear as she allows this great news to sink in.

She is moving to South Carolina, and she will forever more be part of a family.

A real family.

With people who actually love her.

~ CHAPTER 11 ~

After returning from New York, Michelle spent the rest of the summer trying to adjust to the idea of going to high school in Mount Pleasant. The new high school was only a couple of years old, and Michelle already knew lots of people through Joseph, Jake, and Matthew. To make Michelle feel welcome, Uncle Paul had painted and decorated a room for her, and he told her it was hers—her home for as many years as she needed.

News spreads quickly that the summer guest has now become a permanent resident. Michelle starts showing up at summer parties with the guys and starts meeting new people. Mr. and Mrs. Nicholson think it's important for Michelle to be included in lots of summer events, so she'll hopefully have some friends when school finally starts.

One hot, summer morning, sitting at the kitchen table, Mrs. Nicholson asks Michelle about friends. "So, have you met any girls you want to hang out with?"

"Not really. Lots of them seem to be hanging out with people they've known forever … and they don't really talk to me," Michelle shares as Mrs. Nicholson hands her a cup of coffee.

"Have you tried talking to them?"

"Yes, but when I do, it seems that all they really want is to use me to get to Joseph."

"What do you mean?"

"They are all totally in love with the guys. I can't believe you don't know this. I'm pretty sure if they hang out with me, it won't be about me, but about him or Jake or Matthew." She laughs. "Why did I get the best friends that are all the dream guys?"

******

Later that afternoon, the guys are snacking in the Nicholson's kitchen.

"Hey, man, did you see Kevin Brannon talking to Michelle?" Matthew asks.

"No, what's up with that?" Joseph asks, perking up.

"I'm not sure why, but I really don't like that guy. Something about him makes me feel like he's not a good guy," Matthew replies.

"Did you hear anything they were talking about?"

"He was asking her about the Fourth of July party and if she was going," Matthew says. "Kind of like he was asking her."

"What did she say?" Joseph questions.

"She said yes, she was going, and that she'd be there with all of us," Matthew says, laughing.

"Some chance that dude has!" Joseph adds with a big grin.

"I don't know about that, JoBro. She was flirting with him in a big way," Matthew says.

"Remember my dad's words: We have to look out for her, especially now after losing her mom," Joseph explains, hoping he doesn't have to deal with this now.

Kevin is known for his restored 1967 Firebird. The last thing Joseph wants to think about is Michelle in *his* car. He is Mr. Football, big, arrogant, and very good-looking. All the girls fall for him, and most of the girls who fall for him are left brokenhearted.

Joseph knows this type of guy well. He's been playing baseball on select teams for years and has heard it all. The dugout is like a big confessional, and Joseph has never liked what he's heard from Kevin's mouth. Kevin Brannon is a user of girls. He lures them into believing he cares for them, but it's all sexual for him. He's the kind of guy who is heard in the dugout talking about last weekend's conquests. He was the worst kind of kiss-and-tell kind of guy. He's a *namer*, and his stories ruin reputations. Joseph didn't like him before, and he certainly doesn't like him now. Joseph is pretty sure that Kevin knows he can't stand him.

"We can't let her out of our sight," Joseph says.

"That might be easier said than done," Matthew adds.

******

The four arrive at the party as an attention-getting group. The beach party is on Sullivan's Island next to the lighthouse. People from all over Charleston arrive, bringing their own food and drinks, sitting with friends, and enjoying a day at the beach that ends with fireworks over the Charleston Harbor.

The adults usually congregate in groups under colorful umbrellas, sipping fruity drinks or beers. The little children congregate with moms next to the tide pools, which provide shallow water, like a baby pool. The teenagers hang out near the lighthouse.

"No drinking. Remember that, please, when someone offers you a beer," Mr. Nicholson advises Joseph. "Be on your guard. You are the driver today."

Joseph has been working for one of the shrimp-boat captains for a few years. He gradually saved enough money and recently bought his red truck. It's a clunker for sure, but to Joseph, it is a beautiful representation of hard work. Whenever he has time, he's either washing it or making sure everything is in perfect working order. If they all squeeze in close enough, they fit across the front seat.

When they arrive together, they are quite a sight: the beauty and her three handsome jock bodyguards. The girls are all over them. Joseph and Jake start talking to the pastor's daughter. Matthew is laughing with one of the cheerleaders. The weather is a perfect 85° under a spectacular Carolina sky. What could possibly go wrong?

Kevin Brannon.

It was as if someone makes an announcement on a loudspeaker as soon as Michelle arrives. She is instantly surrounded by five of the guys on the football team, one of whom is Kevin Brannon. He's been drinking; Joseph can tell. He's laughing a bit too much and trying to be a little bit too friendly toward Michelle. Joseph finds Matthew and asks him what he thinks.

"She'll be alright, as long as we can see her," Matthew says.

"Just make sure she doesn't leave with that creep," Joseph instructs.

"Amen to that one, JoBro."

At some point, Matthew looks up and sees Michelle holding a beer.

"What are we going to do about that?" Matthew asks, pointing to the beer in Michelle's hand.

"Try not to embarrass her. Let's take her over to get some food with my parents," Joseph suggests.

"Good plan. I'm hungry anyway," Matthew says.

They grab Jake, and the three of them make their way over to where the football team is standing around with Michelle.

"Hey, you hungry?" Matthew asks Michelle.

"Yes, actually I am pretty hungry, and I need some water," she says, following them toward the Nicholson family picnic area.

"Michelle, you need to cool it on the beer. My dad said no drinking," Joseph reminds her.

"It's not like I'm drunk or getting drunk or anything. Let it go, would ya?"

"I don't think I need to remind you that we are all underage, and there are police everywhere," Joseph hands her a cold Coke. "It's not a good idea to be drinking around those guys."

She places both hands on her hips. "Oh, I get it. *You're jealous.* Let me get this straight: You don't want to date me yet, but it's *not* okay for me to date anyone else?"

"Where did *that* come from?"

"I don't know, Joseph. It just seems to me that if you really like me or love me like you say you do, you'd be my boyfriend."

"I'm not ready to be your boyfriend, and you're definitely not ready to be anyone's girlfriend."

"That's for *me* to decide, not *you*. You either want me, or you don't. It's pretty simple." She takes a sip of her Coke and continues, "The way I see it, it looks like you don't want me, but you really don't want anybody else to have me either."

Joseph is at a loss for words. He can't imagine how he'd deal with Michelle having a boyfriend. He'd go absolutely nuts imagining a guy like Kevin Brannon putting his hands all over her, or worse, what if there's a string of boyfriends? What if he had to put up with a new guy all the time? Joseph doesn't believe she's strong enough to resist the pull of a guy telling her what she wants to hear. She'd fall for all of it right now. Like his dad said, she's vulnerable. He can't imagine how he's going to be able to tolerate that. Joseph hopes his dad sets her straight, because he's pretty sure she isn't going to listen to him.

He prays God isn't planning on having him endure all that.

Mrs. Nicholson senses an intense conversation is taking place between the two, and she figures this is neither the time nor the place. "Want a hot dog?" she asks, holding out two plates with grilled hot dogs and chips.

Both willingly accept the plates and angrily take off in different directions. Joseph lets his guard down for just a minute, saying hi to a neighbor, and when he turns back, he can't find Michelle.

"Divide and conquer," he announces to the other two guys.

"Got it," Matthew answers, knowing it's time to look for Michelle.

"Let's do this," Jake adds.

By the time they find her, Michelle has obviously taken in a few beers. She's a little too happy and bubbly. She's stumbling while she's walking, and Kevin Brannon has his arm possessively around her waist. The sun has set, and the fireworks show has just ended. It's time to head home.

"Come on, Michelle. Time to roll," Joseph says to her.

"I'm riding home with Kevin," she says, her words slurred.

"Oh, no, you are not," he says. "You're drunk, and so is he."

"This is none of your business, dude," Kevin interjects.

"The heck it isn't," Joseph firmly says, reaching out to grab her hand. "You are *not* riding home with this drunk guy!"

"You are *not* my boyfriend, and you are *not* my babysitter. Leave me alone," she yells.

She has no sooner finished that last rant before Jake has her by the waist and has picked his cousin up and thrown her over his shoulder, carrying her toward Joseph's truck. At that moment, Joseph could not have imagined a better friend in the whole world. Michelle kicks, screams, and cusses. When they reach the truck, Joseph is thrilled when he realizes that she'll be sandwiched between them and unable to get out.

"Keep her here," Joseph says as he leaves the truck and heads toward Kevin Brannon.

"Seriously, dude, you can't drive," Joseph says to a visibly drunk Kevin.

"What the hell is it to you, Angel-Boy?"

"I don't want you to have a wreck," Joseph replies, taking his tone down. "Can one of you guys please take his keys like a *good* friend should?" he asks, looking at the football players gathered around him.

"I got this," one of the players says, attempting to wrestle Kevin's keys from him.

"Thanks," Joseph says, then takes off running toward his truck.

Joseph is so angry at Michelle he can't even look at her. But he *can* say what's on his mind.

"You're an idiot," he says.

"You're a controlling jerk, and I wish you'd just leave me alone," she fires back.

Joseph drives and picks up the beach road at Breach Inlet headed toward Coleman Boulevard. He is taking deep breaths, trying to calm down.

Turn around.

That voice. Those words. He's heard it before, but it's been years. He looks in the rearview mirror and then turns his head to look out the back window. Nothing. Joseph isn't sure what to do.

"I heard it again," he whispers to Jake.

"What?"

"Turn around."

"Seriously? The creepy *turn around?*" "Yeah, seriously," Joseph says. "Big time." Jake looks out the back window and doesn't see anything. No other cars, nothing but a dark street.

Jake looks out the back window. "I don't see anything."
"You see anything, Matthew?" Jake asks. "What are we looking for?" Matthew questions.

"Remember the story we told you? The *turn-around* story?" Jake asks.

"Yeah, why?"

"Joseph just heard it again."

"What the heck? So, you're saying an angel is talking to you right now?" Matthew asks. He looks over at Michelle who is passed out next to him.

"I don't know who it is, God or an angel, but I heard it, and it sounds just like the last time," Joseph answers.

"Where's the guy in white?" Matthew asks, half joking,

"It's not funny. I can feel it in the air. Something is going down," Joseph says with a nervous tone. "Lord, please show me," he says out loud.

Turn around.

"I think we need to turn the truck around," Joseph says. "I think so too," Jake adds. He looks at Joseph. "I heard it too."

Joseph pulls onto a side street off Coleman Boulevard and makes a U-turn back toward the beach. "You did?"

"Yeah, I did."

And then they see it.

Kevin Brannon's white 1967 Firebird fishtailing down Coleman Boulevard, weaving all over the road.

There's an awful sound of screeching brakes and metal smashing as his car clips a streetlight, followed by a loud crash as the classic car slams into a tree.

Then, complete silence.

Joseph pulls off the road and parks the car. "Everybody out. This is not good," he yells.

Jake is poking at Michelle to wake her up, but she is passed out, so they leave her in the truck.

Joseph runs across the street to the smashed vehicle. The front is completely crushed, and smoke is pouring out of somewhere. Strangely, the radio is still on full blast and is blaring REO Speedwagon.

Kevin is not moving, and his head is bent forward, resting on the steering wheel. Blood is pouring out from a wound somewhere.

Joseph immediately opens the driver's seat door to evaluate Kevin.

"Don't move him yet," he instructs. "I need to make sure his back is okay."

Joseph reaches into the car and runs his hands down Kevin's back. There is so much blood that Joseph realizes bleeding to death is the more critical issue. He gently moves Kevin off the steering wheel and sees the horrible gash on Kevin's right shoulder where blood is pouring out.

"Jake, go get my beach towel."

"Matthew, get in the back seat, sit behind him, and try to hold his head still."

By now, other cars have stopped to look.

"Someone, call 911 *now!*" Joseph yells.

Jake returns with the beach towel, and Joseph starts applying pressure to the wound. "Kevin, can you hear me?" Joseph asks.

"Joseph? What the heck are you doing?" Kevin mumbles in confusion.

"You've had an accident, and you're bleeding. I'm applying pressure to keep you from bleeding out," Joseph explains.

"It hurts," Kevin cries.

"I've got you, Kev. Hang in there," Joseph says in his best reassuring voice.

"Father, we need your help here. Please stop the bleeding and help my friend Kevin. Show me what else I need to do."

"My neck," Kevin moans.

"I got ya, brother," Matthew says from the back seat. "Man, I'm glad you know what you're doing, Joseph."

"I'm trying to remember everything I learned," Joseph says.

The siren sounds are getting closer, and Kevin drifts in and out of consciousness. The EMTs arrive and begin to assess the scene.

Joseph steps back and speaks to the EMT in charge.

"He's bleeding from his right shoulder. I've been applying pressure to stop the bleeding," Joseph offers. "I hope I did the right thing. I told my friend to try to stabilize his neck. His breathing seems good. He hit his head on the steering wheel, and he was wearing a lap belt. He's been drinking."

The EMTs verify all of Joseph's observations and find everything to be correct.

"Hey, man, what's your name?" the older EMT asks Joseph.

"Joseph Nicholson, sir," Joseph replies.

"Nice work, Joseph Nicholson. You saved this guy's life," the EMT says. "Are you trained or something?"

"Yeah, I've taken the basic medic training class at the hospital," Joseph replies.

"Do you mind taking his number?" the EMT says to the ambulance driver, pointing to Joseph.

The ambulance driver writes down Joseph's name, address, and phone number.

"How old are you?" the driver asks Joseph.

"Sixteen, sir," Joseph replies.

"Incredible," he says.

The EMTs remove Kevin from the car and load him onto the stretcher. They turn on the siren and speed off to the trauma center in Charleston.

They hear the scream.

Michelle has gotten out of the truck, crossed the street, and is standing next to the passenger side of the vehicle. Kevin hit a tree going fast. He tried to swerve, so as not to hit the tree head-on. The passenger seat, the place where Michelle would have been sitting, is completely smashed. It looks like the dashboard is in the back seat. If Michelle had been sitting in that seat, she most surely would have been crushed and killed.

Michelle is standing next to the smashed passenger seat as it dawns on her that if she had been left to her own poor choices, she would be dead right now.

Joseph Nicholson saved her life.

"Oh, my God! Oh, my God! I'd be dead!" she cries. "Oh, my God, is Kevin dead?"

"No," Joseph says. "I think he'll be okay."

"I'm such an idiot. You were right," she admits, standing by the car looking like a lost child.

"Come here," Joseph says, holding out his arms to her.

She steps into his embrace and sobs, "I'm so sorry. Please forgive me."

Joseph holds the girl he loves and starts to cry, realizing how close he came to losing her. It also occurs to him how much of his life is being spent rescuing people.

******

When they arrive home, covered in Kevin's blood, Mrs. Nicholson freaks out. Mr. Nicholson calmly looks at his son and says, "You heard it again, didn't you?"

"Yes, sir," Joseph says, crying into his father's shoulder. Joseph doesn't understand why, whenever he hears the voice, he is reduced to tears. The events of this evening feel no different from the day he heard the voice and saved the boy. He's emotionally exhausted.

"Jake heard it too, Dad," Joseph says.

They both look across the Nicholson's kitchen to find Jake choking back tears, just as his father steps into the kitchen.

"Dad," Jake says, crying, "I heard it too!" and he steps into his father's embrace.

Michelle is standing in the corner alone. Matthew holds his arms out to her and wraps her in a hug. She sobs into his chest.

"It's okay. We're all fine," he whispers into her ears. This moment feels better to Matthew than anything he has ever experienced. It's way beyond a physical attraction now. Matthew feels a desire to protect her, to be like Joseph, and to rescue her. Oh, God, how he loves this girl. He drinks in the scent of her hair and the idea that her body seems to fit perfectly into his. The top of her head hits just below his chin, perfect for this kind of embrace. He tightens his hold on her, just for a moment. In this beautiful moment, where he holds the girl he loves, he wonders, deep in his soul, if he'll ever feel this way again. What if he spends the rest of his life comparing anything spectacular to this single moment?

Matthew knows in his heart that someone loved her first and that someone is his best friend in the world, a young man he'd do anything for. Will he be able sit by and watch someone else love her forever? A brutal truth begins to dawn on him. He cannot handle this.

Matthew West knows he needs a plan. He needs a good solid plan to exit South Carolina and this agonizing love he feels for Michelle.

Everyone in the room is crying, even the adults. Joseph looks across the room and sees what his father sees at the exact same moment. Matthew is holding Michelle. Joseph sees the painful truth he's long suspected—a truth he wishes with all his heart was not true.

Everything seems to be spiraling out of control, and Joseph can't imagine a scenario where this will have a happy ending.

Matthew West is hopelessly in love with Michelle too.

~ CHAPTER 12 ~

At her desk in New York City, the recently promoted reporter Jenny Myers is busy looking over local stories for something special to dig into. As she sips her morning coffee, she stumbles upon the story of the teen boy who saves a car accident victim. Something about that name, Joseph Nicholson, sounds familiar. She gets out old files and can't figure out what about that name rings a bell. She goes over to the microfiche machine and looks up the name. Bam! There it is, this is the Joseph Nicholson who heard the angel's voice and rescued the drowning boy a few years ago.

Jenny thinks about it and cross-searches the name, Kevin Brannon. *Very interesting,* this story is getting better by the minute. Kevin Brannon is the youngest son of Senator Jim Brannon. Perhaps she'd search for the little boy he'd saved and follow up with him too. This day was shaping up to be something special.

She goes to her editor's office to request travel to Charleston for a big story.

Two hours later, she boards a plane heading south. Jenny arrives at her hotel and immediately starts making calls. Her first is to the lead EMT on the scene, who she meets at the fire station. He's a friendly guy and seems to want to talk. He quickly fills her in on the details of how this incredible sixteen-year-old guy saved a young man.

She asks him if his friends were there too.

He says, "Yes. Two others? No, there were three. One girl, two other boys. A new member of the group. Why are you so interested in this? I mean you're network and all. This seems like kind of a local story," the EMT says, reaching for his coffee cup.

"Well," she says, "I covered a story once before where this Joseph Nicholson saved a life. At the time, he was only twelve."

"Wow!" he says. "That's incredible."

"That's not all of it," she continues. "Just before that rescue, he heard the voice of an angel telling him to turn around. Only after turning around, did he notice a child at the bottom of the pool."

"You don't really believe that. I mean, *anybody* could have called him, don't you think?"

"That's what I thought until I saw the video that a mom at the pool shot that day," she explains. "The video shows an angel diving in after him and pulling them both up out of the water."

"Dang! I remember that story," the EMT exclaims. "I can't wait to see your piece on it."

"It gets even better," Jenny says. "Kevin's dad is a U.S. Senator."

******

The kitchen phone rings.

"I got it," Joseph says and hops up from his chair to answer. "Hello," he greets, listens to the voice on the other line for a minute, then says, "Sure. See you then." And he hangs up.

"What was that all about?" his father asks.

"Dad, that was Jenny Myers, the reporter from CBS who did the last story on the rescue at the pool. She saw the story about the car accident in this morning's *Post and Courier* and wants to do another story with us," Joseph explains.

"Oh, boy, here we go again," Mr. Nicholson says, smiling. "Are you ready for this?"

"Dad, if this story can bring people hope, I'm all in," Joseph replies, smiling back.

"That's a great way to view this," his father says. "Kind of a reminder that God shows up."

"I guess someone should get the paper," his mom suggests, with a chuckle. "Apparently there's a story on this."

******

Joseph gets up and heads toward the front door. Just as he opens the door to get the newspaper, a black limousine is pulling into the driveway. Joseph stays where he is, waiting to find out who is in the limo and why they are in his driveway.

The limo driver parks the vehicle, gets out, and opens the door for someone in the back seat. A well-dressed man steps out, in a suit and tie, but the clothes look like he has slept in them. There are traces of blood on the fancy white dress shirt. His two-day old beard and bloodshot eyes give him the look of a man who hasn't slept in days.

"Are you Joseph?" the man asks.

"Yes, sir," Joseph replies.

"I'm Senator Brannon," the man says, wiping his eyes on a cotton handkerchief. "I believe you saved my son's life last night."

Joseph never put the two together. The idea that Kevin Brannon's dad is a U.S. senator seemed strange. Kevin is such a screw-up; how could he be related to a senator? But the man before him is none other than the very popular senator from South Carolina. Senator Brannon moves toward the porch and staggers slowly up the steps. He walks toward Joseph with his arms out, and Joseph finds himself in an awkward embrace with a complete stranger.

The senator is crying.

"Sir, it was my honor," Joseph says as he moves out of the embrace.

The screen door slams, and Joseph turns and sees his father step out onto the front porch. It takes his dad a second to put the pieces together. Kevin Brannon is *Senator* Brannon's son.

Mr. Nicholson looks at the crying, visibly disheveled man and says, "Sir, you look like you could use some breakfast."

The senator looks from Joseph to his father, smiles, and says, "I'd love some." He steps into the Nicholson home and is greeted warmly by Mrs. Nicholson.

A few short minutes later, Michelle walks in.

"Somebody should get Matthew and Jake too," Joseph says.

Mrs. Nicholson picks up the kitchen phone and calls his house. Matthew is there within five minutes. Michelle runs next door to get Jake.

Senator Brannon looks at Joseph and says, "Can you please tell me what happened?"

"Yes, sir," Joseph replies and starts with the backstory of the drinking at the Fourth of July party. He includes Michelle's role in the day as well as how they kept her from riding with them. When he reaches the part where he is driving down Coleman Boulevard, he stops.

"Senator Brannon, sir, do you believe in things like angels?" Joseph asks. "Because if you don't, this story will sound crazy to you."

Across the room, Mrs. Nicholson smiles and walks toward the senator. She hands him a steaming cup of coffee.

"I do," the senator replies. "I'm kind of an old-fashioned, church-going guy. Last night, as I was begging God to spare my son's life, I sensed I was supposed to find out what happened.

Maybe that sounds crazy to *you*. But I think God wants me to know *He* saved my son."

"Good to know, sir," Joseph says, nodding. "Good to know. Sir, I was driving down Coleman Boulevard last night, just after the fireworks ended at the Sullivan's Island beach party. The four of us here were in the front seat of my truck. Without warning, I heard a voice saying, *Turn around.* Now, sir, you need to understand that this has happened before, so I had no doubt that it was an angel. I knew it was from God, so I looked in my rearview mirror and saw nothing. I told Jake that it was happening again, and he knew *exactly* what I was talking about, because he was with me the last time it happened. So, Jake turned around too, and like me, he saw nothing.

"A moment later, we *both* heard it: *turn around.* So, I pulled into a side street, made a U-turn, and turned around. We were driving down Coleman and saw Kevin's white '67 Firebird, and he was weaving all over the road. Then, he crashed.

"Sir, the reason God put me there is because I'm CPR trained and have taken advanced lifesaving classes. We arrived at the scene, and we discovered Kevin bleeding out, with his head resting on the steering wheel. He was unconscious. I checked his pulse, stabilized his neck with the help of my friend here, and my other friend here went to get a beach towel to put pressure on the bleed, and then the EMTs arrived. "

"With *God's prompting*, you saved my son's life?" the senator says again, just above a whisper.

"Yes, sir."

"Wait a minute … You said this has happened before. Are you the same kid who saved the boy at the pool a few years back?" the senator asks.

"Yes, sir," Joseph replies.

"Unbelievable, just *unbelievable,*" the senator says, putting his coffee cup down. "I am so grateful to God and to you, Joseph. I need you to know if there's ever anything I can do for you, please just let me know," the senator offers.

Joseph is pleasantly surprised to realize that Senator Brannon is the real deal. He is a great man with a wonderful faith in God. After a few minutes at the table, he feels like they have become friends.

When they are finished eating, the senator stands up, comes around the table, and hugs Joseph again. "Thank you, Joseph."

As Senator Brannon is leaving the Nicholson house, Jenny Myers is walking up the steps to the front porch with her cameraman filming as she moves. When she sees the senator, she stops and observes his disheveled appearance. With a trained eye, she takes in the blood on his shirt and dirty suit sleeves, bloodshot eyes, and day-old stubble. She infers that he has likely come here straight from the hospital, where his son has been in surgery all night.

Jenny thought, *this is golden.*

"Excuse me, Senator Brannon," Jenny says, pointing a microphone in his direction. "How is your son this morning?"

"He will be okay," he replies, raking his hands through his dirty hair. "Do me a favor, will you?"

"Sure, if I can," Jenny says.

"Don't let my son's drunk driving overshadow the real story here. I'm just a senator, and eventually, everyone will lose interest in me, but they never lose interest in angels. Please, tell this story of the angel's voice."

"Sir, I didn't realize you believe in stuff like this."

"Miss Myers, I have a deep belief in God. Just because I'm a senator doesn't mean I can't have a strong faith," he explains.
"I get it," Jenny says.

"We've got a real opportunity here, Miss Myers. We can take the focus off my drunk son and put it on something hopeful. I am not suggesting that you omit my son's faults, and I'm not asking for any breaks there. But please let the beauty of what God has done be your focus."

"Sir, what you might not know is that Joseph has heard this voice before when I broke that story a few years ago. It was that story that got me off the fence about my beliefs. I think just telling the story honestly is enough. So, you have my word, Senator. This is a story of a lifetime," Jenny shares, smiling.

"I look forward to watching it, Miss Myers. Thank you," Senator Brannon says as he moves toward the opened limo door.

"Do you have anything you want to say?" Jenny asks.

"Yes, as a matter of fact, I do," he replies, turning to face the cameraman.

Senator Brannon begins, "Early this morning, my wife and I got the call no parent ever wants to get. Our son, Kevin, had been in a terrible alcohol-related car accident. He was being rushed to the hospital, where he would go straight to surgery. We were up all night waiting for news that he'd survive.

"At about 4:00 a.m., the surgeon came out and pronounced the operation a success and that they expect Kevin to make a full recovery. While I am grateful to the gifted surgical team at the Medical University of South Carolina, I am most thankful to a young man named Joseph Nicholson and to Almighty God who spoke to this young man. I hope you will listen to this powerful story of God's mercy and love. Thank you, and God bless you."

******

After Senator Brannon leaves, Mr. Nicholson goes in search of Michelle. He finds her sitting out on the dock.

"I think we need to talk about a few things," Mr. Nicholson begins, sitting down next to her at the end of the dock. He takes off his shoes and dangles his feet in the water.

"So, I'm guessing Joseph told you?" she asks.

"He did, and just so you know, we will have this talk about drinking and drunk boys *just one time.* Are we clear?" he says, in a harsh tone not typical of him.

"Yes, sir," she answers.

"You are in a vulnerable time in your life right now. Losing your mom is a terrible wound for a young girl."

"I didn't lose anything, Mr. Jeb; you can't lose what you never had."

"That may be so, but nevertheless, a girl needs a mom and a dad. In the absence of them, she will go looking for replacements," Mr. Jeb adds.

"I'm not sure what you're getting at."

"When there's a big empty spot in your heart, you will live with a longing to fill it. And if you're not careful, you will begin to fill it with the same things your parents did," he explains.

"I will *never* drink like they did!" she spat at him. "Sounds to me like you tried," Mr. Jeb snaps back. "I had a couple of beers. No big deal. That's it!"

"Well, then, let me be *perfectly clear*. No drinking. No dating. Period," he says. "I've given the boys instructions to watch out for you."

"You've got to be kidding," she says. "Like bodyguards or something? No wonder no one wants to ask me out. This is *not* fair!"

"Of course, it's fair, because everything you do right now will impact the rest of your life. When you're hurting, the way you process it means everything. I believe you are mourning more than just the loss of your mother; I believe you're also mourning the dream of a real family. And I'm seeing you starting to look for it in the wrong things. Do not act on this desire to chase things to make you feel better. There is no substitution for walking through grief and experiencing sadness. And I promise you, one day it won't hurt as much, and you'll know you're getting better," Mr. Jeb shares.

"I'm not hurting. I'm just angry."

"It's been my experience that anger is nothing more than sadness that didn't get dealt with. And if you're not careful, that anger will set up shop and change you in negative ways. So, I want you to give me your word. No drinking and no boys until you are in a healthy place."

"Wow, you sure can move right into dad mode really quickly," she mumbles, wiping her eyes on the back of her hand.

"You should consider that a compliment. If I didn't really care, this conversation wouldn't be happening."

"So, I'm just supposed to sit home and do nothing?" she asks.

"No, heavens, no. Get out, go running, swim, play tennis, pray, and spend time with my wonderful wife. Cry with people, and share your heart. A lonely heart doesn't heal. Share your grief with people you love," he suggests, putting his arm around her. "I've got a little secret for you."

"What secret?"

"Some incredible things are waiting for you down the road. And in this time, if you heal the right way, you will have a love that was worth waiting for," he says.

"How do you know?" she asks, leaning her head on his shoulder.

"Because there's a young man who is waiting for you," he replies with a smile. "And I'd like to think that it would be just about the coolest thing in the world to know that I got to raise both my son and his wife."

She leans her head against his shoulder and says, "I love you, Mr. Jeb."

"I know you do, and I sure love you, Sweet Girl," he tells her. "Take care of your heart."

~ CHAPTER 13 ~

"Matthew, can I talk with you for a second?" his coach calls to him as warm-ups are about to start.

"Yes, sir."

"I don't want to make you nervous, so I've waited till the last minute to tell you this," the coach says. "We've got some scouts coming out to see you today."

"Oh, wow," Matthew replies. "What schools?" he asks, hoping one of them is a school that will take him far away from Mount Pleasant, South Carolina. He knows he has to get away from the ever-increasing likelihood that people will start to pick up on the fact that he is crazy in love with Michelle. He can't stand the agony of watching this much longer.

"We've got three schools today. The University of Texas, Alabama, and Clemson, but that's not all," the coach says.

"More than three schools in one day?"

"No, Matthew, even better. A scout from the Yankees franchise will be here," the coach says, beaming. "As a senior, you need as many options as you can get."

"What? Wait a minute, as in the Major League Yankees?" Matthew says in shock.

"Yes, I believe he scouts for all their teams, both the major league and the minors. When he called last week, he simply said he'd read about you and wanted to know when your next home game series was and where you'd be starting. He said he wanted to see you with your home team support," his coach explains.

During Matthew's warm-up time, all three college coaches are clocking the speed of his pitch. Matthew's gift of precision and focus is almost more impressive than his actual pitching. He can tune out the world, access the batter, determine possible weaknesses, and pitch accordingly. As the three coaches look on, each takes out small notebooks and starts writing notes. The University of Texas coach produces a video camera and starts filming Matthew. When Matthew has completed his warm-up, The University of Texas scout approaches him about a meeting with the UT coaching staff and Matthew's parents. The game has yet to start, and Matthew has his first meeting.

The Yankees scout never makes himself known. But Joseph sees him the second he sits down. The man has an intensity that makes it clear he isn't just someone's dad watching the game. He makes no notes; he never changes his expression; he simply sits down on the bleachers with the rest of the students and parents, crosses his arms, squints his eyes, and sits in silence for nine innings.

When the game is over, he turns to Joseph and says, "You that kid's friend?" He points to Matthew. "You seem to be cheering for him quite enthusiastically."

"Yes, sir, I am. He's one of my very best friends," Joseph says proudly.

"He always like that?" the man inquires, referring to Matthew's steely resolve on the mound.

"Yes, sir, he is," Joseph answers. "When he has a baseball in his hand, everything he's wired to do comes together in that moment."

"Interesting take. What specifically do you mean?"

"It means he's a focused, absolutely gifted ballplayer, but he is also an incredible man. He's a natural born leader, and he sees people."

"Sees people?"

"Meaning he senses struggles and responds. He cares about people and always goes the extra mile. A bunch of those guys out there made fun of him on his first day of school down here a few years ago. They were pretty mean. Matthew had a stutter. Some of those guys out there don't deserve his kindness, but Matthew understands people. He realized early on that those guys had their own struggles and that's why they were mean." Joseph shares. "Most of those guys out there would do anything for Matthew now."

"Kind of the real deal?"

"And then some," Joseph responds quickly.

The man reaches into his pocket and retrieves a business card and hands it to Joseph.

"You think you could give this to your friend and ask him to give me a call?"

Joseph takes the card and stares at the front.

Marshall James, New York Yankees, Recruitment.

"Yes, sir, I'd be so happy to deliver this card to him," he says, smiling and holding out his hand to shake his. "Nice to meet you, sir. I'm Joseph Nicholson."

******

Marshall James immediately goes back to his hotel and makes some important phone calls. He needs to get this kid signed before he signs with a college. Good ball players are a dime a dozen; good coachable young men with good character and leadership potential are not. Pitchers tended to be cocky guys, and so this combination of character and incredible talent is a rare combo. He wants this kid for the Yankees.

******

"Matthew!" Joseph calls out to his friend from the sidelines. "Dad's firing up the grill with some steaks later. You up for dinner on the dock?"

"Oh, yeah! No sane man turns down a Nicholson steak," he replies. "See you after the game debriefs and showers!"

Joseph is so thrilled for Matthew that he wants to make this a huge deal. He is pretty sure Matthew has no idea a Yankees scout was there. He can't wait to tell his dad. On the way home, he stops by Matthew's house and tells his parents to come on over for a cook-out and the reason. Once in the driveway at home, he runs next door to get Michelle and Jake.

"It's celebration time, guys," Joseph says, explaining what is happening.

Mrs. Nicholson hears the commotion and asks what is going on. She laughs and goes to the refrigerator to add some additional steaks; they are having a big party tonight.

When Matthew arrives about an hour later, the Nicholson house is full. He walks in and looks around in surprise.

"Somebody have a birthday?" he questions. "Did I miss something?"

"I don't know, Jake. What do you think? Did he miss something?" Joseph teases.

"I don't know either... Mr. Jeb, did he miss something?" Michelle says to Mr. Nicholson, laughing.

"I think he must have." Mr. Nicholson says, smiling.

Matthew's parents are grinning ear to ear.

"Okay, what's going on?" Matthew inquires.

"I heard there were some scouts out there today, Matthew," Mr. Nicholson hints.

"Yes, sir!" Matthew says.

"Anything interesting?"

"No one spoke to me after," Matthew replies. "Probably weren't interested. Although The University of Texas wants to meet with me."

"Someone spoke with *me*," Joseph says.

"Who?" Matthew asks.

"Him." Joseph hands his friend the business card that had been in his pocket.

Matthew takes the card and starts shaking. "I don't understand."

"A scout from the New York Yankees figured out that I was your friend, because I guess I was cheering maybe a bit too loudly. But anyway, he introduced himself to me and asked me to give you his card. He asked me to tell you to please give him a call as soon as you get this," Joseph says.

"What do you mean? Like, I'm supposed to call this dude back? Like, you think he might be interested in me?" Matthew asks breathlessly.

"Oh, he's more than just interested. He asked me all about you!" Joseph punches Matthew in the bicep and then asks, "Don't you want to know what I said?"

"I don't need to ask. I know you, bro. You said something great."

"I'm just so proud of you, MatMan," Joseph tells him, with tears in his eyes.

"I knew it!" Mr. Nicholson exclaims. "I knew this day would come the first time you threw a ball back there." He points to the homemade baseball diamond out back.

The next thing Matthew knows, everyone is hugging him. The last in line is Michelle. She steps into his embrace and holds her grip.

"Please don't move far away and forget all about us. Don't forget about me," she whispers. "I love you, MyMatt."

******

After sunset, Michelle is down on the dock alone. She is thinking about all the changes that will be happening once the senior year starts. It feels like they are all losing a piece of themselves, with all of them going in different directions. She can't imagine life with this group split up. Who will she be when there is no longer a happy foursome? Michelle fears that lonely days are ahead. She wonders how the other three could ever understand how vital this foursome is to her. They have families with siblings and other people to love. She does not. Then there is the issue of Matthew. He'll be gone and probably won't look back. If he plays major league baseball, he'll spend his time on the road.

Michelle doesn't realize until now that she has been crying. She always imagined they'd all go to college together. Matthew would be on the baseball team, and they'd go to his games and continue being the foursome they've always been. It had never occurred to her before this evening that Matthew would leave them. He has always talked about it, but she believed he was talking big, but not serious. Tonight makes her realize, he's *actually* leaving—moving on to bigger things. He's leaving her behind. She has Joseph, so this should not bother her ... but it does.

Matthew sees her from the kitchen window, sitting alone on the dock. He steps out the back door, onto the porch, and walks down the well-worn path, through their baseball diamond, and onto the dock. If she hears him, she doesn't look back to check. So, Matthew quietly sits down next to her, assuming the position on the edge of the dock, dangling his feet in the creek.

"When you leave, you'll never be back," she says, matter-of-factly, with a trembling voice.

"I think you're probably right. It's probably best."

"How is that best? Doesn't our foursome mean anything to you? Is it that easy to walk away from all we've become?"

"There's no room for me here, Michelle. I just can't do it," he admits. "I love that guy in there more than anything, and all I want is his happiness." He points back to the house.

"What are you saying? I don't understand," she says.

"That's the problem. You don't get it. Everything I love is right here. But there's one person here that I love very differently, and it can't be. I expect no response to this confession, Michelle, I just know that I need to be honest with you, because your life has been filled with too many people who have rejected you, and I am not doing that," he shares.

Taking a deep breath, he continues, "I remember the first time I saw you. I'd been told the tomboy cousin from New

York was visiting, and then this beautiful young girl with hoop earrings and a pink bikini came down the path toward the dock. I saw you, and I fell hard. In that fantastic moment of seeing you for the first time, I experienced feelings I had never known. I looked up at my best friend, and I saw him watch you too, and I knew I was a few years too late. He already loved you, and you became off limits for me, forever.

"So, I've tried my best to bury my secret, but the older we get, the closer it comes to the time when the two of you will be together. I seriously rejoice in that for Joseph, but I can't watch it … not every day. I guess I never thought that I'd be telling someone I love them, and then, in the same sentence, say that I'm sorry that I do. God, I wish I didn't. I've struggled with these emotions. I've even begged God to take the feelings away. But you are the only girl I can look at. I see you, and I want all the things that a guy who loves a girl wants. Just once, I'd like you to look at me like you look at Joseph. I love you for the right reasons. I wish I'd been the one selected to care for you and protect you, but that's Joseph's job," Matthew explains, struggling against the tears falling down his cheeks.

He goes on, "It feels so unfair to me. I've really tried to do the right thing, even praying about it constantly, but I'm truly stuck—so stuck that a part of me doesn't even want to try to love someone else. Why should someone else have to be my second choice, because I love you, and probably always will? And I love you even more because you've not done anything wrong here. You've never misled me or anything like that."

Michelle blinks her eyes a few times, trying to fight the tears from falling. "I know all this, Matthew, and believe me, there have been many moments where I've looked at you and wondered about us. In my own way, I love you too. At times, it's been confusing, but you are absolutely right about one thing: I loved him first. I have always felt that God gave me Joseph," she says.

"Yeah, me too," Matthew agrees.

"Thank you for telling me this so I wouldn't spend the rest of my life thinking you just left," she whispers through tears. "I can't believe how much I'll miss you, Matthew. You are such a part of me."

"I pray that life is really good to you, Michelle. You deserve it. And if we never have a conversation like this again before the end of the year, just know how grateful I am for this evening, this conversation, and how you've treated me tonight," he adds.

He puts his arm around her, and she leans her head on his shoulder as she stares at the moonlit waters of Shem Creek.

He turns to look at her with sadness etched on his face. She places both hands on his cheeks and pulls his face down to hers. Lost in a moment, he leans in and kisses her gently. In the intoxicating moment, he experiences a mixture of the purest of emotion and the deepest desire. *God, how I love this woman!*

But, in this magical few seconds of his life, Matthew loses a piece of his heart, never to be given back. He knows this kiss will be the benchmark kiss he will compare all others to in the future. And, after imagining this moment for years, *this kiss did not disappoint.*

As he pulls away from her, he stares into her navy-blue eyes, and try as he might, he can't imagine ever feeling this way about another woman.

Matthew stands up, wipes the tears off his face, turns around, and walks up the dock toward the house. He sees Joseph looking at them through the kitchen window.

Joseph greets him in the kitchen. It feels like a friendship Matthew doesn't deserve. "You had to do it, Matthew. She needed to know," Joseph says.

"Yeah, I know," Matthew says. "But it's time to move on."

"Will you promise me something?" Joseph asks with tears in his eyes. "Will you please ask God to show us, as brothers, how to navigate this and stay close?"

"I've been doing that for six years," Matthew admits.

"Well, then, I guess we can expect God to help us," Joseph says. "Because I can't lose you."

As Matthew walks out of the house, he knows he will be spending a lot less time here in the next year. He's sad as he contemplates the ending of the foursome. He reaches down into his pocket and feels for the business card. He silently thanks God for giving him choices and opportunities to take him away from Mount Pleasant—away from the agony of this love. Away from the most beautiful woman he's ever known. Away from watching someone else star in the role he wants to play.

Even though it's painful, he is grateful for the incredible young woman he loves so much. He just wishes he could understand why.

~ CHAPTER 14 ~

Michelle is mindlessly flipping through a fashion magazine, looking at dresses. It seems that once the Christmas season is finished, all discussions center around the prom and graduation. Girls are talking dresses and hairstyles. It's as if that's all the females are capable of doing.

And Michelle hates it.

She's become popular. She knows she's on the top of all the social lists. Michelle gets invited to *everything*, from parties, to boat outings, to girl slumber gatherings, to dances ... But as spring starts, Michelle is outright angry. Several great guys have asked her to the prom. She has given all of them polite no-thank-yous because she is secretly waiting for Joseph. She knows for sure that Joseph won't be able to handle her going to the prom with someone else, but it seems like maybe he's a bit too overconfident that she will say yes. It's as if he knows she'll say yes, and he feels like he can take his sweet time asking. Guys are so frustrating. They are famous for dangling a small cookie of affection to you, thinking you'll wait around. She seriously hopes he isn't going to stick with the idea that she's not ready. Michelle is sick of everyone trying to decide if and when she is ready to date someone. She's almost eighteen, not a little kid anymore. Time is running out. Even if Joseph does ask, she doesn't have a dress.

As the weeks pass, she still has no invite from Joseph. In fact, no one in her friend group has been asked or asked anyone. One afternoon in late March, Joseph, Matthew, Jake, and Michelle are hanging out on the dock, and Matthew makes a suggestion.

"Since nobody has a boyfriend or girlfriend this year, what about we all do the prom as a group?"

"That's a great idea," Joseph says. "A really cool idea." "Who do we want to include in the group?" Jake asks.

After this question, Michelle gets up from the dock and storms off, slamming the back door to the house behind her. She is fuming mad. She makes a decision right then and there: No, she will *not* go with a group. She *will* go with the next guy who asks her. She will not get all dressed up to be part of a group. Don't these people realize prom is a special night, intended to be shared with someone special? Michelle throws herself across her bed, flinging her fashion magazines on the floor. Who needs the *Seventeen* magazine prom special edition? Definitely not her.

She will not be part of a group that will make her look like no one asked her. She's turned people down. She will stay home. Let them pretend that it doesn't feel like nobody cares about you when you're dateless. She will not participate in this lousy night. So much for the prom being one of the great nights of her life.

******

Later that afternoon, Mrs. Nicholson knocks on the door.

Michelle answers and smiles. She loves Mrs. Nicholson so much.

"I was thinking that a certain beautiful young girl I know is probably going to be needing a prom dress. What do you say we head out shopping?" Mrs. Nicholson suggests.

"I don't have a date yet," Michelle confesses. "I'm not going."

"I thought you all had settled on a group night," Mrs. Nicholson says, reaching her hand up to brush a hair from Michelle's forehead.

"*They* did! But no one asked me what I thought about it," Michelle snaps back.

"Well, either way, aren't you going to need a dress? Whether you go with a date or with the group?" she asks.

"I don't think I'll go if it's with a group," Michelle says. "That would make me feel like such a loser, like nobody wants me."

"Let's just go try some dresses on. Come on, it'll be fun!" Mrs. Nicholson says.

Michelle reluctantly agrees, and off they go to downtown Charleston.

"What do you think?" Michelle asks, spinning around outside the dressing room in the department store.

"Well, let's be clear, *everything* looks fabulous on you, but not every dress is *right* for you," Mrs. Nicholson says. "You're *seventeen* not *twenty-five*, so please remember that."

Michelle rolls her eyes at the modesty speech again.

"Why don't you try this one on?" Mrs. Nicholson offers, holding up a different dress.

"Okay, but it's not really my style," Michelle says, reluctantly taking the dress.

"Sometimes someone else suggests a dress, and it's the perfect one!" Mrs. Nicholson says. "Just give it a try, *please.*"

Michelle comes twirling out of the dressing room, and Mrs. Nicholson smiles at her. Michelle feels beautiful in it. The dress is strapless with a fitted bodice and full skirt. The color is an extremely pale blue. The fabric hangs perfectly on Michelle's lean frame, doing justice to her beautiful shape. The pale blue color offsets her gorgeous navy-blue eyes, dark hair, and sun-kissed skin.

"You look absolutely stunning in that dress, Michelle!" Mrs. Nicholson exclaims, with tears in her eyes.

"I really love it, and honestly, I would never have given it a second glance," Michelle says. "But let's wait to buy it until I get a date."

"Okay, Sweet Girl, but it might be gone by then," Mrs. Nicholson comments, following her back to the dressing room.

"Hand me the dress when you get it off," Mrs. Nicholson says, with her hands reaching out over the top of the fitting room door.

Michelle holds on to her stubborn attitude toward the prom, but sadly, no additional offers come in. The evening of the prom, she stares out the window, watching Joseph and Jake in tuxedos posing for multiple photos with the well-dressed friends going with the group. As she sees all the beautiful girls in their gorgeous gowns, showing cleavage, she feels jealous and sad. Why, if Joseph loves her, did he not ask *her* to the prom? Has he changed his mind? Has he decided he wants someone else, but is too honorable to tell her? Michelle can't remember a moment when she has ever felt this abandoned. If Joseph doesn't love her, who is she? She watches them load up the cars. At the last minute, just before Joseph gets in his red truck, he turns and looks toward her window. He gives her a sad smile. He waves, gets in the truck, and drives off.

Michelle is just about to sink into tears when she sees it. The beautiful, pale blue dress is hanging from the hook on her bedroom door. Dangling from the hanger is a beautiful white rose wrist corsage with a pale blue ribbon. There's a card taped to the hanger. She tears it open, and in Mr. Nicholson's neat handwriting it simply says: *Sometimes the smartest men do the stupidest things. Go knock his socks off. Love Mr. Jeb and Mrs. Nicholson.*

Michelle has just finished reading the note when there's a knock on the door. In walks Mrs. Nicholson, followed closely by Kristen, the young girl that cuts and styles Michelle's hair.

"Let the transformation begin!" Mrs. Nicholson says, plugging in the curling iron.

******

Jake, Matthew, and Joseph walk into the prom together. The place is beautiful; the music is electric; and gorgeous girls are everywhere.

"Alright, boys, let's go break some hearts!" Jake says as they look around at all the lonely girls looking for a dance partner.

Jake and Matthew are having the time of their lives. They never leave the dance floor, as one beautiful girl after another joins them for a dance. Joseph, however, is miserable. When a slow song comes on, all he wants to do was smack himself for not asking Michelle. This night should have been for them. What had he been thinking? This prom is turning out to be a bust. The only girl he will *ever* slow dance with is Michelle. He walks off the dance floor with his head down and hands in his pockets as he heads toward the punch bowl.

Turn around.

"What?" he says out loud. "*Here?*" He must have imagined it because that voice is always saved for emergencies. And there is nothing but fun going on here. Nobody needs a rescue.

Turn around.

Bam. There it is again.

Joseph stops and turns around.

And there she is.

Michelle is standing alone, across the room, bathed in a beautiful light falling upon her like heavenly search lights from above. As Joseph looks at her, he has the feeling that everything around her is in soft focus. She is dressed in a pale-blue, strapless dress, and her womanly curves are stunning. Joseph can't breathe or move. At the same time, Jake, Matthew, and their group are making their way off the dance floor toward Joseph. But Joseph never sees them. He is lost in the moment, looking over the tops of their heads at the most beautiful woman he has ever seen. It's as if instantly Michelle has gone from the teenaged girl he's always known to a full-grown sophisticated woman.

The guys try in vain to get his attention, but they can't. One by one, all the members of the group follow his eyes.

And there she is.

Joseph straightens his bow-tie and confidently squares his shoulders.

Her, God? She's my rescue tonight? *Just her*? And Joseph begins to understand.

It's time, but it won't be easy.

But Joseph figured that out a long time ago. It isn't going to be easy to love Michelle, but Joseph is confident it will be so very worth it. Joseph knows God has confirmed that it's time. It's time to love Michelle. Both of them are finally ready.

Joseph begins a confident walk toward Michelle as people around him seem to know they need to clear a path for him. It feels like an eternity before Joseph stands inches from her.

He has no words. He pauses for a moment, looking down into her Carolina sunset eyes. He wants to memorize every detail of what is about to happen. He does what comes naturally. He cups her soft face in his hands, leans down, and kisses her.

He moves his head back, just a few inches, and whispers, "Oh, God, how I love you."

With his hands still cupping her face, he dries her tears with his thumbs, and he kisses her again. The second kiss is different. Joseph feels her kiss him back in an explosion of physical pleasure he will never forget.

In the background, her name is being called. Someone is announcing the prom court. People around them start clapping. Michelle is the Prom Queen. The music begins, and Michelle and Joseph are in the center of the room. The crowd parts for them, and the slow dance begins. Their eyes remain completely focused on each other. Joseph plants his hand in the small of her back, takes her left hand in his, and gently moves her across the dance floor in an incredible moment that Joseph knows will top the best moments of his life list.

He sings the words to the Randy Travis song *Forever and Ever, Amen* into her ear. A song that will from this point on forever remind him of this magical moment.

Across the room, Matthew watches with sadness as the inevitable comes to pass. He is so very happy for his friend. Joseph deserves everything good and loving that life has to offer, but he can no longer stay and watch this. His heart is breaking. Michelle is the most beautiful woman he's ever seen. All Matthew wants to do is take her in *his* arms, with her body close to his, and slow dance. He wants to feel the warmth of her close to him, with her head resting on his shoulder. He wants to inhale the scent of Herbal Essence shampoo as it clings to her hair. *And, oh, how he wants to kiss her.*

Just before his daydream becomes a nightmare, Matthew remembers that he has been given a one-way ticket away from this agony. This sad moment provides the clarity he needs for his final decision. Yes, he will play for the minor league team looking to draft him. Like Mr. Nicholson says, college will be there down the road, but an offer to play minor league ball might not.

Matthew has been putting off this decision for too long, dreaming that somehow it might work out. But, no, that is never going to happen, and it is time for him to move on.

God bless them, give them a happy life together, he prays. *And, God, please take this love for my best friend's girl out of my heart. Please let me love again.*

~ CHAPTER 15 ~

Joseph's eighteenth birthday starts the same way every Nicholson birthday begins. Cake for breakfast.

"Happy birthday, Sweetheart!" his mom says.

"Are you going to spare me listening to Dad sing it?" Joseph inquires, laughing.

"No breaks there, Joseph," his dad says and starts singing, while his mom lights the eighteen candles on the cake.

"Love you so much, Joseph- I can't believe you're eighteen," his mom says.

"Next year on your birthday, you'll be away at college. This is your last birthday cake for breakfast," his dad says.

Joseph had been thinking about that since he woke up earlier. He was reminiscing on past birthdays and how great his parents are about celebrating them. He knows most kids want to get away from home as soon as possible, but Joseph knows he's got it great. And birthdays are just one small way his parents have made his childhood great.

"Thanks, Mom and Dad," Joseph says. "I sure love you guys." "Oh, Sweetheart, we are so proud of you," his mom says. "Thanks, Mom."

Joseph looks across the room at his mom and senses something is troubling her. Although she's been smiling and singing along with everyone, Joseph sees something different—a look in her eyes indicating she might be preoccupied with something. When breakfast and cake is over, Joseph is wondering if his mom is okay. His dad left for the day, and it's just Joseph and his mom left in the kitchen.

"Everything okay, Mom?" Joseph asks in a gentle tone. "It is, Sweetheart. I have something to give you." "A gift?"

"I'm not really sure. It's something that was given to your dad and me in your adoption file."

"What do you mean, something in my adoption file?"

"There was a folder, sealed up, with something inside it," she explains. "There were instructions on the outside of it. It read, *Give to Joseph on his 18th birthday*."

"And that's what you have to give me?" he asks. "What's inside?"

"I don't know for sure. We didn't open it. Your dad and I believe since it was sealed, it was private, just for you, probably from your birth mother."

"Oh, wow. I didn't see that coming," Joseph responds. "I always thought we didn't know anything more than what you've told me."

"It was a difficult decision for your dad and me, but I gave my word that I would honor the one single wish from your birth mother. I owe her everything, Sweetheart. She gave you to us."

"True," Joseph says, but he hasn't been expecting this. It feels like a kick in his gut, and he has butterflies in his stomach. Over the years, he's wondered about his birth mother, but never to the extent that he'd want to try to find her. He feels content with his life and has never been burdened with a deep need to know things. Plus, finding a birth mother in Guatemala would be next to impossible. Right now, though, he feels like someone ripped a scab off a wound that he didn't know he had. Something about this moment feels unsettling.

His mom leaves the kitchen and heads back to her bedroom. She returns with a large manila envelope. It is carefully taped shut with heavy packing tape. Sure enough, on the outside are instructions to open on Joseph's eighteenth birthday. His mom hands the envelope to him.

"I thought you might want some quiet time to look through whatever is inside. I'm going to give you some privacy, but if you need me, you can call me at work." She gives him a quick kiss on the top of his head. "Call me either way, so I know you're okay, please."

Kathleen honestly has no idea what is inside the large envelope. She thinks perhaps it contains some information or photographs. Whatever it contains, it will be emotional for Joseph. They have always known his birth mother died giving birth to him, but that was really all the information they had about her. They never shared with Joseph that she died in childbirth. The adoption agency had been told that her deep desire was for an American family to adopt Joseph—a Christian American family.

Kathleen hugs Joseph close.

"I love you, Sweetheart," she whispers.

"I love you too, Mom," he says back. "Whatever is inside this, you're my mom. Don't forget that.

"I know that, Joseph. I'm just sad for her because she didn't get to raise you," she says.

Joseph kicks off his running shoes; this morning's run will have to wait. He carries the envelope out the back door, steps onto the porch, and walks down the well-worn path across the homemade baseball diamond to the dock. He sits down and puts his toes in the cool water, knowing this simple gesture will ground him.

He looks out over the gleaming waters of Shem Creek and whispers a prayer, "Help me to read this with my heart wide open. Whatever it contains, thank you, God, for this piece of my history."

He rips open the envelope, and something that looks like a short manuscript falls out. Joseph takes a deep breath and begins to read.

Dear Joseph,

My name is Dr. David Green. I am an American doctor who has spent a great deal of time in Guatemala, treating poor women in need of medical and gynecological care. I have delivered hundreds of babies, most born to poor women who could not afford medical care. Many of the babies I delivered were placed for adoption with families in other countries. Most of the women had no prenatal care, and many weren't able to afford proper nutrition. But there was something extraordinary about serving this population of women. And I truly loved my work there.

Each child being placed for adoption was given special treatment by me. Early on, I understood that children who were adopted eventually wanted to know about their birth families. But given the state of poverty here and how many women are squatters on land that doesn't belong to them, it makes it next to impossible for adopted children to search for information on birth families. Birth mothers are often not even documented as citizens. They were so poor that they had no papers or permanent mailing addresses or any conventional way to find them. As their doctor, I felt sad about this. They would give life to a human being, and then it would be as if they never existed. These women deserve to be remembered. They deserve to have their story told.

So, I began to write letters — the 18th birthday letter. These letters were included in the adoption files given to the adoptive families as a means to provide these brave, impoverished women the opportunity to tell their children who they were.

I must admit, your birth mother was very special.

Extremely special.

She named you Joseph. I hope your parents kept the name, but if not, this is the name given to you by her. She said Joseph was the man who adopted Jesus and loved him as his own. She wanted your name to express her up-front gratitude for the man who would take you in as his son.

177

I met your birth mom, Annalisa, on a beautiful sunny morning in San Lucas. You might not know this, but we call Guatemala "The Land of Eternal Springtime" because every day is sunny and seventy degrees. She was sitting on the side of the road, just outside our little clinic. Sometimes, the women were too shy to come in, even after they had walked many miles to get here. I would often see women sitting outside, and I'd quietly go outside and offer food. Feeding them often brought them in the door. Many of the women arrived, and it had been days since they had last eaten.

I could tell Annalisa was hungry. She was well past hungry, and weakness had settled in. So, I reached out my arm; she leaned against me, and we walked into the clinic.

I looked closely at her. She hung her head as if in shame and refused to make eye contact with me. She was skinny and didn't look pregnant. Her frame was tiny, and there were no visible signs of a baby. I sat her down at the table in the waiting room and fed her a bowl of warm beans and rice.

When she had eaten, I asked her why she had come to the Women's Clinic. Most women wait until very late in their pregnancy to go to the missionary clinic. Many of them waited until they could no longer hide it. But this very young woman was either not pregnant or was very early in the pregnancy.

She said she had questions for me, essential questions.

She began by telling me she was fourteen. She was fourteen and pregnant. Her story was not at all uncommon in that part of the world where violence and rape were everyday occurrences. But it made it no easier to hear.

I asked her to start from the beginning. Every woman who showed up pregnant had a story. To help them properly, I asked them to share it with me.

Annalisa looked up at me. What I saw took my breath away. I was looking into the most beautiful eyes I had ever seen on a human. If you could imagine a set of eyes so green that you had to stop and stare. In all my years in Guatemala, I'd never seen a person with green eyes. They were dark green eyes with a gold ring around them. Eyes framed with thick dark lashes and olive skin as smooth as a baby. Her high cheekbones and wide jaw gave her an exotic look. Her long, dark, shiny hair cascaded down her back. The natural color of her lips was a pale mauve, which seemed to set off the green eyes. I'd never seen a more beautiful woman in my life. I sat and stared at this woman child. My first reaction was to want to protect her.

Annalisa wanted to tell her story.

When Annalisa was born, her mom was not sure what to do. Her baby had come into the world perfectly healthy, but with green eyes. Guatemalan people do not typically have green eyes; it's quite rare, especially the Mayan indigenous people. Her mother worried about what people in her village would think. How would they react? Would they believe she had been unfaithful to her husband? How else could a full-blown Guatemalan woman married to a full-blown Guatemalan man have a green-eyed child? Her mom loved her husband and would never consider being unfaithful.

Annalisa's mom instinctively knew that her daughter was special, set apart, and different from others. Her green eyes would always be the first thing people would notice. Her mom understood that these eyes were a gift from God, marking her as unique. When her mom took her out for the first time, people were astonished. The villagers instantly saw her as special. The curandero (folk healer) would not look her in the eyes, and the Guia (spiritual guide) told Annalisa's mom to keep her away from them. They both saw the heart of God in her, and she rendered them powerless. They feared her.

Annalisa grew to be a young girl of hope. All around her was poverty and pain. There was never enough to eat. She lived in a shack made of corrugated metal with dirt floors. The children in her village made textile crafts to be sold in Antigua, where the tourists visited. Tourists rarely visited the poverty-stricken villages. They didn't want to see the faces of the starving children. But when Annalisa walked down the street in her town, people came out to see her. She would greet them with a smile, and they would call out to La Belleza de Ojos Verdes...The Green-Eyed Beauty. When people were sick, Annalisa would pray for them. When their children were starving, Annalisa would give her portion of food to them. When she smiled, people felt hope.

Annalisa's mom knew that Guatemalan life was one of constant hardship. And for many, this exposed the things of darkness. Annalisa's mom knew her little girl was a child of God. She would protect her with her life. So, the night when Annalisa was attacked, her mom nearly died trying to defend her. She was not able to keep her daughter safe that night, and 14-year-old Annalisa was attacked and raped.

A few weeks later, Annalisa knew she was with child. At 14, she was pregnant with a child conceived out of rape.

Her friends in the village told her to go see the curandero and make the baby go away. The curandero had trained with an American team of doctors who taught them how to make a pregnancy go away.

This was why Annalisa had come to the clinic that morning. She wanted to know what it meant to make a baby go away. Annalisa knew there was no money for another mouth to feed at home with her mother, and she also knew that this child, conceived from rape, would be stigmatized for a lifetime. This child stood no chance. She point-blank asked me about what we all know as abortion. My clinic is funded by a Christian doctor group, and I am a practicing Christian, so I had my convictions about abortion. I told her what that means. She was horrified. She instantly placed her hand protectively on her abdomen. I told her that her baby already had a heartbeat.

She asked for my help. She expressed a desire for her child to be adopted by an American family who is Christian. I told her I would help her with that. I told her she needed to take care of herself. I told her that giving birth at 14 is hard enough, but when you consider her lack of nutrition and impoverished environment, it would be even more difficult. At the clinic, we did not have all the modern conveniences American women have in labor and delivery. I told her this would be a difficult birth. She was so tiny and so very young.

I'll never forget what she said to me. She told me she would gladly give her life for this baby, to see him born healthy and given to a family who will love him and teach him about God. I asked her to come to see me every two weeks so we could check on the baby. When she'd leave, I'd give her bags of rice, beans, and flour to bring home. Her pregnancy began to show. And she was confident the baby was a boy.

In her 6th month, she arrived with a headache and swollen ankles. I knew this was not good. I also knew I had nothing to give her to help. We did not have medication to treat this. I advised her to take it easy and not to strain herself, and I told her I'd come to see her next week. I didn't want her walking in her condition.

I made visits to her village until her 8th month when I arrived to find her very sick. She had pre-eclampsia. Her blood pressure was dangerously high, and I knew the odds that she'd survive labor and delivery were very slim.

I brought her back to the clinic with me and took care of her until her labor started two weeks later. One night, a week before you were born, she woke and wanted to talk. She pleaded with me to choose the right family for you. She indicated that God had told her that you were set apart and would be special. She told me that she would place her hands on her ever-growing belly and beg God to bless you and protect you. She told God she was giving you to Him, for His service. She told me that she'd had a dream and she saw a green-eyed man. He was a strong man who loved God and took care of people. She said that in the dream, God showed her that this man would rescue many. She said that what was conceived in sin, God had already redeemed.

Annalisa took a turn for the worse about 6 hours into her labor. She was slipping in and out of consciousness. At one point, in a lucid moment, she looked up and whispered, "Greater love hath no man than this, to lay down his life for his friends." Minutes later, when you were born, she looked up at me with questions in her eyes.

I nodded my head yes. It was a boy, and yes, he had green eyes.

And with that confirmation, she smiled, and young Annalisa breathed her last breath.

I wept as I held you, knowing that one day I would tell you how very much she loved you. I pray that you've come to love God. I believe this would be the most powerful way to honor her.

Annalisa impacted me in a way that no other human ever has. You were born out of love and strength, Joseph, so that you might honor God with your days. You are receiving this letter on your 18th birthday because you are now an adult, making decisions for your life. Please take this story of love and use it to follow God's leading with your life.

Happy Birthday.

You have been set apart, El Hombre de Ojos Verdes.

Sincerely,

Dr. Green

Joseph cries for the beautiful green-eyed woman he will never meet. He cries for the sacrifice she made to give him life. He cries because he will never be able to hug her and thank her for her incredible gift. He thanks God for her strength and courage.

Then Joseph gets up off the dock, walks up to the house, and goes to his bedroom. He stands in front of his mirror, staring at his reflection as if for the first time, El Hombre de Ojos Verdes—The Green-Eyed Man. In that moment, on his eighteenth birthday, Joseph claims his destiny as a man set apart, a man given life for service to God—a man who is to rescue people, a man who, like his birth mother, will lay down his life for his friends. He thanks God for the confirmation this letter provides.

Joseph calls his mom to tell her he is fine, actually more than just fine.

He can't wait for his father to get home; this is a letter he wants to share with him.

"Dad … want to go for a Dock Walk?" Joseph asks his dad when he arrives home at the end of the day.

"Sure, when did that happen?" Mr. Nicholson said. "You calling *me* for a Dock Walk?"

The two head down the well-worn path, through the homemade baseball diamond, and to the stretch of old wood that is home to some of the most critical discussions and events of Joseph's life.

"What's on your mind, son?" Mr. Nicholson asks, sitting on the edge, dangling his toes in the water.

"The letter, Dad, I read the letter," Joseph begins. "And?" his dad inquires. "Did you learn anything?"

Joseph hands the letter to his father. "I'd like you to read it, Dad."

Mr. Nicholson begins to read the letter, and like his son, he openly cries. When he is finished, he looks up into the green eyes he's looked into every day for nearly eighteen years.

"What are you feeling, son?" "Gratitude, Dad. Just gratitude." "For what specifically?"

"I've always felt that there has been a blessing over my life, like God is always there providing. And I've always felt Him leading me in a way that seems so very different from other people. It has always felt like a gift. The voice and all, it feels like a gift."

"You mean like the gift of a power or something?"

"No, like how you would feel if somebody gave you something incredibly valuable."

"That's fascinating. Do you have clarity now of where that gift comes from?"

"Oh, I never needed that. I've always known it comes directly from God."

"Why do you think He gave it to you?"

"Because she asked for it, Dad. She asked Him for all of this," he says, sweeping his arms around to imply everything.

"So, your take on all of this is that your life has been blessed, and you've been given this incredible gift of hearing the voice, all because Annalisa asked God to give it to you?"

"Yes, sir. Without question."

"What does that tell you about God's love for you and the power of prayer?"

"Everything, sir," Joseph says. "Absolutely everything."

Joseph turns to walk away and knows, *this is why. A woman I will never meet gave me life. And she gave me so much more. All because she trusted God and asked for it. She called down a blessing over me and entrusted me to God for His service.*

Joseph has a newfound peace in his soul, and up until this point, he didn't even know he hungered for it.

~ CHAPTER 16 ~

February 1995

In the seven years since Matthew left South Carolina, he has yet to get accustomed to the noise of New York City. In fact, there are days when he finds it so oppressive that he drives out to Long Island in an attempt to smell the salty air. Everything still feels foreign to him, like he is a guest living another man's life. This life, the life he thought he wanted, has yet to come close to his big dream of it. Somehow, in his thought process, he'd convinced himself that he could simply leave South Carolina behind and start a new life. He thought his new life would be fulfilling because of his love for baseball. The game itself still holds the magic for Matthew that it did when he was a child. He loves it, and he could never imagine doing anything else for a living.

But no one told him how lonely this life would be. It had never occurred to him how much he'd miss his home and the people who had anchored him since childhood. As he thinks back, he can still hear Michelle's voice in Joseph's truck, many summers ago, telling them that their foursome was unique and it probably wouldn't happen again in their lifetime. Matthew is lonely, unconnected, and living a life that lacks meaning.

Since he left South Carolina, Matthew has utterly failed in relationships, both with friends and women. He's tried, but quickly learned that his friends in South Carolina are different.

He wonders about the people he's met since he became famous. Do they have an agenda other than to be his friend? Does anyone really like him, or do they just want the athlete on the billboards?

When it comes to women, deep in his gut, he keeps feeling like all he has to offer is heartache. The women he meets want to be the one to take New York's most eligible bachelor off the market, and most of those women quite literally throw themselves at him. It's gotten to the point where he questions if it's him, if he brings that out in people? Does he give off some sort of vibe that welcomes shallow relationships?

Once he started pitching for the Yankees, his life stopped being his own. He was quickly elevated to celebrity status, and he knows he was completely unprepared for it. If he was in South Carolina, Joseph would be grounding him, and Jake would be reminding him of everything that's important. He'd know for sure that someone really loved him.

But in New York? He is flying solo. If it weren't for his long friendship with Marshall James, the man who first recruited him, he would never be able to withstand the lifestyle of a major league pitcher.

The one bright spot is Marshall James. Immediately, Matthew felt a fatherly kind of kinship with him. This middle-aged man with intense eyes seemed to welcome Matthew as the son he never had. And from the moment Marshall saw Matthew pitch in Mount Pleasant, Marshall cautioned him that his strengths were not just on the pitcher's mound. He wanted Matthew to know that character mattered, especially to him.

Matthew always felt Marshall's esteem and protective nature over him. He knows Marshall went out on a limb with a high school player, convincing the Yankees to put Matthew under contract. Marshall advised Matthew to not give his best pitching years to a college team; he didn't want Matthew to throw his arm out.

Marshall also advised the Yankee franchise to make sure this kid didn't sit in the Rookie League or get lost somewhere in the farm league in A or AA ball. After watching him play four high school games, Marshall advised the Yankees to put him on the Prince William Yankees and to watch him closely.

Marshall still laughs when he retells the story of advising the big shots at the Yankees that his kid shouldn't languish in the minor leagues for long. In 1988, without any games in the lower minor leagues, Matthew moved straight to Prince William County, Virginia, and began playing AAA ball in the Yankees franchise.

******

This morning finds Matthew daydreaming of the early days before he became a wealthy professional baseball player. Matthew gets out of bed and presses the button for the electric shades. He is instantly greeted with a million-dollar view of Central Park. The early morning sun gleams off the white marble floors of the vast great room. Floor-to-ceiling windows make the room seem to exist as part of Central Park.

He walks toward the kitchen and pushes the on button to his designer espresso machine. He quietly opens the sliding glass door onto his balcony. After all these years, he still forgets. His gut reaction is always to inhale deeply to greet the day, and it still seems as if somehow, he expects to catch the scent of salty ocean air and pluff mud. Instead, he's greeted with the scent of the garbage truck that recently clanked down the street.

Every time he brought a woman here, he could feel her admiring the view and wanting it, almost as if he was the second thought. When he bought the apartment, he was excited to be able to live in the posh location. Truth be told, he wanted to impress the people who always implied that he was some country boy from South Carolina. Sometimes he felt like giving them a geography lesson, knowing they had no idea he lived on the water in South Carolina.

By New York standards, he is staring at the pinnacle of success. But sadly, most days, as he stares out over the park and the city, he finds himself daydreaming of Shem Creek. He misses the early morning colors and reflections. He misses the peace he felt when he watched a sunrise.

Matthew looks back over his shoulder at a woman he does not love who is sleeping in his king-sized bed, and he wonders if this is all there is. He's got that morning-after guilt that always plagues him. In the moment, when the wine is flowing and he's out with a beautiful woman, nothing seems wrong or out of line. But in the morning, he wants to be alone. In the morning, his thoughts drift to Michelle.

******

When Matthew first arrived in New York in 1991, Marshall James invited him to live with him and his wife. At first, Matthew thought it might be strange, but he quickly realized that this huge city was a lonely place if you didn't have people to come home to. Marshall's wife, Melissa, was a wonderful woman in her early fifties. She came to genuinely love Matthew and became a second mom to him. Marshall quickly became a man that Matthew confided in and sought wisdom from. It was as if God had sent a man to fill the spot that Mr. Nicholson used to occupy. Matthew was grateful.

One evening, Marshall asked Matthew about women and why he didn't have a special girl. Marshall had been so good to him that Matthew finally decided to let someone in. That night, he told Marshall all about Michelle, Joseph, and Jake, and he shared his lifelong love for Michelle.

"Sounds like you're letting yourself stay stuck," Marshall noted.

"Sir, I've tried, really tried, but no matter what I do, I compare every woman to her," Matthew shares truthfully.

"That's okay, son. That just means your standards are high, and you're not willing to settle," Marshall discerns.

Matthew never thought of it that way. Perhaps the celebrity lifestyle had kept him away from the kind of people he wanted in his life. "If you're right, then where does a guy find real people—people who love you wherever you are?" he asks.

"It might surprise you to know that not all New Yorkers are shallow people. I know some pretty great people," Marshall says. "Let me take you to my favorite deli tomorrow. I'm going to introduce you to the kind of people you're missing."

"I'm game," Matthew says, actually encouraged for the first time.

******

The two men leave the apartment at noon and walk north a few blocks. With Marshall leading the way, they step into a deli called Mario's. It's a small deli with six small round tables covered with classic red and white checked tablecloths. The walls are adorned with vintage Yankees' paraphernalia. He winces when he sees a poster-sized version of a baseball card with his smiling face on it.

They are instantly greeted. "Marshall, my friend! Where ya been?" a large smiling man calls out from behind a counter.

"Taking care of this one," Marshall says with a smile. "He's a full-time job!"

"Mario Rossellini," the man introduces himself, wiping his hands on his soiled white apron and reaching for Matthew's hand over the counter.

"Matthew West," Matthew replies, accepting his outstretched hand.

"It's an honor to have you here, Matthew," Mario says. "It's not often that one of the Yankees' finest graces my deli."

"Well, sir, Marshall here tells me I haven't met any of the great New Yorkers. He says that because of my job I'm probably meeting a whole lot of the wrong people. His goal is to show me otherwise," Matthew shares, smiling. "So, I guess you're one of the great New Yorkers?"

Mario laughs a deep belly-laugh, and Matthew instantly likes the man. He has thick, receding, salt-and-pepper hair, a pot belly, and sparkling brown eyes with deep creases in the corners. His smile is genuine, and his deli smells like heaven.

"You aren't one of those picky eaters who doesn't do spicy, are you, Mr. West?" Mario asks with an infectious smile.

"No, sir, I'm not. Did you have something in mind that I should try?" Matthew asks.

"Have a seat, son," he says, pointing to a table. "If Marshall brings you here, then we will treat you like we treat Marshall, like family."

Matthew felt welcome for the first time in years, and he didn't realize how much he'd missed it until this moment. He eats more than he's eaten in weeks. Mario sits down with them and calls out to someone in the back to watch the front counter.

"Marguerite, honey, can you come out and give me a hand?" Mario asks.

A few seconds later, a brown-eyed beauty with a dirty apron comes out front.

"Sure, Dad, and thanks a whole lot for the heads up that *Mr. Baseball* is here," she says, smiling sarcastically. "I'm

Marguerite," she says confidently, holding out her hand to Matthew. "Aren't women supposed to get all fixed up to meet you?" she says, pretending to straighten up her apron and running her fingers through her thick hair.

"I'm Matthew West," he says politely. "It's nice to meet you."

"Yeah, I think we know who you are, but what I don't know is ... *why* are you here? This isn't exactly the hangout I'd expect for New York's most eligible bachelor," she teases.

"Marshall brought him, so he's been properly vetted." Mario says, smiling.

"Got it," she says and goes back behind the counter.

Well, she's a nice change, Matthew thinks. He is so tired of women falling all over themselves to get at him that it's refreshing to meet one who didn't instantly elevate him to something he was not. *This girl is different.*

When they get up to leave, Matthew walks up to the counter to pay and speaks to Marguerite once again. "It was very nice to meet you, Miss Marguerite ..." He smiles, turns, and leaves with Marshall.

******

Back inside the deli, Mario speaks truth to his daughter: "Be careful. I saw him flirt with you. That's probably not the kind of man you want to be involved with. He's got too many women at his disposal," Mario says.

"Dad, I can take care of myself."

"Oh, I know you can, but that one has quite the reputation as a lady's man."

"So, basically, because you read the *National Enquirer*, you know this guy?" Marguerite asks sarcastically. "Do you have any idea how much of that garbage is lies? What if he's a great guy?"

"What if he isn't and you get your heart broken?"

"Dad, it's my heart to break or not," she replies. "Plus, honestly, Dad, I've been hit on by men since I was twelve years old. Believe me, I can spot the difference."

It was true, Mario knows it. His beautiful daughter has been pursued by boys all her life. She has a rare Italian beauty that combines dark brown eyes and a magnificent wide smile. When she smiles, everything seems to brighten up, and her teeth stand at attention in a perfect straight white line. Her wavy dark hair has the look of someone who spent hours trying to achieve a soft curled look, but it comes straight out of the shower that way. *His daughter has style*, New York style, and it oozes out of her in whatever she wears. She has this incredible ability to put things together that others can't pull off, and yet she looks completely put together. She is a natural beauty in form and feature.

"Just promise me you will be careful. There is no doubt in my mind that Matthew will be back, and I'm fairly certain it will not just be for the food." Mario chuckles.

"Right, Dad, like some celebrity baseball player is going to come back for some poor law school student working in her daddy's deli."

"You have no idea," Mario says. "And that makes you even more attractive."

"Daddy, you're just biased because you love me, but I sure do appreciate it." She plants a kiss on her beloved father's cheek.

"I always said, the first time I saw your momma, God rest her soul, that she nearly knocked me out. You, my beautiful girl, are a carbon copy of her."

******

When Matthew returns the following day, claiming to be hungry, Mario laughs to himself, knowing he was right. He watches as Marguerite joins him at his table for lunch that first day. They talk and laugh, and Mario has to force himself to realize that his worries might be without merit. Matthew seems to be a genuinely nice guy.

Marguerite falls hard and fast. She, too, has spent a lifetime being chased. Most of the time, men only seemed to want one thing from her. So, when Matthew starts hanging out at the deli every day, talking to her and her dad, she gets the feeling that this guy is the kind of man she's longed for.

"Will you come to watch me this weekend?" Matthew asks her over lunch, a few weeks into his daily visits.

"To be honest, I'm going to need a baseball lesson or two."

"It's not rocket science. Just watch a couple innings, and you'll figure it out. Hopefully, you'll get hopelessly hooked on it."

Matthew pulls out some tickets and a couple of passes, which will get her into places reserved for wives and families of the team—box seats. There are two of everything, one for her and one for her dad.

"And don't worry, you'll be with Marshall," Matthew says.

Marguerite knows what this will mean. If she and her father walk in with Marshall, the press will know they are guests of Matthew West. She isn't quite sure if she's ready, because although they have not actually been on a date, she has no doubt where this is going and what his intentions are. She is quite sure that he's been spending time at the deli not just for her benefit but for her father's as well. He probably guesses that her overprotective father isn't thrilled about a celebrity dating his only daughter. So, Matthew has decided to take some time and put the man at ease.

This gesture captures Marguerite's heart. It isn't just that this man is handsome and successful, but also somewhere along the way, he has learned the value of family. Marguerite hopes that one day she'll be able to meet this family—the really extended one that he speaks of so lovingly. She has a feeling that these people have shaped who Matthew is.

Matthew hands her a Yankees cap. "It might help you hide a bit," he says sympathetically.

"Am I going to need to be hidden?"

"You might want to be, so I'm offering it up—this and a pair of shades. You can walk in and out under the radar screen, and no one will have to know who you are," he explains.

"Are you hiding me?"

"Absolutely not! I just want to give you privacy if you want it," Matthew adds. "The press follows me, and most of the time, they write lies. I don't want you mixed up in it," he says.

The press relentlessly follows Matthew, trying to pair him off. Who Matthew appears to be dating, or not, is always news. Matthew doesn't want the press to mess this one up; he has started to believe this might be something wonderful.

Marguerite catches the baseball bug right away, and Matthew starts her baseball education. It isn't long before she can talk very intelligently about his game, how he throws, and his stats. Matthew loves it.

******

Marguerite will never forget the moment when she knows—the moment she realizes she's fallen hopelessly in love with Matthew West. It was a rather romantic moment as baseball goes, and she realizes, as it is happening, that it is also recorded for the world to see.

Marshall, Mario, and Marguerite were headed to one of the club suites for an afternoon game. Marguerite loves her Yankees hat and shirt and has become quite the fan now that she is crazy about their star pitcher. She has her look styled perfectly. Her hair is in a ponytail, hanging out of the back of an adjustable hat. She's wearing diamond stud earrings, the team shirt, and white shorts. She has new aviator sunglasses, a touch of pink gloss on her lips, and a pair of heeled sandals that make her tanned legs look a mile long.

She likes to be right up at the glass window of the suite when the announcer calls Matthew's name. She loves to watch him arrive on the mound, ready for the game. She is standing at the glass, smiling down at him, but this time, he stops, as if looking for something. He scans the audience until his eyes land on the club box where they are seated. He looks up and sees Marguerite at the window. Without a thought, he smiles broadly, points to the box, and taps his hand on his heart. In return, she smiles and does the exact same thing back to him. All of which is caught from multiple camera angles and broadcasted all over the country.

Back home in South Carolina, Jake, Joseph, Mr. and Mrs.

Nicholson, and Michelle are tuned into the latest Yankees game.

"What on earth was that? Is our boy in love?" Joseph says with a smile.

"Dang! I hope so," Jake says, smacking Joseph on the back.

"Did he RSVP yet?" Mr. Nicholson asks Michelle.

"He did not, but since he's in the wedding party, I'm thinking that lazy boy thinks that's not necessary." Michelle's says, laughing.

"I mean, did he give you a plus one?" Mr. Nicholson asks, wondering if Matthew is planning on bringing this woman.

"Her name is Marguerite," Jake shares.

"Wait, you knew about this?" Joseph asks.

"Yeah, he called a few months ago to talk about her. She's in law school, and her dad owns a deli. He says when he met her and her dad, it was the first time since he'd moved to New York that he felt like he'd met some real people," Jake explains.

"Probably helps that she's gorgeous," Michelle comments.

"Well, we all know Matthew. He's got great taste in women!" Joseph says poking Michelle.

******

Later that evening, Matthew and Marguerite are driving back to Matthew's apartment. Matthew feels uneasy. He is concerned that people would see this as some huge profession of love. When he did it, that really wasn't what was on his mind. He was simply feeling flirtatious with his pretty girlfriend. At the moment, he'd been caught up, just looking for Marguerite and Mario. *How do you backtrack from what people think they saw on the camera? And what must Marguerite be thinking?*

He was thankful for the break in his thoughts. They had the radio on … and Matthew heard it. "A moment of silence please … for The Dogs," he says, laughing.

"What on earth?" Marguerite looks at him quizzically.

"I'll explain when the song is over, but for now, a moment of silence, please!" And Matthew sings out the song.

"Okay, okay, what's the story?" she asks him when the song finishes. "You singing out, driving through New York, is not your usual act."

"True. Just a group of teenagers, growing up on the banks of Shem Creek, singing out as loud as we could, on a fabulous summer day—making memories. My friend Joseph has this habit of saying 'a moment of silence please' in this announcer's voice whenever one of our favorite songs comes on. It's like code to sing it out. Joseph, Jake, Michelle, and I were a foursome, always together and always having each other's backs. We all lived within a few houses of each other. We all pretty much grew up together," Matthew explains.

"Are you sure it isn't more than that?" "What do you mean?"

"Well, we had a pretty spectacular day. The world now knows we are a couple. I was feeling pretty great," she says. "But then you start to share this memory of this time in your life, and I've lost you."

"I don't understand," Matthew says. "Why do women always need to analyze stuff like this and pick a fight?'

"A woman can tell. I'm sitting here beside you, and it's as though you left," she replies. "I'm thinking we are connecting here, and you're finally sharing something with me about your past. But it feels like that in sharing it, the connection between you and me is lost."

"I have some great childhood memories. What's wrong with that? Why are you making this into a fight?"

"I'm not, and it's not a fight to ask a question to someone you care about," she says, choosing to drop the subject. She knows when a man has shut a door. She'd just like to know why.

The following morning, the sports section carries the photo of Matthew West smiling and tapping his heart. It didn't take the press long to figure out who the woman was. Before long, Mario's deli is packed every day. All of a sudden, it becomes a baseball-lovers' hangout. Mario installs a large TV, and families come to watch Yankees games with Matthew West's girlfriend's dad. Mario loves it.

~ CHAPTER 17 ~

The two have been an item for almost a year, and Marguerite spends most nights at Matthew's new apartment. On some level, Matthew knows it's wrong to have a woman basically living with him who isn't his wife, but with the hours he keeps and his travel schedule, if she wasn't spending the night, he wouldn't get any time with her. And to be honest, she's Italian, with a more European view on things like sex. She is very unencumbered. Secretly, Matthew worries she's doing whatever is in her power to get him to really love her.

The difference between Marguerite and all the other women is her sincerity. She truly loves him; he can tell. There are days when Matthew genuinely thinks he loves her too or at least is heading that way. But then there are so many days he just wants to be left alone. Often, he yearns for the days when she wasn't around. Guilt overwhelms him at times, knowing he *should* love this wonderful woman, and yet he does not.

Matthew is out on the balcony overlooking Central Park when he hears the sliding door open. Marguerite steps out with two mugs of coffee. She is holding an envelope.

"Are you bringing me to this, or am I being hidden for some reason?" she asks, holding out the invitation to Joseph and Michelle's wedding.

"No, I'm not hiding you, but there's a part of me that thinks you'll think where I came from is kind of back-woodsy, from the sticks," he says. "You're such a city girl, and you might not fit in."

"Seriously? You're really saying that?" she asks. "You met me wearing a dirty apron, working in my dad's deli. Are you sure that's the real reason you don't want to bring me?"

"I didn't say I didn't want to bring you." "Does anyone there even know I exist?"

"Um, everyone knows you exist. They all saw it on national television." Matthew winks at her.

"You know what I mean. Like, have you had a conversation with any of them about me?"

"Actually, yes, even before you came to your first Yankees game. I spoke with Jake," Matthew says, "and then I told Mr. Nicholson."

"Okay ... I feel a bit better then. I kind of thought you were hiding me."

"No, but it's a big deal for me to go home at all, and it would be a huge deal if I came home with a woman," Matthew explains. "Would you even want to go?"

"*Of course I want to go!* It's like there are all these missing puzzle pieces that seem to be located in South Carolina. I feel like you don't really know a man till you've been home with him."

"Then I'll RSVP with a plus one," Matthew replies, instantly feeling better about not standing at Joseph and Michelle's wedding alone and feeling like a loser. But if the truth were to come out, he'd be horrified. Even though he hasn't gotten over Michelle, at least he'd look as if he had. He sincerely hopes that seeing the two of them get married will once and for all provide closure. Maybe knowing for sure that she will never be his will finally open his heart completely to love Marguerite the way he wished he did. Because God knows, *she loves him*. And most of the time Matthew feels like the luckiest man alive, but it's in the moments when he tries to contemplate marrying her that he feels somehow disloyal to Michelle, which is ridiculous, because she is marrying someone else.

Although Matthew is very fond of Marguerite, it still feels like she is in second place. Matthew *knows* he's only with Marguerite because he can't be with Michelle.

"A couple of warnings before you go to Mount Pleasant with me," Matthew begins, with a smile. "It's wardrobe warnings. First, this is an outdoor wedding, and the ground is always mushy in The Low Country, so heels aren't going to cut it. Second, 'dressed up' in South Carolina is your leather flip flops, and casual is our canvas ones. Seriously, this is an outdoor wedding in the most humid place on the earth. Nobody dresses up there."

"So, what am I supposed to wear? Shorts and a tank top?"

"Not *that* casual, but you're getting closer. Do not even think about a New York wedding when you contemplate what to wear. It's likely that Joseph will either have flip flops on, or he'll be outright barefoot. Michelle will probably have a sundress/beach wedding kind of dress. So, think sundress ... and NOT black."

"Seriously? People will be *that* casual for a wedding?"

"So, here in New York, you women wear navy blue, gray, brown, or black, and that's it. Southern girls wear colors ... pink, purple, light blue ..." he explains. "It's like happy colors there, and sad colors here."

"So, if I buy a colorful cotton dress, I'd be okay?" "Yes, and sandals."

"Got it." She smiles, excited for the new adventure.

******

From the moment Marguerite steps off the plane at the Charleston airport, she feels the oppressive moisture in the air. The humidity in June makes things outright sticky. As they drive over the rickety Cooper River Bridge, Marguerite feels herself holding on to the hand rests for safety. The bridge doesn't exactly make her feel secure.

As they cross into Mount Pleasant driving onto Coleman Boulevard, Marguerite starts to see the charm. Palmetto trees are everywhere, and lush vegetation seems to grow wild. When they turn left onto Simmons Street and make the quick right onto Rue de Muckle, Matthew starts to inhale and exhale as he rolls all the windows down.

"Good God in heaven!" he exclaims. "I'm home!"

As he pulls into the driveway, two men who must be Joseph and Jake come running out, and Matthew is wrapped into the most loving man hug Marguerite has ever seen. And these two men are *gorgeous*. She quietly gets out of the car, and immediately sees what was so captivating about this spot of heaven: her first glance at Shem Creek. As the gentle breeze off the ocean hits her nostrils, she smells the salty air and finally understands what Matthew is always talking about. This looks like a place where any boy would want to grow up.

"Well, if the men aren't going to bother," Michelle says, "I will. I'm Michelle," she introduces, sticking out her hand.

Marguerite is at a loss for words. Matthew failed to mention that this woman is absolutely stunning. For reasons that Marguerite doesn't understand, she has always pictured Michelle as some plain-looking country girl. She had certainly not imagined her to be this stunning dark-haired beauty. Marguerite is very much taken in by the heavy lashes and the navy-blue eyes.

"I'm Marguerite Rossellini," she responds, while taking Michelle's hand in her own.

"It is so nice to finally meet you, Marguerite. The cameras do not do you proper justice," Michelle adds, smiling warmly.

"Thank you," Marguerite replies.

Marguerite turns and sees Matthew enfold Michelle in a big hug and swings her around. She watches with keen interest as she notices the placement of Matthew's hand on the back of Michelle's hair. "You're really doing it, huh? Marrying this creep?" he teases.

"I sure am, and I've waited long enough," she says, winking at Joseph.

Marguerite watches as a middle-aged man with a huge smile comes walking toward them. Marguerite watches as Matthew smiles in response and receives a loving hug from someone who has genuinely missed him.

"I've missed you so much son," says Mr. Nicholson. "And who is this lovely creature who is so obviously out of your league?" he asks, looking at Marguerite.

"Mr. Nicholson, this is Marguerite," Matthew introduces.

"Jeb, please," he says, taking her hand.

Marguerite's initial thought is this man reminds her of her father. She knows at first glance that she will like this man. Mrs. Nicholson is right behind him, and she takes Marguerite into a hug.

"Let's get you two inside and changed into something comfortable. Tonight is the rehearsal dinner. That's a joke, Marguerite, but it is the night before the wedding. We're having a cookout on the dock," Mrs. Nicholson explains. "If Mr. Baseball over there hasn't explained it to you yet, we're a bit casual down here in South Carolina."

******

Marguerite makes her way downstairs in shorts and a t-shirt. She's headed through the family room to the screened-in porch off the back. She walks out onto the porch and out to the backyard. She stops as she observes that the remains of the old baseball diamond are still there. The weeds are trying to overtake it, but too many years of wearing down the path make it still visible. She notices a well-worn path heading toward the dock, and she follows it down to where all the adults are. She is introduced to Matthew's parents and finally has a moment to talk with Jake and Joseph. A stunning blonde has joined the group, and Matthew appears to be meeting her for the first time.

"This is Christina," Jake says, with his hand on the small of her back.

"I'm Matthew, a nd t his i s M arguerite," M atthew greets, taking Christina's hand. "Jake, out of your league, bud ... totally out of your league," Matthew teases as he elbows Jake in the ribs.

Marguerite walks to the edge of the dock, takes off her sandals, and sits down, dangling her feet in Shem Creek for the first time. She breathes in deeply, catches the fragrance of the pluff mud, and begins to understand what Matthew meant when he said that New York City air smells like pollution compared to this. Having grown up in the city, Marguerite can't imagine how wonderful it must have been to have this as your home. She is utterly at a loss as to why someone would ever want to leave here. She begins to wonder if something chased him off, or if it really was baseball.

"What do you think?" Matthew asks as he sits down next to her.

"Magical, absolutely magical. Why on earth would you have ever left this paradise?" she asks, only half joking.

"Oh, just a little job as a pitcher for the Yankees ... just that," he responds. "I had always intended to return here, especially knowing how short the career of a professional athlete is."

"Good to know. I never realized that was your long-term plan."

"I always thought I'd want to raise my kids here," Matthew shares honestly. "It feels like a better place than New York."

"You're probably right," she replies, splashing her feet in the warm creek water.

Matthew stands, facing the creek, and all of a sudden, two guys are behind him.

"Bet he can't …" Jake says.

"Bet he won't … unless we push him in!" Joseph says.

Both grown men tackle their lifelong friend, and the three of them go splashing into the water, fully clothed.

"Don't worry. Girls stopped being required to do that about fifteen years ago," Michelle says, laughing. "Usually, they are stripping off their clothing as they run toward the edge."

Marguerite watches this with happiness and curiosity. This is so wonderful. She has a fleeting thought of how wonderful it would be to return here with Matthew and raise a family. She just hopes that when Matthew returns, it will be with her. She notices that everyone is very affectionate with each other. She likes that a whole lot. There are also moments when she has no idea what anyone is talking about, for they are all so lost in a lifetime of memories. But that doesn't bother her at all. This group is family, and Marguerite has always wanted to be a part of a large family. She's so glad she came to this wedding.

"What time does everything start tomorrow?" Matthew asks.

"The decorating folks arrive at about 2:00, and the wedding will be just before sunset," Michelle says. "We will be stringing up lights all along the dock, and the preacher will be standing right here tomorrow evening. We've got chairs arriving, and they will be placed at the base of the dock."

******

The following day, as the sun is setting, Marguerite sees the beauty of Shem Creek come alive. Tiny white lights are lining the walkway down to the dock. The gazebo at the end of the dock has white lights around the top. The rails have lights and bouquets of wildflowers tied with white satin bows adorning them. The preacher, dressed in jeans, seersucker jacket, and flip flops is already waiting under the gazebo as the groomsmen slowly walk up the dock to join him. All of the men are wearing blue and white striped seersucker jackets, white shirts, white bowties, white shorts, and flip flops. The scene is stunning as the sun is slowly setting over Shem Creek. The men are all extraordinarily handsome.

The music starts, just a single violin, playing the traditional wedding song. Marguerite is in the front row closest to the gazebo with a clear shot of Matthew. She thinks that a few years ago, if anyone had told her she'd consider a wedding like this to be absolutely fabulous, she'd have laughed. Her idea of a wedding was always very New York, formal dress, church, and an expensive reception. She smiles as she realizes how falling in love with a man can make you want what he likes.

She is busy contemplating her own wedding someday on this very same dock, when she looks at Matthew again. She smiles at him. He looks so handsome with his tanned skin next to the blue of the seersucker jacket. His sandy hair has natural summer highlights. He is standing up straight, hands clasped in front of him, shoulders broad, looking serious.

Michelle finally appears on Mr. Nicholson's arm. Marguerite turns to gaze at the gorgeous bride. The simplicity of her dress is perfect for this sunset wedding on the dock. The dress is a cotton lace sundress with a completely open back. Around Michelle's tiny waist is a pale pink band that ties in a bow in the back. Her dark curls are falling out of an updo with baby's breath woven in. Michelle has a suntan that highlights the pure white dress. Her makeup is light and soft, and her lips have a gentle pink gloss. Her bouquet is a handful of tiny white roses.

Marguerite smiles to herself as she realizes that Michelle is barefoot. She is simply the perfect bride. This is precisely what Marguerite wants some day, and she is enjoying her little daydream.

Marguerite turns to face the men again, and her little daydream abruptly ends. When she looks at Matthew, she sees everything that she has never understood before. She's watching him look at another woman in the way in which she wants him to look at her. The truth becomes painfully clear as the tears stream down Matthew's cheeks unchecked. This is the reason Matthew can't love her. This is the reason that, although he is a wonderful, giving man, he has never given himself entirely to her. This is the reason he hesitated to bring her to this wedding. Someone already has his heart, and she is marrying his best friend.

Marguerite finds herself fighting back tears. It's okay to cry at a wedding, but what's welling up inside her is a heartbreak so great that if she gives into it now, she will make a fool of herself.

Her pulse is racing, and she feels physically ill. Oh, God, how will she make it through this day? On one hand, why hadn't he been honest with her? But on the other, she feels protective of Matthew in this moment, because she is sure this is not something Matthew has done on purpose. In fact, she remembers hearing the stories of Matthew joining this group after they had all been friends for a few years. Maybe it had been Matthew's bad luck to fall for his best friend's girl. Either way, one thing became crystal clear: Matthew loves another woman, leaving no room for her. She glances around at the group. Is she the only one seeing this?

Marguerite makes a decision. This is a choice she's making because she truly loves this man. She will not spoil this for Matthew by making some sort of emotional scene. He's broken enough, and she loves him too much to add to this pain. In this moment, she fully understands what it feels like to love someone who doesn't love you back. As the vows are spoken, it becomes abundantly clear that Michelle and Joseph adore each other, and Matthew's feelings are not reciprocated.

As Joseph watches his father escort his beautiful bride down the dock, he can't compose himself. He glances at his two friends and is grateful that he's not the only emotional one in this moment. It feels as if he's waited a lifetime for this moment. He considers how many of his life's best moments have taken place in this very spot, and he thanks God as his beautiful Michelle's hand is placed in his by his teary-eyed father.

"This is a dream come true, son. The son I raised is marrying the woman I helped raise. God is in this moment, Joseph. Thank you for waiting," Mr. Nicholson says, knowing for certain that his son had waited.

"I now pronounce you husband and wife," the preacher announces with joy.

The fifty friends and family members gathered to celebrate this moment break into applause.

Joseph kisses his bride, turns to face his guests, and speaks: "My wife and I would like to thank each and every one of you for the role you've played in this day. I am grateful beyond words. Today is the Dock Walk of a lifetime for me. Most of you here know what the Dock Walk has been for us guys here. I learned everything I needed to learn about life and love so far on this very dock. I saw this gorgeous woman for the first time on this dock; I fell in love with her on this dock; I've made and cultivated the two best friends of my life on this dock; I was told to wait on this dock; I've laughed on this dock and cried on this dock; and today, it is only fitting that I've gotten married on this dock. Lord willing, this is where I'll teach my kids about love.

This place feels like sacred ground to me. I just have one more thing to say. This is my wife!" Joseph cries out.

As the happy couple walk back down the dock as husband and wife, Joseph's world changes.

"Why is it pink?" Michelle asks, holding up her hand, looking at the gorgeous new pink diamond ring in a gold setting that Joseph has given to her.

"Because every woman has a white diamond, and you are special and set apart. So why on earth should you wear what everyone else wears?" he explains. "Like this stone, you are a rare and unique treasure."

Michelle has no words. She looks at this man, the one who chose to show her what love looks like, and realizes for the first time that he is now her husband.

"Do you like my dress?" she says with a wink.

"Yes! You look absolutely gorgeous!" he says.

"Wait till you see what's under it," she teases with a very sexy undertone, which leaves Joseph standing there with his mouth open.

"Have mercy!" he says, catching up to her, looking down at his watch. "How much longer till we can get out of here?"

******

"I don't think we will see her again," Jeb says to his wife, pointing at Marguerite.

"I don't think so either. She saw it," Kathleen discerns.

"That poor guy—Joseph's best day is his very worst," Jeb says sadly. "I'm a bit worried about him."

"Me too."

"I think I'm going to have a talk with him later." "I think that's a good idea."

******

After Joseph and Michelle have left for their honeymoon, the guests are gone, and people have retired for the night,

Matthew steps out the back-porch door, heading down the well-worn path, through the old baseball diamond to the dock. He sits down on the edge, dangling his feet in the water. The moonlight reflecting on the high tide is beautiful. The nighttime creatures of Shem Creek are playing their music. Matthew bows his head and starts to cry with his shoulders shaking and a pain so deep that it all seems to pour out through his eyes.

"Why, God? Why?!" he cries. "Why would you give me such a deep and pure love for someone I cannot have? God, I've begged you, please take the feelings away. So, why, God?" he sobs. "I can't do this anymore. My heart is broken. I love her so much, God. Please, help me."

Matthew is very embarrassed when he hears Mr. Nicholson walking down the dock towards him. Truth be told, he just wants to be left alone. Maybe if he finally cries this out, he can move forward.

Mr. Nicholson sits down on the dock next to Matthew and gently puts his arm around the young man. The two of them just sit, looking at the moonlight dance on the water, and Matthew cries even harder.

"What am I supposed to do?" Matthew asks, wiping his eyes on the back of his hand.

"Love God as much as you love her," Mr. Nicholson quietly said.

"What?"

"Give all your love to God. I know you've walked away from your beliefs. I know you and Marguerite are living together, and it's not fair to her. So, I am going to challenge you, in your grief, to make things right with her and God. You are in no place to be in a relationship with a woman when you carry so much love for another. And believe me, she saw it tonight," Mr. Nicholson shares.

"What do you mean she saw it?"

"You didn't even realize that when I walked Michelle down the dock, you were crying. Everyone, including Marguerite, saw it. I know you didn't plan this, and I also know you haven't done this to her on purpose. Honestly, the only way you ever know if you can love someone is to try, but she deserves more. So, I want to challenge you, Matthew. Let her go, and stop trying to love someone else. Just run as fast as you can towards God. Pursue Him with a passion. I promise you, your ache will subside," Mr. Nicholson says.

"You honestly think the absence of God in my life is making all this worse?" Matthew asks.

"I do," Mr. Nicholson replies gently. "He's a jealous God, Matthew, and you've walked away from Him. He wants you back. I firmly believe that until that is your priority, you'll never have the love you so desire."

"Where do I begin?"

"On your knees," Mr. Nicholson says, standing. "I'm going to leave you alone here to do your own private business with God. In a month, I'm coming to New York to see you, and you are going to take me to church in whatever church God settles you in."

216

"You'd actually come to New York for me?" Matthew asks.

"You are a son to me, and you're struggling. Of course I'm coming."

"Oh, Mr. Nicholson?"

"Yes?"

"I thought you might like to know that I asked the owner of the backwards house to let me know if he ever wanted to sell it. I don't know why, but I guess I always thought I'd get married and move back here to raise my family. Anyway, I've already written a contract, and Old Man Nelson is going to stay in it as long as he wants," Matthew says.

"Now, that's the best news I've heard in a long time!" Mr. Nicholson responds, smiling. "Just knowing you'll be back here someday is about the happiest news I could get tonight."

Matthew spends a few hours on the dock by himself. As the sun rises over Shem Creek the morning after Joseph's wedding, Matthew feels a new resolve for the first time in years, and the deep pain inside seems manageable. For the first time in many years, Matthew is going to dust off his Bible and see what God has in store for him.

*****

When Matthew and Marguerite arrive home at Matthew's apartment, things are strained. Marguerite has spent way too many hours fighting off tears that she desperately needs to shed.

"It's okay, Matthew. We don't have to have a big discussion about this. I really understand," she says quietly.

"I think you deserve an explanation," Matthew says and begins the story for her. "I arrived in Mount Pleasant a few years after Jake and Joseph had become best friends. They were so good to me. When I arrived, I had a terrible stutter, and I had basically been a hermit. I didn't have any friends. When I arrived, they reached out to me, and before I knew it, my stutter was gone. They are the brothers I never had. Michelle is Jake's cousin, and she had been coming every summer. At first, we were all still young enough that I thought either my crush would go away, or Joseph would decide that she wasn't his girl. But they were one of those couples who meet and just know it. They always knew they were supposed to be together. And everyone around them thought so too. I was fooling myself, and with each passing year, the two of them just grew closer, and I knew. They loved each other as far back as either of them can remember. They have never been with other people, and they waited till their wedding night for sex. It's a pure love. And honestly, I've felt the same pure love for her. Mr. Nicholson told us all to keep our hands off her, that she was vulnerable and that we were to be her protectors. So, we did. That helped us through the teen years because nobody could date her. I tried to have girlfriends, but every girl I met I kept comparing to Michelle. They never matched up, partially because I didn't want them to. As the end of high school came around and the Yankees wanted me, I guess I thought that if I moved away and started a new life that I'd get over it. I've actually prayed to have God remove the feelings. So, basically all of my adult life, I've loved a woman I can't have, because Joseph is my very best friend in the world."

"That's really sad, but beautiful. Not many men fall in love for life," she says sadly. "And the only way you ever know if you can love again is to try it. So, I have no hard feelings here, Matthew. I love you too much. I just want you to be happy. Honestly, like you, I don't think I can stay in New York and see you in every paper all the time. Since passing the bar exam, I've been offered a job in Boston. I think I'm going to take it. They have a New York office, so when I'm in a better place, I can come back. I'm just going to get my things and head over to my dad's."

"I'm so sorry, Marguerite, for everything. I haven't treated you honorably, and I am so sorry."

"You're a wonderful man, Matthew, and I'm going to miss you," she says through tears. "I won't be keeping in touch. I hope you understand."

~ CHAPTER 18 ~

Jake was home, waiting for his dad to arrive. The ring in his pocket felt like a one-hundred-pound weight. He was so excited. Tonight was the night; he was going to ask Christina to marry him.

Jake laughed to himself at how very different he and Christina were from Joseph and Michelle. It made him smile to think that, initially, he didn't like Christina one bit. When Joseph, Jake, and Michelle had shown up at The University of South Carolina for college, the annoying Christina had been Michelle's roommate. Michelle and Christina had become fast best friends, and it felt like there was an ever-constant pressure for Jake and Christina to become a couple. After all, how cool would that be?

Jake's first impression of Christina made any idea of that an absolute no. Christina had the look of one of those high maintenance Charleston girls who were full of themselves. She was gorgeous, but Jake got the impression she knew it. She was the typical Charleston blonde, with long hair, blue eyes, perfect white teeth, and the year-round suntan. She was always wearing something monogrammed. Jake thought that was just plain stupid. She had perfect hair and nails at all times. She always looked like she was ready for someone to pick her up for a date. She wore pink lipstick that always made Jake wonder what would happen to it if someone kissed her.

And she was a born performer. It oozed out of her rather loud personality. Everyone was "sweetie" or "darling," and she drank a steady diet of sweet tea. She had the very annoying habit of wearing her cowboy boots with a sundress. Although Jake had been raised in the South, he never did like most of the women's fashions. He had gotten too used to his cousin Michelle and her tomboy ways.

She was a transfer student from some school up North, which made her a year older than Jake. Truth be told, that intimidated him a bit. They had asked her what that was about, and she simply said it was a change in major. Jake always had the idea that there was something more to it than that.

They ended up spending a great deal of time together because the girls were inseparable. Jake made it very clear to Joseph and to Michelle that he had absolutely no interest in this girl whatsoever.

Jake had heard she was musical and that she liked to sing. He hoped no one ever forced him to listen to her, because he was scared he'd have to lie and say it was good. The one positive was that she was a very loyal friend to Michelle. Since Michelle had grown up with few female friends, Jake thought this was good for her. However, it annoyed Jake that it seemed like there was an ever-present agenda to get the two of them together.

Jake's plans had altered somewhat from his first days at USC. He had arrived believing that he would study history and eventually become a teaching professor. He loved education and loved to teach. But within the first month of his arrival at USC, he had joined a men's Bible study and had begun to feel the first stirrings of a call into ministry. He enjoyed the impact that God seemed to be having on the college students and thought that it was almost more impactful than the education they were receiving. So he joined a local church in Columbia and became very involved. He loved church culture and loved how the music seemed to draw people in. He began to believe that he was being called to preach. He was quite sure that Christina was not pastor's wife material. She was far too materialistic.

It was a stormy Easter morning, and the four college students had planned to go to church together and have some brunch after. They arrived at church, only to realize that the power had gone out. The general feeling in the church building was one of panic. Everything that the church did was run on electricity. Everything from the electric keyboard to the microphones to the electric guitars to the air conditioning required power. People were filling the large sanctuary only to realize that there was the distinct possibility that Easter church might not happen.

At precisely 10:00, when the service was to start, the senior pastor came up to the front and attempted to speak. Without a microphone, it was hard to hear him. "I apologize that we have no electricity, and I'm guessing that half of you can't hear me. In the absence of electricity, we won't be able to have any music this morning," he said, sadly. "Everything about our music program here runs on power, and no one here is in a position to sing without accompaniment. So, I'm going to start the service by reading a few Psalms to you," he continued.

Christina was horrified. How could you have Easter church without music?

Jake, Michelle, and Joseph watched in silence as Christina got up and started climbing over people in their pew to get to the center aisle. Once she reached the center aisle, she started walking forward towards the pastor, who was reading Psalms that people could not hear.

"Excuse me, sir," she whispered to him. "We cannot do Easter service without music. I can sing any hymn you'd like, and I can guarantee that everyone will be able to hear me," she offered.

She grabbed a hymnal from the first row and said, "How about we start with 'Because He Lives'?"

The pastor seemed at a loss for words and not sure exactly what to do about this offer. He didn't know this young girl, but he *had* begged God to turn on the power so they could have music.

"You can do this?" the pastor questioned.

"Absolutely! In fact, I'm pretty sure that most of my training was probably about this moment," she said with a smile.

"Okay, ladies and gentlemen, it seems that God has given us a worship leader today, who can sing without any of our electrical instruments to back her up," he said. "I'm sorry ... I don't even know your name," the pastor said.

"I'm Christina," she introduced as she walked onto the stage. "This is going to be old-school, so if all of you would grab your hymnals and turn to number 124, we can get started." She gave them all a minute to find the hymn in their books, and she closed her eyes, looked up to heaven, whispered a soft prayer, and began.

She never opened her eyes. She spread her arms out wide, head facing heaven and began. Her voice, pure and powerful, filled the church with Easter music the likes of which none of them had ever heard. Her voice was magical, and she could sing out every hymn from memory. She didn't need the book. All around the church, people were wiping their eyes on the backs of their hands as they joined in with her song.

And that was the day that changed everything for Jake. As he listened to her sing, he realized that he was hearing genuine worship. This girl knew God. All of a sudden, things started to make sense. This was why God had given Michelle this beautiful blonde roommate.

The ride home was fascinating. Jake felt like he'd just met a new woman. It was almost as if blinders had been taken off. Jake realized that Christina Miller was an absolutely gorgeous girl.

"I definitely didn't see that coming," Joseph said in the car on the ride home.

"What, you didn't realize I could sing?" Christina teased.

"Yeah, kind of," Jake added.

"I told you all I had transferred from a school up North, but none of you all ever asked which school," she shared.

"Where did you transfer from?" asked Jake. "Juilliard," she told him. "I transferred from Juilliard."

"Seriously?" Jake added. "Like as in the Juilliard that's the top music school in this country, that Juilliard?"

"Yes," she answered. "Juilliard was my parent's dream."
"Not yours?" Jake added.

"No, I never saw myself singing at Carnegie Hall or performing for a living," she explained. "I always thought that my parents wanted that more than I did."

"So why did you leave?" Jake asked. "What changed your mind?"

"I began to feel that my music was a gift, something given directly to me by God. And if that was the case, then I should use it for him," she said.

"I seriously get that, in a major way," Joseph responded.

"I've heard about your voices from God," she added.

"How come you've never shared this with us before?" Joseph asked.

"Timing is everything. It's hard just to come out and say. Hey, I sing great, but I think I'm supposed to do it for God," she added.

"That's true," Michelle chimed in. "It would be hard to say that and not have it sound like you're prideful."

"Exactly," Christina smiled, feeling understood. "I want to help people with my career and bless people with my music. That's it. No big stage. No bright lights. No fancy music degree."

"Sounds like you've given this a lot of thought," Jake said.

"I have, and I've prayed and prayed about it. I'm not supposed to be some music star. My music is supposed to be free," she explained.

"When we drop you off, do you want to go for a walk or something?" Jake asked.

Michelle and Joseph looked at each other and smiled.

And Christina looked at Jake and said, "I'd love to. Just let me run upstairs and change into something comfortable, please."

"I'll wait down here," Jake said.

When she stepped out of her dorm with her hair in a ponytail, in cutoffs and flip-flops, Jake felt like he saw Christina for the first time. It felt only natural that he should reach out and take her hand in his. When she turned to him and smiled, Jake fell in love with the beautiful blonde.

******

He touches the ring in his pocket now, knowing full well that Christina has no idea that tonight he is going to propose to her.

When Jake's dad arrives home, he takes one look at his son and asks, "What are you up to?"

"Why, Dad? What makes you think I'm up to something?" Jake asks, puzzled.

"Son, you have a look on your face that says something is going on!" Jake's dad replies.

"Dad, I stopped by to tell you that I'm going to ask Christina to marry me tonight," Jake shares.

His dad wraps him in a huge bear hug and says, "It's about time!"

~ CHAPTER 19 ~

Joseph is bone tired after a twelve-hour shift. Working rescue is a dream come true for him, but it is physically exhausting.

Accident season is upon them, with proms and spring breaks, and people are passing through on their way to Florida; the shifts seem to be a nonstop whirlwind of tragedies. But Joseph loves the work, especially since he knows he is doing the work God has asked him to do. But lately, things seem to be getting more dangerous, as if God is asking much more of him.

Michelle seems like she is constantly worried about him, and Joseph wonders why she always fears the worst. Joseph feels confident that if God called him to do it, it is God's job to see him through it. To Joseph, it is quite simple. But Michelle sees too much in her role as an ER nurse. She sees all the mangled bodies, and she faces the loved ones in a way that Joseph's job rarely requires of him. Very often, Michelle has had to console the parents of a dying college student.

Michelle's worries seem to escalate ... since she has discovered she is pregnant. It's as if she expects Joseph to stop rescuing and focus exclusively on the fact that he is going to be a father. They weren't exactly fighting about this, but there is some strain, to be sure. Joseph understands that with Michelle's history, she has fears. She's dealt with the long-term ramifications of a childhood filled with rejection. Her greatest fear is being left alone. Joseph does his best to reassure her and listen to her. Joseph knows he can't possibly understand what it was like to grow up as she did, and it seems to Joseph that marriage has brought out some more of those fears.

He picks up his cell phone and calls her. "Hey, Babe, I'm just heading home. Do you need anything?" he asks.

Michelle laughs. She knows exactly what he's referring to. "Yep, go ahead and stop and get me a pint of mint chocolate chip."

"Will do. See you shortly. Love you." "Love you too, Boo," she says back.

Joseph gets in his red truck and checks his gas gauge. He decides to stop at the gas station on the corner of Highway 41 and Highway 17. He has finished his day with some additional deep water rescue training near Awendaw. He is sore from all the swimming today. The gas station is right next door to the all-night Waffle House, and it has a convenience store where he can get Michelle's ice cream.

Joseph pulls up to the pump, parks his truck, gets out, and heads into the convenience store to pay for his gas. The parking lot isn't full, and there are no other people pumping gas. There are a few cars parked on the far end near the Waffle House.

Joseph thinks it smells like rain. Being aware of the changing weather patterns helps him in his job. He is always concerned about heavy rain approaching if the Charleston area is at high tide. Flash floods always ensue.

When Joseph gets back to his truck, he sees the first flash of lightning. The storm is quite far off still, so he is confident he'll get home before it pours. As he starts to pump the gas, the air begins to feel electric, as if there is static in the air. The first feeling Joseph has that something is going on is the moment the hair on his arms stands up straight. He feels a shiver, although it is a balmy 70. He has a strange feeling that something evil is lurking, although he isn't sure why he feels that way.

While he is pumping gas, he takes in his surroundings. He has a strange feeling that one of those moments is upon him, but before this experience, he's never had any forewarning feelings. It has always just been the voice. For the first time, Joseph is truly scared. And for the very first time, he feels guilty, because he truly wishes God wasn't asking him to do this.

He whispers a prayer: "If You need me, God, I'm here, but I'm so scared. Please show me that You're here with me."

Again, he feels the chill and a shivering sensation. Instead of relief from God, his fear intensifies. He is almost finished pumping when he hears it:

Turn around. Joseph turns, and as usual, he initially sees nothing. There are two cars parked behind him. One is a newer model truck and the other is a beat-up old station wagon with wood paneling on the sides. The station wagon is parked in the corner, almost in the way you'd park a newer car you didn't want to get dinged. Nothing. He sees nothing that gives him any cautionary signs, and yet, he feels paralyzed with fear. He glances into the Waffle House, and several men are eating at the counter, talking with the waitress. A man on one of the barstools turns around. Joseph quickly looks away, not sure what is happening, but he is getting a strange feeling that this man is somehow part of this current calling. Joseph keeps his eyes peeled on the parking lot and his surroundings.

There it is again… *Turn around* Joseph turns back, looks at the old station wagon, and at the same time, there is a flash of lightning.

Joseph rubs his eyes. There is no way he saw what he thinks he saw. Inside the bright flash of lightning, just for a brief second, Joseph saw the car surrounded by an army of angels dressed in white, holding swords. They were guarding the car.

Just as soon as his brain registers this thought, the angels are gone. Joseph thanks God for the visual proof he'd asked for.

Joseph takes out his cell phone and calls Jake.

Jake answers on the first ring. "Jake, it's me. I'm at the convenience store at 41 and 17, call the police and get them here. If I call because I've heard a voice, they will think I'm nuts. I need you to make it happen, Jake. Something bad is going on. I've heard the voice, and I've seen angels," Joseph explains quickly and hangs up.

Joseph puts his phone in his pocket and scans the area again. He hears a tapping noise. He looks around and can't determine where it's coming from. The gentle tapping becomes what sounds like someone banging on a door. He grabs a flashlight and a crowbar out of his truck and begins to walk towards the old station wagon. "Help me, God," he whispers.

As he reaches the station wagon, he turns on the flashlight and looks inside the car. It's filthy. There's trash all over the front seat, empty food wrappers, Styrofoam coffee cups, and beer cans, lots and lots of beer cans. He moves his flashlight to the area beyond the second-row seat.

A little face looks up at him—a filthy face. A little girl about three or four, with blonde hair, is pounding on the window, looking like a caged animal. Her eyes are filled with terror. There's a bruise on her left cheek. She's wearing filthy PJs, and Joseph vaguely recognizes the outfit.

She's sobbing and banging on the window. "Get me out!" She is frantic to get Joseph's attention.

Joseph uses the crowbar and breaks the driver's window, unlocks it, and reaches in the back to grab the little girl, just as he hears a click.

He then feels the cold muzzle of a gun touching the back of his neck.

"You got no business here," the man, who Joseph had seen inside the Waffle House, says. "Leave her be, or I shoot," he adds.

The little girl is screaming. Joseph realizes this is the missing little girl who was kidnapped five days ago. There has been a massive search going on for her. The TV has been filled with clips of her parents begging for her return. There are pictures of her stapled to telephone poles and hanging in shop windows all over Charleston and the surrounding areas. Joseph knows he cannot let this man leave with this girl. Joseph feels the electricity in the air again.

"I'm going to tell you something, but you won't believe me. I'm not scared of your gun. This car, this entire parking lot, is filled with an army of God's angels sent to protect this child you've stolen. You stand absolutely no chance against them," Joseph says with confidence, even with the gun touching the back of his neck.

"Nice story. Don't make me shoot you," the man growls, and Joseph feels the evil.

There's an invisible battle going on at this moment, and Joseph feels it—a battle between good and evil. Joseph senses the electric charge in the air again, and he feels the sparks.

"I am not scared of you or your gun," Joseph repeats. "You will not win this battle."

The little girl is still screaming and crying.

"Shut up! Or I'll shoot you too!" he yells at the little girl.

"You won't shoot anyone here today," Joseph says, calmly turning around.

As if in slow motion, Joseph turns and sees the man. Just behind the man is a large angel, and the angel's arm is on the man's gun. As the kidnapper tries to shoot, a mighty hand, invisible to the kidnapper, reaches out and crushes the man's fingers. There's a terrible crunching sound, as multiple fingers are broken, and the gun falls to the ground.

The man crumples to the ground, crying out in agony, looking at his crushed, mangled fingers, bent in various wrong directions. His hand has been rendered useless.

The angel is gone, and the police cars are pulling into the parking lot.

Police surround the crying man with the destroyed hand, who is in so much pain he is unable to put up any sort of fight.

They push him face down on the ground and cuff his hands behind him, which causes the man even more pain.

Joseph reaches inside the filthy station wagon and grabs the hysterical little girl. Her eyes are wild with fear. She grabs Joseph as if she's holding on for life. She wraps her body around him, arms and legs, as if she's trying to attach herself to him physically. She is safe. She is sobbing, and Joseph is crying now too.

"I saw them," she whispers in his ear.

"So did I. So did I." he whispers back.

The ambulance arrives; the scene is chaos. The FBI is there, but the little girl refuses to let go of Joseph. Out of the corner of his eye, Joseph sees Jake. He is so grateful for Jake. Only a lifelong friend would respond in such a way. The two lock eyes; both men are visibly shaken.

"Why don't you go with the little girl?" Jake suggests. "I'll let Michelle know."

"Thanks, Jake," Joseph says. "Thank you for convincing them to come." He waves his arm over all the police cars present.

"They all know you, Joseph. They know your history. I didn't have to convince anyone of anything. They all believe God speaks to you," Jake says and turns to head back to his car.

Joseph looks at the little girl in his arms and tries to smile.

"Are you Lauren?" Joseph asks the little girl.

"Yes, how did you know?" she asks, still sniffling.

"We've been looking for you," Joseph says. "You and I are going to take a ride in that ambulance to the hospital, and your mommy and daddy are going to meet us there, okay? How does that sound?"

"My mommy and daddy are alive?" she asks with tears in her eyes. "The man said they were dead, and they would never come looking for me."

"Oh, no, my little one, they are on their way, and they haven't stopped looking for you," he says back to her.

By the time the ambulance arrives at the hospital, the place is crawling with media. When news gets out that the little girl had been found alive, it becomes the story of the year.

Little Lauren will not let go of Joseph, so he finds himself at the center of the media circus as he steps out of the ambulance. He covers the little girl's face with his hand and runs straight for the emergency room doors, amidst flashbulbs going off and microphones being pushed towards them.

Once inside the emergency room area, Joseph is greeted by Lauren's parents, hysterically crying, with arms outstretched. The little girl is gathered into her parent's embrace, where she immediately feels safe again. Her mom is looking over at Joseph, with tears streaming down her face. "How did this happen? How did you find her?"

"Momma, the angels did it," the little girl says, matter-of-factly. "I saw them."

"I don't understand. Can someone tell me what happened?" the mom asks. "What are you talking about? The police said you found her."

"I did find her, ma'am, but only after God had sent an army of angels to protect your little one," Joseph explains, openly crying. "Yes, God told me to turn around as I was pumping gas. If God had not spoken to me, I would not have known. When I turned, there was an army of angels dressed in white, surrounding the car. You need to realize that the supernatural God of the universe intervened to save the life of your child today. She's seen angels too, ma'am, and she's never going to be the same."

"But we ... we aren't religious," the woman replies.

"That's not necessary, because this isn't about religion. It's about God's love for you and your daughter," Joseph testifies, then adds, "Now, I need to go home and reassure my pregnant wife that I'm okay."

"Ask him about all the other times this has happened," a female reporter interjects.

"What does she mean, the other times?" the mom asks, looking surprised.

"God speaks to him and tells him who to rescue," the female reporter says.

"I really need to get home to my wife," Joseph repeats. "God bless you, Little Lauren. Don't ever forget that God saved you tonight. He really loves you." He ruffles her hair then turns to leave.

"Mr. Joseph?" The little girl stops him with her tiny hand.

"Yes, Sweetie?" Joseph says.

"Can I hug you?" Lauren asks.

Joseph gets down in a crouched position, and Lauren leaves her mom's arms, running straight into Joseph's outstretched ones.

"Thank you for bringing the angels with you, Mr. Joseph," she says.

"God did that, Sweetheart. God did it," he explains.

"But you listened, Mr. Joseph," Lauren tells him.

"Yes, I did, Miss Lauren, and you are a very smart little girl," Joseph adds.

She kisses Joseph on the cheek and goes running back to her mom and dad.

Joseph knows he needs to get out of the crowded waiting room, because he feels the tears starting again. He needs a good cry. He is reminded of how grateful he is that he and Michelle have built a house on his dad's land on the creek. He feels the deep need to talk with his father. He needs his father's shoulder tonight.

As he heads out the door, he suddenly realizes he doesn't have his truck. He reaches in his pocket to pull out his flip phone to call someone for a ride.

"You looking for a ride, son?" his father asks, stepping out of the shadows.

"Yes, sir." Joseph says, as he steps into his father's outstretched arms.

"How about I just take you home, and we go get your truck in the morning?" Mr. Nicholson suggests.

"Good plan, Dad. Would it be okay if I spent a few minutes with Michelle when I get home, and then you and I head out to the dock? Tonight was a completely different experience, and I need my sounding board dad," Joseph says.

******

The strain of the evening takes its toll on Michelle too. She has seen the news and now knows enough about what has transpired. All she wants is to take her husband in her arms and thank God he is alive. Tonight is the first time she has wondered if God will ever ask her husband to give his life for someone. It is one thing for him to be told to rescue a drowning child or help a car accident victim, but it's an altogether different experience when someone pulls a gun on you.

The evening leaves Michelle feeling conflicted. On the one hand, she knows God is in control of all things and is leading her husband. But on the other hand, she knows that evil is out there, and sometimes, evil overpowers things.

At this moment, she chooses to be grateful. A little girl has been rescued from horrors, and God protected her husband.

"Thank you, God," she whispers. "Thank you."

******

"I saw things tonight, Dad. I felt things that I have never before felt," Joseph confesses to his father out on the dock later. "I've never known fear like I experienced. It was as if I was tasting the evil that lurked."

"What kind of things?" Mr. Nicholson questions.

"At first, I experienced what felt like an electrical charge in the air. It made the hair on my arms stand up. Initially, I thought it was because a thunderstorm was approaching, but inside a flash of lightning, I saw the kidnapper's car completely surrounded by an army of angels dressed in white. When the man pulled the gun on me, I had no fear. I understood that God had sent angels for my protection, to give me courage. But, Dad, it was the sense that I felt the forces of evil fighting the forces of God that made me uneasy. We all know that the evil spiritual world exists, but to feel it in such a tangible way is scary," Joseph says, fighting back the tears.

"Was there a voice this time?" Mr. Nicholson asks.

"Yes, sir, the same voice I've always heard, saying the exact same thing," Joseph answers.

"Well, son, God is challenging you to a deeper level of obedience. Most of us don't hear a voice as you do, but we still are required to do what God asks. And most of us aren't given visual proof that God is with us, either. He showed you angels to bring you confidence tonight, but son, it may not always be like that. In fact, it probably won't."

Mr. Nicholson puts his arm around his son and continues, "I can honestly say that I believe God is going to ask even more of you now. I think God is purposefully showing more of Himself to you because of that. Joseph, in the end, God wins. For some reason, God seems to want you to understand this. Son, you need to be asking for wisdom now."

"Although I felt God's protection tonight, Dad, I also felt a new fear that I haven't experienced before. I felt as if God might be telling me I might need to give more. Honestly, Dad, I don't mind giving my life for God. I'm absolutely not afraid to die," Joseph explains. "What I am afraid of is His possible exit strategy."

"What do you mean, son?" Mr. Nicholson asks.

"I don't fear what happens after death. I fear the pain of getting there ... like what I might be asked to suffer through. Does that make sense?" Joseph asks.

"That makes perfect sense. I don't think any of us want to have cancer, a painful accident, or a debilitating disease," Mr. Nicholson responds.

"Just please pray for me, and pray for Michelle. I feel how uneasy she is, ever since she found out she's pregnant," Joseph says.

"I will step up my prayers," Mr. Nicholson reassures. "Obeying God comes with a high price tag. Loving God with all your heart, soul, and mind isn't for a weakling."

"Amen, Dad. Amen." Joseph replies, with a grin.

"Joseph, this one isn't going to go away. This kidnapping has been all over the networks for a week now. Every reporter is going to want this story, Joseph. And you are going to need to decide what you will do about it," Mr. Nicholson says.

"I think I got away tonight, Dad. I think I've dodged this one," Joseph responds.

"Jenny Myers has already called … twice," Mr. Nicholson tells him.

"Then she's the only one I will speak to," Joseph decides. "She loves God and will shine His light on this."

"I think that's a good call, son," Mr. Nicholson says. "But you are still going to be faced with fielding all the reporters that I'm pretty sure are going to be parked out front by morning."

"Thanks, Dad. I'll deal with it as it comes. I think I'm going to go inside and give Matthew a call before he sees this on the news," Joseph says.

"He already called, son," Mr. Nicholson tells him. "But that's a great idea. You should call him."

"Love you, Dad."

"Love you too, son," Mr. Nicholson says, as he hugs his son.

*****

At 2:00 a.m., Matthew's phone rings. He is so grateful to hear the voice of his friend, Joseph. God, how this moment makes him miss home!

It has been a long time since Matthew has felt such a strong pull toward South Carolina. And for the first time in a very long time, that pull has nothing to do with Michelle. It has to do with Joseph and Jake—his friends who are his family.

Unconsciously, Matthew rubs his very sore shoulder. Up until this moment, Matthew has assumed he'd have the rotator cuff surgery, do some physical therapy, and hopefully return to baseball. His physicians thought he could make a complete recovery. But what if he doesn't want to return to the game?

What if it is time for something new? What if this is the moment that Matthew is supposed to act on some of the new yearnings he's had? All Matthew knows is that ever since he has returned to church, gotten into a Bible study, and returned to his faith, he has begun to think of doing something with children. The idea that had been percolating in his head was something with kids and baseball. His contract with the Yankees is up for renewal. Is it time for something new? Maybe he'd run some of these ideas by Jake and Joseph when he went home next month for Jake's wedding.

~ CHAPTER 20 ~

True to his father's predictions, there was a media circus surrounding the safe return of Lauren, and the news spread quickly. It became known as The Band of Angels Rescue. Jenny Myers of CBS News was given the exclusive interview with Lauren, her parents, and Joseph. The world watched as an innocent little girl, with absolutely no reason to lie, told the world that she'd seen an angel dressed in white for five days straight. Her kidnapper had tried to hurt her repeatedly, but the angel in white had stopped him every time.

Until the camera was running, and Lauren was allowed to speak the truth, Joseph had no idea that she had been protected the entire time.

Late in 1997, two significant life-changing events were happening in South Carolina. First, Jake and Christina were finally getting married, and second, Joseph Nicholson became a father.

After ten hours of agonizing labor, Annie Elizabeth Nicholson is born at six pounds, five ounces. Joseph watches in amazement as the baby is released from Michelle's body. As the doctor receives the baby, Joseph reaches out his hands.

"First things first," Joseph says as he takes the baby into his arms.

With the delivery team looking on, waiting to take the baby to clean her up and do APGAR scoring, Joseph holds her up with his arms extended, over his head. He kneels down, bows his head, and prays, out loud, for all to hear: "Lord God, the Giver of Life, I thank You for entrusting me with this life. My wife and I dedicate her to You for Your service. May she know and love You, and may she serve You, Holy God, with her life. Speak to her, God, show her who You are, and surround her with love. Protect her, and keep her safe. Father, may she help heal hearts and bring many to You. In Jesus's name, I pray. Amen."

He looks down at this dark-skinned, curly-haired little girl and can't believe what he sees. Joseph Nicholson sees a carbon copy of his very own eyes staring right back at him. Annie Nicholson has her daddy's green eyes. From the very first moment of Annie's life, she is entrusted to God.

******

When Matthew arrives back in South Carolina for Jake's wedding, he is in a much better place emotionally. Although he knows he still loves Michelle, he is better equipped to be her friend. He finds that seeing her with baby Annie brings him immense joy. Matthew has fun laughing at how crazy in love Joseph is. The wedding coupled with the new baby makes this time one of joyous celebration.

Joseph is proud to toast his best friend: "Family and friends, thank you so very much for celebrating Jake and Christina's special day. I'd like to take a moment to celebrate a truly wonderful man, one who has always taken up space in the background. Jake, as far back as I can remember, you have been my best friend and brother. All my life, you've had my back, loved me, and cared for me. I cannot thank you enough for all you have done for me.

"Christina, I know you know this, but it doesn't get better than this man! There is nothing I wouldn't do for him. I would give my life for this man. So, today, I pray God's blessings over your marriage and future family. I pray that every day you grow closer to each other and closer to God. And, Jake, I pray in thanksgiving to God for the gift of your friendship."

Joseph held up his glass and said, "To a long and loving life together. Cheers!"

As Joseph and Matthew sit out on the dock long after all the guests have gone home, Joseph notices the difference in his friend. Changes are taking place, and Joseph is overjoyed.

"What's new, Matthew? You seem like you're doing better." Joseph notes.

"I am. I've gotten some things straightened out, mostly my faith," Matthew says honestly. "I've made the decision not to renew my contract with the Yankees. I had this surgery on my rotator cuff, and although the physical therapy has gone well, I don't think I want to return. God's got me thinking about kids

...not necessarily like I want to have a bunch of my own, but more like how I could help kids. I'm giving some thought to starting The Matthew West Baseball Academy. I'd like to start with my first branch in New York, but I'd like my second one to be here in Charleston. I'm thinking it would combine stellar baseball training with a little Jesus."

"Wow! I'm impressed, Matthew," Joseph responds. "You know, I'm on board to be a part of this and help you in whatever way I can. I think this idea of baseball and God would be a bit like how we were all raised right here."

"Thanks, man," Matthew says. "I'm really excited to get things rolling. It feels like the right time to leave professional baseball … you know, before I stink at it. I'd like to leave it on a high note. It's funny … I really feel this calling to help kids."

"Have you dated anyone special?" Joseph asks.

"No, I've stayed away from that. A wise man I know, someone you call Dad, told me to give all my love to God and the rest would fall into place. So that's what I'm doing. And honestly, it's filling a spot that I always yearned to have filled," Matthew explains.

"I never knew my dad said that to you. I know when you left here last time that you were not in a good place emotionally. I know my dad has been reaching out to you, trying to help you, and I love him for it. I'm so grateful for this right now. I feel so blessed that you and I can be close like brothers again. I've missed you, friend," Joseph shares.

"Yeah, I've really missed you too, JoBro. I always felt disconnected without you. Something about your friendship has always given me a sense of grounding. Maybe it's because my stutter stopped when I met you and Jake. I don't know. I just understand that Michelle was so right years ago when she said you don't get what we've all had more than once in a lifetime. It's taken me a long time and a lot of wrong roads to realize that. I've hurt some people along the way, mostly Marguerite. I deeply regret that and have tried to make restitution as best as

I can. I do believe that God will let me love someday, and I just need to wait on His timing—His perfect timing," Matthew says.

"But you think that you'll return to Shem Creek someday?" Joseph asks.

"I do," Matthew replies. "Once I get the first academy up and rolling in New York, then come back to my house."

"Wait ... your 'house'?" Joseph asks.

"Oh, yeah. I guess I never told you. I bought the backwards house a few years ago. I've just let Old Man Nelson live there until he's ready to move on. Once he leaves, it's going to need some work, so I'll probably get rolling on that as well when the time is right." Matthew tells him.

"Oh, my goodness! Did you know Jake is building his house here too?" Joseph asks.

"So, you're saying when we're all old and gray, we are all going to be living on Shem Creek together?" Matthew responds in amazement.

"Yep, raising our kids together." Joseph laughs. "Wow! I'm feeling pretty blessed right now."

"Me too, bro. Me too!" Matthew hugs his friend.

~ CHAPTER 21 ~

"Daddy, is it time yet?" a very impatient 3-year-old Annie asks.

"Patience, Miss Sparkles ... patience ..." he says back. "Did you get all your stuff?"

"Yes, I packed my little beach bag, got my towel, and got my sand shovel and bucket," she answers.

"I don't see your baseball cap," Daddy says.

"Oh, yeah! I almost forgot!" Annie never goes anywhere without her cap.

"I'm going to grab a few sandwiches and chips, and then we're good to go!" Daddy announces.

They climb into the red truck. Joseph straps Annie in her car seat next to him in the front seat. He loves looking across the seat and seeing her. Joseph takes a second to load a CD; Annie loves the CD of "The Moment of Silence Collection."

"I wanna hear the Daddy Song, Daddy!" Annie says excitedly, clapping her hands.

"Oh, you do, do you?" he teases.

"Yes, Daddy! You know it's my most favorite song!" Annie exclaims.

Joseph adjusts the CD track to Annie's favorite.

"A moment of silence, please! George Strait is on, ladies and gentlemen!" Daddy says, in his very best announcer voice, and Annie giggles. "*A Father's Love* is the best Daddy song there is."

Annie and her daddy have the windows down, stereo blaring, and the two are singing out at the top of their lungs.

The perfect day, Annie thinks to herself.

Annie is so excited. Whenever Momma has a Saturday shift at the hospital, she and her daddy go to the beach together. Annie loves this time with her daddy. She adores having his undivided attention, and sometimes she wonders if she'd like it or not if she had a baby brother or sister.

The days at the beach are magical. They build sandcastles, splash in the ocean, go on shell walks, and sit and talk. As she sits next to her daddy in the front seat, she feels like his best girl. Annie knows she has the best daddy in the world.

They had just had a long swim time. Annie loves to climb on her daddy's back as they ride the waves in, one after another. They are finally taking a much-needed break, sitting side by side, toes in the ocean.

"Daddy, how come sometimes I don't hurt myself?" Annie asks looking at the ocean.

"I'm not sure what you mean, Sweetheart. Can you explain it?" Daddy questions.

"Well, I kinda don't want to get in trouble," she answers.

"Did you do something wrong that you need to tell me about? You know we talk about how important it is to say when you did something wrong. Remember what we call that?" Daddy asks.

"You mean confess?" she replies. "Cause that's not what I'm talking about."

"Well, then, you better tell Daddy what you're talking about, Miss Sparkles." He smiles at her.

"Well," she begins then stops for a moment, before adding, "you know how you don't like it when I climb too high?"

"You mean in the tree by the dock? The one I tell you that you could fall out of?" he questions.

"Yeah, what if on accident I climbed too far up?" she asks.

"Well, that probably wasn't on accident, was it?" he says. "We like you to tell the truth."

"The climbing part wasn't the accident. It was the falling part," she says, timidly.

"How far up did you climb?" he asks, seeming more concerned.

"All the way, Daddy," she confesses. "And when I got to the tippy top, I got scared."

"Why were you scared?" he leads, wanting her to speak out what she'd done.

"I was scared 'cause I couldn't get back down. It's lots harder to get down when you can't see where you're going. And nobody was playing with me."

"Okay, but you look like you got down okay. Did momma come out and help you get down?"

"No, Daddy. I fell from the tippy top," she says, sounding scared. "I was all the way up, and my foot slipped, and I fell."

"What? Are you hurt? When did this happen?" Daddy fires away questions at her, imagining how far the fall from the top of the live oak next to the dock is.

"I didn't get hurt, Daddy. That's why I asked the question," she says, giving her daddy that look when a kid thinks they know better than a parent.

"What question?"

"I asked you how come sometimes I don't hurt myself," she repeats.

"So, you're asking me why you fell from the tippy top and didn't get hurt?"

"Yes. How come I didn't get hurt at all?" "Maybe God protected you," he answers. "But what if it was kinda funny like?" "What do you mean? kinda funny like?"

Annie explains, "My foot slipped. And I was falling, and I was screaming 'cause I was gonna fall on my back and bump my head."

"What do you mean you were 'gonna fall on your back and hit your head'?" he questions.

"Daddy, somebody caught me."

"Who caught you, Annie?" He turns to see her eyes.

"Nobody, Daddy. Nobody was there, but it felt like your strong arms caught me and put me down on the grass next to the tree," she tells him, now crying. "I don't know, Daddy. It was kinda scary but really neat at the same time."

Joseph pauses for a moment to consider the ramifications of what he had just heard. *Was his daughter telling him that an angel had caught her and placed her down on the ground?* He stops and thanks God for saving her from such a terrible fall. *But what does this mean? Was this a one-time thing, or was Annie's life going to be like his? Was she already being set apart?* He doesn't know the answers to any of these questions, but he knows he needs to explain some things to his little girl.

"Sweetheart, I think it was an angel sent from God to help you," Daddy tries to explain.

"Yeah, me too," she replies.

"You already thought that?"

"Yeah, Daddy, sometimes He whispers stuff to me."
"Really? Tell me more, Sweetheart."

"You know when I go to preschool, and we are supposed to play outside?" she asks.

"Sure, like recess?"

"Yeah. Well, sometimes kids don't have someone to play with, and I hear someone tell me to go play with that girl," she shares.

"Is it the teacher?"

"No, I hear it here." She taps her heart.

"Me too, Annie. Me too."

"Another thing we're twins about, Daddy?"

"Yes, Miss Sparkles. And remember what Daddy says. Sparkle on the outside means it's shining through from the inside. Always listen to the voice coming through your heart." He places his arm around her tenderly.

Later that evening, Joseph finds himself out on the dock, talking with Jake. Since they both are dads now, their individual time together is rare. Joseph is thankful for this time alone with his friend. He tells Jake about his conversation with Annie.

"So, history repeating itself?" Jake says laughing at their two daughters growing up together with one hearing from angels.

"I don't know, but I'm sure grateful that these two little girls love each other!" Joseph says back. He loves Jake's daughter, Bridget, like his own child.

"I guess it's going to be time for the next generation of Dock Walks," Jake smiles. "I sure hope we can do it as well as your dad does it."

"We've been trained by the master!" Joseph exclaims.

"Who is the master?" They hear Mr. Nicholson ask, coming down the dock behind them.

"You are, Dad!" Joseph says, smiling.

Mr. Nicholson joins them down on the dock, and Joseph shares the conversation he had with Annie earlier.

"Well, son, you asked for it. Didn't you?" Mr. Nicholson questions.

"What do you mean?" Joseph asks.

"The day she was born ... didn't you tell me that you held her up in the delivery room and dedicated her to service to God? Did you not expect Him to take you up on it?" He chuckles. "You, of all people should remember to be very careful what you pray for."

"You're right, Dad. As usual. I guess I do keep praying for God's safety over her," he says.

"Why do you think the knees of my jeans are so worn out?" Mr. Nicholson asks. "Once you started hearing from God, it just meant that I had to intensify my prayers for you. Son, God loves the prayers from the heart of a parent, and He loves our repeated prayers."

******

Little Annie stares intently at the glass; she wants to be absolutely sure. She bends down so she is eye level with the spot where she will insert her quarter. She looks through the glass and sees all the prizes inside the clear, plastic, egg-like containers. She needs to make sure that the one she wants is near the bottom. Daddy says that's the only way she has a chance of getting the exact one she wants. And Annie knows *exactly* which one she wants. She dreams of it. It's the same thing she hopes for each and every week as she stands before the collection of gumball and trinket machines at the grocery store.

She doesn't want another bouncy ball. She has quite an extensive collection of them stored in a Mason jar on top of her dresser, and besides, Momma yells at her when she bounces them in the house. Annie told her momma it wasn't the ball's fault that the blue vase was in the way. Momma said that little girls shouldn't speak to their mommas like that.

And although she loves it, she doesn't want another piece of bubble gum, even though it's probably Bazooka and comes with a tiny little comic in it. Daddy says bubble gum is a waste of time and has no lasting value. Annie thinks that means it stops tasting good, and she doesn't understand why. She thinks that's stupid. Why make something perfect and tasty when the flavor isn't going to last?

She definitely does not want a package of SweeTarts; they make you spit. Whenever she eats them, she feels like she did the time she tasted grapefruit. It was so disgusting that it made her have too much spit in her mouth. She didn't know what to do with all that spit, and she knew she didn't want to swallow it. Momma had gotten mad at her when she accidentally coughed and spat chunks of grapefruit out on her plate and the table. Annie did not want that to happen with SweeTarts.

She desperately wants the gold ring with the big pink stone, the one that looks sparkly and grownup. The one just like her Mamma's ring. When she sees it through the glass, it seems like something a princess would wear. The stone is round and flat on top, and when she looks down on it, it forms a circle. The stone is light pink. The edges are cut like a diamond, and she feels confident that if she wore it on her hand that it would sparkle like a million stars in the nighttime sky. Happily, it looks as if today might just be her lucky day. The clear plastic container with the ring in it is very near the bottom.

******

Last night, Daddy said he was sure today would be the day. He was so sure she was going to get the gold ring with the big pink stone that he had painted her fingernails. He said her hands have to be beautiful and ready for the ring. He said that's like being prepared for life. Annie isn't sure what being prepared for life is. She does think people might want to look at the ring when she wears it, and she wouldn't want her fingernails to look dirty and gross.

"Come here, Miss Sparkles!" Daddy yells from the hall bathroom.

Joseph Nicholson is the kind of dad every little girl wants.

Annie runs down the hallway, following her father's voice. She is always excited to see her daddy. When he calls her, she feels all happy inside. She arrives in the bathroom and sees her handsome daddy, looking funny, standing beside the vanity with all the girly stuff on top. Daddy says he can't imagine how such a pile of bottles and junk can make Momma beautiful. He says Momma is already gorgeous. Annie agrees.

She looks closely and sees Daddy has something in his hand. She realizes he is holding the most glittery bottle of pink nail polish Annie has ever seen. She can hardly contain herself. It's not just that it's her favorite color of hot pink, but it's glittery too. Every girl loves glitter. Annie does her little self-clap thing. This always makes Daddy laugh.

Momma won't buy the glittery polish; she says it looks cheap. Annie doesn't really know what that means, but she thinks it might mean something bad.

So, she is amazed to see that Daddy has a bottle of glitter nail polish.

"Oh, Daddy! Is that for me?" she squeals with delight, even though the answer is obvious.

"What do you think, Miss Sparkles?" he replies with a wink and a smile.

"Yes! Yes! Yes! I know it's for me!" she says, hugging his leg.

Daddy shuts the lid on the toilet seat and tells her to have a seat. She uses the little step stool and climbs up. He places a towel down on the vanity counter.

"Let's do it," he says, shaking the bottle of nail polish to mix the glitter and nail polish properly.

Annie places both hands down on top of the towel. She spreads her little fingers out wide and watches in amazement as Daddy begins to paint her fingernails, carefully and skillfully. He blows on them gently to help them dry.

"But what about the quarter?" she asks, feeling antsy after having to sit still.

"Patience, my little girl, patience."

"What about the calendar with the doors?" she asks. "What did I tell you about that?"

"We open the first door four weeks before Christmas."

"And when did I tell you that?" Daddy says with his gentle voice.

"Yesterday," she replies, rolling her eyes. "And how many days have passed?" "Just one more."

"So, we still have three more days to wait."

"But, Daddy, I'm so excited to know all the secrets behind the doors!" Annie says.

"Patience, my little girl … patience."

Joseph finishes painting his daughter's nails, and then he pulls the blow dryer out from under the cabinet, puts it on the cool setting and dries all ten of her little fingernails.

Annie watches in wonder. Momma says Annie is Daddy's girl. Momma likes to point out that she was Daddy's girl *first*, but she's absolutely fine with losing that spot to her daughter. Annie loves the feel of her Daddy's whiskers against her cheek, and she loves that he smells like a mixture of hair gel and new lumber. She loves the one dimple that sits on the left side of his face and makes his smile light up the room. Annie loves that she owns the very same set of heavily lashed green eyes. She loves it when people say she looks just like her Daddy.

But what she loves the most of all is when he calls her Miss Sparkles. She knows what that means. He tells her people sparkle on the outside because of what's on the inside. Annie doesn't know what that means, but she knows it's good because Daddy said it and she knows that she feels good on the inside. She knows this is his special name for her, and no one else gets to use it, not even Momma. It's just for him. He says she's just like a precious diamond, rare and sparkly.

That's why she wants the gold ring with the big pink stone. She imagines how much it will sparkle. And since Daddy keeps giving her quarters, it's like he's buying it for her. She believes that she will feel special when she wears it—extra loved by Daddy. Every time she looks down at her hand, she will be reminded of it.

*****

She *really* wants that ring.

She thought about making it her birthday wish this year, but as she blew out the candles, she wished for a baby brother instead.

"I think they are just about dry," Daddy says, pointing to her fingernails.

"Is it time?"

"Yes, I do believe it is!" he says with a wink.

Daddy reaches into the pocket of his worn-out jeans and pulls out a single quarter. He places it in the palm of his hand, face side up. He pretends to spit on it for good luck. Then he proceeds with the game they play every Wednesday evening. He turns his back to her and shuffles the quarter between his two hands. He turns around, holding both hands out in front of him with his fists closed, faced down.

"Okay, Miss Sparkles, guess which hand has the quarter in it," he tells her, with a look of mischief.

"That one!" She taps his left hand gently. Annie thinks that secretly there is a quarter in both of Daddy's hands because she never misses, but she doesn't care. As long as she gets the quarter, she's happy.

Daddy turns over his left hand, and there is a shiny quarter.

Annie grabs it and tucks it carefully in the pocket of her jeans.

"Love you, Miss Sparkles," he says.

"Love you more, Daddy-O!" She takes off running down the hall to show Momma her glittery pink nails.

******

At the store, it's finally the moment of truth. Annie takes the shiny quarter out of the pocket of her jeans, pretends to spit on it for luck, and gently inserts it into the slot on the machine. She turns the metal handle and quickly puts her hands down to catch the prize as it comes out of the slot.

She stares down in utter delight.

"Momma, Momma, Momma!" Annie yells as she turns toward the check-out line, where Momma is just finishing up paying for the groceries. "I got it. I got it!"

"Aren't you going to open it up?" Mr. Fisher asks.

"Not yet," Annie says. "Not 'til my Daddy gets home tonight. We're going to open it together, and it's going to be like a party. Momma is making a cake."

Michelle Nicholson is the kind of momma that bakes cakes from scratch, not from the boxed mixes.

Annie looks up and smiles big at Momma and puts the bulky plastic container in the front pocket of her jeans. She can hardly wait to show Daddy.

~ CHAPTER 22 ~

2000

The season has brought unusually chilly days for South Carolina. People are sharing stories of winters past with temps in the twenties, but not in years.

Joseph is at work, looking over the tides for the day, due to an impending thunderstorm heading their way. It leaves Joseph feeling very concerned. Several times a year, the locals refer to a tide called the King Tide. It coincides with the moon. They are not quite at King Tide stage, but this evening's tide is looking to be about six feet above normal. In the Low Country, this can mean trouble if this high tide accompanies a thunderstorm that is producing lots of rain. Tonight looks like it might just be the perfect storm—all of the challenges coming together in one hour.

They are calling everyone into work this evening, knowing that the possibility will exist that water rescues will be necessary. Joseph doesn't like when the winds are high. This can push water inland that would typically stay put. It has been an unusually rainy autumn as well, meaning the ground is quite saturated. This leaves little or no room for additional water. The marshes are very wet. Tonight will be difficult. Joseph says a quick prayer, asking God to use him to help people tonight.

He is a little worried about Michelle and Annie, so he picks up the phone.

"Hey, Babe," he greets. "Tonight's storm is gonna be a tough one. I'm glad you're off today. Do me a favor, please?

You two stay put this afternoon, then I'll have two fewer people to worry about." he says to Michelle on the phone.

"Okay, sounds good, Sweetheart. What about this evening?" she asks.

"I know ... Annie's big ring night. I'm thinking things might pass right at or before dinnertime, so pending no big issues, I should be home in time for the big celebration," he lets her know.

"She's so excited she's out of control." Michelle laughs.

"Oh, yeah. I gathered that based on the phone message she left me earlier." Joseph smiles thinking about his sweet girl.

"Be careful, Joseph. You know I worry about you, my love," she says.

"I will. Just please stay at home. It's looking ugly for the late afternoon," he cautions again.

"Yes, sir!" she teases. "Love you, Boo."

"Love you too, Sweetheart. See you later!" He says before hanging up.

The tides rise, and the wind begins. The rain is falling in sideways pelts. Visibility is zero. And yet, all the team sits and waits for the calls, waiting for the emergencies, but it is a shockingly quiet night as far as rescue goes. It feels like the worst of the storm has passed. Joseph checks his watch; his shift is over in ten minutes.

"What do you all think? Did we dodge this one?" he asks, wondering if he could go home for the evening.

"I think everything looks clear," his boss says. "And the next shift has arrived, so we're okay."

"Well, all right then, I'm heading home," Joseph grabs his bag that contains all his personal rescue items—things he only brings to the station when storms are on the horizon.

The rain has stopped, so he decides to stop for gas. He is pumping gas when he looks up and sees Christina's car pass by. He waves and sees Bridget in the back seat.

Life in a small town, he thinks. He finishes pumping gas, gets in his car, and heads down the road.

He is headed up Highway 41 towards Highway 17, trying to make his way towards South Mount Pleasant. Highway 41 is a two-lane road that meanders through marshes. The road has many low bridges crossing over mostly dry marsh areas. Joseph has a fleeting thought that it looks as if it has rained a whole lot more in this area. The marsh waters are high, and they are lapping the road.

He does a quick mental exercise, reminding himself of what is ahead: several very low bridges. He wonders if enough time has passed since the drenching rain. *Were the waters receding yet?*

Out of caution, he slows down considerably. Darkness has settled in, and he doesn't want to come upon high water moving too fast. You never want to hit high water going fast, you will quickly lose control of your vehicle.

Joseph knows he is coming up on a creek, and a swollen creek is a dangerous thing. He puts on his brights to see in front of him. The road is invisible about fifty yards in front of him. A strong current of water is flowing across the street. On either side of the now covered bridge lays a creek bed and surrounding marsh. On the other side of the bridge is a visible shoreline. Between Joseph and the shore is a raging stream that is dragging tree limbs with it.

Joseph slows his vehicle to a crawl, wanting to check and see how deep the water is. Suddenly, he feels the pull of a hydroplaning vehicle. He immediately hits the brakes, checks his rearview mirror, and puts it in reverse. When his truck reaches the road that is not covered with the swollen stream, he turns his vehicle around. This is too dangerous to pass. He will have to go back the direction he came.

He is only a quarter of a mile down the road when he hears it: *Turn around.*

A feeling of fear creeps up Joseph's spine, as a thought occurs to him. Hadn't he waved at Christina's car as she drove down this road just minutes before him? He looks in his rearview mirror, but sees nothing. No cars. No lights. Nothing to turn around for. He slows down and asks God, "What do you need me for?"

Turn around.

"Lord, this is unsafe, and that swollen creek is scaring me, God. Are you here? Are there angels around that I cannot see? What are you asking for, God?"

Turn around.

Joseph fishes out his cell phone and makes two calls. The first call he makes is to 911, because Joseph knows that if God was asking him to turn around, it probably means that someone is in trouble in that creek. And, oh, God, it may be his best friend's family. The second call he makes is to Jake; he wants his friend to pray.

Thankfully, Joseph immediately feels Jake's prayers, and he feels confident. Next, he gets on his handheld radio in the car and calls out to anyone in the area with a boat who can help with a water rescue and can get there now.

Then, despite his fears, but in obedience to God, he turns his truck around, heading back towards the bridge over the swollen creek. He decides to park his vehicle in the middle of the road and put the flashers on. He doesn't want any additional cars to drive over the bridge. He reaches in the back and pulls out his big flashlight. He steps closer to the water and shines the light downstream. Then, he hears the sounds of people screaming, screaming for help.

Multiple cars appear to have gone in the raging creek.

Joseph never thinks twice about jumping in to rescue. Even though the water is near freezing, he knows this is his mission.

God has made that clear. His flashlight is waterproof, so he brings it in with him.

When he hits the water, the cold feels like knives stabbing him.

He can see headlights in the water, so he swims towards the first car he sees. Joseph dives under the water. Two people are just making their way out of a submerged car. Joseph can see it is a woman and a small child. The woman is holding her child, frantically trying to use her other arm for swimming against the raging current, but she is sinking. Joseph grabs the woman around the waist and begins to swim against the current towards the shore slowly.

The woman is Christina, and the child is Bridget. The current took them downstream a ways, but when he reaches the shore, freezing and breathless, he deposits Christina and Bridget on the muddy shoreline. Christina is amazingly calm, but Bridget is screaming, freezing, and dangerously close to shock.

"Another car went in after me," Christina tells him, shaking from the cold.

"Wrap your body around Bridget. Unbutton your jacket and get her next to your skin. You both need the body warmth," Joseph instructs. "I've already called for help, so it shouldn't take long. Are either of you hurt at all? Did either of you hit your head, anything bleeding?" he asks.

"We're fine ... go get the others!" she responds.

Joseph turns and scans the water. He sees someone bobbing up and down. Without another thought, Joseph dives in again.

He feels a searing pain in his shoulder. Debris is floating everywhere, and something has stabbed his shoulder. He makes it to the frantic woman, and she appears to be injured. So much debris is floating that it is like a minefield. The woman has been hit by something too.

With his good arm, Joseph grabs her around her waist and begins the painful swim to the other side. Joseph swims to the edge and deposits the nearly unconscious woman on the shore, just as the first red flashing lights are approaching.

"There's another car!" The woman coughs.

Joseph turns around once again, looking at the raging waters and feels the first hint of fatigue. He notices he is bleeding from somewhere near his shoulder. There is a lot of blood. Joseph knows he needs to stop his own bleeding, but there isn't time.

He scans the waters and sees what appears to be someone clutching onto an overhanging tree. Joseph doesn't know if he can do it. But he can tell time is running out for this person hanging.

Joseph dives in again. Just swimming to what turns out to be a teenage boy hanging from the branch takes most of what he has left. He grabs him by the waist and begins the challenging swim back to the opposite shore. He has lost a lot of blood and is now carrying the dead weight of a nearly grown man.

Three times he goes under, gulping in large amounts of creek water.

Three times he fights against fatigue and comes back up.

He is finding it difficult to swim with the searing pain in his shoulder. A fear begins to take root—fear that God is asking him right now for the ultimate sacrifice.

"Let me save him, God. Please, help me, Lord!"

A newfound strength surges through him, and he makes it to the opposite shore. He pushes the teenage boy up onto the sand with all the strength he has left. He is vaguely aware that people are running toward them.

Joseph can't get his footing to stand. A hand reaches out to him.

With all the strength he can muster, he holds out his hand. He makes contact with the hand, but a moment later, he finds himself submerged in the icy waters, floating downstream. In that moment, it occurs to him that he has no energy left to swim to shore. He feels himself beginning to lose consciousness. He blacks out for a second, but then the cold water brings him back immediately.

He sees the limb, an overhang. If he can just grab onto it, he might be able to buy enough time.

He is not able to grab the overhanging tree, but his jacket somehow catches on it. Joseph stops moving downstream. He has no idea how far he is from the rescue workers, has no idea how far he'd moved downstream. He does know that he is absolutely stuck on a piece of wood. He thought they would be there quickly, but Joseph realizes it is possible they can't see him. Then, he starts seeing things—things not of this world. His shoulder hurts. Something is broken. Bone is exposed.

******

Bright lights are flashing, and the scene is chaotic. Rescue workers everywhere.

Jake arrives on the scene at the same time as most of the rescue vehicles. He runs down the embankment to the shoreline, where to his absolute shock, he sees his wife and daughter being treated for hypothermia.

"Oh, God, are you two okay?" he asks with panic in his voice.

"I think we are both okay. The car hydroplaned and went into the creek. We were able to get out just as Joseph showed up. Jake, he saved us. Joseph saved us. If he hadn't come, right at this time, we'd be dead," Christina cries, holding a crying Bridget closely.

"I need to find him," Jake says.

"He went back in after the others," Christina tells him.

"What? There were others?" Jake asks with a feeling of fear. He turns and looks at the freezing waters raging by and thinks, *A person won't have much time in that kind of water.*

"Yeah, he got me out too," says a woman sitting close to Christina. "And he went back in for that teenage boy over there. He was bleeding a lot then, though. You all need to look for him to make sure he got out."

"Joseph!" Jake yells at the top of his lungs. "Joseph!"

"Everyone," Jake calls out "look for Joseph! Did anyone see him get out?"

A few yards down, a fellow rescue worker says he had reached out his hand, and Joseph grabbed it, but lost his grip.

"Oh, God, please, no. Please, God, no." Jake prays.

Jake takes off running downstream, screaming out for his best friend.

"God, please ... *please,* help us here!" he begs. "Joseph! Joseph! Where are you?"

Everyone is combing the shoreline looking for Joseph. They've got lights, beams pointed at the swollen stream, looking for him.

"Anybody see anything?" Jake shouts. "All eyes on the water, everyone! Joseph is a great swimmer. Also, look under the overhanging trees; if he's tired, he might hold onto one and await rescue."

All the rescuers are watching Jake with pity knowing exactly who these two men are to each other. Jake is frantic, thinking that too much time is passing. If Joseph has washed downstream, the water is too cold. If he's injured, he's going to be out of time soon.

Jake is wet, freezing, and shaking ... and he's frantic. "Lord, where are you?!" Jake cries out in agony. "Please, God, he's done everything You've asked him to do. He's saved my family. Lord, please, don't take him!"

At that moment, Jake looks down and sees what seems to be a shirt or coat caught on a piece of overhanging wood. Jake wades into the icy water and puts his hands under Joseph's arms and pulls his limp body from the freezing water.

But Jake knows.

He feels it deep in his soul.

He is too late.

Joseph has a compound humerus fracture. Bone is exposed, and at some point, during his rescuing the others, he had begun to profusely bleed from his brachial artery. Joseph's face is ashen, and his lips are blue.

Jake sits down on the shoreline. He has Joseph in his arms, leaning up against him. He is holding Joseph up in what he hopes is a life-giving embrace.

"I got you, Joseph. I'm here. I'm here. Please, don't leave me. Bro, stay with me," Jake cries, looking down at an unresponsive Joseph. "Oh, God, no ... please nooooo. Please, don't take him, Lord. Please!" Jake sobs as he rocks his best friend back and forth in his arms. Jake sees the massive blood loss and the hypothermia; he just barely has a pulse. Joseph is dying in his arms.

"Tell him," Joseph says, barely audible in a breathless whisper. "Tell him."

"What? Who?" Jake says. "Stay with me, JoBro. Don't leave me."

"Matthew," Joseph answers.

"What do I tell him?" Jake asks, knowing these are going to be Joseph's last words.

"This is why ..." Joseph tries to speak through difficult inhales and exhales. "When it's time ... Tell him this is why ...

This is why he has always loved her. Tell them ... it's a gift." Joseph's last words are caught inside his final breath of life.

"I'll tell him," Jake says, openly sobbing, vaguely aware that he now has an audience. Joseph's fellow EMTs, police officers, and firemen are all standing helplessly by, watching a man whom they all know and respect, die. Every man is crying, hats off, heads bowed in respect.

"I love you, Joseph. I'll see you again, my friend," Jake whispers. And his best friend dies in his arms.

Jake doesn't know how long he holds Joseph's lifeless body, while crying out in sorrow. He just remembers that at some point, Joseph's fellow rescuers take Joseph's body out of his shaking arms. Jake lets go of the best friend he will ever have.

Nobody seems to notice a teenaged boy standing by, watching in horror, as the man who just saved his life has died. This troubled young man is at a crossroads. From somewhere deep within, he understands that his life must be different from this point on, for he will be living for two people now. His second chance needs to matter.

******

On "The Day of the Black Car," everything changed.

Annie's life seems to be divided into two very different parts—life before The Day of the Black Car and then life after it. In life before, she sparkled. In the life after, she not only has stopped sparkling, but she also even forgets what it feels like to sparkle.

It is supposed to be the best day ever. Four-year-old Annie has waited patiently for this day to arrive. She is so excited.

"I need you to wait inside today, sweetheart. It's too cold," Momma says.

"But, Momma, I wanna be ready and waiting for Daddy!" Annie replies.

"It's so cold out there. It reminds me of when I was a little girl living in New York," Momma tells her, "and you know I don't miss that."

"But I'm so excited, and I always wait for Daddy outside …" Annie pleads. "Can I at least put on my coat and wait on the couch by the window?"

"Okay, sure, sweetheart." Momma watches Annie put on her warm rain jacket with the hood.

"Is it time yet?" Annie asks, facing the window with her hands on the back of the couch.

"I already told you, Daddy must be running late," Momma answers.

"Did you call him?" Annie asks, now on her knees, on the couch, bouncing up and down with her hands on the seat back.

"Yes, Annie, I called him," Momma replies with a tone of annoyance.

"What did he say?" Annie asks.

"He didn't answer."

"Why didn't he answer?" Annie questions.

"Sweetheart, *I don't know.*" Momma is starting to sound very annoyed.

"If I stay at the front window, I'll see his red truck as soon as he turns into our driveway," Annie says, trying to reassure her momma.

Annie overhears her momma calling Daddy's work.

Subconsciously, Annie fingers the round plastic container in her front pocket. Just touching it fills her with such excitement. Momma keeps saying that Daddy must be running late because of the weather. He is usually home by now. Daddy gets off work at 6:00, and he is home by 6:15 every night. Momma says Daddy's schedule is like clockwork. And, if Daddy is running late, he always calls momma. Annie always knows it's Daddy because Momma says, "I love you too," in that soft voice.

By 7:30, Momma is calling Daddy's work. He left on time.

By 8:00, Momma is calling Mrs. Jackson next door to see if Mr. Jackson was home. Nobody answers.

By 8:30, Momma is visibly worried. Dinner is cold, and Annie begins to get a strange feeling in her stomach. Momma doesn't look right. Something is wrong.

"Where's Daddy?" Annie asks in a pleading tone.

"For the tenth time, Annie, *I don't know!*" Momma snaps back.

By 9:00, Momma is crying.

"Why are you crying, Momma?" Annie asks, fighting back her own tears.

"This isn't like Daddy. I'm worried," Momma answers softly.

"He's coming home soon, Momma!" Annie indignantly says. "He knows about the ring."

Annie never moves from her kneeling position on the couch facing the front picture window. Maybe if she stays in the very same spot Daddy expects to find her in, Daddy will show up. Momma gets up and turns on the porch light.

At 10:30, Annie finally sees the headlights of Daddy's truck turning down the long gravel driveway.

"He's home! He's home!" Annie squeals with delight.

Momma gets up and moves over to the window to look out.

But it isn't Daddy's red truck.

It's a black car.

Two men get out and walk toward the door.

Momma lets out a sob and wipes her eyes on the back of her sleeve.

The men knock on the door.

"Don't move, Annie," Momma says sternly. "Stay right where you are."

Momma opens the door, steps out, and gently closes the door behind her.

From the window, Annie watches the two men on the porch talking to her momma. Annie tries to imagine what the two men in the black car might have to talk to her momma about. It is kind of late for visitors. And Momma never answers the door to strangers when Daddy isn't home.

Don't they know she and Momma are waiting for Daddy? Momma doesn't have time for visitors in a black car. They have a busy evening ahead of them. They are going to eat dinner, open the clear plastic container in Annie's front pocket that contains the ring with the big pink stone, and have cake. It's going to be an evening that feels like a party, and it isn't even anybody's birthday. She wishes Momma would hurry up and finish talking with the two men in the black car so her momma could come to sit next to her on the couch, where she is patiently waiting.

She has the same scary feeling in her tummy that she had when Daddy took her to the amusement park, and they rode the roller coaster. She's a little bit scared that something is wrong.

She's not quite sure what that might be, but maybe the men in the black car know. She misses her Daddy, and right now, she needs her momma. For some reason, Annie feels like crying. It always helps when Momma puts her arms around Annie.

Momma will tell her everything is okay, but her stomach doesn't seem to agree. Her stomach now feels like it did after she and Bridget held hands and faced each other and spun around and around. She feels dizzy.

Annie sees the men begin to walk away, down the porch steps. She hears the front door slam shut, and Momma walks back inside.

Annie looks at her momma, but it doesn't look like her momma anymore.

Her beautiful momma's sparkle is gone.

And so was Daddy.

******

Christina and Bridget are taken by ambulance to the hospital to be treated for hypothermia. Jake takes off towards the hospital, knowing he needs to be there for his family.

A few hours later, the doctor says both Christina and Bridget will be okay, but he still would like them to stay the night for observation. They are safe for now, and Jake knows he needs to step up for Joseph's family.

As he turns onto Simmons Street and then on to Rue de Muckle, the sobs begin. As soon as he pulls into the driveway,

Mr. Nicholson comes running out. It isn't until he sees the horrified expression on Mr. Nicholson's face that Jake realizes he is covered in Joseph's blood. The two men embrace, both inconsolable.

"Are Christina and Bridget okay?" Mr. Nicholson asks, openly crying.

Jake nods. "Yeah, he saved them, Mr. Nicholson. My best friend in the whole world gave his life for my family," Jake shares. "He had called me earlier and told me he heard the voice. He was scared this time; the creek was crazy swollen with debris everywhere. He'd seen Christina's car pass earlier. I think he knew they'd gone in the creek," Jake continues, choking back tears. "I'm so sorry, Mr. Nicholson. I'm so sorry."

"You don't need to be sorry when a man has done what God called him to do. And we know Joseph was completely in God's will tonight. Joseph knew that God was calling him to much more difficult things. He also knew that for the believer, heaven is the final goal. I am certain that Joseph willingly gave his life, and God called him home. It was his time and God's plan. I don't know what we will all do with the holes in our hearts, but God promises us hope, even in the most difficult circumstances. Let's just try to figure out how to help that young woman and her little girl in there," Mr. Nicholson says, pointing to Michelle's house.

"My poor cousin ... who will she be without Joseph?" Jake says with fresh tears.

"She will be a woman held up by us, Jake," Mr. Nicholson encourages, crying again. "There's a little girl in there who will never get the gift of years we were given, so we must give her everything that Joseph was given. Give her this life, and help her live it. Show her who God is."

"Has anyone spoken to Matthew yet?" Jake asks. "No, I thought this needed to come from you." "First, I need to see Michelle and Annie."

Jake runs home to change and wash up. Annie doesn't need to see her daddy's blood all over him.

Jake walks into the house and finds Michelle and Annie on the couch together. There are no words being spoken, just two people holding on for life, crying their eyes out, not knowing what to do. Annie jumps up into her uncle's arms.

"My daddy ..." she cries. "My daddy ..."

"I know, sweetie, I know ..." Jake whispers into Annie's hair as he hugs her tightly.

"Are Christina and Bridget okay?" Michelle asks.

"Yes, they are being treated for hypothermia, but they should both be home tomorrow," Jake tells her. "He saved them, Michelle. I'm so sorry. I'm so sorry that saving my family cost him his life."

"Jake, don't you ever say that or think that again. Joseph was part of God's army here, and God asked him to do it. I know he heard the voice tonight. I have peace about that. I'm terribly sad, and I probably always will be. But Jake, he was doing what God asked him to do," Michelle says with tears streaming down her face.

"And I can't go see him now, Jake" Michelle says. "I don't want to remember him this way."

"I understand completely," Jake says with a sob.

Jake hugs his cousin and decides that this woman is stronger than he ever thought she could be. With God's help, they will survive this.

"I need to call Matthew, so I'm heading home for a bit," Jake says. "I'm so sorry, Michelle and Annie ... so very sorry."

******

Matthew is just finishing a late dinner with Marshall James when his cell phone rings. He glances at the caller ID and sees Jake's number. He has a feeling that even though it may seem rude to Marshall, he should take the call.

"I'm sorry, Marshall. I need to take this." He hands Marshall his credit card. "Go ahead and pay the check? I'll be back in just a few seconds."

"Hey, Bro!" Matthew says answering the phone as he heads out the restaurant door.

"Hey, Matthew ..." Jake's voice cracks. Try as he might, he can't stop himself from crying.

"What's wrong, Jake?" Matthew asks as fear creeps up his spine.

"It's ... It's Joseph," Jake says. "We lost him tonight, Matt."

Matthew feels his heart sink like a rock. "What? I don't ... What do you mean?!" Matthew says, already crying.

"He heard the voice ... There was a storm ... The creek flooded on Highway 41, and several cars had gone in the water. Joseph dove in and saved everyone, including Christina and Bridget," Jake explains, openly sobbing.

"Oh, God, no, no, no!" Matthew cries out in agony.

"He died saving my family, Matthew," Jake says just above a whisper.

Matthew is standing out in front of the restaurant in Manhattan. People are walking by, and everyone knows the New York Yankees' own Matthew West. Some people have stopped and some just stare a little too long as they pass him, while he uncontrollably cries. A piece of his heart has just been lost.

Marshall comes out the door and sees the crowd gathered around a sobbing Matthew. He shoos them away. Marshall has no idea what is happening, but he knows he needs to get Matthew to a quiet place. He flags down a cab, pushes an inconsolable Matthew into it, and they head towards Matthew's apartment.

At some point, Matthew knows he got off the phone with Jake, but he doesn't remember. The thought that keeps going through his head is they are no longer a foursome.

Marshall stays the night with Matthew and gets him to the airport the following morning. Even in his sorrow, Matthew sees God's hand in the moment. He thanks God for allowing him to be with Marshall when Jake called with this tragic news.

******

It's been three days since The Day of the Black Car. Three long days. Annie sits at the kitchen table looking down at her soggy Corn Flakes. She tries to think of something else, anything else, but all her thoughts come back to her Daddy. Annie knows that her head can usually house all sorts of happy thoughts, especially when she's playing with Bridget. She knows that at any given moment, there are so many things going through her head. And she loves to daydream about happy things like the beach with her Daddy or playing catch with Uncle Matthew or her birthday. She loves to think about her birthday. And usually, when she's sad, she can choose to think about one of those things and she's not sad anymore. But, The Day of the Black Car takes up all the space right now. It's like it fills her head and crowds out everything else. And try as she might, she can't think about anything else. She wonders if the rest of her life will be like this. Does your Daddy going to heaven do this forever? Do you get another Daddy or do you just learn to not have one? Annie has so many questions. And Daddy was her question person. Anytime she needed to understand something all she had to do was ask her Daddy. He knew *everything*. And now there's nobody to answer these questions.

Everyone does the fake happy when they get near her. She knows this. She *feels* it. Everyone is crying. Nonstop. And they try to pretend they weren't just crying, but Annie knows. And they all cry differently. Some people cry with their whole face, leaving their nose all snotty and their eyes puffy and red. Some people wipe their eyes on the back of their sleeve and sniff their snotty nose as they break into a smile. Then they act like she didn't just see them cry. Some people do the shake cry, they hug you and they seem happy but you feel their middle start to shake like they are trying to hide it. And right now her mom has her back to Annie with her hands in the sink and her mom thinks Annie doesn't know she's crying. She's doing the silent shoulder shake cry.

Annie is supposed to have gotten dressed for the funeral. But she can't even think about the dress Momma wants her to wear. The last time she wore it, she was with Daddy at Thanksgiving dinner. But instead of getting dressed, Annie is wearing an undershirt, tights and the cute shoes with bows on top. She wanted these shoes so badly and they used to make her smile just to look at them. Today, they have no power. Annie knows she's going to her Daddy's funeral and she's very confused about this. Why are they going to church because her Daddy went to heaven? She can't imagine how they are going to sing out all those happy church songs when Daddy is gone. And Uncle Jake is preaching and she knows he's the worst shoulder shaker of them all. Can you stand in front of everyone like the Pastor and shoulder shake at the same time? Annie doesn't think that's going to turn out good.

She hears the front door open and in walks Uncle Matthew. *He* might be different. Annie knows he shakes from the middle, but he lets the tears fall. He doesn't try to do the dry cry. She likes this about him because it makes her believe him. She thinks it's funny that he doesn't even knock on the door. He just comes in.

"Anyone home?" Uncle Matthew calls out from the den.

"I'm here in the kitchen," Annie answers.

Uncle Matthew walks in the kitchen and looks down at her soggy Corn Flakes and then looks back at Annie. This is the kind of moment where her Daddy would be funny and fill the room. Daddy did that. He filled a room. Her Daddy would say, "do you think those Corn Flakes are going to jump up from that bowl into your mouth?" And he would be laughing and he'd probably pick Annie up and swing her around and her momma would be rolling her eyes telling Daddy she needs her breakfast.

"How's my Sweet Annie?" she hears whispered in her ear. Uncle Matthew kisses the top of her head. "Looks like somebody isn't all the way dressed. Need some help with that?"

Annie's momma turns around from the sink, and although she was at the table with Annie earlier, Annie can tell her Momma hasn't actually *seen* her. She's stomach crying, with her head bowed and her hand over her stomach. Uncle Matthew jumps up and hugs her, putting one hand on the back of her head. It's like a daddy hug. Annie likes watching him take care of Momma.

Uncle Matthew turns to Annie and says, "let's finish getting you ready."

Annie follows Uncle Matthew up to her room. He opens the closet and reaches for the dress. Annie shakes her head no.

"Why not?" Uncle Matthew asks gently. "Because I wore it for the last time with Daddy."

"Did he tell you that you looked pretty?" Uncle Matthew asks. "Yes."

"Well, that's as good a reason as any to wear it. Today is a day that all of us are going to get dressed up and honor your Daddy. I'm going home to put my suit on and you *know* I wouldn't do that for just anyone. So, what about you and I get really dressed up? People are going to be looking at you because you are Joseph's little girl, I think you should look pretty," Uncle Matthew says with an unchecked tear slipping down his cheek.

Annie reaches up and wipes the tear away. She raises her hands over her head and Uncle Matthew slips the dress over her shoulders. He buttons the back of the dress and ties the sash. And to Annie's complete shock, Uncle Matthew takes her brush off the dresser and proceeds to gently brush Annie's dark curls and clips the matching bow on the side. Annie smiles as she watches him in the mirror.

"You look so pretty Annie, your daddy would be so proud," he says.

Annie does a little twirl in the dress and says, "I'm gonna be pretty for Daddy today."

"That's my girl," he says with watery eyes.

"Will you sit with me?" she asks.

"I will sit with you and will even carry you if you get sick of all the huggers," he says with a faint smile.

"Thanks Uncle Matthew," she says grabbing his hand as they walk down stairs.

******

286

The Church smells like wet people and burning candles. It makes Annie's stomach feel sick and she's glad she didn't eat the Corn Flakes. It's a cold and rainy day. The church is filled to overflowing. People are standing around the edges. The front row is filled with all of them: Momma, Annie, Uncle Matthew, Aunt Christina, Bridget, Grandpa Jeb, Grandma Kathleen, and a space for Uncle Jake who was preaching. When Annie looks down the row, everyone has a tissue in their hands. Annie feels cold and small. It seems like this is a gathering for adults. Annie still can't figure out why she has to be here. No one is paying any attention to her. They are all hiding their eyes like you do when you cover your eyes because you are the counter in hide and seek. Everyone is paying attention to themselves, like when you have a tummy ache and only you know what to do about it. It makes her feel lonely. Annie leans closer to Uncle Matthew searching for warmth and someone who tells the truth because it's like everyone else is lying. Pretending. They are all so sad right now, but later, they will pretend they are fine and fake smile at her as if that makes it feel better. It doesn't seem like anyone cares about *her* today. Do they all think she's okay? Does she need to be snot crying for them to know how much she hurts? Is everyone so sad that there isn't anything left over for her? Don't they know how forgotten she feels? Uncle Matthew does. He reaches over with his strong arms and picks her up and puts her on his lap. Annie settles in, resting her head in the soft muscle of his shoulder with her forehead touching his neck. She can feel the pulse in his neck. He grabs her hand. She can feel his stomach cry as it bounces up and down. He pulls her closer and kisses the top of her head. She feels his tear as it drops onto the side of her neck. She doesn't brush it away. She likes that her tears are mixed with his.

As if he knows she needs this, Uncle Matthew carries her for the rest of the day. At first, she feels like he's treating her like a baby, but then she starts to think he needs her too. Annie smiles at people, but she's sure they don't believe her. She can tell everyone feels sorry for her, as if the sight of her causes them to cry more. Puffy faced, teary-eyed people try to touch her and Annie doesn't like it. She doesn't think most people loved her daddy enough to cry that much. She doesn't understand *all* the people crying like that. She needs her Daddy now. This is one of those times he'd know exactly what to do to make her feel better. And if he was here, he'd make everybody smile again. But that doesn't make sense either, because that's why they are all here, *because* Daddy is not. Thankfully, Uncle Matthew holds her the whole time they stand in the long line. People try to do a double hug to get both she and Uncle Matthew. It doesn't work well. Most of the time she gets a nose full of hair smell which because of the rain smells like a wet dog. It feels weird to hug all these people she doesn't even know. She doesn't understand why they act like they know her. She recognizes the guys from the station because they all have their uniforms on. She's okay with them. The only one who doesn't try to hug her is the teenage boy with the bandage above his eye.

He just stares at her with a ghostly white face and says, "I'm sorry."

His words make Annie extra sad. He doesn't look at Uncle Matthew at all. He gives all his attention to Annie. And Annie is sure she doesn't know him. She would have remembered this guy because he isn't old and he has sad eyes and pale skin. His face is handsome but he has no sparkle. The part of his eyes that's supposed to be white is red like momma's eyes after she cries a lot. She sees dried tear stains on his cheeks. Annie feels sad for him because she can tell that like Uncle Matthew, he is telling the truth. He doesn't look at Annie and try to be fake happy. Annie doesn't know why, but she gives him a half smile. She thinks he needs it. After she smiles, the teenage boy does the shoulder shake cry without tears. She wants to ask Uncle Matthew who he is but Uncle Matthew is talking to someone else. She'll ask him later. Maybe Daddy had been really nice to this teenage boy.

Uncle Matthew holds her as the rain falls at the graveside. She watches as they take the big box out of the Black Car. She is in one of Matthew's strong arms and in the other, he holds the umbrella to keep them dry. She remembers him putting her down, handing her a flower and everyone looking at her funny like she knows what to do. Uncle Matthew takes her hand and shows her how to put the flower on the box where Daddy is sleeping. She wonders if Daddy is cold and will the big black box leak? Is Daddy getting wet? She hopes not. She's still trying to understand how Daddy can be in heaven and in a box at the same time. Maybe Uncle Jake can explain that. But she doesn't think she should ask anyone yet.

She turns to look at her Momma. And usually when Annie turns to her Momma, it's like Momma has super powers because she always *knows* and looks back. Momma doesn't do that today. Aunt Christina is standing beside her in a black raincoat and Annie thinks Aunt Christina is holding Momma up. She looks at Grandpa, he's crying. It's a scary thing when grown-ups cry. Annie thinks they really aren't supposed to cry. Especially Grandpa Jeb. He's like the leader of everything and if he's crying, Annie wonders who is going to take care of things.

She holds her arms up to Uncle Matthew. He instinctively knows she wants to be held again. Once again, she rests her head on his broad shoulders. She's safe in his arms.

"Thank-you," he whispers into the top of her head. "For what?"

"For sticking with me today," he says with his stomach shaking. "I couldn't have done this without you."

"Me neither," she says as she finally gives into the sobs that have been threatening to overtake her all day.

"We're going to be okay," he whispers. "We'll stick together, okay?"

"Love you, Uncle Matthew," she whispers.

"Oh, I love you too, Sweet Annie," he whispers as he tightens his grip on her.

******

After the funeral, Matthew, Jake, and Michelle find themselves on the dock on a chilly night, with jackets on. Despite the cold temperatures, the three of them need to be in this spot on this night.

"What are we going to do without him?" Jake asks in a desperate tone.

"I keep asking myself the same question," Michelle says with fresh tears.

"I mean, seriously, what will we do?" Jake repeats.

"We are going to LIVE!" Matthew says. "We are all going to grieve, then pick up the pieces ... and live."

"You're right," Jake agrees. "We are not going to just live; we are going to honor the memory of our friend by devoting ourselves fully to God. There would be no better way to honor Joseph."

"There is a little girl in that house right there who needs all of us to stick together and love her," Jake says. "The only way she will see her daddy is in the three of us. We are the best of what he gave us."

"Amen," Matthew says. "Amen."

"I wanted to let you all know I did not renew my contract with the Yankees. I'm done with baseball. I feel God moving in my heart about kids. So, I've started a new venture: The Matthew West Baseball Academy. I'll be bringing Jesus and baseball together for kids. I've launched my first one in New York, and now seems like the right timing to start the second one here. We all need to be together and help each other through this. I'm moving back to be supportive in any way that I can," Matthew shares. "I had already told all this to Joseph, but ... this is where I intend to live, and I bought the backwards house awhile back."

Both Michelle and Jake get up at the same time and hug Matthew.

"You can't know how much I needed to hear this tonight," Jake says.

"Me too," Michelle says, tears rolling down her face. "Oh, me too."

~ CHAPTER 23 ~

Life has a way of moving on, sometimes without our permission.

There were jobs to return to, bills to pay, children to raise, and the need for joy. Everyone seemed to want to fall into the new normal, despite the intense grief. Years down the road, when the adults were asked how they survived it, each of them would say one word: "Annie."

At first, it was out of a sense of duty. All of the adults felt the deep need to make certain that Annie had a good life, even in the sadness. But in stepping out in faith to do right by her, the feelings gradually began to follow.

******

Michelle has a few very dark weeks—weeks where she questions her desire to move forward. She has moments when she doesn't think she wants her life if it doesn't include Joseph. Her entire life has been spent with him, and the loss of him feels like a part of herself has been taken. She feels herself start to become blinded to joy, as if she lost the ability to feel it.

Annie simply says that her mom "forgot how to sparkle."

"I won't wear that, Momma. It doesn't have pockets!" Annie nearly yells at her mom.

"Sweetie, it's your favorite dress ... you love this dress," Momma says back sadly.

"I told you. Pockets, Momma!" Annie says back indignantly.

"Why do you need pockets?" Momma asks.

Annie reaches into the pocket of her jeans and pulls out the egg-shaped plastic ball that contains the gold ring with the pink diamond and says, "because this needs to go in the pocket every day."

Annie really doesn't know why she wants the ring close by at all times, but ever since The Day of the Black Car, she can't stop looking at it. It is as if she wants it with her in case Daddy shows up. Annie knows her daddy isn't going to show up—Momma said he had gone to heaven—but still, her last moments with Daddy were all about the ring. If she lets go of the ring, was she letting go of Daddy?

Sometimes, when she is really sad, she puts her hand in her pocket, feels the ring, and thinks of Daddy. Sometimes this makes her wonder where he is. *What is heaven like? Is it so much better than here? Is that why Daddy left?*

In the first few weeks after The Day of the Black Car, Annie just cries. Sometimes she cries because she is sad and misses her daddy, but other times she cries because Momma cries all the time. She doesn't like crying all the time; it isn't fun.

One morning, a new feeling starts. She feels herself begin to get really mad at little things. She has a feeling in her stomach like she wants to punch something. When her momma tries to talk to her, she just wants to push her away. She feels like she is just mad, but Annie doesn't understand this. She doesn't really feel like she is mad at somebody; it's more like she is mad at everybody.

She knows she can't really talk to Momma about this. Annie also realizes that whenever she didn't understand something, she used to ask her daddy. She decides that maybe Grandpa has answers. Maybe if she asks her grandpa, she can have a Dock Walk with him. Maybe he can help her understand.

Annie leaves her house and walks next door and knocks on the door.

"Hey, Little Sweetie," Grandpa says smiling. "Come on in.

Honey, Annie's here!" he calls out into the house.

"It's okay, Grandpa. You don't have to call for Grandma. I just need you," Annie tells him.

"Oh, well then, what can I do for you?" Grandpa asks, looking at Annie with sad, red eyes.

"Am I old enough for a Dock Walk?" Annie asks.

"Well, sure, I suppose so. I never set an age on it. I think I did your daddy's first Dock Walk when he was a year or two older than you, but we have no rules on it. If you need a Dock Walk, you need one. So, would you like to do it now?" Grandpa asks her, with a wink.

"Yes! I think I'm a really big girl now, and it's time for me to get to do a Dock Walk," Annie says happily and with resolve.

"Okay! Let me get my baseball cap," Grandpa says.

The two walk out the back door, just like her daddy had done hundreds of times in his childhood. They walk through the back porch, across the baseball diamond, to the well-worn path that leads to the dock. Annie grabs her grandpa's hand. He looks down at her and smiles as they walk to the end and sit down. There is a chill in the air, so they keep their shoes on.

"What's on your mind, Little Sweetie?" Grandpa asks.

"You know Daddy used to call me 'Miss Sparkles', right?" she asks.

"Well, yes, I do seem to recall hearing that a time or two." He smiles.

"What do I do if I've lost my sparkle? How do I get it back?" she asks. "So, I got this kind of feeling inside, like I'm mad at everybody. But nobody did anything to me. Sometimes, I feel like I want to punch somebody. It makes me feel like I'm in a bad mood and makes other stuff not fun. What do I do?" she questions.

"Have you talked to your momma about this?" Grandpa asks.

"It's kind of a daddy question," she responds.

"Like it's something you'd ask your daddy, but you can't now?" Grandpa tries to clarify.

"Yes. When I had stuff like this, he always talked to me. I didn't talk about stuff like this to Momma," Annie explains.

"Well, let's take a look at this for a minute," Grandpa suggests. "So, you're mad, and you can't figure out who you're mad at?"

"Yep." Annie nods.

"Are you blaming somebody for what happened?" Grandpa asks, wondering if the girl had started to blame Christina and Bridget because Joseph saved them.

"No, I don't think so. Like, I don't feel madder at anyone more than somebody else. Everybody has the same amount of mad right now," she answers honestly.

"Have you ever thought that maybe you're mad at God?" Grandpa asks.

"Why would I be mad at God?" Annie ponders. "Daddy told me all about God."

"Well, everyone has been talking about how your daddy heard an angel tell him to turn around. When he did, he saved the people, but he didn't survive. Do you think maybe you are mad at God for telling him to turn around?" Grandpa suggests in a soft voice.

Annie starts crying then, really crying hard. Fighting to get words out, she questions, "Grandpa, why did God have to use *my* daddy? Why couldn't he have used somebody else's daddy?" The little girl sobs.

Grandpa reaches over and lifts her up onto his lap. He lets her cry until she calms down a bit. "Little Sweetie, I've wondered that myself ... because I am really sad too. He was my little boy. But here's the thing: Your daddy was special, really special. From the time he was not much older than you, he started to understand that he was going to be used by God for things. He accepted it. He actually liked it. Sometimes the kids made fun of him. Sometimes he didn't want to do what was asked of him. But he trusted God and knew there was a plan. His job was to do what God asked of him. So, in a way, you and me, we should be smiling about this, because how many other people do you know that hear from God that they are supposed to do something?" Grandpa speaks softly while smoothing down her hair.

"Well ... me," Annie says, matter-of-factly.

"What do you mean 'me'?" Grandpa asks.

"I hear things sometimes, and I feel things here." She taps her heart. "Then when I feel it, I know I'm supposed to do something," Annie shares. "And since The Day of the Black Car, I'm scared about it."

"I can understand that perfectly," Grandpa says in a reassuring voice. "I think that knowing your daddy lost his life doing what God asked might scare me too if I thought the same thing was happening to me."

"Daddy understood stuff like this, Grandpa. When I told him about falling from the tree and being caught but nobody was there, he didn't seem surprised at all," Annie tells him.

"Yes, your daddy told me about that, and you know what?" Grandpa asks.

"What, Grandpa?" Annie says.

"He was so proud that you were just like him!" Grandpa smiles.

"He was?" Annie asks, looking into her grandpa's happy eyes.

"Oh, Sweet Annie, he even called his own Dock Walk over it," Grandpa says.

"Did Daddy sometimes get sad about it?"

"Yes, every time something happened, he would cry like a baby."

"That's funny, Grandpa: Daddy like a baby." Annie laughs.

"I've got an idea," Grandpa says.

"What, Grandpa?"

"Well, I know I'm not your daddy, but you know I raised him. I got to see this up close. Maybe I could help you. Maybe I could be the person you come to about it. What do you think about that?" Grandpa asks gently.

"You mean like Dock Walks to help me?"

"Exactly. Oh, and one other thing, Annie. Be very careful about letting yourself stay mad. You know, when you get really mad about something, and you leave it there, it can block out God's voice in your heart. So, I'm really proud of you for coming to me so that we could talk this out."

"I don't want to be mad, Grandpa; I want to be just like my daddy," Annie admits.

Grandpa smiles at her, then asks, "Have you been saying your prayers?"

"Not really, Grandpa. Daddy did that with me."

"Well, there you go. You have to say your prayers. You should talk to God and tell him that maybe you're a little mad at Him, but you really don't want to be. Daddy taught you about confessing, right?" Grandpa asks.

"My daddy taught me all about that," Annie says with confidence in her voice.

"Well, then, you know exactly what to do," Grandpa smiles. "But, Annie, it's okay to be sad, and you might be sad for a long time. You and your daddy had something pretty special, and I know for a fact that he loved you to the moon and back. You know what?"

"What, Grandpa?"

"He still loves you. Even though you can't see him, he's still here." Grandpa taps his heart. "And he will always be there."

"I guess that's why I like this so much," Annie says, pulling the plastic egg with the ring inside it out of her front pocket. "When I touch it, I think about him, and it reminds me of that feeling I used to get when Daddy was around."

Grandpa knows all about the little ring, and the night she was going to open it with her daddy. He knows how heartbroken she is that he never saw it. "Well, then, I guess you better keep that close by for a while. What do you think?"

"That's why I need pockets. I never opened it up, Grandpa. Daddy was supposed to be there when I did. I never wore the ring. I just feel it in my pocket and look at it."

"Maybe someday you'll be ready to open it. It's a beautiful ring, Little Annie, and your daddy would be so happy to know that it makes you think of him."

"Yep. Hey, Grandpa, I'm a big girl now." She smiles broadly. "I had my first Dock Walk!"

"That makes you special, Little Annie, because you're my first Grandchild Dock Walk ever." Grandpa winks at her.

"I am special, Grandpa. Daddy told me so."

"Oh, yes, Sweet Annie, you are so very, very special. And you know what?"

"What, Grandpa?"

"I love you till infinity," Grandpa says as he gives her a big hug.

"I love you till infinity, and I said it last!" Annie giggles, playing along with their game, and hugs her grandpa right back.

******

Annie and Bridget like to play outside all the time. Inside is for all the adults, and they are just too sad. Annie wants anything that belonged to her daddy, so she takes to wearing his old baseball glove. She and Bridget started tossing the ball to each other one day, and it's now become their habit. Annie likes how she feels when she is on her daddy's baseball diamond. It feels like he is with her.

One Saturday afternoon, Christina looks out the window at the girls tossing the ball, and she says, "It's a shame that nobody has taught those girls a thing about baseball. A girl should never throw like *that*." And she points to a couple of girls throwing the ball shamefully.

Jake comes over to the window, watches, and says, "Oh, dear, that is shameful."

"We cannot let Matthew see this!" She laughs.

"Maybe he needs to see this and can help. For now, though, I'll go get my glove," Jake says, smiling. Even the smell of his glove reminds him of Joseph.

"Who wants to learn how to pitch better than Uncle Matthew?" Jake questions as he's walking towards them.

"We do! We do!!" they all yell back.

And so, it begins again. The next generation is playing on the old baseball diamond facing Shem Creek. It doesn't take long before the well-worn diamond is back. It's as if two little girls told the weeds to get lost.

******

One evening, Annie is over at Bridget's house playing.

"Uncle Jake, can we call Uncle Matthew?" she asks.

"Sure," Jake responds with curiosity, and he dials the number.

"Hey there," Jake greets. "Somebody here wants to talk to you." "Okay ..." Matthew says.

"It's me, Uncle Matthew!" Annie says into the phone. "I just want you to know I don't throw like a girl anymore."

"Well, what do you know?" Matthew says, and he feels his smile down to his soul. "It's about time, because nobody likes a girl who can't throw a ball."

"When you coming home to see it?" she asks.

"I don't know ... soon? How about I arrange it with Uncle Jake?" he suggests.

"I think you should live here, or none of us will play good baseball. Uncle Jake is good, but he wasn't a Yankee." She giggles.

"What's in it for me?" Matthew teases.

"Me! Of course! And Bridget!" she exclaims. "You don't have kids, so you can have us!"

"Now *that's* a good offer, Annie. I think you sold me on it." "Really, Uncle Matthew? You gonna come home soon?"

"Yep, I'm coming home." He marvels at how she understands that South Carolina is his home, even though she's never known a time when he lived there.

"Yeah! Love you, Uncle Matthew."

"Love you too, Little Annie," he says back.

Secretly Annie thinks she has a crush on the handsome Uncle Matthew. Whenever he comes, he calls her Little Annie, and she likes that a whole lot. He's really nice to the kids, and he always plays with them. Annie thinks it will be fun when he lives in the backwards house, because every time she hits a home run over his house, he'll see it and maybe he'll come out and play. Momma says that Uncle Matthew is coming back soon, and she can tell because the men have been fixing up the house.

Michelle has a small concern. Joseph has been gone for two months now, and she started to notice that she feels awful in the morning. At first, Michelle just assumes it's the crushing blow of grief, until she realizes she's late.

She decides to go to the pharmacy for a pregnancy test.

She stands at the sink, waiting for the results. The pink line appears.

She feels equal parts of joy and dread. Truth be told, she feels she lacks the ability to do this alone. Joseph had been such a full partner in parenting. So much of who Annie is right now is due to his love and attention. How can she do this alone? It is difficult enough to contemplate raising Annie by herself, but another child?

Michelle keeps looking at Annie. Annie seems to be better able to smile, despite her pain. But honestly, it is hard to look at Annie, because her eyes are Joseph's. She is the female version of Joseph Nicholson. She even seems to be hard-wired with his faith, and that faith intimidates Michelle.

Michelle is worried about Annie. She refuses to say that her daddy died. She always refers to it as The Day of the Black Car. In some small way, she seems to blame the men in the black car for her father's death. Michelle worries that she is too young to try to understand such things.

Shortly after Joseph's death, Annie had announced that she would only wear clothing with a front pocket. She doesn't allow herself to ever wear the gold ring with the pink stone. It hurts her too much because her daddy never came home to open it with her.

Every day, she puts the egg-like plastic container in her front pocket. Michelle watches her reach her hand into her pocket just to feel it. Michelle gets the feeling that somehow it makes her feel better to touch it. Michelle just wants to make sure none of this is too weird or a sign that Annie needs help. Other than those two quirky things, Annie seems to be doing as well as can be expected.

Michelle feels lost. She knows if Joseph were alive, and he'd just found out she was expecting, he would have picked her up, swung her around, and danced with her in the kitchen over this news. He would have been out the door to tell his dad and Jake and on the phone with Matthew. This moment would have been so joyous. He would have come up with some incredible way to tell Annie, and the two of them would be squealing with delight. All of this just makes Michelle even sadder.

Michelle just wants to know how to get her joy back. How do you force yourself to continue when a part of you dies? In dark moments, she remembers back to her mother's death. This time reminds her of all the days she spent alone, with two parents who didn't love her. She starts to feel rejected again, as if only through Joseph had she been validated, as if his love alone had pulled her through. His love was always a strong dose of hope in dark times.

"God, how does this work? I feel no joy," Michelle prays, and she feels guilty, as if she is dishonoring Joseph by her attitude. She also feels guilty because Mr. and Mrs. Nicholson have always been there for her and she has done nothing for them. She has not reached out or offered her love and concern. They have lost a son. It makes her feel selfish.

Michelle makes a quick decision. She goes to the closet, where she keeps the wrapping paper and gift boxes. She fishes the pregnancy test out of the trash can, puts it in a box, and wraps the box beautifully. Then, she gets in the shower and does her makeup and hair. She goes to her closet and pulls out a sundress, puts on some earrings, and looks at the results in the mirror.

Not great, she thinks, *but much better.*

Annie had stayed the night at Jake's, so Michelle is free to go over to the Nicholson's.

She knocks on the door, and a very tired looking Mrs. Nicholson answers. Kathleen looks like she has aged twenty years since Joseph died.

"Who's at the door, honey?" Michelle hears Mr. Nicholson call out from the other room.

"It's Michelle!" She answers as she pulls Michelle into an embrace.

"How are you doing, Sweetie?" she asks Michelle as she leads her into the living room.

"It's rough. Up and down is the best description I've got." Michelle sits down on the couch. "But, honestly, more down."

"Same here," Kathleen admits sitting down in a rocking chair. "Some days, I feel like I can't do it. I don't know what I'd do without Jeb. He can be so sad, but still have hope. I'm struggling."

"Me too," Michelle shares. "I worry that I'm being a terrible parent to Annie."

Mr. Nicholson enters the room with a big smile on his face. Michelle thinks to herself, *Why have I not realized how much I need these two?*

Michelle stands to greet him, and he takes her in his arms, giving her one of those hugs that feels like it restores you.

"You sure look pretty today, Michelle," he says, taking a step back.

"You sure know how to make a girl feel good, Mr. Jeb," she replies, smiling and really feeling the smile.

"Oh, hey, sweetheart, have you had lunch yet?" Mrs. Nicholson asks.

"If you're offering, I'm staying!" Michelle feels happy for the first time in weeks.

They all head into the kitchen. Mr. Jeb and Michelle take seats at the kitchen table, while Kathleen pours some sweet tea for both of them.

"I've got some leftover fried chicken, or I can make you a sandwich. What are you in the mood for?" Kathleen asks.

"Actually, can you come sit down for a second? I have something for you," Michelle announces.

"Oh, okay," Kathleen says, setting the pitcher down on the table. She sits down across the table from Michelle, next to her husband. Unconsciously, she takes her husband's hand.

"This is for you." Michelle pushes the wrapped box across the table to them. She smiles. "Go ahead. Open it!"

"Why don't you do the honors, honey?" Mr. Jeb suggests to his wife.

She takes the box, unties the ribbon, and unwraps it. She opens the box and sees the contents. Without a word, she passes the box to her husband.

In that moment, joy returns. It's not a big overwhelming joy, but a little trickle of it seeps into their lives again. And it feels like every day, a little more gets added.

"I cannot imagine a greater gift," Kathleen cries and gets up to give Michelle a hug.

"Oh, Lord, we love You, and thank You for this incredible gift of love. Lord, this piece of Joseph is truly from You. Thank You, God!" Mr. Jeb has tears rolling down his cheeks too.

He gets up and takes Michelle in his arms again. "We are in this 100 percent. You are not alone. Kathleen and I will take turns spending the night to help. We will fill in the gaps that Joseph's absence left. We are family. We are at your disposal for whatever this road brings," Mr. Jeb tells her.

"I am scared. But for the first time in weeks, I feel hope again," Michelle admits. "I keep thinking that if Joseph were here, he'd be shouting and hollering all over the block. He'd be dancing around the kitchen, and most of all, he'd dream up something to make this moment incredible for Annie. Can we dream up something perfect? I want to tell her this with joy in a way she will always remember."

"You're such a great momma, Michelle," Kathleen encourages. "I'm so proud of you."

Kathleen has no idea how desperately Michelle needs to hear those words.

"How about we cook this up so it's a surprise for everyone?" Mr. Jeb suggests. "I think we could use a reason to have a small party."

"You know, Matthew is coming home in a few weeks," Michelle tells them.

"Let's do it then!" Kathleen can feel the excitement building. "That's a great idea!"

******

It's an early March evening, and everyone is gathered for a barbecue on the dock. It is the first gathering since Joseph died.

It feels like they aren't quite sure what the rules are. Is it okay to laugh? Is it okay to feel a bit better in a moment? Is it time to start telling Joseph stories?

After dinner, everyone is lingering on the dock, and Michelle speaks up: "I have a gift for someone here, and I'm trying to see what the name on the box is ..." Michelle holds up a beautifully wrapped box, with a big bow and a tag on it.

"I can't seem to read the tag. Can you?" She passes the box to Christina, who willingly plays along.

"Hmmm ... I don't know. I think I need my glasses ... I can't read it well. Can you?" Christina says and passes it to Jake.

"Maybe it's for me!" Annie jumps up and down. "Let me see!"

"I don't know ... I don't think you can read yet, Little One," Jake teases, passing the box over her head to Mr. Jeb.

"Well, now ... wait a minute. I think Uncle Matthew can read. Can't you?" Mr. Jeb passes the box over Annie's head again.

Annie is giggling now "I think it's for me." Annie says again.

"Well, let me see here ..." Matthew turns the tag over and hands the box to Annie. "Can you read that?"

Annie grabs the box and says, "it *is* for me! I told y'all, it's for me! I can read my own name, Uncle Matthew. I can even write it now too."

She turns to her momma. "Can I open it, Momma?" "Of course you can, Sweetheart," Michelle answers.

Annie rips open the package and discovers a very pink t-shirt with glittery letters on it. "Um ... I can't read that much, Uncle Matthew," she says, moving over beside him. "Can you tell me what the letters say?"

Michelle has noticed that Annie seems to single out Matthew for things. Jake has even mentioned that she had wanted to call Matthew several times.

Matthew takes the shirt out of her hands and holds it up. The t-shirt says: "I'm the Big Sister" on it.

Everyone looks at Michelle in stunned silence.

"I don't understand, Momma," Annie says. "I don't have a brother or sister. Why did you get me this?"

"Because, My Little Love, your Daddy left you one, and *she* is growing in Momma's tummy," Michelle explains.

"I'm getting a baby sister?" Michelle nods, and then Annie understands. She screams out, "Yaaaahoooooooo!" and jumps up and down, clapping.

"Yes, you are! And you are going to be a big sister." Michelle beams.

Annie touches the pink ring inside her front pocket and thinks of her daddy. She remembers how much she wanted the ring in the gum machine. Even though she wanted the ring so bad, on her birthday last year, when she blew out her candles, she had wished for a baby brother. Even though this is a sister and not a brother, it feels like God answered her prayer. Her wish is coming true.

Before she knows it, everyone is jumping up and down with Annie, celebrating her baby sister. Annie notices that everyone is crying, but no one is sad crying. They are all happy; Annie can tell.

When she looks at her momma, Annie sees it again. A little of Momma's sparkle is back.

~ CHAPTER 24 ~

On September 13, 2001, just two days after the terrorist attacks in New York, the world around them seems to be going crazy, and Matthew just wants out. This is the final straw for him.

New York has never been his home, and there is absolutely no reason to stay. The frantic calls he's been getting from Michelle, Jake, and Mr. Nicholson have been enough to show him that home is where the people who love you are. They all want him home.

Marshall James shows up at Matthew's apartment. Since Matthew had left the Yankees, he doesn't see Marshall as much. But when Matthew answers the door, with no advance call, he thinks that perhaps something is happening. He is shocked at Marshall's appearance. He looks like he hasn't slept in weeks.

"Come in," Matthew says. "Are you okay?"

Marshall comes in, goes straight to the couch, and sits down, looking weary. He rakes his hand through his hair and says, "Listen ... um ... I don't know how to tell you this."

"What? Who?" Matthew says, knowing death is all around him, and it is apparent that Marshall has lost someone.

"Matthew, it's Marguerite. She was on American Flight 11. She was headed out to LA on business. Matthew, she's gone," Marshall says, openly crying. "I've been trying to console Mario, but it can't be done. He's lost, Matthew."

"Oh, dear God, no, no ... Oh, poor Mario. She's his everything," Matthew starts to cry now.

After a few moments, he asks, "What can I do?"

Marshall sighs then answers, "Nothing. I'm not sure he'd be ready to see you. I just know she was important to you, and I didn't want you to find out when you watched the news. You've been through quite a bit this year, and I'm worried about you," Marshall sympathizes.

"Thank you, Marshall. The events of this week have just served as a reminder that I don't belong here anymore. You are the only thing I will miss," Matthew tells him.

"I just don't know what poor Mario will do. He's got no one left," Marshall says.

"He probably hates me, or I'd reach out to him. Should I stay away from her funeral?" Matthew asks.

"Yes, probably. I think he feels like you broke her heart. He has never actually said that, but I'm thinking that you there might make him hurt even more. If you feel the need to reach out, maybe send him a card or something," Marshall suggests.

"I'm going to go with what you advise here because Mario is your best friend. You know him best. I just can't stand the thought that he'd think I don't care. I really came to love that man," Matthew admits.

Marshall stands as if to leave. "I hope you stay in touch with me, Matthew. You're the son I never had."

"Sir, my home is your home, and I hope that you will come to see me and soak up some South Carolina sun."

The way Matthew saw it, he had about three weeks left of work to tie up the loose ends on the first Matthew West Baseball Academy. He decides that the academy will be a series of two-week camps throughout the summer and during Christmas break. With the dual purpose of baseball and Jesus, Matthew thinks he can make a difference in the lives of kids who are fatherless or at risk somehow. He sincerely hopes that God will place kids in his path that need help. He has his staff up and running, busy registering kids for the upcoming summer break. He is thrilled to have several ex-pro baseball players on board.

It is early October when Matthew receives a phone call. A lawyer representing the estate of Marguerite Rossellini called requesting a meeting with Matthew. There will be a reading of her will, and Matthew has been named. The meeting is the following morning at 10:00 at the offices of her law firm in New York. Matthew writes down the address, planning to be there.

Matthew feels guilty that he hadn't loved her well, and yet here she is leaving something to him in her will. He is trying to figure out why he'd been called to the law firm.

At 10:00 a.m. sharp, Matthew arrives at the law firm. He is greeted and escorted to a room with a large conference table. Around the table are chairs, and in front of each chair is a folder. Matthew assumes that her colleagues are handing her estate and perhaps they all felt the need to be there. He still can't figure out why he is there.

Matthew sits down. A clerk comes in and offers coffee. Matthew begins to feel nervous.

A few minutes later, the clerk brings in his coffee. She is immediately followed by the arrival of Mario Rossellini. Matthew stands, and any fear he had that Mario carried ill feelings toward him disappears the minute he takes Matthew into a loving bear hug. "I've missed you, son," he says with tears in his eyes.

"Me too, sir," Matthew replies, openly crying. "I'm so sorry, Mario. Just so sorry."

Both men are unable to control their emotions for a moment, but then they wipe their tears, take deep breaths, smile at each other, and take their seats at the table.

They are at a loss for words. It appears that they are waiting for the rest of the attorneys to join them, but they don't know why. Matthew feels nervous, and the others appear to be late.

"Now? Can I go in now? Is it time? I've been waitin' like you told me." A little boy is standing just outside the doorway. The boy is about five, and he has thick, dark hair sticking out of a New York Yankees baseball cap, which he is wearing backwards. His eyes are a deep smoldering blue. He's holding a baseball glove and standing completely still, as if he's surprised. He looks straight into the eyes of Matthew.

Matthew stands. An overwhelming feeling comes over him. He has butterflies in his stomach; his heart is palpitating in his chest; and he knows. He absolutely knows. An intense desire to protect overtakes him. He does not need anyone in the room to tell him. He feels it, sees it, and knows it deep in his soul. *This is his son.*

"This is the best day of my life," Matthew says in a whisper.

Matthew walks over to the little boy, crouches down eye-to-eye with him, and holds out his arms. The boy pounces into Matthew's arms with all the joy a five-year-old can muster.

The little boy pulls back and looks at Matthew up closely.

"You're him?" he asks puzzled. "The guy in the posters on my wall?"

By this time, Mario is crying as he sees this exchange.

"Matthew, this is JW," he introduces. "JW, this is your daddy, Matthew West."

"My daddy ... is the pitcher?" JW asks, thrilled.

Matthew is so overcome with emotion. He simply stands in awe of this gift of life that he didn't even know about.

"Hey, JW, what does that stand for?" Matthew asks.

"Well, I'm Joseph West Rossellini, and I'm five!" JW says, putting his hands on his hips.

Matthew crouches down again and takes the boy in his arms. She had named her son after him and his best friend — amazing. "You're gonna have to be patient with me. I'm probably gonna have to hug you a lot to make up for the lost time," Matthew tells him, while wiping his eyes with the back of his hands.

"Why are you crying?" JW asks. "Aren't you glad to see me?"

"That's why I'm crying, JW. I am just so happy that it's spilling out," Matthew explains.

Just then, the rest of the attorneys walk in and begin to take seats around the table.

A young woman comes in and says, "JW, you want to go watch a movie, while these adults talk about boring stuff?"

"Sure, but that's my daddy. Did you know that?" He points back at Matthew. "He plays baseball, and I got a poster of him," JW tells them proudly.

Mario speaks first. "There are lots of legal papers here, and we could go through it all if you'd like, but if you want, I can just summarize them for you, Matthew."

"I'd like that, sir. I'm in shock at this moment, good shock, but just surprised," Matthew admits, honestly.

"She knew she was pregnant when she went with you to South Carolina. She planned to tell you when you all got home from the wedding, but when she realized that you loved another woman, she said she didn't want you to be stuck doing the right thing with the wrong woman. So many times, Matthew, she said that she didn't blame you. She said that it wasn't your fault. Long story short, that's why she left for Boston."

Mario paused a moment to let that sink in before continuing, "She desires that you take full custody of JW, with one important stipulation. Marguerite said that if you agree to take full custody, you must move him to South Carolina and give him that life. She did not want him raised in New York. She said that Shem Creek was everything she ever wanted for her son. She made it clear: She loved everyone she met there. She was positive they would open their hearts to JW, and he'd have a great childhood. Most importantly, she knew you'd be a great father.

"This was all in her will. If she had lived, she was going to head back here at Christmastime to tell you about JW. She had been closely watching your work with children and knew it was time and that you were ready," Mario says.

Matthew looks Mario in the eyes and says, "Sir, I can absolutely agree to all of that, with one request of my own."

"Okay, what might that be?" Mario asks, still fighting back the tears.

"Will you come with us, sir?" Matthew asks. "I'm going to need this boy's grandpa with him. And, sir, on this earth, I did not do right by your daughter. I know that. I also know that out of the mess I made, something good will happen. Our family in South Carolina needs you, Mario."

"Oh, I couldn't do that. You don't need to feel like you owe me anything," Mario says with tears running down his wrinkled cheeks.

"Sir, this child needs you. I need you. And quite frankly, you need us," Matthew says. "Please, sir, come with us. I have a

318

large house, and you can have your own space. And I promise you, you will love everyone."

"Thank you, Matthew," Mario whispers. "Thank you. Just being near that boy will feel like I still have a piece of Marguerite."

"Then it's settled," Matthew says. "We will work out those details over dinner."

Mario smiles. For the first time in his life, he feels ready to leave New York. He is tired, ready to retire, and the events of the past month have made him realize life is short, and it means nothing if you aren't with the people you love.

Marguerite left everything to Matthew. As soon as the meeting is over, Matthew starts making calls to have the contents of Marguerite's home shipped to Mount Pleasant. Mario finally agrees to sell the deli to a baseball fan who has kept approaching him with offers. Plans to leave New York quickly fall into place.

Matthew arrived at the law firm alone, and he leaves with his son. Mario says his goodbyes for just a little while to go to his little apartment to start the job of packing up.

Matthew tries to figure out who to call first. His parents? Jake? Mr. Nicholson? Michelle? He cries like a baby when he realizes the one person he wants to tell is Joseph. He looks up towards heaven and whispers, "I've got a son, and he's named after you, JoBro. I wish you were here."

When JW and Matthew arrive back at his apartment, it becomes evident that Matthew needs kid stuff. JW runs through the apartment saying, "Yay, my daddy's house."

"We won't be here long, JW. We are going home to South Carolina," Matthew explains. "I can't even tell you how great it is! You just gotta trust me."

"Okay, cool! When do we go?"

"Well, I'm thinking I need another week to get things in order. So, in the meantime, do you think you'd mind sleeping in my bed with me, just us guys?" Matthew asks.

"Just like with mommy when I get scared?" he asks, and then gets teary-eyed.

"Yes, just like that. I'm so sorry your momma went to heaven, JW," Matthew says. "I promise you I'll take good care of you, okay? We're gonna have a lot of adventures, you and me."

"Okay." JW says, and the tender moment is apparently finished, because he goes running down the hall to Matthew's king-sized bed, climbs onto it, and starts jumping on the bed.

Matthew smiles and stares in awe at this beautiful, resilient child.

~ CHAPTER 25 ~

"What's a road trip, Daddy?" JW asks over breakfast. "Well, it's when you get in a car or truck, and you drive a long way," Matthew explains.

"Are we gonna have an a'venture?" JW asks.

"You bet ... lots of adventures." Matthew answers.

The truck is fully loaded. The apartment is cleaned out. A new chapter is about to begin. Matthew tells everyone he is moving back, but he decides to save the news of JW. He decides to surprise everyone. Mario is going to be stuck in New York for another few weeks, tying up the paperwork on the sale of the deli, but he will be joining them as soon as possible.

"It's gonna take us two days," Matthew says. "Do you like cheeseburgers?"

"Duh, Dad. All kids like cheeseburgers. I really like Happy Meals," JW tells him.

"Good to know, buddy. Good to know." Matthew smiles, then says, "Off we go."

As Matthew drives out of New York with his son in the front seat of the Ryder truck, he feels no need to look back. His time playing baseball has been good to him, but it is time to go home—home to the beautiful waters of Shem Creek, where the air is salty, and the sky is blue, where nighttime sounds are crickets and frogs, and where baseball is the language of friendship.

"You okay, Dub?" Matthew asks, using his new nickname for JW.

"Yeah ... I'm just thinking of Mommy," JW says.

"Me too," Matthew responds. "How about you tell me a silly Mommy story?"

The little boy begins what would be the first of hundreds of Mommy stories Matthew asks JW to tell him. He wants to make sure that JW always knows that his momma is part of their lives. Matthew instinctively knows that healing happens best together. The more Matthew asks his son about his mommy, the closer the two become. And in hearing these stories, Matthew begins to see what an incredible mom Marguerite had been. Matthew is so impressed at JW's ability to love new people. Matthew is so grateful that the little boy quickly bonds with him. He knows that speaks volumes of how well Marguerite loved him and made him feel secure.

The second day on the road, Matthew says, "I'm gonna call them and tell them I'll be home at 6, but *you* are the big surprise! What do you think?"

"I'm gonna be a great surprise!" JW says. "I wanna meet Annie and Bridget 'cause they play baseball."

"It's gonna be awesome. Hey, buddy, do you swim?" Matthew asks.

"Yep," JW answers. "I swim good."

"What did I tell you about 'yep'?" Matthew asks with a slight smile.

"Yes, sir, Dad," JW says, grinning back at him.

"Well, now, you sound just like a Southern gentleman," Matthew tells him.

As they cross the Cooper River Bridge going towards Mount Pleasant, Matthew opens all the windows in the front cab of the truck.

"Breathe this in, JW. This is the smell of The Low Country. This will be the smell of home for the rest of your life," Matthew says with excitement.

"Dad, look at all those boats. Can we ride in one?" JW asks.

"You bet, Dub. We are going to do it all!" Matthew smiles.

As they make the left-hand turn from Coleman onto Simmons Street, Matthew thinks back to a day, long ago, when a lonely stuttering boy arrived here. He smiles as he remembers the "baseball day," as it had come to be known. He silently asks God to give all of this to his son—the place of belonging, family love, and a desire to serve God. As he turns onto Rue de Muckle, the street where it all happened, he finishes his prayer with: "He's Yours, God. Please help me to be the kind of father that he needs."

As soon as they turn the corner, Matthew starts honking the horn, and JW starts clapping. "We're home! We're home!" JW gleefully cheers.

As they drive down the long driveway, flanked by live oak trees and mature azalea bushes, the backwards house comes into view. It has been freshly painted, and someone has planted flowers.

As he pulls the truck to a stop, it's as if all the front doors on the block open. Everyone comes running towards the truck. As Matthew climbs out of the driver's seat, there is quickly a semi-circle surrounding him, and he finds himself welcomed home in a way that brings tears to his eyes.

Jake, Christina, Michelle, and Mr. and Mrs. Nicholson are all hugging him and laughing.

Annie, on the other hand, sees something suspicious. Although Uncle Matthew is her most favorite man, she walks to the other side of the truck and is very curious about a little dark-haired boy, who is currently struggling to get out of the truck. In all the commotion, no one sees Annie jump up onto the cab, open the door and let the little boy out. She grabs him by the hand and comes around to where all the adults are standing, laughing, and talking.

"Uncle Matthew brought a boy with him, Bridget!" Annie exclaims, clapping and jumping up and down.

All heads turn towards a joyful Annie, holding the hand of a little dark-haired boy with a backward baseball cap and navy-blue eyes.

"Well, well, well ... who do we have here?" Mr. Nicholson asks, crouching down to get a better look at the boy.

"I'm JW," he announces. "He's my daddy," JW matter-of-factly points at Matthew.

"Oh my! What a surprise." Mrs. Nicholson says, followed by Jake, who barely gets out a, "Wha—?" before Annie excitedly asks, "Can he stay, Uncle Matthew? Please, please, please ... we need a boy for baseball."

Before another word is said, everyone turns to watch a very pregnant Michelle crouch down and open her arms. A little boy who has been missing his mom very willingly climbs into the arms of Michelle. He likes the way it feels when Michelle hugs him, kind of like when his mom used to do it, and he thinks, *This nice lady even smells like a mom.* She has shiny dark hair, just like his mom, and JW decides he likes her. Maybe, when he misses his mommy, this lady will hug him.

"I'm Michelle, and you are just the very best surprise I could imagine." She smiles at him and then adds, "I live right there." She points to her house. "Please come and visit me anytime. Your daddy is one of my favorite people in the whole world."

"You gotta baby in your tummy," JW states with a smile.

"Yes, I do, and it's another girl, so we sure need a boy around here," she tells him.

"I like you, Can I play at your house?" JW asks.

"You better, or my Annie will probably have a fit." Michelle teases, putting her arm around Annie. "JW, this is Annie, and this other little crazy is Bridget."

"Do you play baseball?" Annie asks hopefully.

"Oh, yeah. My daddy is a pitcher," he says, as if they might not know.

"Hey, take off your shoes, JW," Annie orders.

The boy sits down and does what he is told, stands up, and looks at Annie for further instructions. She kicks off her flip flops at the same time as Bridget. Then, each of the two girls grab a hand, and the three of them go off running towards the dock.

Three adults, lifelong friends, stand by and watch the next generation fall in love with the beautiful waters of Shem Creek.

JW sits on the edge of the dock with his two new friends on either side, and he dips his feet into the warm waters of Shem Creek for the first time. Before long, they are all wet. JW decides that kicking and splashing in the water is the best thing he's done in a long time.

Meanwhile, Matthew turns to his friends and begins, "After the wedding, Marguerite and I broke up. I was not aware that she was pregnant. I guess she felt like my heart was someplace else and felt the need to move on. She wanted something from me that I didn't have to give. Then ... well, she was on Flight 11. In her will, she made it clear that JW was to be raised on Shem Creek and given this life." Matthew waves his arm around.

"What about her father? Didn't he want his grandson?" Jake questions.

"We solved that little issue at the lawyer's office. I told Mario that he was coming with us. I told him that JW needed his grandpa, and I told him he'd be welcomed into this large family," Matthew explains.

Matthew continues, "He's still in New York tying up the sale of his deli, but he is a very grief-stricken and broken man. He lost his wife when Marguerite was just a little girl, so he has no one else. Honestly, you all are going to love him … he's us with a New York accent."

Later that evening, Matthew was tucking JW into bed for the first time in his new room.

"Daddy?" JW asks. "Am I gonna get another mommy?"

"Only God knows that, but we can never replace your mommy. You know that, right?" Matthew replies.

"I know. It's just that my mommy said that sometimes kids get two mommies and two daddies."

"She did?" Matthew asks curiously. "What else did she say?"

"She said it was really cool," JW says. "She said that she was almost sure I'd get another mommy. She said that I would love her lots too."

"Hmmm, that's interesting. She seemed to have a whole lot figured out," Matthew notes.

"She said that one of my daddy's friend's went to heaven and that my other mommy might be Michelle," JW shares. "Is that why she hugged me? 'Cause I liked it."

"Whoa, Dub. I don't know about all that. What I do know is that your mommy is right; some kids do get two sets of parents. And it's all good. Michelle's mommy went to heaven too, and she moved down here and got all of us as her family. So maybe Michelle understands. What do you think?"

"I think it would be good if she were my mommy," JW answers.

"How about let's settle for her being your friend Annie's mommy, who lives right next door? And you know, you can go over there whenever you want," Matthew tells him.

"Really?" JW asks.

"Oh, yeah. Playing with Annie and Bridget, you'll be all over this block having the time of your lives." Matthew smiles down at him and musses his hair.

"Stay here till I fall asleep?" JW asks.

"Of course, but you better scoot over and make room for me," Matthew says, sprawling under the blankets with JW.

"Daddy?" JW says. "It's okay with me if you get us another mommy. I think sometimes you're lonely."

"Well, that's good to know, Dub," Matthew kisses the boy on the head. "Sweet dreams."

"Daddy?"

"What, buddy?"

"I love you," JW says.

"Oh, Dub, Daddy loves you to the moon and back!" Matthew responds.

"Is that a lot, Daddy?"

"Oh, yeah! It's big time!" Matthew answers.

"Okay, me too," JW mumbles as he closes his eyes.

Matthew encircles JW's little body and inhales the scent of his hair. Part of him is sad that he missed the baby years with this incredible child, but he's made a decision not to dwell on that. At this moment, with this child, Matthew feels a contentment that he has never known. He feels so grateful to Marguerite for this gift. He only wishes he could have told her.

~ CHAPTER 26 ~

A nnie is at school one day when she hears it.

Mrs. Forrester is the best teacher ever. Annie loves her because she is like a grandma. And maybe she knows that Annie's Daddy has gone to heaven, because she always does nice things for Annie. Mrs. Forrester is one of those teachers who really loves kids. All of the children in Annie's kindergarten class hug Mrs. Forrester as they arrive daily and as they leave as well.

Annie is at the clay table during centers time. She is busy working on a pinch pot, squeezing the clay between her thumb and index finger. There is lots of talking and laughter in the class, and Mrs. Forrester doesn't mind if the kids are sometimes loud.

But, even through all the noise, Annie hears: *Look into Mrs. Forrester's eyes.*

"What?" Annie says, looking around at her classmates at the table. "What did you say?"

"I didn't say nothing," a little boy says.

"Me neither," says a little girl in a pink dress.

Annie reaches her hand into her pocket to feel the plastic egg, because she has a scared feeling in her tummy.

Look in Mrs. Forrester's eyes.

She hears it again, but no one else does. It doesn't seem like anyone else is talking to her. *Should she just do it? Go up and look into Mrs. Forrester's eyes? Will her teacher think she's weird?*

Annie gets up from her chair and heads up to the front of the class. She stands in front of Mrs. Forrester's desk, and her teacher looks up. When her teacher makes eye contact with Annie, it's as if somehow information is transmitted without words. Annie knows that something is wrong with Mrs. Forrester, even though she seems fine. Annie feels nervous, and her heart is racing. She feels like she has just run to the back fence in the schoolyard and back. Her cheeks are hot.

"Do you need something, Annie?" Mrs. Forrester asks in her sweet voice.

"Um ... I need to go to the office, my tummy hurts," Annie answers.

"Okay, let me write you a pass, Sweetheart," Mrs. Forrester says.

Annie runs out of the classroom, down the hall, and into the office.

"My tummy hurts! I need to call my grandpa right now," she says in a panic.

"Okay, I know your momma is at work, Sweetie ... just one minute ..." the office lady says.

"I need to talk to him, *please*," Annie says, now crying.

"Are you okay, sweetheart? What's going on?" the office lady asks.

"I just need to talk to my grandpa. He'll come get me, but please let me talk to him now," she says, openly sobbing.

"Okay, Sweetheart, let me get him on the phone," she says, getting out the directory and calling her grandpa's number.

"Mr. Nicholson?" the office lady says into the phone. "This is Mrs. Wilson at Annie's school. She's saying she has a tummy ache and needs to talk to you. She's quite upset about something. I'm going to put her on, okay?" She hands the phone to Annie.

"Grandpa, I'm scared," she cries. "I heard it, but I don't know what to do."

"Tell me what you heard, honey," Grandpa says.

"The voice said, 'Look in Mrs. Forrester's eyes.' That's my teacher," Annie explains, regaining some composure. "So, I went up front and looked in her eyes, and she looked okay. It's just ... I don't know why, but I know something bad is wrong with her. Grandpa, can you help? You believe me, don't you?"

"Yes, yes, I do," Grandpa replies, then adds, "What do you think we need to do?"

"Call Daddy's work friends," Annie says. "Call them right now."

"Okay, I will, and I'll be there in five minutes," Grandpa reassures.

Mr. Nicholson hangs up with Annie and has no doubt that Annie has been given directions by God. He calls down to the station and relays the message to them.

"We are on our way," the captain says, with no questions asked. If this is Joseph's daughter, she may be just like him. The captain smiles to himself as he looks at Joseph's uniform hanging on the wall in remembrance. He grabs his team, turns the sirens on, and heads towards the elementary school.

The captain and his best EMT arrive at about the same moment that Mr. Nicholson is walking up towards the school. "This isn't the first time this has happened to her," Mr. Nicholson shares.

"I trust you, Jeb," the Captain replies.

The three of them enter the school and head towards the office. Annie's phone call has created a bit of a scene in the office, and everyone remembers how this frequently happened to Annie's father. They aren't sure if Annie is making something up, because as of yet, Mrs. Forrester seems just fine.

"Maybe we should bring Mrs. Forrester down to the office?" the captain suggested.

The principal agreed, and she volunteered to get her.

As she turns the corner, heading down the hall towards Mrs. Forrester's class, she is greeted by a group of screaming kindergartners. "Mrs. Forrester fell asleep!" they are yelling, and one little girl is crying.

The principal turns around and runs back to the office.

"She's passed out or something," the principal says. "Hurry!"

The captain and his team run toward the classroom and arrive in a scene of complete chaos. There are little children trying to wake their teacher up. Some are crying; some are screaming.

"Everyone, outside in the hall, please," the principal says with a calm but firm voice.

The EMT team quickly assesses an unconscious Mrs. Forrester. Heart attack.

The team goes to work quickly, with CPR and heart massage and begin mouth to mouth resuscitation.

"We need to get her to the trauma center now," the captain yells.

Within seconds, Mrs. Forrester is loaded onto an ambulance, racing toward the emergency room.

Annie stands in the doorway crying, with all eyes on her.

She feels Grandpa's hand on her shoulder. "Let's get you home, sweetheart," he says. He picks her up like she's still a baby, and walks out the front door of the school.

"Is she dead, Grandpa? Did I not do it right?" she asks. Daddy would have known what to do.

"Sweetheart, you did everything right, and I am so proud of you," Grandpa says. "I'll call down to the hospital when we get home to find out how she is, okay? Can you tell me exactly what happened?"

"I heard a voice, Grandpa," she says, crying again. "It was telling me to look in Mrs. Forrester's eyes, so I went up to her desk. She looked up at me, and when I saw her eyes, it was like a secret message got delivered ... like on TV or something."

"So, what did the secret message make you think?" Grandpa asks, noting how different this was from his son's experiences.

"It was like I knew she was really sick and something bad was going to happen to her," Annie explains. "Really bad. Like I needed to get help. So, I told her my tummy hurt, and I needed to call you."

"You made some really smart choices, Annie, and I'm very proud of you," Grandpa encourages. "I'm so glad you and I had our Dock Walk, and I knew all about this."

"I didn't know what else to do, Grandpa," she says, crying.

"From now on, Annie, if this happens and you don't know what to do, you can always call me," Grandpa tells her. "We will handle it together, okay?"

"Okay, Grandpa." She gives him a little smile and begins to calm down.

******

Michelle is on duty in the ER when Annie's teacher is wheeled in. Michelle has come to love this precious teacher, who has always taken such good care of her daughter, but especially since Joseph's death.

"What's going on here?" she asks the captain.

"Heart attack," he says. "She's conscious. I think we got to her just in time. If we hadn't been at the school, she would not have made it."

"Why were you all at the school?" Michelle asks.

"Mr. Nicholson didn't call you yet?" the captain questions.

"I've been tied up with patients. He may have tried ... What's going on here?" she asks with concern in her voice. "Is Annie okay?"

"She's just like her daddy," the captain shares.

"What do you mean, 'just like her daddy'?" Michelle asks.

"She heard a voice," the captain explains. "She called Mr. Nicholson, and he called us, instead of calling 911, knowing that no one would have come out because when Annie called, the heart attack hadn't happened yet."

"Oh, my God," Michelle says, takes a moment, and then immediately turns to help with Mrs. Forrester.

As soon as Mrs. Forrester is stable and headed to surgery, Michelle goes to the shift supervisor's office, briefly explains what has happened, and tells her she needs to go home.

Michelle arrives home to find Annie and Mr. Nicholson out on the back dock. Annie is on his lap, with her head resting against his chest, and she looks like she has been crying.

"Annie, what happened, Sweetheart?" Michelle asks.

"I'm just like Daddy. That's what happened," Annie cries as she runs into her mother's arms.

"I know, you look just like him, but what does that have to do with today, Sweetie?" she asks.

"I heard a voice. And when I went to Mrs. Forrester's desk and saw her eyes, I knew," Annie shares.

"What did you know, Sweetheart?" Michelle asks in a gentle, loving voice.

"That something was wrong with her, and something bad was gonna happen," Annie explains.

"Is that why you had the school call Grandpa?" Michelle asks.

"Yeah, Momma. I had told Grandpa about the voice I heard once before. And Grandpa already knew 'cause Daddy told him," Annie tells her mother.

"How come nobody told me?" Michelle asks, puzzled.

"I'm sorry, Michelle. I didn't realize no one had told you.

I'd never keep something like that from you," Mr. Jeb chimes in.

"I didn't think so," Michelle says, sounding relieved.

Michelle sits on the dock and pats her lap for Annie to have a seat. "I want you to know how proud of you I am. I want you to know that the more of your daddy I see in you, the more I love you. Your daddy was just about the best person I've ever known, and I loved him to the moon and back. It doesn't surprise me at all that God is working through you too.

"I was there when you were born. I heard Daddy's prayer to God the second you came out. So, Sweetheart, you listen for God, you obey Him, and you do everything He tells you to do. Do you hear me?" Michelle tells her. "If God set you apart to do stuff for Him, I think that I could not be more proud, Annie."

Mr. Nicholson sits there and listens to Michelle breathe life into a scared child. He always knew Michelle was strong, but today she shows him that she is strong in faith too. He had worried that she might fall apart without Joseph, but today she proves she is going to be just fine.

"Momma, you're not mad at me?" Annie questions.

"Of course not. Why would you ask that?" Michelle asks.

"Because Daddy went to heaven because he heard God's voice, and that makes you sad. And I don't want to make you sadder," Annie cries.

"Oh, Sweetheart, I'm sorry you've seen Momma cry so much. But you need to know that sometimes when I'm the saddest because of Daddy, all I have to do is look at you, and I can find a smile again. Did you know that?" Michelle tells her.

"I make you smile?" Annie asks.

"Every single time I look at you!" Michelle answers.

"Now that's one terrific momma and daughter combo, ladies," Grandpa says.

"Hmm, I'm thinking maybe Miss Annie here is going to be a doctor someday," Michelle smiles.

"I love you, AnnieGirl." Michelle kisses the top of Annie's head.

"Love you back, MommaGirl," Annie says, laughing.

A few hours later, Michelle calls down to the emergency room to check on Mrs. Forrester. The attending physician tells her that Mrs. Forrester will be just fine. Because she was treated quickly by the EMT team that was already at the school, they were able to take her to surgery and correct a blocked artery.

Michelle hangs up the phone and takes Annie in her arms. "Sweetheart, you saved her. Mrs. Forrester is going to be just fine because of you," Michelle says.

At some point, Matthew begins to serve Michelle. She no longer has a man around the house to do the stuff that Joseph used to take care of. He cuts her grass, takes care of her car, does odd repair jobs for her, and generally starts to look out for her. Matthew is concerned that she is alone, pregnant, and in charge of a very active five-year-old. A new baby is coming, and Matthew worries about her. She looks tired all the time, and the grief is still etched on her face.

"Uncle Matthew, can I help you?" Annie asks, looking up at him.

"Well, probably not while I'm on the ladder. It's kind of high up here," Matthew is changing a lightbulb in a fixture on Michelle's kitchen ceiling.

"What can I help you with then?" she asks, sounding hurt.

"Well, I was going to do some yard work next and maybe rake out Momma's flower beds. Want to help with that?" he asks.

"Yes, I'm a very big help in the yard, Uncle Matthew!" she happily answers. "I'll go get the stuff from the garage."

Matthew smiles at the sweet girl. He can tell that she is really missing her father and the influence of a man around her. He can also see what a good job Joseph had done with her. She is such a sweet little girl, and she follows Matthew everywhere. It seems to Matthew like she wants to be around him all the time. *It's an honor,* he thinks.

Joseph's daughter has developed a special affection for him, and he really feels blessed. He plans to run with that because, in the absence of a father, a girl can go looking for that in boys. Matthew has made the decision to fill in whenever he can.

Even chilly days in Mount Pleasant find the kids outdoors playing. One afternoon, Bridget brings a soccer ball out to the baseball diamond.

"What's that?" Annie asks, looking at the soccer ball.

"It's a soccer ball, dummy!" Bridget teases.

"I'm not a dummy!" Annie says back, sounding hurt.

"Oh, I know. It's just everybody knows this is a soccer ball," Bridget responds quickly.

"I know *that*. I'm just trying to figure out why you got that out on the baseball diamond," Annie clarifies.

"Daddy says when it's chilly, a softball will sting your hand. So, I thought maybe we can play soccer today," Bridget suggests.

"I'll play with you," JW chimes in.

"Okay, I guess I will too," says Annie.

JW runs to the other end of the yard and places two rocks about ten feet apart, claiming it as the goal. "I'll be goalie first," he offers.

"Cool!" says Bridget, and she starts to strut her stuff. Annie and JW stand by and watch Bridget dribble and handle the soccer ball like a champion.

"Wow, Bridge ... you're already really good at soccer!" JW encourages, smiling.

"Sometimes baseball is too slow for me. I like the speed and the running!" Bridget shares.

"Well, I'm just fine and happy with softball," Annie pouts.

"How about when it's cold, we play soccer, and if it's warm, we play softball?" Bridget suggests.

"I'm good with that," JW agrees.

"Yah, me too," Annie says.

Just then, the kids hear a loud horn honking repeatedly. A car with New York tags is pulling into the driveway.

"That's my grandpa," JW cheers, with a huge smile. He drops his glove and goes running toward the driveway, just as Mario is parking the car and opening his door.

JW jumps into the smiling man's arms and says, "Everybody, this is my grandpa! He's the best, and I bet he won't mind being your grandpa too. Isn't' that right, Grandpa?" It seems like JW has a hundred words coming out all at once.

"Well, that's just about the best deal I ever heard. I now have *three* grandkids!" Mario says. "I'm Grandpa Mario, and you must be the famous Annie I've heard so much about." He holds out his hand in introduction. Annie wants no part of an introduction that's a handshake. She wants the full treatment that JW got.

"Aren't you supposed to hug your grandkids?" she says, opening her arms to Mario. Mario leans down and picks up the precious little girl. Something cuts loose in his grieving heart. She hugs him with a fierceness that warms his heart immediately. She kisses his wrinkled cheek and says, "I *am* Annie, and I'm one of JW's best friends!"

"Well, hello, Little One," he says with a funny accent that Annie instantly likes.

"And this must be the famous Bridget." Mario looks into the blue eyes of a sandy-blonde-haired little girl who is feeling left out.

Mario puts Annie down and picks up Bridget.

"I'm Bridget, and I'm going to marry JW someday," she announces, giggling.

"Well, that is good to know," Mario laughs, again feeling a happiness he didn't think would ever return.

Mario looks up, and the driveway is filled with people. Everyone has come out to meet him. Mario looks around and thinks, *This sure is different from New York, where everyone is so guarded.*

Matthew reaches for Mario and takes him into a bear hug. "Welcome home, Mario! Welcome home." Matthew sweeps his hand out over the landscape.

"It sure smells better here than back in the city," he jokes.

A very pregnant Michelle steps forward and hugs Mario. "I'm so honored to meet you. Matthew has nothing but great things to say about you."

Mario looks at the raven-haired beauty and knows beyond a shadow of a doubt that this is the woman who has always held Matthew's heart, and he understands why. He can see that, in some ways, Michelle is like his Marguerite. Both women are stunning, but they seem to have no idea that they are. Both women exude a warmth that draws people to them. Mario decides in that very first moment of meeting her that he really likes her.

Matthew does the rest of the introductions, including Mr. and Mrs. Nicholson, who seem to be genuinely happy to have another person in their age group join the family.

"Daddy!" JW says. "We decided to make Grandpa everybody's grandpa, okay?"

"I think that's a great idea," Matthew replies.

Mario looks over the heads of the adults, glancing for the first time at the beautiful waters of Shem Creek. He breathes in deeply, notices the baseball diamond, and smiles. He thinks to himself; *this is a magical place for a little boy to grow up.*

He silently thanks Marguerite for knowing this. One glance at JW, and he can tell that this place and these people are good for his soul.

"I'm sorry your little girl went to heaven," Annie says. "My daddy did too."

Mario is so taken aback by the sincerity and concern in the little girl's voice that, for a moment, he is at a loss for words. After he wipes his eyes on the back of his hand, he says to her, "Well, aren't you a special little girl? Grandpa Mario is sorry about your daddy too."

When Mario looks up again, Michelle is wiping her eyes too.

"Mario, how about I show you your room?" Matthew suggests, trying to divert the emotions of the moment.

Matthew heads toward the backwards house that is now the place he calls home. He opens the front door, and once again says, "Welcome home. It's an honor to have you live with us."

He shows Mario around the main level, which has a large eat-in kitchen, a big family room with an old brick fireplace, a very casual dining room, and two bedrooms—one for JW and the master bedroom. He leads the way upstairs. When they reach the top, Matthew turns to Mario and tells him, "The entire upstairs is for you."

Mario looks around at a beautiful space. Matthew has converted the upstairs into a mini-apartment for Mario. There is a large bedroom with a private bath. Attached to the bedroom is a large sitting room with a couch, coffee table, ottoman, and a TV. One full wall is nothing but windows overlooking Shem Creek. In one corner is a built-in bookcase. Displayed on the shelves are multiple framed pictures of Marguerite, JW, and Mario. Matthew had found the photos in Marguerite's shipment of household things from Boston. Mario sees the images and gets fresh tears in his eyes. On the far end of the sitting room is a cased opening into a mini-kitchen with Mario's own coffee pot, microwave, sink, and refrigerator.

"The furniture is all old, Mario," Matthew says apologetically. "I thought you might want to put your own things up here, so it would feel more like home. And I have all of Marguerite's furniture in the garage, so you can furnish this however you want. Jake and I will move everything around to suit you. I just wanted it to be furnished when you first arrived since your shipment won't be here for a week."

Mario looks around in awe and then finally says, "I know why she loved you so much."

"Yep. My mommy loved my daddy!" JW chirps.

Matthew looks over at JW with a surprised look on his face.

He had never heard JW say that.

"It's true," JW says. "Sometimes she would stand in front of your poster on the wall in my room and touch it like she was touching your face."

Matthew smiles at the little boy and then admits, "JW, I loved your mom too."

"I know," JW replies. "Because Mommy said that when two people love each other enough, sometimes there's enough left over to make a whole new person. That's me." He smiles at the two men from ear to ear.

"Your momma was exactly right." Matthew chuckles and ruffles the boy's hair.

"Thank you so much for creating this apartment for me. I was not expecting anything like this. I love it," Mario says.

"You are so welcome. I hope this space will be well lived in, Mario." Matthew gives him a sincere smile. "We are all family here."

Mario smiles to himself, feeling grateful for this man that his daughter had loved and lost. And for reasons he could not explain, he feels like he is home, maybe for the first time in years.

He realizes how lonely it has been since Marguerite had grown up and left home. He realizes how much he missed family life and having a lot of people around, since his wife passed. Things had been far too quiet for the last several years. He has a good feeling about his future. He has a new home and a new chapter in his life. For the first time in months, he feels hopeful.

~ CHAPTER 27 ~

"Let's get outside, this is driving me nuts!" JW says to Bridget.

"It's too cold!" she responds.

"It's not cold. You should see Boston; now that's cold! Come on, this is so boring," he says, referring to the video they are watching.

"Okay, okay. I'll get my coat," she reluctantly agrees.

The two leave Bridget's house, heading towards the dock. Bridget keeps thinking about something her momma had said earlier. Her mom had said to be very kind to JW, because his heart is sad. Bridget thinks she knows what that means, but she isn't sure. Bridget always thinks that if something hurt, someone cried, and JW was not crying all the time.

Her mom said that a boy would be very sad for a long time if his mommy went to heaven. Bridget asked her mom if it was the same for Annie because she lost her daddy. Bridget's mom answered yes, Annie is very sad and misses her daddy every day.

Bridget had a crazy thought that she was scared to say out loud, especially in front of grownups. They made stuff so hard that should be easy. And they always want to talk too much about stuff. The way Bridget saw it, if Annie needed a daddy and JW needed a mommy, then why didn't Uncle Matthew and Aunt Michelle get married? This seemed so simple to her, especially since she always noticed them looking at each other.

Bridget and JW reach the dock and sit down on the edge.

"My daddy and all his friends grew up here. Did you know that?" Bridget asks.

"I know … my mommy told me that," JW replies.

"I never met your mommy. Was she pretty?" Bridget asks.

"Yes, she had hair like Aunt Michelle's, but different eyes," JW tells her. "Sometimes I feel like I forgot her. It seems like so long since I saw her."

"JW, my momma says you have a hurt heart. Is that true?"

"Yeah, I guess so. Sometimes I cry in bed at night. Daddy usually hears me and comes to sleep with me. I feel a little better after that," JW shares.

"I'm sorry your heart hurts. I don't know what that feels like, but I think it's bad," Bridget says. "I know your momma went to heaven, and that's the reason you're here, but I sure am glad you're here." She turns to JW and adds, "'Cause I really like you."

JW turns to look into the light blue eyes of this girl sitting next to him, and he is glad he is here too. He misses his mommy every day, but he also likes his new life here with his daddy. In Boston, he only played with boys, and at the time, he thought girls were gross. But Bridget is different. She doesn't act all stupid like girls usually do, and she wears a baseball cap and can play lots of sports. So, even though she is a girl, it isn't like she is a girl. When she smiles, JW likes the one dimple on her left side. He thinks it makes her look really happy.

Sometimes when he looks at her, he feels funny inside. He's even found himself thinking about her. He thinks he should ask his daddy about this. This seems like something a daddy would understand.

"I like you a whole bunch too," JW replies.

Bridget feels her cheeks get warm, and a smile emerges out of a sad conversation. "I'll be your friend when you're sad, okay?"

"Okay." JW feels a smile on the inside as well.

Matthew spends a Saturday moving all the office furniture out of Joseph's spare room. After the furniture is in the garage, he puts down the paint drop cloth and reaches for the can of pink paint.

He had finally convinced Michelle to let him get the nursery ready for the baby. She tried to say that the crib in the office would be just fine, but Matthew wouldn't hear of it. This baby deserves all the bells and whistles. The two of them went to the hardware store and picked out paint and a wallpaper border, and Matthew was hooked. He had never done girly stuff, and the idea of turning this dark blue room into a girly pink nursery made him smile like he hadn't in weeks.

The room is warm, and Matthew opens the window to catch the breeze off Shem Creek. He has his music playing loudly, and the door is closed, so he takes off his shirt. Matthew is standing on a ladder, with gym shorts on, singing along with the radio. He doesn't hear the door open and doesn't realize that Michelle is standing in the doorway watching him.

Michelle had heard the music from down the hallway and decided to go check on the progress. She opened the door and quickly realized that Matthew hadn't heard her enter. Instead of calling out to him, she stops and takes in the sight.

The room is looking adorable in pink. But what really catches her attention is Matthew. It feels like she is seeing him for the first time. She had never looked at him closely, like a woman would view a man. He had always been her husband's best friend. But as she stands in the doorway with her huge pregnant belly, she feels embarrassed to admit that she really likes what she sees. Matthew's years as a professional athlete have made him someone who takes excellent care of his physical body.

Standing in the doorway, she notices how slim his waist is and how broad his shoulders are. His height only enhances the overall effect.

Matthew turns around and sees Michelle standing in the doorway, and Michelle feels herself blush. Matthew climbs down off the ladder to get more paint and sees her in the doorway.

"Sorry," he says, while leaning over to grab his shirt. "It got warm in here."

"Don't bother putting that back on because of me. I may be the world's most unattractive beached whale female right now, but I still have functioning eyes!" She laughs, not feeling guilty.

Matthew has no idea what to say. He is caught off guard and feels his heart start to race, and an old feeling he had long ago packed away takes root.

"Let's be clear about one thing, Michelle," Matthew says smiling. "There is no set of circumstances that could ever make you unattractive. Even pregnant, you're the most beautiful woman I know."

She places her hands under her belly. "You are too kind to this beached whale here, and you're probably lying, but I'll take it. I've missed having someone tell me I'm attractive," she says, with a melancholy look.

"I'm happy to tell you that you're beautiful anytime you need to hear it," he says softly. "Come here." Matthew holds out his arms to Michelle.

She climbs into his embrace and genuinely likes how it feels, especially when she inhales the scent of this man. She feels her heart speed up. It feels strange, but not wrong, to have her face resting against the bare chest of another man. She tightens her arms around his waist.

"Thank you for everything you've done for me," she whispers. "I don't think I would have survived this time if you hadn't returned." She backed away, turned, and walked out of the room with a smile on her face.

Matthew stood still for a moment, trying to figure out what just happened. Had she just admitted that she thought he was attractive? He was sure he'd seen something different in her eyes. She had looked at him like a woman looks at a man, not like a friend does.

Something shakes loose inside Matthew's heart. Feelings he had shut off and packed away long ago quickly reemerge. He feels sixteen again, only this time, she hadn't looked that way at Joseph. She had looked at him.

Matthew feels confused. *Is this wrong? Should I keep my distance? Lord, what do I do? And he knows.* The answer he hears in his heart: *Continue to serve her and take care of her. The rest, if there is more, will come.*

Matthew finishes painting the room and assembles the crib. He brings the dresser/changing table combo in and sets it up. He goes to the laundry room and collects the stacks of new baby clothes that Michelle has pre-washed in preparation for the new arrival. There is only one thing missing, and that will arrive tomorrow. Matthew smiles; this is such a charming room for a little baby girl to come home to.

The next day, Matthew's baby gift to Michelle arrives. It's a glider chair to rock her baby in. He had shopped for it after they had picked the paint color. The fabric on the chair has little pink hearts. He sets it up while Michelle is out running errands.

******

Mario has taken to cooking for everyone on the block. He is quick to remind Matthew that he owned and operated a deli for thirty years, and he can't just stop cooking all together. Matthew happily agrees to Mario's Italian meals. Every afternoon, when he finds Mario in the kitchen, he always has a separate dish cooking for Michelle.

After a few weeks of this, JW comes in one afternoon with a question. "Daddy, if Aunt Michelle and Annie are eating the same dinner as us, how come they don't eat here?"

"That's a good question," Mario says, "and one I've asked myself as well. How about I set the table for all of us tonight and you go over and get them?"

Mario smiles to himself. There is nothing he'd like to see more than these two people together. Sure, this woman had cost his Marguerite her love, but Mario understands that neither of them did it on purpose. Matthew had been good to Marguerite. Mario hopes that one day soon, Michelle and Matthew will be husband and wife. These kids need the two of them together. Mario smiles, knowing Marguerite would love this.

"Daddy, can I go get them?" JW asks, jumping up and down with excitement.

"Sure, Dub," Matthew says. "Ask Aunt Michelle politely. Tell her if she doesn't feel like it, Mario will still bring dinner over."

Michelle hears the knock on the door and assumes that Mario is bringing her another delicious meal. When she answers and sees JW, she says, "What a great surprise! How are you doing, JW?"

JW smiles. "I'm here to invite you over to eat with us, but Daddy said if you don't wanna come, we will still bring dinner."

He speaks so fast, without stopping, that Michelle starts laughing.

"Come on, Annie!" she calls out. "A good-looking guy is at the door, inviting us to an Italian dinner!"

"Over at JW's?" Annie asks, bouncing into the room, looking surprised and happy. Dinners are too lonely now that Daddy is in heaven, and she misses the funny stories at dinner.

"Sure, Sweetie, that sound good?" Michelle asks.

"You bet!" Annie grabs JW's hand and heads out.

Michelle hadn't realized how quiet dinners had become until she steps into Matthew's home. Growing up in New York, she had always eaten alone in front of the TV. But once she arrived in South Carolina, dinners were terrific. Someone was always joining them, or they were at the Nicholson's. Dinner was loud and entertaining, and she loved it.

After everyone greets each other, they all sit down, with Matthew at the head of the table and Michelle sitting next to him. He grabs her hand, bows his head, and prays, "Father God, thank you for this meal and the loving hands who prepared it. Thank you, Father, for family and friends, and thank you so much for Annie and Michelle being here with us tonight. We love you. Amen."

Mario looks around the table and smiles. Just one more seat needs to be added, and that seat would be filled with a highchair for a while. Somehow, Mario thinks this all feels just right. This family, his new family, should sit around this table, overlooking Shem Creek, and enjoy dinner every night.

This is the first night of many, and Michelle starts to feel very spoiled.

~ CHAPTER 28 ~

"Momma, can I go now?" Bridget calls out to Christina. "I wanna take my suitcase to Grandpa's house." Even though Bridget was not an official grandchild of Mr. Nicholson's, he loved her the same. All the kids called him and Kathleen Grandpa and Grandma.

"Sure, Sweetheart, do you have your toothbrush and jammies?" Christina asks.

"Yes, Momma. I'm so excited!" Bridget says clapping. Jake had surprised Christina and booked the two of them a four-day weekend on Hilton Head Island. Kathleen and Jeb were more than willing to have Bridget stay with them. Bridget loves the bunk beds in the guest room, and most of the time, if Bridget is there, Annie gets to sleep over too. It is so much fun.

"I need to stop in and say bye to Michelle, okay? I'll meet you at Grandpa's in a second," Christina tells her.

Christina heads down the block to Michelle's.

"Hey, there, you all ready for your weekend getaway?" Michelle asks, seeming genuinely excited for Christina.

"Yeah, I am. Jake's had a hard few months. I think some romance time might do him good," Christina shares. "I got the

357

cutest new bikini. Check this out!" she says, opening a bag and pulling out what looks like strings to Michelle.

"Well, I guess you're gonna cause that poor man to have a heart attack," Michelle teases, looking at the adorable bikini that will look fabulous on her gorgeous friend.

"I hope so," Christina smiles. "Nothing like a romantic weekend to restore the soul."

"I envy you," Michelle admits, with a sad look in her eyes. "I miss that."

"I can only imagine. You going to be okay with me going?" Christina asks, pointing to Michelle's stomach.

"Of course! I'm still three weeks out, and Kathleen and Jeb are here," Michelle reassures.

"And ... Matthew?" Christina smirks at her friend.

"And Matthew," Michelle says, grinning right back.

"So, if you need me, here's the number where we will be. Call me anytime if you need me."

"You are the best friend a girl could ask for, Christina, but get lost!" Michelle laughs, then adds, "And remind that guy why he married you."

"Will do," Christina says, really looking forward to a weekend alone with Jake. He is still hurting so much about Joseph, and

Christina senses that something is bothering him. She hopes to be able to have some good talk time while they are there.

"I think I'll send Annie over for the night. She loves the sleepovers with Bridget," Michelle decides.

"Poor Kathleen. She's got to keep up with those two." "Oh, she loves it. Have a wonderful weekend. Love you."

"Love you back, girl." Christina does a little wave over her shoulder as she walks to meet Jake at the end of the driveway, and they head out.

Christina is a bit nervous leaving Michelle so close to her delivery time, but as Jake pointed out, she is going to need lots of help after the baby comes. No one will want to leave town then. The time to go is now, and Christina agrees. Besides, Annie came two weeks late.

As they are about to turn out of the block, Jake turns to Christina and says, "I need to do one more thing. Sorry."

"Ok, what?" Christina asks.

"I need to tell Mr. Nicholson something," Jake says, pulling back into the driveway. "Give me ten minutes, okay? I'll be right back."

Jake rings the Nicholson's doorbell, and Mr. Nicholson answers.

"Got a second?" Jake asks.

"Sure, son. What's up?" Mr. Nicholson responds and steps outside onto the front porch.

"I've needed to tell you something, and I think it's time," Jake begins. "And this is a conversation between you and me now, and at the right moment, for others."

"Okay, sounds serious. Everything okay?" Mr. Nicholson asks.

"Yes, it is. But this might be hard for you to hear, so I wanted to say this without anyone else around," Jake shares.

"Okay if I pray then?"

"Sure, go ahead. Please."

Mr. Nicholson puts an arm around Jake, bows his head, and prays, "Father, I sense that Jake is troubled. Will you please be with him and calm his spirit. And Lord, whatever he has to say, please be with us at this moment. Amen."

Jake wipes his eyes with the back of his hand and then says, "Okay ... Where to start ... Um, okay, so, we have spoken of Joseph dying in my arms." Jake pauses and takes a deep breath then exhales. "What you don't know is that Joseph had some pretty profound final words, and if it's okay, I'd like to share those words with you now."

"Okay, son, I'd be honored if you'd share those words with me. A man's final words are some of the most important he will speak in his life," Mr. Nicholson says.

Jakes tells him, "So, at first, he said, 'Tell Matthew ... this is why ...' Then, he coughed and was really struggling to breathe, and then he said, 'Tell Matthew this is why he's always loved her.'"

Mr. Nicholson stands there, tears stinging the corners of his eyes, and he smiles. A million memories are flashing through his mind, the most significant being the conversation he had with Matthew just after Joseph's wedding. He remembers consoling a broken Matthew, who could never understand why he had this love for Michelle. He remembered how even Joseph knew and understood this love. Truth be told, Mr. Nicholson had often wondered why God had placed this burden of love on Matthew's heart if he was never going to be able to love Michelle. And when Matthew had confided in him that he had been praying for years for the feelings to be removed and yet they remained, Mr. Nicholson had wondered about that.

Could this possibly mean that God never removed those feelings because Matthew will one day love Michelle as *his* wife? Mr. Nicholson grins and says, "This is just like our Joseph, isn't it? That he would give words to release his lifelong friend to marry Michelle. It is so beautiful how Joseph understood Matthew had loved her for years, because God's perfect plan included Joseph's early departure."

"Are you okay?" Jake asks.

"I'm more than okay. That was like Joseph's final blessing. Honestly, I think Matthew will need to hear this before he moves forward with Michelle. Incidentally, I give this union my full blessing. But I'm curious, why are you telling me now?" Mr. Nicholson asks.

"Because Christina and I are leaving town, and it feels like part of a plan. You and Kathleen are taking the kids. So, if

Michelle goes into labor, Matthew will be the one at her bedside during labor and delivery. If the two of them marry someday, this will be Matthew's child, and a man should be present at the birth of his child," Jake explains.

"I never thought about that. You're so right. So, I guess I'm going to need to keep Kathleen away," Mr. Nicholson says. "She has a bit of a cold anyway, so she is probably not the best person to have near a newborn."

"Yes, somehow this seems like the right thing to do. I've watched Matthew serve her and take care of her with no agenda of his own. I've watched him step up to the plate with Annie. He drives Annie to school. He's become such a faithful man of God. And everything he's done has been out of a desire to serve. So, I'm asking God to lead them to one another," Jake shares.

"You know, after Joseph's wedding, Matthew really took my words to heart. I told him to focus all his love on God, and I told him to chase God and God alone. In doing so, it has led him right back to the woman he's always loved. If it's possible to love my own son more, at this moment, I believe that I do," Mr. Nicholson says, choking up. "Only a strong man of God would be able to see this. Only a strong man could accept that another man would marry the wife he adores. I am so grateful for the peace I know this must have brought to Joseph in his final minutes of life. Thank you for telling me."

Jake hugs Mr. Nicholson. "I love you, Mr. Nicholson, like a father. Don't ever forget that."

"And I love you too, son," Mr. Nicholson says.

Jake says goodbye and gets back in the car to a face a very perplexed Christina.

"What was that all about?" she asks.

"I'll tell you later, that okay?" Jake says.

"Sure, Love, that's fine," she replies, knowing something significant had just been announced.

******

Michelle seems really tired, so the following afternoon, Matthew decides to get the kids outdoors so she can rest.

"Alright, everyone ... out to the baseball diamond," Matthew orders

"Yay! Baseball!" JW squeals with delight.

"Don't forget your gloves," Matthew reminds.

Michelle mouths a silent thank you to Matthew, holding her lower back. She had told him earlier that her back was hurting.

No wonder, Matthew thought, *her small frame seems to be struggling under the weight of the baby.*

Outside, Matthew was busy setting up today's game.

"Annie, you cover the outfield," Matthew says. "You're our best glove!"

Annie smiles and takes off to stand near his house.

"JW, you got some heat for me?" he asks his son.

"Sure, Daddy. You know I love to pitch," JW says, and Matthew winks at him.

"Bridget, you are first up to bat. And I'll cover the infield," Matthew coaches.

The first pitch zips by Bridget. She swings and misses. For the second pitch, she is paying closer attention and connects with it. It sails down the first base line, and she takes off running. Matthew pretends to stumble so that she makes a base hit.

He had taught them all how to chatter, so they are making a lot of noise.

Matthew turns to look in the outfield. He smiles to himself. Annie is out there, talking to herself. She is such a whimsical, happy child.

He turns back to the infield, just in time to see her come running by.

"Hurry, Uncle Matthew. Hurry," she yells as she runs past him towards her back door. "It's Momma."

"JW, go get your grandpa. Bridget, go get Grandpa Nicholson. Hurry, " Matthew tells them with confidence, understanding that once again Annie had heard something. She wasn't talking to herself in the outfield; she had heard a voice.

Matthew goes running for the back door. He arrives in the kitchen to find Annie staring at her mom, who was on the floor with blood coming out of a cut on her forehead.

"I'm fine ..." she says, unconvincingly. "I just slipped on an ice cube on the floor and fell."

Matthew grabs a paper towel and leans down and gently wipes her forehead.

"It's not deep. Let me just give this some pressure, and it should stop bleeding. Does your head hurt?" he asks.

"Honestly, no, it's fine," she replies. "I'm just a little embarrassed that I'm going to need some help getting up off the floor." She attempts a chuckle. "Help me get to the couch, please, will you?" she asks Matthew.

Matthew leans down, as if to pick her up, and he stops.

"We aren't going to be putting you on the couch right now, okay? Looks like we are going to the hospital to have a baby!" Matthew tells her. "Your water has broken."

"No, no, no. It's too early. Christina isn't here. Oh, no! She thought this would happen," Michelle says, sounding like she is panicking. Anxiety washes over her. She keeps thinking of racing down Highway 17 with Joseph driving, heading towards the hospital to have Annie. They were so in love, and they were about to have their first child. She had packed a suitcase in advance, and they'd done childbirth classes. Joseph had been as ready for that moment as she was.

Today is so very different. This moment serves as a harsh reminder that no one is going to be there to share this moment with her. Even if Christina makes it back in time, it would be a distant second to sharing the moment with the baby's father.

Michelle starts crying. For the thousandth time since Joseph died, she whispers, "Why, God?"

Matthew notices the tears streaming down her face. "Don't worry. You're in good hands," he reassures.

Matthew feels so sad for Michelle. Childbirth is supposed to be one of life's most joyous moments, but somehow, this time, it is going to be another tragic reminder that Joseph had died.

Matthew looks up, and Mr. Nicholson walks in, followed by Mario.

"It's a good day," Mario smiles. "A perfect day to have a baby." "Want to help me?" Matthew asks, looking at Mr. Nicholson. The two men each take an arm and help Michelle to her feet.

"I'll take her to the hospital now," Matthew says. "And, Annie, how about you stay by the phone at Grandpa's house? When it's time for you to hold your sister, Grandma and Grandpa will bring you, okay? It will probably take a while, and you might get bored waiting at the hospital."

"Okay," she agrees, then adds, "Will you call me and tell me how it is?"

"Of course, Sweetie," Matthew replies.

"Come here. Give me a hug," Michelle says to Annie. "Are you ready to be a sister?"

"Yes! I'm gonna be the best big sister ever!" Annie cheers.

They all help Michelle into Matthew's car. Everyone stands in the driveway, waving and feeling sad and joyful at the same time. Joseph's child is about to be born—his final gift to all of them.

As they are driving to the hospital, Matthew digs out his cell phone and calls Jake. It goes to voicemail. "Hey, Jake. It's Matthew. The baby is on the way. Try to get here. Michelle needs Christina."

After leaving the message, Matthew starts to get really nervous. No one else is with them. Who will be with Michelle in the delivery room if Christina doesn't make it in time?

Matthew prays, "Your will, Father. If you need me to do this, I will, but I'm scared."

The pains are starting, and Matthew has no idea what to do. Every few minutes, Michelle tenses up and does her best not to scream. They pull up to the emergency room entrance, and Matthew puts the car in park, runs around to the other side of the car, and helps a moaning Michelle to her feet.

As they turn around, they happily discover a nurse with a wheelchair, waiting to take Michelle in. The nurse starts firing away questions to Michelle, and Matthew feels very out of his element. He doesn't know the birthing language and has not gone through childbirth classes. Christina had taken the childbirth classes with her. Matthew begins to feel panicky. Christina had prepared for this moment, not him.

He pulls out his cell phone and tries Jake again.

Again, it goes to voicemail.

Matthew starts to really panic. What if he is the only person there? What should he do? Then he remembers this process usually takes a long time, and hopefully, Christina will be back by then. He needs this process to take several hours, giving plenty of time for Christina to arrive. Jake and Christina are only about an hour and a half away. So the sooner Jake hears the message, the faster they will be here.

******

Jake and Christina never hear the cell phone ring, because they are out on a boat, gazing at the beautiful shoreline of Hilton Head Island, watching dolphins jump. They are leisurely sipping red wine, having a glorious romantic evening, watching the sunset.

They put Michelle in a birthing room. It seems like just a few minutes before a doctor comes in. Matthew guesses they are trying to figure out if she is officially in labor yet. Matthew thinks that it's rather obvious as Michelle let out another scream.

"Michelle, I'm Dr. Reid. I'm going to need to examine you to see how dilated you are," he informs.

Matthew excuses himself and closes the door behind him. He is really anxious now. His heart is racing, and his stomach feels like he is on a roller coaster. Initially, when he decided to handle all of this, it was under the belief that Jake and Christina would be here. He had imagined labor and delivery going on in one room, and he and Jake in another, preferably the waiting room. He had imagined Christina in with Michelle, helping her and encouraging her, and generally doing what a best friend would do.

What he is now having trouble imagining is the intimate nature of such an event. Will Michelle be embarrassed? Will he? Does he really want to see Michelle like this so soon? Will his presence be a complete invasion of privacy? He feels like it would be. This was his best friend's wife, not his.

"Sir, could you come back in?" Dr. Reid requests.

"Uh ... sure ..." Matthew says nervously.

"She's about six centimeters dilated; it appears she's been in labor for a while. I'm guessing this back pain she's been having was back labor pains," the doctor tells Matthew.

"So how much time does she have till the baby comes?" Matthew asks, trying to keep his nerves under control.

"It usually speeds up pretty quickly at this point," Dr. Reid explains. "I'm thinking the baby will be here in the next couple of hours."

Matthew went from panic to outright fear. That means if Jake isn't on the way, they aren't going to make it in time.

Oh, Lord, what am I supposed to do? Matthew prays, and then he wonders what Michelle thinks. Should he ask her? Would this all be too weird of a conversation to have?

He fishes his phone out of his pocket and tries Jake one last time. It goes straight to voicemail again.

He decides to call Mr. Nicholson.

"What's the good word?" Mr. Nicholson asks.

"I'm kind of panicked, because I can't reach Jake and Christina. They are supposed to be here," Matthew blurts into the phone. "What am I supposed to do? The doctor says the baby will be here ... *within a couple of hours.*"

"Calm down, Matthew. Maybe this is God's plan. Maybe you're supposed to be there when this child is born. You'll be okay," Mr. Nicholson encourages, with a smile in his voice.

"What do you mean 'I'll be okay'? Michelle needs someone else in the delivery room with her!" Matthew says a little too loudly. "Can you send Kathleen?"

"Honestly, no. She has a cold, and that's not good for the baby or anyone at the hospital," Mr. Nicholson tells him.

"Just try and calm down and pray. God will work something out ... and keep us all posted!" Mr. Nicholson says cheerfully before hanging up the phone.

Matthew stares at the phone in his hand for a few blinks. He takes a deep breath, and then goes back inside Michelle's room. He can tell she's scared.

"They are getting ready to give me an epidural," she tells him. "I need it baddddd... ohhh, God!" she scream-prays as a more extended contraction wracks her body.

Matthew has no idea what to do. He is unprepared for this moment, and she is in so much pain.

Thankfully, the medical team arrives quickly. Once again, Matthew leaves the room. He begins to pace down the hall.

He finds the men's room, leans over the sink, and splashes water on his face. He looks up at his reflection. There is a truth he needs to face here; something he knows for sure. Matthew has put aside feelings for Michelle in order to survive, but they have always been there, right under the surface. They were safe and controlled under the surface, and he'd figured out how to manage his life without her.

If he goes back in that room and walks with her through the most challenging moment of her life, he will not be able to stay at a distance. He will feel her vulnerability and want to be the one to rescue her. In unleashing his heart to rescue her, the uncontrolled love will return and, with it, all the hurt. The ache he'd felt for years will return, and he's not sure he'll be able to take it this time.

Filled with fear and anxiety, Matthew calls out to God. *Lord, I can't do this. My heart, God ... it cannot take the torture of unleashing my feelings again. I cannot do this again, God. I'm so scared that I'll never recover from it this time. The only way I can do this, Lord, is if you let me love her. Give her to me to love and cherish, and I promise you I will care for her always. But, Lord, please don't send me in there only to have my heart broken. Please, God. I know you hear us when we cry out to you, so please have mercy on me and show me what to do.*

As Matthew stands in the men's room, a warmth settles over him, and something that feels like a warm blanket encircles him. At that moment, his fears are calmed, and a gentle peace washes over him.

Matthew returns to the hall outside Michelle's room, and a few minutes later, they are finished with the epidural. Matthew re-enters her room, and Michelle seems to be calming down with the pain now under control.

"I'm sorry you have to be here ..." Michelle says, with sadness. "This isn't your job. I'm not your problem."

At that moment, Matthew knows she needs to see an attitude adjustment in him. He needs to do whatever he can to put this scared woman he loves at ease. *Is it time, Lord? Is it time to be completely emotionally vulnerable with the woman I love?*

A few minutes later, the doctor returns to examine Michelle again, and Matthew steps out into the hallway once more.

There is a flurry of activity in the hallway as carts and trays are moved into Michelle's room. Matthew hesitates. He doesn't want to be in the way, but wants to be there for her when she needs him.

A nurse leans out the door and says, "Dad, we're ready to push. The baby is coming!"

"I'm not the dad, but can you ask her if she needs me?" Matthew asks.

The nurse disappears for just a second to ask Michelle, and she returns furiously nodding. "Sir, she needs you right now!" the nurse tells him.

Matthew enters the room and sits in the chair next to her. At that moment, it's as if everything around them, all the nurses and trays and carts and monitors, slows down, just for them to have a few seconds to connect.

Michelle turns to him with the saddest eyes he has ever seen and says, "Please, don't leave me. I'm so scared, and I feel so alone at this moment. Don't leave me, Matthew, please, please ... *please!*" Her voice is on the edge of hysteria.

"But ... um ... I don't want you to feel embarrassed, Michelle."

"Matthew, I can't bring a child into the world without someone I love with me. I know you love me, and I would never take advantage of that. I can't do this without you. You're supposed to be here, Matthew. Don't you see?" she cries. "Please, do this for Joseph."

"I don't know what I'm supposed to do, Michelle," Matthew says, honestly tearing up and feeling a well of emotion explode within him.

"Just start by holding my hand," she says, reaching out her hand to him.

He sees how vulnerable she is, and it is as if at that moment he remembers how very much he has always loved this woman. All his life, he has wanted to be the man who cares for her, and now here she is asking him to take care of her.

"How about we pray?" he suggests, taking her hand, with what he hoped was a comforting smile on his face. "Let's invite God to be with us here. This is a sacred moment for us."

"Yes ... yes, please ..." she agrees, sounding calmer, looking into his eyes, and feeling protected.

"Father God, thank you for the gift of life. Father, I give this time of labor and delivery to you, and I ask you to bring Michelle and Joseph's child into this world healthy and safe. Please be with Michelle and give her peace during delivery. In your name, we pray. Amen." It is only after he stops praying that he realizes both of them are crying, united in a moment that causes each of them to remember the man they both deeply loved and missed.

Matthew thinks, *Joseph, I'm taking your place here, but only because you're gone. You know me, Joseph. I would never take what was yours. I've always honored that, even when it hurt. Joseph, she needs me now; she can't do this alone. Please, God, show me this is okay. God, if I watch this child be born, there will be no turning back for my heart. God, please? Show me.*

"Is the father on the way?" one of the nurses asks.

"No, he isn't," Matthew answers. "We wish he were, but he's gone to heaven."

"I'm so sorry ..." the nurse replies, pauses just a brief moment, then says, "Okay, then ... are we ready to push?"

Michelle nods, and the nurse gives her instructions on how to push. Matthew listens closely.

"How can I help her?" he asks the nurse.

"Just stay up close to her there. When she pushes, she will sit up a bit almost like doing a sit up. Just help support her back," she instructs.

"Are you ready for this, Michelle?" Matthew says to her gently.

"With you here, I am," she replies, giving him a small smile. "Let's have a baby!"

"Okay, let's try a push," the nurse says, and Michelle pushes. "And, yep, you're a great pusher," the nurse encourages Michelle.

"We're ready to go here, Dr. Reid," the nurse says. She then moves out of the way, and the doctor takes her place.

On the fourth push, the doctor announces, "There we go ... I see the head! One more now ..."

On Michelle's fifth push, the head is delivered.

"You're doing great, Michelle," Matthew whispers in her ear. "You're not alone. You can do this, strong momma. One more ..."

On the seventh push, the baby arrives.

Matthew doesn't fully understand why at that moment his instincts take over. He reaches out his arms, and the doctor places the baby girl in *his* arms and not Michelle's. God shows Matthew precisely what he needs to see.

With all eyes in the room on him, Matthew kneels down, holds the baby up, and prays, just like he knew Joseph would have done. "Father, thank you for this gift of life. She is a perfect gift from you. Father, at this moment, I give her to you for your service. Father, love her and guide her all the days of her life.

Please send angels to protect her always. May she know you early in her life, and, Father, teach her how to serve people. Amen."

As Michelle watches this magical moment, she realizes that this birth moment has gone from being something of fear and sorrow to something of profound joy. With a smile on her face and tears streaming down her cheeks, Michelle falls fully in love with Matthew West.

Matthew turns to Michelle and hands her Joseph's child. "She's perfect," he says, openly crying. "Absolutely perfect."

Michelle takes the baby into her arms and sees a mirror image of herself, a shock of dark hair, royal blue eyes, and a small dimple on her chin.

"Her name is Annalisa," Michelle announces. "Annalisa Joy."

Matthew leans down and kisses Michelle on the forehead. "You did great, Michelle, Joseph would be so proud."

As Matthew looks down at the woman he loves, holding her newborn baby, something is confirmed deep in his heart: Annalisa Joy is his daughter too.

"Thank you, Matthew, for being here. Thank you for sharing this moment. Thank you for always taking care of me and loving me. I know it's been hard," Michelle says with tears streaming down her face.

"I've waited a lifetime to be able to take care of you, Babe. I'm honored," he replies. "She looks just like her beautiful mother."

Michelle hears something different in his voice, an intimacy, and it feels good. And he's never called her "Babe" before. She hopes he'll always call her that, in the soft tone he is using.

"I think it's time to call Annie." Michelle beams. "She needs to meet her sister."

"Would you like me to go get her? I was thinking it would be important to make her feel special, maybe not arriving with everyone else. What do you think?" Matthew asks.

"That's a great idea. I'll call her and let her know you're coming. Thank you."

When Matthew leaves, Michelle lets go of the final round of tears that are inevitable. She will always miss Joseph, but she has a strange feeling of protection come over her, as she contemplates what just happened. *Did You set Matthew apart for me? Did he suffer for years, loving me, because You had this plan, God? Is it possible to love Joseph with all my heart, but love Matthew too? Is it okay, God?*

Michelle knows in her heart that she has never before witnessed a love like Matthew has demonstrated over the years. As she holds her new baby girl, she realizes how sad she's been for months, because her child would come into the world without a father. But today, she is given a glimpse of what God has always had in store for her. She will have hope and a future.

For the first time, in a very long time, Michelle feels completely happy.

Annie comes slowly into Michelle's room, holding Matthew's hand. Michelle loves the sight of it. As she looks at them, she is reminded of how much time and energy Matthew has invested in Annie. She is reminded of how much Annie loves her Uncle Matthew and has always seemed to set him apart. The pieces of the puzzle feel like they are coming into place.

The first thing Annie notices is Momma's sparkle. Her momma is sparkling brighter than Annie has ever seen. The second thing she notices is that Uncle Matthew is sparkling too. Annie likes this a whole lot.

Matthew hoists Annie up onto her momma's bed. Annie looks down at the tiny, dark-haired, little baby and says, "Hi, my little sister! It's me, your big sister!"

"Isn't she beautiful?" Momma asks.

"She looks like you, Momma. Pretty, just like you, Momma," Annie says, hugging her momma close.

"What's her name?" Annie asks, touching the top of her sister's fuzzy little head. "Ooooh, she's so soft!"

Michelle laughs, then tells Annie, "Her name is Annalisa Joy Nicholson."

"Can we just call her Joy, Momma?" Annie suggests.

It had never occurred to Michelle to call her by her middle name, but after the day she had just experienced, she thinks, *Yes, this child represents joy, pure joy.*

"I think that's a wonderful idea, Annie," Michelle replies. "How about I let you tell everyone all about her name? Could you be the big sister helper and do that for me?"

"Yes, Momma. I can help you all the time."

Just then, Matthew's cell phone rings. "It's Jake," Matthew tells Michelle.

Michelle's smile gets even brighter. She winks as she teases, "Well, tell them to hurry up already. They're missing all the cool stuff."

Matthew chuckles as he answers the phone: "Hey, man ... she's already here," Matthew says in a dreamy tone. "And she's perfect. Eight pounds, two ounces. Mommy and baby are doing great."

"Were you with her?" Jake asks.

"I was, and it was an honor."

"Congratulations, Matthew! We're on our way, and we'll see you in a couple of hours," Jake tells him.

When Jake hangs up, he turns to Christina and says, "Matthew says she's here already, and all is well with their souls."

Christina gives a little happy clap. "Oh, praise Jesus!"

Jake takes a deep breath. "I think it's time I share with you what I was talking with Mr. Nicholson just before we left. I haven't yet shared with Matthew, so please don't tell Michelle anything just yet."

"Ok. You have my word," Christina says.

"When I pulled Joseph out of the water that night, he had a few last words. He was barely able to speak, but through a breathless whisper he said, 'Tell Matthew this is why he always loved her.'"

Christina's eyes well up with tears. "Oh, wow ... so Joseph gave Matthew his blessing to love Michelle? And he did this with his last words? That is amazing."

"Yes, it's like pieces of a puzzle fit together for Joseph finally. I could tell it gave him peace, like he knew Matthew would take care of Michelle."

"When are you going to tell him?" Christina asks.

"Well, he's just become a father for a second time. He just doesn't know it yet." Jake chuckles. "So, as soon as we get home. Something spectacular has just happened with the birth of a beautiful baby girl. God's great love is shining down at this very moment. All along, He's always had a plan and purpose for them ... for all of us."

"You are so right, Jake," Christina says, excitedly. "We are living in a divine moment for sure." She ponders that for a moment in silence. Then she looks at him with a twinkle in her eye. "And I cannot wait to get my hands on that baby. Drive faster," she teases.

******

As they arrive at the hospital and step into the elevator, Christina has the quick flash of a thought: *There is going to be a very special wedding soon. God, you are so great.*

When Jake and Christina step out of the elevator and onto the maternity floor, the lobby is filled with this glorious family that God has put together.

Kathleen approaches them quickly and says, "Let Annie tell you the story."

"Okay. Annie, what's the news?" Christina asks.

"I have a baby sister. She looks exactly like my mommy, which means she's pretty. And her name is Annalisa Joy ... but I decided to call her Joy." Annie blurts out. "Momma says Joy is the perfect name, because today God gave her joy."

"Oh, what a beautiful name you picked, Annie. May I go in and see her?" Christina asks. "Will you show me where to go?"

"Sure!" Annie says, grabbing Christina's hand and walking her down the little hallway.

When Christina steps into the room, it's as if the world has tilted on its axis. Matthew is sitting next to Michelle, while she holds their newborn baby.

When they both look up, Christina can see it. Annie leans over and whispers into Christina's ear, "They both have sparkle."

"I think you're right about that, Annie. You are a very smart little girl," Christina says with a wink.

"Come over here, Christina. I'll get out of your way," Matthew says. "I'll go say hi to Jake."

Matthew gets up and leaves the room, and Annie gets up and follows him, grabbing his hand.

"Oh, can I hold this little bundle of perfection?" Christina asks.

"Of course." Michelle hands her Joy, and Christina's heart overflows.

After a few moments, she wipes the tears from her eyes. "You did it, Momma. I'm so proud of you. She is just beautiful, Michelle. She's like a mini-you!"

Christina continues, "Okay, friend, I have to ask ..." She points to the door that Matthew and Annie had just walked out of. "What is going on there? Hmm?" Christina asks, with a big smile on her face.

Michelle blushes a bit, then answers, "He's my hero. He's the man who has done everything for me and never asks for anything in return. The man who has always loved me. The man who loved my husband so much that he never betrayed him. Matthew is such a loyal and selfless man."

"I think it's time to love him back, Michelle," Christina discerns.

"I already do," Michelle says in a whisper. "And I'm pretty sure he knows."

"Oh, this is just wonderful! I'm just so happy!"

"Oh! I almost forgot to make proper introductions here," Michelle jokes. "Joy, this is your crazy Aunt Christina. Aunt Christina, meet our Joy."

Christina looks again at Joy in her arms and truly feels joy to her core. This baby is God's healing tool. This baby girl, conceived in love, has been sent to bring them all back from grief.

With tears streaming down her face, Christina says, "God, you are so very good. Thank you."

******

Matthew joins everyone in the lobby, still holding Annie's hand. Jake walks up to Matthew and gives him a bro hug. After they both chuckle and wipe away tears of shared happiness, Jake says, "Hey, let's go for a ride, okay?"

"Um ... Sure ... What's up?" Matthew asks.

"I just need to talk to you about something," Jake says.

"Okay, yeah, let's do it. " Matthew turns and asks, "Mr. Nicholson, can you please keep an eye on Annie and JW for a little while?"

"Sure thing," Mr. Nicholson answers, noticing how Matthew takes responsibility for Annie too.

Matthew and Jake head out the door and get into Jake's truck. Without any words, Jake drives out of downtown Charleston, down Coleman Boulevard, takes a left on Simmons Street, and then makes a quick right onto Rue de Muckle.

Jake parks the truck, gets out and heads for the dock, their dock—the place where everything happens. It's where they all met and became friends, and the place where two men fell in love with the same woman. It's the place of their lives.

Matthew and Jake walk through the yard, down the path, and onto the dock, and they sit at the dock's edge.

"I need to share something with you—something that's really been heavy on my heart," Jake begins. "I've wanted to tell you for a while, but I knew that I needed to find just the right time for these words. I think tonight is that night. I also think that it's very fitting that you hear them on this dock, our dock, overlooking Shem Creek. This is where our foursome began."

"Okay ... Is something wrong? I'm starting to get a little nervous here," Matthew responds, trying to get a feel or a clue for what's about to come.

"Oh, no, man, nothing's wrong. I didn't mean to worry you. It's actually the exact opposite; it's something really right, Matthew. I need to share with you some details about Joseph's last moments," Jake explains.

"Oh, wow. Okay ... I'm listening," Matthew says, leaning forward slightly.

Jake continues, "When I pulled Joseph out of the water, I thought he was already dead. His face was white, and his lips were blue. He had lost way too much blood to still be alive. Plus, he had rescued four people in those rough waters. I guess what I'm trying to say is that I think he held on so he could say these words."

"What words, Jake?"

Jake takes a deep breath and then goes on: "Matthew, a man's last words are what he holds most dear, what is most important to him. You might think that he would have chosen to say something like, 'Take care of Annie and Michelle,' or something like that. But that's not what he said."

Matthew furrows his brow and really tries to understand what his friend is telling him. "Okay, so, what did he say?"

Jake answers, "He said, 'Tell Matthew this is why ...' Then, he gasped for breath a couple of times, coughed, and said his final words: 'Tell Matthew this is why he's always loved her'."

"Whoa ... I don't know what to ..." Matthew's sentence trails off while his mind reels. The tears begin to flow.

"Do you understand the magnitude of his words, Matthew?"

"I think so," Matthew says, just above a whisper. His shoulders are shaking.

"He's telling you, Matthew, that the reason you could never love another was that God set you apart for Michelle for such a time as this. He's telling you it's okay to love her. In fact, I believe the reason he said this was because he knew that if you loved Michelle, Annie would be cared for too. His last words were both a blessing and an assignment," Jake explains.

Matthew stares at Shem Creek. Slowly, his mind puts all the pieces together, and he begins to sob. "Oh, God, I never knew that the only way I'd get to love her was if Joseph was gone. Lord, I miss him so much!"

Jake pulls his friend into a hug and says, "Be happy, brother. You've been given the blessing to marry the woman you've loved all your life. Can you even comprehend the love that man had for you?"

Matthew shakes his head, trying to clear his thoughts. He wipes the tears off his face, and says, "Is it okay to be happy about it, Jake? What about Mr. and Mrs. Nicholson?" Matthew asks, seeming concerned.

"I shared this with him already. I felt that as Joseph's father, he should hear it first." Jake says. "His response was joy, complete joy."

"Wow. That man never ceases to amaze me," Matthew says, wiping his eyes.

"True, true," Jakes replies, then adds, teasingly, "What are you still sitting here for, brother? Go on and chase your dream, Matthew. You've waited a lifetime for her!" Jake pats him on the back and then gives him a playful shove.

"Thanks, Jake," Matthew says, sincerely.

"Oh, and congratulations! You became a father again tonight!"

"I have to tell you, Jake, God confirmed this in the delivery room. She really is my daughter," Matthew shares, beaming.

~ CHAPTER 29 ~

Michelle is in such a deep sleep that when she awakes, she forgets where she is.

It is daylight and she is home in her own bed, but things are foggy. She feels like she has slept forever, which is a rarity with a newborn.

She turns over and checks the clock on the nightstand: 9:00 a.m. She had completed Joy's last feeding at about 10:00 p.m., and the baby should have awakened three or four more times since then.

Michelle jumps out of bed and quickly checks the bassinet at her bedside. It's empty. Kathleen is probably downstairs with the baby. She walks to her bedroom door, opens it, and leans out to see who is there. She doesn't hear anyone.

She turns, grabs her bathrobe, and heads down the hall to check Annie's room. She peeks in, and shockingly, Annie is still asleep at 9:00 on a Saturday morning. *Poor thing*, Michelle thinks, *the baby has been keeping her awake.*

Michelle makes her way down the stairs to the family room. She can't believe her eyes. The reason she has slept peacefully for nearly twelve hours straight is Matthew. She finds him stretched out on her couch, sound asleep, with baby Joy resting on his chest. Several empty bottles are on the coffee table in front of him.

Michelle tiptoes into the hallway and opens the closet, where she stores her camera bag. She quickly takes out her camera and shoots multiple pictures of this beautiful sight. She wants to remember seeing Matthew this way. She looks around at the family room, and everything is tidy and picked up. She heads for the kitchen to start the coffee and notices all the bottles cleaned and drying on a clean dish towel on the counter. The kitchen is clean, no dishes in the sink, and the dishwasher has been run. She walks through the kitchen into the laundry room, knowing a pile of dirty clothes is waiting for her, but everything is clean and folded, ready to be put away.

Michelle can't believe it. For the first time in the nearly two weeks since Joy came home from the hospital, she feels rested. And, of course, she has Matthew to thank for that. His kindness humbles her.

"Good morning, beautiful," she hears from behind her.

"Good morning back at you. Look at you!" she says, absolutely loving the site of this tiny baby resting on his broad shoulders. She has a fleeting thought of how unfair it is that he looks gorgeous just rolling out of bed. She feels like a troll in her old bathrobe, messy hair, and new mom dark circles under her eyes.

"How about some of that coffee?" He smiles at the thought of waking up in the same house as Michelle. He has to laugh; this sure is backwards.

She hands him a cup, remembering how he likes it, and simply smiles up at him.

"I feel like a new woman. I haven't slept for that many hours straight since I can't remember when. You are such a doll. Thank you," she says.

"Well, I am kind of in love with this little bundle here, so don't give me too much credit." He pats Joy gently on her bottom.

Just then, Joy gives out a cry, letting everyone within earshot know that she is ready for breakfast. "Let me grab a bottle and feed her. Why don't you head upstairs and get a shower? Take your time, I know a long shower is a luxury when you have a newborn. If Annie wakes up, we will make some pancakes," he tells her.

"I guess I must look like a train wreck," she says, suddenly feeling very self-conscious, knowing he must think she needs to fix herself up. Truth be told, she feels bloated and unattractive. The baby weight is coming off just fine, but a man like Matthew can have any gorgeous woman he wants. He is breathtakingly handsome, kind, wealthy, and has the physique of an athlete. Not for the first time, Michelle tries to imagine what he saw in her. She feels like a nursing cow.

"No, you do *not* look like a train wreck. In fact, you are one of those rare women who is a natural beauty. To me, you are always gorgeous. I didn't mean to offend you about the shower. I just know with two kids needing your attention all day long it's probably hard to work in a shower. And this Little Lovebug here does *not* like to be put down.

"You looked tired yesterday when I stopped by, so I wanted you to get some quality sleep last night. And as long as I'm here, just get the shower done.

"It was kind of funny last night when I snuck into your house. I didn't hear any baby noises downstairs, so I headed upstairs. I guess Annie hadn't fallen asleep, and she came out in the hall. She said, 'Momma's really tired.' I said, 'Shh.' I tiptoed into your room and took Little Joy. Annie didn't want to be left out, so she followed me downstairs. After I fed Joy, we all fell asleep on the couch. I have to admit, I sure do love your girls."

"Matthew, thank you for all you do for me," Michelle says. "You have no idea how much you mean to me."

The sweet moment is interrupted by a delighted Annie, who woke up to discover her favorite Uncle Matthew is in her kitchen.

"Uncle Matthew's here," she says, doing a little clap.

Matthew leans down to give her a little good morning hug and says, "Momma is going to head up and shower. I'm going to feed the little princess here, and then you and I are going to fire up some pancakes. How does that sound, Miss Annie?" He winks and smiles.

"I'm a good pancake maker!" Annie announces.

"While I feed Joy, how about you run over to my house and see if JW wants some pancakes with us?" Matthew suggests.

She doesn't even answer Matthew, nor does she even think about changing out of her PJs, before racing next door. Annie finds JW watching Saturday morning cartoons with Mario. She doesn't even knock; she just opens the door and calls out orders: "Everybody, come over to our house! Uncle Matthew and I are making pancakes!"

"That's awesome. I'm hungry!" JW says, turning to his grandpa. "Can we go?"

Mario thinks about it for a second. This has the makings of their first Saturday morning breakfast as a family. Mario thinks that maybe he should just stay home and have some cornflakes. Perhaps today was a good day for the five of them to do a little dress rehearsal for their future.

"You know, I got up early today, JW, and already ate," Mario said. "Why don't you go with Annie, and I'll see you a little later?"

"Ok, Grandpa," JW walks over and kisses his grandpa on the top of his head. "Let's go, Annie!"

******

An hour later, Michelle comes downstairs wearing a pale blue sundress. Her hair is washed, and it is air drying, hanging down her back. Her legs are shaved, and she has put a touch of makeup on. She has to admit, the shower worked wonders. She actually feels human again.

When she walks into the kitchen, Matthew whistles. "Now that's one pretty little momma right there, people!" he says, making Annie and JW laugh.

Michelle looks around her kitchen and the family around her. This moment feels right, like it is a sweet movie trailer of a film yet to come out. Not for the first time this morning, she quietly thanks God for this man.

Matthew starts doing the night shift every other night so Michelle can get rest. He sneaks into her house, head upstairs, take baby Joy out of her bassinet, and bring her downstairs.

Matthew learns to love the nighttime with Joy when no one else is awake. He loves her fiercely. Sometimes, he finds himself staring at her in wonder, feeling such a protective love over her. And sometimes she looks up at him, and his heart melts. She is an excellent little baby, who really only cries when she's hungry. With a bottle, a little bit of rocking, and a clean diaper, she almost always goes right back to sleep.

******

A few weeks later, Michelle turns over and checks the clock: 4:00 a.m. She looks over at the empty space in the bed next to her. She misses a man to snuggle with at night. She misses knowing there is another human within arm's reach. She misses the feel of a man's arms around her, spooning at night.

As the moonlight is peeking through her window, Michelle has a startling thought. As her thoughts and daydreams play out, Matthew is the man she imagines in the bed next to her; Matthew is the man spooning her; Matthew is the man snuggling with her and whispering in her ear. For the first time, she imagines what it might be like to share his bed as a man and a woman do. Michelle smiles to herself and realizes Matthew is probably downstairs with Joy. At that moment, she feels a deep need to see Matthew. She wants to be near him.

Michelle tiptoes downstairs. The moonlight is bouncing off Shem Creek, providing just enough light through the windows to see Matthew sleeping on the floor next to Joy's Moses basket. He is stretched out on an old quilt, resting on his side, facing the Moses basket, with his arm protectively on its edge.

Michelle grabs a blanket from the couch, and she gets down on the floor, lying down right behind him. She covers them both with the blanket. She puts her arms around him and nuzzles up close to his neck, spooning him. She inhales the scent of him, pulls herself close to his sleeping body, and feels the warmth of him.

With her face right up next to the back of his head, in a barely audible voice, she whispers, "I love you, Matthew West."

Matthew thinks he is dreaming. There are so many nights as he climbs into his empty king-sized bed that he imagines what it would feel like to sleep next to Michelle, to hold her, to whisper in her ear ...

Matthew turns over to face Michelle, and it's as if she knew exactly how he'd imagined this moment, because she instinctively turns over as well. Matthew is behind her now, pulling her close to him. With her back against his chest, they fit together perfectly. He encircles her with his strong arms. He nuzzles his face into the back of her hair and side of her neck. He inhales the scent of her, wanting every part of her touching him.

Although he had intended to tell her he loves her, the words never come out. Instead, as he holds her close, twenty years of longing begin to spill out. As Matthew West holds the woman he loves in this intimate way for the first time, he shakes with sobs as a lifetime of love can finally be unleashed.

Michelle tightens her grip on the strong hands holding her. She can feel his body shake with emotion. His tears are spilling out on her cheeks, mingling with her own. He tightens his hold on her, finally closing all the distance between them. The only words she hears from Matthew on the night she professes her love for him are the words, "Thank you, God," that he whispers softly as he cries.

For the first time, Matthew West falls peacefully asleep, holding the love of his life.

~ CHAPTER 30 ~

"I'd like this dock to be larger than the one next door," Matthew instructs the contractor, pointing at the Nicholson's dock. "I'm looking for a walkway with safety rails, but a much larger area under a gazebo. I'd like for the space under the gazebo to be special, with a custom woodworking design on the underside."

"Are you going to want a boat lift?" the contractor asks.

"Yes, and I'd like some sort of platform for the kids to dive off of, a slide, and a ladder to climb out of the creek," Matthew says. "I'd like a grill here, and a built-in bench right here."

"Okay, and electricity?" the contractor asked.

"Yes, of course," Matthew says.

"Okay, let me get working on the drawings and the estimate," the contractor tells him. "Anything else?"

"Yes, I almost forgot ... I'd like a flagpole," Matthew adds.

"That will look great. I'll get these to you by the end of the week. And if everything is to your liking, I can get my team started next week."

"That sounds really good," Matthew says. "And one more thing, I need you to install swings from these two trees."

"This sounds like a place that some kids are going to love!"

"I grew up here, and there's no better place on earth." Matthew smiles.

******

Michelle knocks on Christina's door. She has a whole lot to tell her.

"Well, well," Christina says, smiling. "Isn't somebody I know just glowing this morning. Get in here. Spill it!"

"That obvious?" Michelle asks.

"Yeah, it's bad." Christina laughs. "Where are the girls?" "Where do you think?" Michelle asks.

"With Mr. Baseball?" Christina responds.

"Yeah, he sure loves those two." Michelle says.

"Coffee?"

"Always."

They sit down at the kitchen table, gazing out over Shem Creek. The sky is Carolina blue with white puffy clouds dotting the horizon. The day is warm already, and the humidity is threatening to arrive early for the year.

Across the table, the best friends are okay with a quiet moment. Years of a close friendship between the two have proven that sometimes just being in the same room is okay.

Christina waits patiently for Michelle's words.

"I was asleep last night. I awoke, and it was 4:00 a.m. I was thinking to myself how very much I miss the closeness of a shared bed, not necessarily the sexual part, but that cozy feeling that your partner is close by. You know?" Michelle shares. "And honestly, as I was daydreaming about my empty bed, I realized there was a face on the person in the daydream. It was Matthew."

She looks at Christina for a minute, then continues, "So I figured he was downstairs, and I just wanted to see him asleep on my couch, holding Joy. For some reason, I just wanted to be close to him. When I got downstairs, he was asleep on a quilt on my floor on his side with one hand resting on Joy's Moses basket."

"What a sweet sight, Michelle," Christina says. "He is so good to Joy."

"Well, I didn't exactly leave it alone, Christina. Without any thought, I grabbed a blanket, got down on the floor behind him, put my arms around him, and snuggled him close," Michelle admits.

"Oh ... oh my, you kind of stepped over a line neither of you has crossed yet," Christina observes. "How'd that go?"

"Well, I pulled myself close to him, and you know how you inhale the scent of a man? You know that moment you realize it's his scent and only his?" Michelle asks.

"Yeah, I know exactly what you mean," Christina says dreamily.

"I needed to experience his scent. It mixes with your feelings and just becomes that person. Does that sound nuts?" Michelle asks.

"No, not at all. But it's a very intimate thing, probably not something to take casually. You know?"

"I don't know how it happened, but once I inhaled the scent of him, I took it into my soul, I had to say it. I had to tell him, Christina. So, I just whispered into the back of his neck, 'I love you.'"

"Oh ... wow. Hmm ..." Christina chooses her next words carefully. "It's just ... this is a huge deal, Michelle. Are you sure? Because, you can't not be sure, you know?

"I know, but I've been feeling this way for a while. I'm sure. I've known I needed to be all in if I was going to allow Matthew in," Michelle explains. "Does that make sense?'

"Yes, perfect sense," Christina replies "How did he react?"

"Well, he turned around to face me, and I just knew I needed to turn around too. So, with my back to him, he took me in his arms, and he pulled me close."

"Oh my! What a moment!" Christina says. "What did he say?"

"Oh, Christina, he couldn't say a word. He pulled me even closer, and we fit perfectly together. And I felt his body shake as he cried into my hair and neck," Michelle says, and tears roll down her face. "He cried so hard, Christina, and I only now have a small glimpse of what loving me all his life has cost him."

"He is one incredible man, Michelle. A real Boaz." Christina smiles.

Smiling back, Michelle tells her, "I knew that I needed to break the ice with us, like open the door, you know what I mean?"

"Then what happened? Did he tell you he loves you too?"

"No, he wasn't able to; he was so overcome with emotion. All he could get out was, 'Thank you, God.' Do you think all this is okay?" Michelle asks. "Do you think Mr. Jeb will be okay with it?"

"You know, I think that both he and Kathleen would like nothing more than to see you both happy," Christina expresses. "And I am so happy for you both."

"I don't deserve the two men God has given me," Michelle says, with tears in her eyes again.

"None of us deserve all these blessings, Michelle. Our job is to be grateful for them," Christina says. "Were you aware of the rough time Matthew went through?"

"Probably not. I mean it's not exactly what your husband would talk to you about when it concerns someone that loves his wife," Michelle says.

Christina nods, then shares, "He really crashed at your wedding. Apparently, he didn't even realize he was crying as you were walking down the aisle. Marguerite saw it and pretty much took the hint. But Mr. Nicholson had a long talk with him on the dock after you all left. He was absolutely inconsolable, and he kept asking God to take the feelings for you out of his heart. He begged God for years to help him stop loving you. Mr. Nicholson told him to get right with God again. He told him to give all that love to God."

"Oh, my God, I never meant to hurt him in that way. I never knew it was this awful for him," Michelle cries. "Do you think it's possible to try somehow to make it up to him?"

"I think you're doing it already."

Michelle didn't think she could love Matthew more, until Christina shared his struggle. Michelle marvels at how God had set a plan in motion that included her Joseph's early departure. Michelle decides that her job is to love Matthew tenderly. He deserves it. She will do her very best to make up for the years of heartache he experienced.

******

"Wanna go fishing, JW?" Matthew asks "Yeah! Where are we going?" JW replies.

"Let's take a boat over to Caper's Island. Remember, the Dinosaur Boneyard?" Matthew says, referring to the trees that storms had washed up on the shore. The trees are buried in crazy angles and have turned to driftwood creations. The locals call it the Dinosaur Boneyard.

"Yay! Just you and me?" JW asks. "Yeah, unless you want to ask Annie?" "Yes! Let's ask Annie! Can I go get her?"

"Sure, but let's make sure it's okay with her momma, okay?"

Both guys leave their house and walk next door. Of course Annie wants to go. And Michelle thinks it is a great idea. Matthew had bought a fishing boat a month ago, and he loves taking the kids out.

"Let's get some snacks and drinks to bring with us. Don't forget your sunscreen too. And both of you two need your life jackets," Matthew instructs, sounding like a father.

They leave in the boat and head up Shem Creek, under Coleman Boulevard, passing by the parked shrimp boats and heading out to the open sea, going towards Isle of Palms. They need to catch the Intercoastal Waterway. One of Matthew's favorite fishing spots is just past the Isle of Palms. He decides to anchor the boat there and do some fishing.

The kids are all set with lines in the water and a crab cage dangling over the edge.

"Hey, I've got a question and a secret," Matthew says. "I love secrets!" Annie responds. "Is it a surprise?" "How about the question first?" Matthew asks. "Okay!" JW agrees.

"What would you all think about all of us becoming a family, you two, me, Joy, and Aunt Michelle?" Matthew asks.

"And Grandpa Mario?" JW asks. "Absolutely, Grandpa Mario, too."

"Like I'd get you as a new daddy?" Annie asks with serious eyes.

"And like I'd get a new mommy?" JW chimes it.

"I don't really like saying a new mommy or a new daddy. I like saying another one," Matthew explains, tenderly. "Because both of you had them already. But, Annie, I'd like to know if you have room for another daddy, because if you do, I'd like to be your daddy."

Annie drops her rod into the water, turns around, and jumps into Matthew's arms. "Would I be able to call you Daddy?" she asks honestly.

"Only if you want to. But there is nothing I'd like more than for people to think I was your daddy. I'd be so proud." Matthew holds her back to look in her eyes for a moment, and then he hugs her.

"Would Aunt Michelle be my 'nother mommy?" JW asks.

"Yeah, if that's okay with you," Matthew says. "She sure loves you, JW."

"I totally know that already," JW says proudly. "She hugs me like my mommy used to."

"Do you love *me*?" Annie asks curiously.

"Oh, Sweet Annie, I surely do," Matthew answers, "lots and lots and lots."

"We're gonna be a family! We're gonna be a family!" Annie sings out.

"Okay, now the secret," Matthew says. "Can you two kiddos keep a secret?"

"Yes!" Annie says. "Tell me!"

"Me too!" JW answers.

"Okay, if you absolutely promise you won't tell. Annie, I bought your momma a ring, and I'd like to ask her to marry me. Would that be okay with you both?" Matthew asks them.

"Will Momma get to be a princess?" Annie asks.

"Oh, I sure hope so," Matthew says. "So, I'm going to ask you to keep this secret, because I need to make it an extraordinary moment. Can you promise me that you will not tell her?"

"I promise!" Annie agrees.

"Me too!" JW answers.

"You know what this means?" Matthew asks, looking at Annie.

"What, Uncle Matthew?" Annie replied.

"It means that JW will be your brother," Matthew explains.

"Awesome. I never had a brother!" Annie says clapping.

"And I never had a sister!" JW bobs up and down in excitement.

"This is the best day ever!" Annie exclaims. "How long do I have to wait to call you Daddy?"

"Until Mommy says yes!" Matthew replies. "And I couldn't ask your mommy to marry me unless it was okay with the both of you first."

"Oh, Uncle Matthew, I love you." Annie places a sticky kiss on his cheek. And she reaches into her front pocket and pulls out the egg-like plastic container that holds the gold ring with the big pink stone. The container has never been opened.

"If you're gonna be my daddy, we can open it now," she says, presenting her most prized possession to Matthew.

Matthew takes the plastic container into his hands and tries to comprehend the magnitude of this moment for her.

"Annie, I am so honored to open this with you," he says. "Shall we?"

Annie takes Matthew's hand and covers it with hers. Matthew twists off the lid. Annie reaches in and pulls out the gold ring with the pink stone. She puts it on her finger, holds out her hand, and smiles.

"I think it's kinda big to wear. Don't you think, Uncle Matthew?" she asks.

"I have a great idea, Annie," Matthew tells her. "You know that sparkly crystal candelabra Momma has?"

"Yes," Annie answers.

"Why don't we attach this beautiful ring to it and put it out with all your momma's pretty things. That way anyone who comes to visit will see it. And it's so pretty, they will ask about it. And you can tell them all about your first daddy," Matthew suggests.

"That's a great idea," Anne says.

******

When they arrive home a few hours later, Annie goes running into the house.

"Momma, Momma! Look how pretty it is! I always knew it would be!" She holds out the gold ring with the big pink stone.

Michelle covers her mouth and backs up. "Sweetie, you opened it!"

"I did, and Uncle Matthew helped me," Annie tells her. "He told me that since it's so big, we can attach it to this." She runs into the dining room and points at the sparkly candelabra. "And people who come see it will ask about it, and I can tell them all about my first daddy who went to heaven."

Michelle looks across the room at Matthew, and a million unspoken words are shared. She understands the profound significance of this moment for Annie. She is ready, ready for a new chapter.

"I think that ring is going to be the perfect addition to our dining room, Annie!" Michelle says. "Do you know how much I love you?"

"Yes, Momma, you tell me every day!" Annie answers, then adds, "But you can say it again."

Michelle takes her daughter in her arms and kisses the top of her head.

"I love you to the moon and back," she says with a very full heart.

******

When Matthew's new dock is completed, he decides it's time for a summer party. He is going to go all out. Great food, great music, and sparklers for the kids. The gazebo at the edge of the water is stunning with a high cathedral ceiling with beams crossing. Matthew had speakers installed outside so dock parties could include music. Everyone on the block is coming, even Matthew's parents.

The evening is perfect. The hot temperatures of earlier in the day subside, and a breeze picks up, just as Matthew throws the first steaks on the grill. He wouldn't let anyone cook except him and Mario. It is a feast. Everyone is sipping wine, playing with kids, and laughing on the dock, overlooking Shem Creek. Matthew thinks the music gives it a festive feel.

"I really like the dock." Mr. Nicholson tells Matthew.

"Thanks. I think the contractor did a great job," Matthew replies. "I just pray that this dock brings us all the same kind of happy memories your dock did."

"I think that it probably will." Mr. Nicholson smiles, looking over at Michelle.

JW is off to the side convincing Bridget and Annie that they should be dancing. JW loves to rock out. Matthew is glad he has loaded five CDs into the CD changer so that he could play continuous music. Matthew smiles. Life was good.

"Excuse me, please!" JW hollers, while jumping up on one of the benches. Everyone turns and quiets down, and he says, "A moment of silence, please … The Dogs are on!"

And the little boy starts singing out at the top of his lungs to the music coming out of the CD.

He sings out the words to the song *Joy to the World.*

Matthew reaches out for Michelle and Jake. Standing in the middle of the two, arms around them both, and missing their best friend Joseph, they sing out like they are sixteen again, driving down Coleman Boulevard in an old red truck, heading to Sullivan's Island.

Mr. and Mrs. Nicholson stare silently, drinking in the memory of a time years ago when their beloved Joseph was sixteen. Then, they start singing too, and Mario and JW know all the words as well. When the song is over, it gets really quiet. Everyone is looking at each other wondering the same thing.

"JW, who taught you to say that before this song comes on?" Matthew says curiously.

"My mommy did. She says that one of her friends that she loved a whole lot sang this with his friends just like this. And she said she thought the song deserved a moment of silence too, so every time we heard it in her car, Mommy pretended she was the announcer just like I did," JW said.

"Thank you, Dub. Do you want to know something?" Matthew asked.

"What, Daddy?" JW says, wondering why his daddy has tears in his eyes.

"That friend of mommy's was me. And the guy who used to stop us all and say 'a moment of silence, please' was Annie's daddy Joseph. And you just made us all so happy reminding us of some of the most carefree days of our lives. Thank you, JW." Matthew says, hugging his son. And he silently thanked Marguerite.

The kids were getting tired, and the party was coming to an end. The sunset was spectacular, with pinks and golds fading into the horizon.

"Hey, why don't you let me take the kids home with me tonight," Christina suggests with a wink.

"Really? That sounds like heaven!" Michelle replies with a smile. "You really don't mind?"

"I know my way around your house and know exactly where everything is for Joy. I'm going to kidnap her and take Annie too. We will have an all-girl sleepover!" Christina says enthusiastically.

Meanwhile, Kathleen and Jeb are busy getting things cleaned up.

Matthew is out on the dock alone, hands on the rails, facing the water. He is taking in the last moments of the spectacular sunset. He whispers a quiet thank you to God.

"You know what I'd really like?" a voice says from behind him.

Matthew turns around to see Michelle standing at the other end of the dock, bathed in moonlight.

"What would you really like?" Matthew asks back playfully.

"I would like for you to kiss me. Not on the forehead. Not on my cheek. But really, really kiss me, like you love me, Matthew West," she tells him.

Matthew's breath catches in his chest, but manages to get out the words, "Oh, yeah? You sure?"

Michelle nods.

Matthew quickly closes the distance between them and then stops. He gathers her hands in his, holds them up to his lips, and kisses them.

He cups her face in his hands and says, "Let me just look at you for a second."

He stares down into the blue eyes that have captivated him for more than two decades. Slowly, ever so slowly, he bends down, barely touches his lips to hers, pulls back, and looks at her again, dropping his hands. He brings his left hand up and strokes her cheek. He then brings the right one back and pulls her face to his.

"With all my heart," he answers, and he kisses her with a force and a passion that leaves both of them breathless and dreaming of what is ahead for them.

They both stepped back, seeing each other in a whole new light.

Matthew thought to himself, *It was worth the wait. All of it.* Because he knew God had saved him for Michelle. All the days he prayed to be delivered from this love made sense to him now. Not only had God given this beautiful woman to him, her touch and her kiss exceeded his wildest dreams.

He pulled her towards him, and she rested her face on his chest.

He was finally home.

And as he looked up, he realized that like every other significant event of his life, he was standing on a dock overlooking the beautiful waters of Shem Creek. Only this time, the girl belonged to him.

~ CHAPTER 31 ~

Everyone is at the beach because Matthew has called a family beach day.

"Can I ride on your back, Uncle Matthew?" Annie asks, looking at the waves crashing on the shore of Sullivan's Island.

"Sure, hold on tight, though," Matthew replies.

"Hey, me too!" JW calls out, and Matthew scoops him up onto his back too.

Mr. Nicholson is lounging in a chair beside the water, and he looks up and marvels at what God has done in this man. He has gone from a heartbroken, selfish professional athlete, seeking his own agenda, to this godly man, who is clearly ready to take on a wife and her children. He has a fleeting thought that somehow Joseph knew this, had full confidence in this man to do this job. His last words had made that clear. Mr. Nicholson prays a silent thank you to God.

"Okay, break time, kids!" Matthew says. "How about we work on a sandcastle?"

"Uncle Matthew, will I get a ride?" Bridget asks.

"You bet, Sweetie," Matthew replies. "But right now, this old man is tired."

Matthew looks up at Michelle. She is a marvel. She is wearing a blue bikini, standing beside the ocean, with her mane of dark hair hanging out of a Yankees hat. The sharp angles of the teen body have been replaced with the curves of a mother.

Matthew thinks it looks gorgeous on her.

"Hey, Mister, aren't you Matthew West?" a little boy asks.

"Yes, I am. And who are you?" Matthew says to the child with a smile. Most of the time when they were out somewhere, people recognized him. Matthew is always kind and gracious.

"Will you sign my hat?" the little boy requests.

"Absolutely!" Matthew says, taking the hat and the pen the little boy gives him.

His privacy that day is now lost. Other kids are approaching him, and some of the adults on the beach want to say hi. Matthew keeps smiling, but he has another agenda up his sleeve.

"Aww, someone is going to get family pictures!" Michelle says as she watches a photographer get his equipment ready.

All the family is staying and moving in behind her. She is standing at the edge, where the waves kiss her feet. In a flurry of excitement, Matthew is down on one knee with a tiny box in his hand.

"Michelle Nicholson, I have loved you since I was thirteen years old. You are the most beautiful, loving, wonderful woman in the world. Would you please do me the honor of being my wife?" He opens the box containing a stunning vintage Art Deco ring with a three-carat diamond in the middle.

She is crying. "Oh, Matthew, I would be honored to be Mrs. West!" She cups his face in her hands and kisses him.

The first cheer is from Annie, and it is a loud and beautiful sight to see as she jumps up and down yelling out, "Daddy! Daddy!"

"Hey, Annie, would you come over here, please?" Matthew asks.

Annie walks over to Matthew and stands in front of him, looking up at this tall man she loves. Matthew pulls another box out of his pocket and gets down on one knee again.

"Annie, my sweet Annie," he says with tears in his eyes. He opens the tiny box. "Will you be my daughter?" As he opens the box, everyone gasps. Inside the box is a small ring. It is a gold ring with two small pink stones.

"This is for you, Little One. With two stones, for your two daddies," he shares, gently placing the ring on her little finger.

"So, you're marrying me too?" she asks.

"I am marrying you too," he says back in confirmation.

"My daddy!" she says with her arms around the man who would take over the job left vacant by his best friend.

Mr. Nicholson is speechless, as is everyone watching.

"And I'm getting two sisters!" JW cheers.

"Yes, you are!" Michelle takes the dark-haired boy into her arms.

"You're gonna be my new momma," he says.

"I really like the sound of that, JW." She wipes her eyes

The entire scene is all perfectly captured by the photographer, who thinks it is really cool that *the* Matthew West called him to do his engagement pictures. He thinks maybe the local sports commentator might like to see it too. When they look back on this fabulous picture, with the ocean in the background, and everyone cheering, they all see it with a touch of sadness too. The only reason this incredible celebration is taking place is because someone they all love had given his life for them.

******

Early the following morning, Matthew's cell phone rings.

"Son, what's this I'm reading in the morning paper?" Marshall James says, laughing.

"Sir, I don't know what you're talking about," Matthew jokes back.

414

"Well, son, I'm staring at a picture of a gorgeous woman on the beach in a Yankees hat, and a certain former Yankees pitcher is on one knee. The headline says: 'Yankees' Matthew West Proposes to His First Fan'," Marshall says.

"Yes, sir, I did propose to her, and thankfully, she said yes," Matthew tells him.

"This is her, isn't it?" Marshall asks.

"It is, sir. She's the most incredible woman I've ever met," Matthew replies back.

"I guess so, since she captured your heart decades ago," he says back.

"Marshall?" Matthew asks. "Would you do me the honor of standing with me in my wedding party?"

"Oh, son, I wouldn't miss it for the world," Marshall says. "Congratulations! And Matthew, enjoy the ride!" he adds, smiling at his wife of thirty years.

~ CHAPTER 32 ~

Her hands are shaking. She is alive with emotions she can't seem to put in check. She feels honored and humbled.

Ever since the day at the beach when Matthew asked her to be his wife, she has been filled with an immense sense of gratitude. Michelle decides early on that she wants to make this day incredible for Matthew. She wants to be able to present herself to him, giving all of herself. She wants this man to have everything that twenty years of loving someone unselfishly should bring.

Her dress is the palest of blush pink, with a portrait neckline exposing her shoulders. The bodice is fitted, tightly encircling her tiny waist, with a beaded lace overlay highlighting her curves. All of it is giving way to a full skirt of soft, airy chiffon fabric that moves with the breezes off the water. Her hair is down, natural, and cascading in waves being lifted off her bare shoulders by the gentlest of breezes. She is wearing a crown of tiny roses in her hair. On her feet are a stunning pair of sexy high-heeled silver sandals. Her legs are bare and golden tan. The slit down one side exposes one long leg as she walks. She is carrying a bouquet of fresh flowers she cut from the yard earlier that morning.

Michelle feels like a mature woman walking towards her man. She feels the power of the intense attraction. Michelle wants Matthew to see this moment in his mind's eye for years to come. She wants him to anticipate the thrill of what is to come fully.

As Matthew sees his bride walking down his dock with their home in the background, he is overcome with emotion. Briefly glancing to his right, he remembers a day, years ago, when he watched this woman walk towards another man. Matthew remembers the grief he felt in his heart. He turns back towards the gorgeous woman walking towards him, and once again, he's on the dock seeing her again for the first time.

This time, she is walking towards him, with her eyes entirely focused on him, with a purpose in her step that leaves no room for doubt that she plans to love him. Matthew can't help it; tears cascade down his cheeks unchecked. As she gets closer, he sees her tears as well. In the fading light, this creature in pale pink glows before him. As Mr. Nicholson places her hand in his, he turns to Matthew and says, "She's finally yours."

The rest of the service is a blur to Matthew. All he knows is that, at some moment, he was looking into her eyes and promising his life to her. When she promised hers back to him, Matthew felt like he could finally breathe. It is real. This is happening.

"I now pronounce you husband and wife," Jake says. "You may kiss the bride."

Matthew leans down and takes Michelle's face in his hands. He stops briefly, just savoring the moment. He smiles and says, "Hello, Mrs. West." And he kisses his wife.

The yard erupts in applause. There is a large crowd in attendance, many of whom are, or had been, professional baseball players. Most of the Yankees coaching staff is there, as are many of Joseph's friends from the station. All of Michelle's nursing friends are present, as is Mrs. Forrester, who had been saved by Annie. The crowd is cheering, with Annie and JW being the loudest.

In the spot where the dock walkway connects with the grass, Matthew stops, looking at the hundreds of white chairs on his lawn, flanked by twinkling white lights strung up in a square shape surrounding the event, and he speaks: "I have loved this woman since I was thirteen years old, but I had the world's most unfortunate timing. She had already met and fallen in love with my best friend, Joseph, a man I loved like a brother. I always thought that my teen crush would go away. Because of my fierce loyalty to Joseph, my feelings would be kept silent, and I would never attempt to act upon them. But as the teen years went on, my feelings for this woman only intensified. I was unable to enjoy the company of any other girl, because my heart always belonged to Michelle. My love for this woman, now standing next to me, became a painful burden.

"When the Yankees drafted me, I thought I could leave this all behind, begin a new life, and the feelings would finally dissipate. I not only left my home behind, but I left my faith too. I began to allow all the trappings of fame to lead me away from God.

"I remember watching this woman marry my best friend. It was the lowest moment of my life. But a wise man picked me up and dusted me off. Mr. Nicholson, my best friend's father, found me out on that dock over there, crying out in agony, trying to understand why I would be cursed with love for a woman I could never have. Mr. Nicholson, my mentor and other father, gave me a cold shot of wisdom and truth. He told me to return to God, to give all the love that I had in my heart to my heavenly Father. He told me to pursue God with a passion, and he told me that if I did, I'd be in a better place to manage these feelings I had.

"I arrived in South Carolina that weekend a broken, wandering man. I returned to New York as a man with a mission. What I learned is that *who we are while we wait is more important than what we receive when the prayer is answered. Waiting matters. Waiting refines us. Waiting transforms us.*

"A short period of time later, my career as a Yankee was winding down. And in that time, my friend Joseph died, saving the lives of four people he pulled out of a swollen creek. My best friend in this life gave his life for his friends. Two beautiful people here today are alive because he was the kind of man who would lay down his life for a friend. I moved back to South Carolina and made a decision. I would honor the memory and sacrifice my friend made.

"Surprisingly, when I returned, I was in control of the feelings that had once destroyed me. I understood my role. God showed me that I was to serve Michelle and her children. And honestly, I didn't have any ulterior motives. I was not thinking about she and I being together. God had given me peace. All I was doing was honoring my friend by helping his wife. It felt good to do something of value. The truth is, this love I feel today for this woman, grew fresh and new from the ashes of suffering. At this moment, I will tell you that if anyone had offered me this moment in exchange for the life of my friend and brother, Joseph, I would have gladly turned it down. That's how much I loved that man.

"Joseph's parting words were a message. He said, "This is why ... Tell Matthew that this is why he always loved her.' So, we are only here today because someone else is not. Joseph gave his blessing, and after sorrow, God brought us joy. Today, I am the happiest man alive, and my friend, Joseph, is looking down from heaven, giving us two thumbs up. Thank you all for being here. Now let's celebrate!"

Michelle and Matthew stepped off the dock and began their life together.

EPILOGUE

*A*s Joseph is drifting in and out of consciousness in his final moments, he hears it one last time.

Turn around.

Joseph turns around and sees a glorious angel standing before him. The angel, whose voice he had heard all his life is finally revealing himself to Joseph.

"Joseph," the angel says, "God has something to show you." "Okay," Joseph says to the angel, feeling humbled and scared.

To Joseph, it feels like he is in front of a huge movie screen, vibrant and colorful, with multiple camera angles playing at once, yet somehow, he is able to register it all. He's watching a wedding. Joseph sees the back of a man walking someone down the aisle.

The camera angle changes, and he sees the front of them. Matthew is walking someone down the aisle. Joseph struggles to figure out who it is, but he feels a familiarity. He looks closer, sees the green eyes, and knows he's watching Annie's wedding. Matthew places her hand in the hand of the man waiting for her in the front of the church.

The camera angle changes again, and Joseph sees the front row of the church. Matthew is seated next to Michelle, holding her hand, with their wedding rings visible. Joseph smiles to himself. Next to Matthew is a beautiful dark-haired young woman with navy blue eyes. Joseph doesn't know who she is, nor does he know the young man sitting next to her.

The angel explains, "That is your daughter, Joy. Michelle was pregnant when you died, Joseph. The young man is Matthew's son, JW. Matthew returned to South Carolina with a little boy."

Joseph is overcome with emotion. He will never meet his daughter.

He never even knew about her.

Joseph continues to watch, enjoying the scene, watching all his family members years down the road.

The camera angle changes once again, and Joseph looks at Annie in front of the church, taking her vows. Joseph feels sad—sad for all he missed. Joseph wishes he had been able to meet the man Annie married.

The rest of the scene feels familiar, but not the sight of this man marrying his daughter. He looks a few years older than Annie.

Joseph voices his thoughts to the angel. "I wish I could have met the man Annie is marrying."

The angel looks at Joseph and smiles.

"You did meet him, Joseph," the angel says. "He was just one of the many people you rescued in your lifetime of service to God, the boy in the creek."

"Thank-you for showing me this," Joseph says.

"God has one final message for you, Joseph," the angel says.

"What is the message?"

"Well done, good and faithful servant."

~ THE RESCUE ~

Book Club Questions

1. In the life of Joseph Nicholson, what role did his adoption play?

2. What were some of the positive things to come out of the childhood friendship circle?

3. What is your response to Michelle's claim that God seems to love some people more than others? Has this been your experience?

4. Why did Mr. Jeb Nicholson tell the boys to not act on their feelings for Michelle?

5. What were some of the ways Joseph showed his love for Michelle?

6. What were some of the ways Matthew showed his love for Michelle?

7. Was Mr. Jeb Nicholson a good spiritual leader of the family? Why or why not?

8. What are some of the major themes of this book?

9. How has the idea of sacrificial love impacted your life? Who in your life showed you that kind of love?

10. Was there anything in this book that you could personally relate to?

11. What was the key to Annie's ability to love another father?

12. Have you ever had an experience that led you to believe an angel was involved?

13. Have you ever experienced a voice from God?

14. As Christians, we know there is a spiritual world going on all around us. Why do you think people are so fascinated by the demonic side vs. the angelic?

15. How can faith in God help you survive a painful loss or tragedy?

16. Share a time when you came alongside someone in a completely sacrificial way?

17. What changed inside Matthew that allowed him to serve Michelle without ulterior motives?

18. Do you pray regularly? Pray for your children/grandchildren? Have you ever prayed that God would use them?

19. Would you rather be married to a Joseph or a Matthew? Why?

20. Have you ever been in a time in your life when God asked you to wait? What did you learn about God and yourself during that time?

21. Have you ever prayed to God for something and you did not get the answer you wanted? How did you respond to God?

22. Do you find it difficult to live for God? To be obedient?

23. If you read this book alongside a young unmarried woman, what advice would you give her about choosing a mate?

Karen O'Neill Velasquez was an artist, author, speaker, wife and mom. On any given day, you could find Karen either in her basement studio working on something colorful, inspiring others on Facebook where she set to interrupt the negative narrative with her message of love or meeting with others. She liked to connect with people who would never set foot in a church and respectfully treated everyone as a friend.

After decades of being cancer-free and impacting countless lives for the Kingdom of Christ, Karen went home to her Savior on April 17, 2021.

Karen's battle with cancer began years ago as a recently married young woman. She had just returned from her honeymoon in the Greek Islands when she received the devastating news that she had Stage 4 Melanoma. She was given only six months to live yet after more than twenty-two weeks in the hospital doing a clinical trial drug that nearly killed her, fifteen operations, radiation, and immunotherapy she survived.

Karen realized she had a powerful story of hope to tell and was featured on Dateline, Nightline, The Oprah Winfrey Show, Dr. Phil, CNN, PBS, Newsweek, The Washington Post and in many local news segments. Karen believed that *hope* is the most powerful drug of all.

Karen spread her message of faith, hope, and love for nearly thirty years after God healed her from her first battle with cancer. She taught bible study, spoke at women's events, captured others beauty in her photography, and painted Christian themed and South Carolina Lowcountry art. She touched the lives of so many with her message of hope.

Karen lived with her family on the harbor in Charleston, South Carolina, a few miles from Shem Creek. To learn more about Karen's amazing life journey, please connect with her family on her website, social media, or via email.

Email: karenvbooks@gmail.com

Website: www.karenvbooks.com

Facebook Page: karen v books

Instagram Page: @karenvbooks

Made in United States
North Haven, CT
10 November 2021